THE MONTANA M

TATE

BOOK TWO

SUSAN MAY WARREN

SDG PUBLISHING
A division of Susan May Warren Fiction
Minneapolis, MN

Tate
Montana Marshalls series
ISBN: 978-1-943935-27-7
Published by SDG Publishing
15100 Mckenzie Blvd. Minnetonka, MN 55345
Copyright © 2019 by Susan May Warren

Scripture quotations are taken from the King James Version of the Bible. Scripture quotations are also taken from the Holy Bible, New International Version®, NIV®. Copyright© 1973, 1978, 1984, 2011 by Biblica, Inc®. Used by permission of Zondervan. All rights reserved worldwide.
For more information about Susan May Warren, please access the author's website at the following address: www.susanmaywarren.com.
Published in the United States of America.

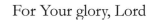

For Your glory, Lord

Excerpted from Knox...

Someone, namely him, Tate Marshall, security for the Yankee Belles country music group, had to raise his hand and point out the obvious—someone had tried to kill them—and that someone was still on the loose.

His brother Knox and band member Kelsey sat on the white leather sofa overlooking the massive fountain of the Bellagio hotel in Las Vegas. Knox's friend, former bull rider Rafe Noble, had pulled connections to secure a two-bedroom penthouse suite and gifted it to Knox to give to the Yankee Belles.

Tate and Knox had nabbed a similar suite, so Tate wasn't exactly complaining, but just being in the Bellagio, or even in Vegas proper, raised the little hairs on the back of his neck.

The sooner they hit the road, well, the more likely he'd live through his under-the-radar return.

"Room service show up yet?" Blonde and sassy bandmate Glo Jackson came out of a bedroom wearing a fluffy white bathrobe, her hair wet and tousled as she dried it with a towel. She hadn't cinched the robe, and he spied a T-shirt and a pair of yoga pants underneath, so maybe she was simply basking in the luxury. She slid onto a green leather high-top stool pushed under the granite countertop of the long, mirrored bar.

"Not yet," Tate said, the scent of her catching him, and he had to look away.

The adrenaline of tonight's events still spiked his system, and he'd barely stopped himself from grabbing Glo and holding on when she walked offstage.

Just because.

Knox got up, his hand woven into Kelsey's. "We're going for a walk."

A walk. Right. Euphemisms. But he could play along. "The fountains go off every fifteen minutes."

Knox grinned at him.

Lucky dog.

Dixie had gone out with Elijah Blue and Carter to check out the famed chocolate fountain.

Which left—aw, shoot. He hadn't done the math in time. The door clicked behind Knox and Kelsey.

Glo was still drying her hair with the towel.

Now she looked over at him, her hair in short, almost white-blonde curls around her head. "How do you know so much about the fountains?"

Oh. He walked to the window, stared down at the night, the strip alive and always moving. The 460-foot Eiffel tower replica sparkled gold against the pane of night in front of the Paris Las Vegas. At its feet, the Chateau Nightclub was rocking, spotlights alerting the world to some headliner, and to the left, a little farther, blue light cast upon Bally's casino. The real action was happening just northwest of Bally's at Drai's nightclub in the front yard of the Flamingo.

He knew every cranny and dark alley on the Vegas strip, not to mention what happened under the bright lights.

"Tate?"

He hadn't noticed Glo come up beside him. She had stuck her hands into the robe, and without her boots on, she seemed like a tiny, delicious package of curves and smarts and talent.

For a second, he was standing offstage, watching her sing her solo. So much of her heart on the outside of her body, her voice sweet and honest and…

And the words felt like they might be for him.

But you don't know if you don't start
So wait…for one true heart…one true heart…

He knew, right to his bones, that Glo was the one he'd waited for. Wanted to start over with. And he would. As soon as they got clear of the specter and the death threats stalking them, he would quit this job.

Create his own sappy, happy ending, hopefully.

But until then, he had to keep his hands fisted in his

pockets.

"I used to work here," Tate said, finally answering her question.

"Doing what?"

He simplified his answer. "Protecting people." And other things.

"Of course you were." She glanced up at him then. Such beautiful hazel-green eyes, with tiny specks of gold. He could forget the past, the knot in his gut, even his sins, when she looked at him like that. With trust.

As if he might actually be a hero.

He couldn't move, his heart nearly frozen in his chest.

Especially when she touched his arm. "Thanks for taking down Russell tonight. You set Kelsey free."

"I didn't—"

Her hand touched his chest. "Yeah, you did." She stepped in front of him, her back to the window panes. She put her other hand on his chest. "Thank you."

The heat of her hands turned his entire body to fire. He swallowed, stared down at her. "Glo—I—"

"Kiss me already, hero."

Oh, uh—

But she wasn't hesitating. She leaned up, running her hands around his neck and pulling his head down, and then her lips were on his.

Sweet, tasting of toothpaste, and soft against his.

And it just took a second for him to catch up, because he had to get past the warning bells clanging in the back of his head.

The past, rising to convict him.

But he ignored it and swept his arm around her back, pulled her against him and returned her kiss. Let all the emotions of the past month sweep through him, flood over him, and pour out in his ardor.

She made a sound, something of desire deep in her bones, and it only sparked heat in his own, only made him press her against the glass, move his other arm around her.

Glo—

The knock at the door was a hand between them, and he came up breathing hard, his heart pounding. Glo, too, and she bit her lip as if struggling with her own emotions.

Yay for pizza, because yes, he needed a deep breath, something to help him tuck his emotions back inside and escape the hot temptation that he knew could only cause trouble.

Maybe he and Glo needed a walk, too, and pronto. "Get dressed," he said over his shoulder as he headed into the foyer. "I'll show you the strip after we have pizza."

"It's about time." She headed for her bedroom.

Lock the door behind you, honey.

She did, as if reading his mind. He heard the click just as he opened the door to the suite. "Room service. Finally."

Except it wasn't a waiter with a white-clothed serving cart containing pizza and drinks.

Unless the Bellagio had upgraded their room service staff to a six-foot-five Russian dressed in a black turtleneck, a suitcoat, and missing a right incisor.

Tate's reflexes let out a word. "Slava—"

"Look who's back in town." He shoved a foot in the door before Tate could slam it.

Then the Russian's big hand hit the door, banged it open, and Tate had just a second to brace himself as Slava sent a fist into his gut.

It doubled Tate over, knocking him back into the suite. He fell to the floor as Slava stepped over him. Knelt and fixed his cement mitt on his chest, pinning Tate as he tightened his fist.

"I warned you what would happen if you ever came back to Vegas," Slava growled.

He had. Oh, he had.

Please, Glo, stay in your room…

SUSAN MAY WARREN

1

Some guys had all the luck.
        Got the girl of their dreams.
        Didn't live with the past haunting them.

Some guys were the heroes of the story, who saved the day and rode away on their white horses, the princess tucked behind them.

Some guys were Tate's big brother Knox.

And then there were the other guys. The ones who couldn't help but walk right into trouble, no matter how much they tried to dodge it.

This was Tate's only thought—well, right after how in heaven's name had Slava Gregorivich found him?

He didn't have time to ask, however, because the gigantic Russian who had helped train Tate back in the day had slammed his iron fist into his gut, knocking Tate back from the open hotel room door and into the grand presidential suite of the Bellagio.

Tate tripped on the sofa going down from Slava's shove and ker-thumped on the floor, nearly knocking the wind out of his body.

Slava took two giant steps and landed on top of him, one of his beefy, scarred hands square on Tate's chest. The other hand reared back for a punch, and that's when Tate's mind went to Glo.

Gloria Jackson, his client, and more importantly the

woman he just might be starting to love. She was in the next room, changing clothes to join him for pizza—oops, um, *not* the room service guy, honey—and maybe a late-night romantic walk under the fountains and along the strip.

He wanted to yell, *Run, Glo!* But that would only one, alert Slava to the collateral damage-slash-leverage should Tate not dispatch this guy successfully. And two, bring Glo out of her room to the rumble happening in the thirty-sixth-floor suite. And knowing Glo, she *wouldn't* run. She'd do something heroically stupid and pick up a vase or a pillow or even use her petite body to try to take down Slava, head henchman of Yuri Malovich and protector of Yuri's local entrepreneurial activities.

A man who had more blood on his hands than Tate, and a death threat to make good on.

No, Glo. Stay put.

Tate thought of Knox next, only because his bona fide heroic big brother was already down at the fountains on his romantic walk with the woman *he* loved.

By the time Slava's fist came at him, Tate was wrangling with his thoughts about trouble and how he probably knew this was coming, if he were honest with himself.

Knew the minute he stepped back in Vegas that Slava and the old crew would find out about it and hunt him down.

Which was why his instincts, his reflexes kicked in and galvanized him to throw up his arm.

Deflect the killer punch.

And with his other hand, deliver one of his own, right to Slava's jaw.

It knocked the big bear back, just enough for Tate to wiggle out, spin, and find his feet.

And this day had been going so well. He'd even felt a little like a real hero, catching a killer.

Okay, that had mostly been Knox, too, but Tate had shown up to cuff him and bring him to justice.

Score one for the good guys, and it confirmed for him that he could actually do the job he'd been hired for—keep the Yankee Belles, an all-girl band out of Nashville, safe. Next on the list was finding the two bombers who had nearly killed them at an NBR-X bull riding event a month ago in San Antonio, a couple of domestic terrorists who worked for an ultra-left-wing group of radicals.

Slava found his feet and charged Tate, tackling him back onto the top of a round glass table. The table shattered and Tate's back stung with the shards of a thousand fragments of glass. But he got his knee up and flipped Slava over his head.

Freed himself from the jagged grip.

Yeah, that hurt. He wanted to shout, but a glance at the closed door kept it in.

Slava rolled off the sofa and landed on his feet, breathing hard. A smile tipped his lips. "Still the scrapper."

Tate backed up, a glance at his weapon, still in his shoulder holster and hanging over one of the countertop chairs. He shouldn't have let his guard down.

But his brain had been caught, painfully so, on Glo and that dangerous song she'd sung tonight. The one that had made him throw away caution and kiss her.

Oh, how he'd kissed her. Like he might be a man with second chances.

A man who could be the hero.

Probably his first mistake—thinking that a guy like him might escape his storyline.

Tate had been wooed by the Belles from the moment he'd met them—right after the bombing, when his brother was frantic to find the girl he'd saved. But even before then, when he watched them perform from the wings of the arena where he was working security, he knew they possessed a magic. Their voices, their sound had woven into his soul, making him feel alive, free, and new. As if he didn't have chains of regret wrapped around his throat, digging into his chest.

Then the bomb had gone off, terrifying everyone. Thankfully, no one innocent had died, but it left the band shaken, and of course he'd taken them on as clients.

If he were honest, he saw a chance to be a champion.

Someone's hero.

Glo's hero.

She'd hired him because she'd been afraid—not for herself but for her bandmate Kelsey, who suffered from panic attacks.

It was a simple gig that got more complicated when he discovered Kelsey's fears were founded—a man she'd put in prison was out and on her trail. Add to that the very real bombers who had issued death threats to Glo's mother, Senator Reba Jackson, and the job went from babysitting to close and personal protection.

Very close, very personal because Glo's smile, her teasing, and even her bravery had dug under his skin, found his bones, and edged dangerously close to his heart.

And then came tonight's song. The hit single about loving and losing and trying again.

She...don't wanna try,
It's too hard to fall for another guy.
But you don't know if you don't start
So wait...for one true heart...one true heart...

Maybe his wait was over.

Slava kicked the table aside and advanced on him. "Yuri died in prison," he said, giving an update. "But the Bratva remembers."

Tate put up his hands. "He killed Raquel. What did you want from me?"

Slava threw his punch. Tate blocked it. Slava rebounded on the other side, and Tate blocked that, too, then slammed the edge of his hand into Slava's throat.

Slava stepped back, gagging, and Tate sent his foot into his chest.

Slava flew back onto the sofa.

Tate should grab Glo and run. He was turning toward her room when—

"Loyalty," Slava growled, his voice gravelly. "You pledged

your life to the Bratva."

That spun Tate. "Are you kidding me? The things I did for Yuri out of loyalty make me sick!"

"You went to the FBI." Slava got up, his dark eyes flashing.

"They came to *me*. And I *turned them down*!" A stupid, stupid decision. But that's what loyalty got him—betrayal, a broken heart, and the death of the woman he loved.

He couldn't let that happen again.

He advanced on Slava. "Yuri should have trusted me." He grabbed Slava around the waist, hooking his foot behind his leg. The big man went down, his arm around Tate's neck.

Tate landed on top of him just as Slava clubbed him in the ribs. The pain woofed through him, thick and bracing, and he knew he'd probably injured a few vital organs. Especially when the second punch landed in the same area.

Slava's arm noosed his neck, but Tate managed to get a fist into the big man's jaw. His hold loosed, and Tate broke free and rolled off, gritting his teeth.

Bad move. Slava rolled too, now on top of him, and grabbed his shirt. Tate put a hand on his wrist, but Slava's fist found his face, and a white-hot flash of pain exploded as his nose broke. The room turned woozy, the pain cascading over him.

Blood gushed, but the smell of it galvanized Tate, and he roared through the haze and kneed Slava. Clipped him in the soft parts.

Slava cursed, and Tate battered his fist into his face enough to dislodge the Russian.

Tate rolled over onto his knees, scrambling away.

He just had to get his head clear. He'd fought Slava before—a few times, although never with his life—and Glo's—at stake.

He knew exactly who had tracked Raquel down that night, who had made her suffer, who had left her broken body for Tate to find when he returned home.

Slava took his job very seriously.

The Russian grunted, and Tate glanced at him just in time

to see the man sling a vase at him. It slammed against Tate's hard head, shattered, and Tate went down, the room spinning.

Get up. Get...*up*.

And oddly, it wasn't Glo or even Knox or even some key figure from his past in his head—his deceased father or Major Jaster, his Ranger instructor—but the random, misplaced voice of a twelve-year-old.

What was Jammas doing, rising from the dead now?

Get up!

For a second, Tate was back in Afghanistan, sand in his eyes, choking on smoke, Jammas's hands tugging on his body armor.

Get up!

He staggered to his feet just as a lamp crashed down in his shadow. But Slava was off-balance, and Tate kicked him, sent the man spinning.

He might not win this. The thought cycled through Tate even as he lunged for his gun. The chair toppled over, and the holster went spinning across the floor. Tate went after it, but Slava grabbed his shirt and hauled him up, shoving him against the bar.

Slava's bearish two-handed grip clamped around Tate's neck, a hint of vodka on his breath as he leaned close to Tate. "In the end, she cursed your name."

Yeah, well, he did too...too often.

Tate ducked his chin and grabbed Slava's elbows, bearing down to dislodge the grip, his air trickling down to a sip. He hammered his fist into the big man's ribs, but Slava was a bull, unmoving.

Tate's vision turned gray, splotchy.

Sweet Glo's voice found his ears, the vision of her onstage flashing behind his eyes. Dressed in black, her dress short to show off those amazing legs, her eyes closed, the lights turning her hair a white-gold. So breathtaking, his heart had nearly stopped in his chest.

Her voice had lifted, mournful and sweet, so much heart spilling out into the song, he'd nearly teared up.

She met him on a night like any other
Dressed in white, the cape of a soldier
He said you're pretty, but I can't stay
She said I know, but I could love you anyway

He could have, would have loved her.

And finally, maybe, become the hero of the story.

He hit Slava again, one more useless punch as his world began to blacken.

———————◆———————

Oh, this was really going to hurt.

Glo closed the bathroom door behind her and stared into the wide, gold-framed mirror. The Bellagio spared no expense in these top floor suites. It rivaled any exquisite New York or even DC hotel with its white leather sofas, plush bedding, and spa tubs.

And some thirty-six floors below, the night was lit up with the florescence of the strip, buzzing with life.

Not unlike every cell in her body. Her face was flushed, and she could nearly see the pulse in her neck.

Thumping away as her rebellious, foolish heart ran away from her.

Outside the posh suite, across the patterned black-and-white carpet, past the massive king bed with the padded gold-fabric headboard, and through the towering mahogany doors, the man she shouldn't give her heart away to waited with pizza and the stated intention to take her on a walk down to the courtyard.

Maybe catch a romantic view of the Bellagio's majestic fountains.

And under the cascading kaleidoscope waters, she'd find herself repeating all her deadly mistakes.

She couldn't fall for a man who would die. Not again.

Glo shucked off the bathrobe she'd pulled on after her

bath, a late-night luxury following the Yankee Belles' first official gig for NBR-X—a professional bull riding tour to rival the PBR. The female trio had toured, submitted tapes, auditioned, and nearly been killed trying to land the six-month weekly gig. Frankly, the band should be together celebrating tonight.

Instead, Dixie, their fiddle player, had disappeared with Elijah Blue, their drummer, to check out some famous chocolate fountain, which might be code for finally declaring their love for each other. And their lead singer, Kelsey, would right now be watching the fountains arc through the night sky in the arms of Knox Marshall, the man who had found and stopped a killer from her past striking again.

Kelsey's real-life hero. The man she deserved.

Which had left Glo alone in the penthouse suite with the only other person in the after-gig entourage—their bodyguard, Tate Marshall.

Younger brother to the hero of the hour.

And the man she was currently hiding from. Sorta hiding, really, because a big part of her wanted to rush back out there and continue what they'd started.

Namely a very long-overdue kiss.

She pressed her fingers to her lips, felt Tate's touch still buzzing them, like the neon lights of the strip, alive and full of promise.

Oh, what was she getting herself into?

She wore a T-shirt and a pair of yoga pants under the bathrobe and ran her fingers through her hair, combing it after the towel dry earlier. Maybe she should brush her teeth.

There she went, getting ahead of herself.

It was just a walk.

And he was probably eating all the pepperoni pizza he'd ordered from room service. They'd knocked on the door just as she went into her room.

She checked her bandage—the gunshot wound was healing. She'd never forget the look on Tate's face when he'd found her, shot, at his ranch.

Neither of them had realized that *she* was the target of an attacker who wanted to intimidate her politician mother from running for president.

No, all she'd cared about right then was the broken look on Tate's face and the fact she had practically felt her heart leave her body.

Flinging itself into Tate's arms.

Oh, no, *no*—

Her phone pinged from where she'd left it on the counter, and she noticed the screen listed a dozen or more tweets she'd been tagged in. She tapped one and it opened.

A picture lit up the screen of her onstage, dressed in tonight's short, black tiered dress with flouncy long sleeves, her hands around the mic, the lights turning her hair to gold.

Glo brought down the house tonight. #YankeeBelles #Country-Music #LoveSong

She scrolled down and looked closer—yes, this shot caught Tate in the wings, those blue eyes pinned to her, his arms folded across his chest as if on watch for danger.

But he looked stripped, something raw and vulnerable on his handsome face.

Oh, it could wreck her all over again, seeing this powerful, brave man undone.

She blamed it on the song. The stupid, sappy, tear-her-heart-out song that Kelsey made her sing tonight. A chart-topper that Glo had written after the man she loved had died in the sands of Afghanistan.

One she hadn't been able to sing until tonight as she'd glanced at the wings, at Tate, and realized that maybe her heart had healed, just a little.

Tate had done that with his frustrating, charming smile. Those devastating blue eyes, the way he laughed at her jokes and didn't let her rile him.

The way he was both dangerous and safe and exactly the man she'd waited for.

Yes, this could really hurt.

And it was all Kelsey's fault.

Glo pushed her speed dial and wandered out to the bedroom as Kelsey's phone rang. She heard a strange thump emitting from the next room and imagined it might be the room service cart bumping the door.

"Are you okay?" Kelsey came on the line without a preamble. She sounded a little breathless. And now Glo felt like a jerk.

But, "No."

A pause, and Glo realized— "Sorry, yes. There are no domestic terrorists on my doorstep ready to kidnap me."

A forced chuckle on the other end, and maybe it wasn't a funny joke because, well, they'd all survived a domestic bombing a few weeks ago and… "It's not that. I…" Her voice dropped, turned to a whisper. "I kissed Tate."

Now a real chuckle emerged through the line, and she heard her admission whispered to someone else, probably Knox. She could imagine her friend, hand in hand with the tall Montana rancher, her dark hair caught in the night air, her eyes finally free of the fear that had held her hostage for the past twelve years.

Glo should probably hang up. Nearly did, but Kelsey came back on the line. "Okay, so, it's about time—"

"He works for us!" Glo stepped up to the window. The fountains had begun their hourly dance, pulsing to "Singin' in the Rain." The water rose and fell in time, cascading from one end of the massive trough to the other.

The music filtered through the phone. Beyond the fountains and across the street, a miniature Eiffel Tower glittered, its lights blinking against the night.

"So fire him," Kelsey said.

"That's a little harsh, Kels. This is his *job*. Besides, we need him."

"Glo." Kelsey must have cupped her hand over the phone because the music muted. "There comes a time in every girl's life when she has to take a chance on love. To stop living in fear that it's all going to crumble, and start over. To trust a little in love. C'mon. We both know his working for us isn't why you're—where are you?"

"I'm in my room. Hiding."

"Stop hiding. Stop running."

Glo wanted to raise an eyebrow because, really? This from the woman who had turned running into a full-time career?

But maybe that's what love did. Made you brave and strong and willing to start over.

"Tate is crazy about you."

"Tate could get killed. Whoever bombed the venue in San Antonio was trying to discourage my mother from continuing her run for presidency. They were after *me*, and they haven't been caught. Which means that every minute Tate hangs around me, he's in danger."

"He's a *bodyguard*. He signed up for this."

"Besides," came a male voice through the phone, and clearly Knox was listening in, "Tate knows how to handle himself."

Another bump came from the other room, this time with a shout.

She frowned. "I know that. But...I just can't..." She sighed. "I can't watch a man I could...care about...die. I can't go through that again."

"You won't." Kelsey again. "Don't let your fears keep you from loving a man who loves you back."

Right. Yes. Because David had been a soldier, running into trouble.

Tate's job was to keep them *away* from it. He was careful, prepared, and anticipated trouble.

He wasn't looking for a fight.

A crash sounded. She startled, paused. Maybe he'd dropped a glass.

She headed toward the door. "Okay. Yes. You're right... I'm just freaking out. Overthinking this—"

She opened the door.

The sofa lay askew, the green counter chairs were toppled to their sides, and glass from the round coffee table in the middle of the room glinted under the overhead lights.

One of the tall flower vases had hit the floor, also shattering, water and lilies scattering.

And Tate...*what*—?

Tate was backed up against the wet bar, one hand gripped on the arm of a huge, balding man dressed in a suitcoat, trying to pry the man's beefy hands from his throat.

The other was balled and hammering away at the man's ribs.

Glo couldn't breathe. Or maybe she was simply taking a breath to let out the mother of all screams—

"Glo—?"

Her scream ricocheted off the thick panes of the picture windows, through the glass chandelier, and across the expanse of the room enough to jerk the fighters apart.

She dropped the phone.

"Glo! Get out of here!" Tate's words emerged choked, on a wisp of breath, and he glanced at her long enough for her to see the damage done to his handsome face. He bled from the nose, his mouth, and from a cut over his eye, which turned him into some nightmarish, blood-crazed ninja. Especially when he turned back to Bald and Beefy and slammed his fist into his jaw.

The man staggered back, loosening one hand, and Tate cuffed off his grip from his neck.

Tate ducked away, breathing hard. Glanced again at her, his eyes just a little crazy. "Run!"

But— "Behind you!"

He turned just in time to step away from a bone-crushing fist to the face. He caught the man's arm and held it there while he delivered a backhand to his face, his gut. Then, in a move that had her hands to her mouth, he flipped the big man right there onto the floor.

The man let out an epithet that sounded Russian. Or maybe Polish. Whatever it was, she got it.

Run!

She started for Tate, probably galvanized by the same thought because he held out his hand, as if to take hers. But

Igor the Russian reached out and tripped him. Tate went flying.

In a second, the big man was on him, a knee in his back. He grabbed Tate's arm, twisted it behind him, and Tate howled.

Glo just reacted. She picked up a green lamp on a nearby table and crashed it over Igor's head.

It dazed the brute enough for her to kick him—the power of it stunning even her when he lost his grip on Tate.

Tate rolled, landed a fist in the man's throat, and scrambled to his feet. "Glo, get out of here!"

He kicked the man in the jaw, but Igor had rebounded— probably rage—and resembled a bull, crazed with blood. Unstoppable.

Deadly.

He came at Tate, his nose bleeding, his eyes red. Even Tate's fist to his face didn't faze him. He pushed Tate back, hard.

Tate slipped on the waterfall of glass and went down.

Igor landed on his chest, his knees on Tate's arms. Igor's big, bloody hands found Tate's throat, both thumbs pressing into the well of his neck. Tate was writhing, slamming his knees against the big man's back, but he couldn't dislodge him.

"Get off him!" Glo found a vase and threw it at Igor, but it bounced off him, like it might be a Nerf ball.

Tate was choking, fighting for his life.

Glo leaped on the man, her arms around his neck. "Help!" She hit him in the ears, wrapped her arms under his jaw, tried to pull him away.

It worked.

At least long enough for Igor to slam his fist straight back, right into her face.

The world flashed gray, then black, the pain exploding through her. She fell back, off the beast.

Maybe Tate had gotten a slip of air, because she heard his voice, one last time— "Glo—"

Then Igor wrapped his deadly hands again around Tate's throat and squeezed.

She was screaming now, her hands over her head, frantic. Her face throbbed and the room spun. *Get up. Save Tate.*

He was kicking the floor, his movements jerky.

Fading.

No—please. *Help!* She rolled over to her hands and knees, about to leap again on Igor when she spotted the man. Tall, wide shoulders, and built for hard work, running cattle, and once upon a time, riding bulls.

Knox.

He roared and leaped at Igor, tackling him off Tate. Landed square on the Russian.

Big brother. Furious, protective, and fresh in the fight, Knox sent his fist into Igor's face once, twice, and Glo turned away from the violence, crawling over to Tate.

He wheezed, rolled over, trying to catch his breath.

Not dead—*oh, thank You, God.*

Then footsteps, voices, and hotel security flooded the room. White-shirted Bellagio rescuers leaped on Knox, pulling him off his victim.

"It's not him!" Glo shouted, but Kelsey was already informing them who was the good guy. And who was the assailant.

Glo gripped Tate's shirt, pulling him over to herself. She shook as she wrapped her arms around his chest, clamping tight.

He leaned his forehead on her shoulder, still gasping for breath.

"Are you okay?" she managed, tears washboarding her voice.

Tate's shoulders shook, his breathing raspy, but he raised his head.

Blood smeared his battered face. He found her eyes. "Are *you* okay?

She could barely look at him. The rising purple on his cheek, the split lip, his nose, clearly broken, and the open cut over his eye, as if he'd been hit by one of those lamps.

And she could bet he had internal bleeding, if not a slew of wicked bruises on his body, given the size of Igor's fists. Never mind the damage to his windpipe, or… "Is your shoulder dislocated?" His arm hung loose and grotesque.

He drew in a breath. "Maybe." He touched her face, ever so gently. "He hit you."

She nodded, her eyes filling.

One of the white shirts was hauling him out past them. Tate tensed, glancing up at him. "You're going to pay for that."

Slava's spittle landed on the floor next to Tate. "You come to town again, and I won't just hit her. Or you."

Tate's jaw tightened and Glo froze. This was because Tate had come with them to Vegas? Because he was trying to protect them?

Knox knelt next to them. "Who is he, Tate?" The man had lost his Stetson but hadn't a scratch, otherwise, on him. Except maybe for bruised knuckles.

Oh, the Marshall men were tough and handsome, with those square jaws, eyes that seemed to look right into a woman's soul. While Knox's dark brown hair was threaded with the finest shades of red in the sunlight, Tate's dark brown hair was laced with glints of gold, his beard hazed with a richness when he let it grow, his blue eyes holding a mystery that she very much wanted to solve.

He would still be handsome, maybe more rakishly so, with a broken nose.

"Old score," Tate muttered.

"I think you're even."

Tate made a face.

"He was sent here to *kill* you, wasn't he?" Glo's voice emerged in a whisper of horror.

Tate drew in a breath, and even Knox looked away as Tate nodded.

Oh, she knew it. Apparently, she had a type.

The kind of men who didn't care what trouble—or

death—might be waiting for them. Who turned their face to it and charged ahead.

The kind of men who died for what they believed in.

The kind of men who would break her heart.

No, oh no…

Tate turned to Knox. "Thanks, bro."

"We need to get you to a hospital."

Tate met Glo's eyes, touching her face ever so softly. "I'm sorry, Glo. I…I never meant for you to get hurt."

Maybe not, but apparently that was how all her love stories ended.

Because yes, this was really, really going to hurt.

2

Tate would probably never admit how close he came to dying.

To being *beaten to death.*

But one look at his chart of injuries had Glo nauseous. Two broken ribs, internal bleeding that included losing his spleen, and his throat was so swollen that the EMTs had to put a breathing tube down it to keep it from closing. Never mind the bruises that covered his body, his puffy purpled eye, complete with eight stitches dissecting the brow, and the splint that protected his nose, recently set. His dislocated shoulder had been stabilized, his arm in an immovable sling, and he'd slept most of the last six hours.

Just the tiny squeeze of his hand in hers convinced her that he might live. That he knew she was there.

It made her want to weep every time.

And settled deep in her gut the fear that if he woke and she wasn't here…

Or worse, if she left him, he just might not ever wake up again.

"You need sleep. Or at least a shower."

Kelsey's voice came as a whisper over her shoulder, and Glo lifted her head from where she'd cradled it in her arms on the lip of the bed, next to Tate's blanketed leg. Her hair probably stuck up on end, creases heated her cheek, her eyes felt raw and puffy, and yes, her body buzzed, her veins a mix

26

of coffee and Diet Coke, a handful of antacids her only recent meal.

Kelsey set a muffin and a cup of coffee on the bedside table, and Glo nearly leaped for the breakfast. "Thanks." She released Tate's hand and opened the muffin wrapper, sitting back in the padded recliner.

"He looks brutal," Kelsey said as she stood at the foot of his bed. The haunted expression on her face betrayed her own brush with death over twelve years ago.

Except, Kelsey had been fourteen and in a coma for twelve days. And she had awoken alone.

Glo wasn't going to leave Tate. Not yet, at least.

But Kelsey was right—Tate looked wrecked. Even with his bruises, however, Tate had a rough beauty about him, his face in repose possessing a sort of eerie calm, long lashes against his cheekbones that made her want to kiss the soft wells under his eyes. A fallen warrior.

If only she could erase the image of his bloody face, the fierceness in his eyes when he'd struggled against his attacker, the way he fought for his life.

Maybe it should offer her a morsel of reassurance—after all, Tate didn't go down easily.

But the fact that he hadn't called out for help—for Pete's sake, she'd been in the *next room*—the fact that he'd ordered her, more than once, to simply run and leave him to his fate...

If she'd ever doubted if he had what it took to protect her from whatever terrorists had threatened her life, at least according to her mother, those doubts died on the Bellagio tile floor.

Tate would easily—too easily, maybe—give his life for her.

She took a bite of her muffin, then washed it down with a bracing slosh of coffee. It did nothing to stop the pitching of her stomach, so she put them both back on the tray.

Kelsey walked away, over to one of the padded chairs near the window, saying nothing more. She wore a pair of cutoff shorts and a gray T-shirt with an oversized sweater

and her signature turquoise cowboy boots. She smelled freshly showered.

Outside Tate's private room, the Desert Sunrise Hospital
overlooked the sprawling city, with the vista of Red Rock
Canyon in the far horizon. A scorching sun hung high in the
sky—Glo had no doubt that Vegas was starting to blister
under the springtime desert sun.

But a ruthless chill had slid into her bones, taking root as
she sat through the night.

She couldn't live like this.

Knox, wearing a clean snap-button shirt and a pair of
jeans, had come in behind Kelsey and now stood on the other
side of the bed. He reached down and squeezed Tate's leg.
"Sorry I didn't show up earlier to stop all this, bro."

Glo hadn't been a firsthand witness to Knox's meltdown
when Tate had been taken in for surgery. No, he'd hid that
until he'd gotten to some remote stairwell. Although probably
not his best choice because the yell of frustration had echoed
down the corridor and sent Kelsey fast-walking his direction.

The big cowboy seemed back in control, only the fatigue
on his face betraying his own sleepless, pacing night. He must
have left in the wee hours, after Glo had dozed off.

"I called Ma to let her know what happened," Knox said,
although Glo wasn't sure whom he might be talking to. "Although I lied a little about the extent of your injuries."

Oh. Well, she'd simply avert her eyes to this apparently
private family conversation.

"Ma wanted to jump on a plane, but I told her you were
going to be fine, so don't make me a liar."

Amazingly, Tate seemed to stir under Knox's touch, his
words.

Knox waited, but when Tate's eyes didn't open, he made
a grim line with his lips and nodded. "Okay, well then, we're
not going anywhere, bro, so take your time."

Not going anywhere. Fact was, it took everything inside
her not to flee.

Only twelve hours ago, she'd been clinging hard to the

fantasy that she might actually deserve a happy ending.

Right.

"Tate was always the tough one," Knox said quietly. "He hated ranching, but by golly, he'd stay in the saddle longer than any of us if Dad asked him to ride fence or hunt down a stray. He doesn't know the word quit, Glo."

Oh, now Knox was talking to her. She looked up and nodded. But that was sort of what she was afraid of.

Because it was time to fire her bodyguard.

"You're not going to believe this, Glo." Kelsey held her phone up and flashed the screen at Glo.

Glo shook her head, the screen too far away for her to read.

"We're up for New Group of the Year with the Country Music Guild! Carter just texted with a link of Carrie Underwood announcing the list. He wants us to go to the CMG awards."

Glo stared at her, trying to wrap her brain around— "The CMG awards?"

"They're in Nashville. End of May. I gotta text Dixie."

Dixie. The third member of their band, who had returned to the hotel room right around the time the EMTs were trying to force an oxygen tube down Tate's swelling throat.

Their first official awards show, and frankly, Glo should be on her feet, fist-pumping the air.

Instead, the cold simply shut her down, the triumph bouncing off her. "Yeah. Sure."

Kelsey frowned, glancing over at her, then back to her phone.

Tate stirred again, and his eyes moved under his lids.

Glo stood up, bent over him. "Hey, tough guy. You're okay." She pressed her hand to the center of his chest, glad to feel the steady rhythm of his heartbeat. "We're with you."

His good eye opened, and for a moment, he seemed far away, the texture of confusion, even horror, in his eye.

"Bro. You're in the hospital," Knox filled in, probably deducing the same from Tate's widening eye.

Tate's gaze flashed to Glo, the past knitting together in his blue eye.

Then he started to gag.

"Tate, calm down!" Knox pressed his hand on Tate's uninjured shoulder. "Just let the machine breathe for you—"

Kelsey had gotten up and pressed the nurse call button.

Tate writhed on the bed, reaching for the tube as if to pull it out. Knox grabbed his hand, pinned it.

The white of Tate's eye showed, and Glo pressed her hands over her mouth to keep from crying out.

His agonized grunts tore through her, and she took a step back as Knox leaned over him, talking to him, his voice low, like he might be talking to one of his ranch animals. "Bro. Just breathe. We'll take it out. It's okay—you're okay—"

"What's going on?" A nurse in green scrubs pushed into the room. With short dark hair, she looked lean and strong enough to handle her writhing patient. She stepped up to Tate's bed, grabbed his wrist, and took his pulse. Tate was emitting a strange, deep moan.

She pulled out an iPad and scanned it. "Okay, Mr. Marshall, I'll call the doctor and see if he can take out that tube. You're due more pain meds, so I'll order those for you, but you need to calm down or you're going to hurt yourself more."

He looked at the nurse, breathing hard through the tube, then his gaze fell on Glo.

Maybe he hadn't seen her before, because he simply affixed on her. Held on. And as he did, his panic seemed to drop away. He stopped writhing, his keening died, and his breathing evened out.

Whatever he'd been dreaming, whatever nightmares followed him from his slumber broke away.

Then his eyes filled, and maybe that scared her even more. Tate didn't do tears.

Glo stepped up to his bed, taking the nurse's place as she left, and ran her hand over his trapped in the sling. "I'm here, Tate."

His gaze slipped to the purpling bruise over her eye, and he closed his eye as if in pain.

Yeah, well, she knew how he felt.

"Slava is in custody. And both Knox and I gave statements to the police. He's not going anywhere."

Tate opened his eyes and looked at Knox, who was nodding at her words.

But that wasn't the end of trouble, was it? Because it didn't solve the bigger problem.

The looming death threat against Glo and her family, one that Tate had vowed to protect her from.

What, from his hospital bed? With two broken ribs?

In a way, she was relieved. In her worst nightmares Tate stepped in front of a bullet or protected her body as a bomb exploded around them.

For years she'd gone to sleep with the images of David's death in her brain. No details, just an IED on the side of some road in Afghanistan.

It left her imagination way too open.

Tate had added brutal, vivid color to the scenarios in her head.

She ran her thumb over his hand, pasting on a smile. If she'd learned anything from her senator mother, it was to deflect, deny, and pretend. "We're safe, tough guy. Shh…"

The hospital room door opened again, and a doctor came in, followed by the nurse. A lean, blond man with a short haircut, he looked like a marathoner. "Let's check that throat of yours, Tate, and see if we can't get that tube out."

Glo moved away, her arms folded across her chest as the doctor gloved up, then probed Tate's neck. Knox, too, had stepped back, allowing the nurse to take Tate's blood pressure.

"I think the swelling has gone down sufficiently." He turned to the visitors. "Can you step outside? Just in case he vomits."

Glo felt like vomiting herself as she nodded. "I'll be right back, Tate." She met his eyes, then took a breath and exited the room.

Knox and Kelsey followed her into the hallway.

Glo leaned against the wall, her entire body vibrating.

"You need sleep," Kelsey said.

"He'll be okay, Glo," Knox said and put one of his warm hands on her shoulder.

She nodded but sank down onto the floor. Sighed. "I have to fire him."

A pause, then, "What?" Kelsey crouched before her. "Why?"

Glo raised an eyebrow.

"Fine. I get it. But...we can't go to the CMGs without Tate."

"Then we don't go."

Kelsey considered her, her mouth tight. She scooted beside Glo and leaned her head on her shoulder. "Maybe we need a break. I know we just landed the NBR-X tour, but Knox was talking with his friend Rafe, who is on the board, and given last night's events—"

"The one that included your stalker trying to kill you?"

Kelsey sat up, glanced at Knox, who'd given her a grim look. "Yeah. That. And the rest of it—the past six weeks of shaking off the bombing in San Antonio, not to mention the news about the threats from the Bryant League against you and your mother."

Yeah. Some ultra-left radical group wanted to keep her moderate-leaning mother from running for president. Clearly, they didn't know Reba Jackson like Glo did.

Nothing ignited a fire under her mother more than controversy and opposition. It was akin to waving a red flag in front of a bull.

"Knox and I were thinking that maybe we'd ask NBR-X to postpone our contract for six months. Give us all a chance to breathe. Maybe write some songs, get into the studio and record that album we've been talking about."

It sounded like a good idea. "Will you take Tate back to the Marshall Triple M?" Glo asked. The Marshall family's spread in west-central Montana would be the perfect place for him to find his feet again, maybe escape the haunted expression in his eyes.

At least it had been for Kelsey.

"Yeah, if that's what he wants. You could come with us," Knox said.

"She's coming home with me."

Oh hallelujah, Senator Jackson was in the building. Glo didn't even start with surprise, not one question entering her mind at how her mother might have not only found out about Tate's attack but landed here within twelve hours to rescue her. In other words, take over her life.

She was even dressed as the shining knight, in an all-white pantsuit, her amber red hair down around her collar, tall and striking, and who would ever dare to argue with the powerful and beautiful Reba Jackson?

Glo pushed to her feet. "Mother. Hi."

Reba stopped ten feet away, her mouth opening. "Oh my…what *happened?*"

Oh. Glo's hand nearly went to the bruise on her face, the blackened eye where Slava had boxed her. "It looks worse than it is."

"How could it?" Reba advanced to her and pulled her daughter to herself, holding her so tight Glo nearly believed it was authentic.

Wanted to, really, because she was so tired and overwhelmed, and wouldn't it be nice if her mother had actually shown up because she was *worried* for Glo?

But her mother always, without exception, had a hidden agenda.

Glo hugged her back because she was in the middle of the hallway, in semipublic view, and she didn't need to alert Knox to their family's dysfunction.

The little performance wasn't fooling Kelsey for a moment, however, and out of the edge of her periphery, Glo saw Kelsey rise. Raise an eyebrow.

Reba held her daughter at arm's length. Scrutinized the wound. Shook her head. "I just knew something like this would happen. What, did he involve you in a barroom brawl?"

Glo's eyes widened. "No. He was attacked. In our suite." And she didn't bother to explain how the suite wasn't actually theirs and, oh, never mind. The important fact here was, "This wasn't Tate's fault."

"Sure it wasn't." Reba looked past Glo down the hall, and Glo followed her glance to her mother's security boss whom she'd assigned to work with Tate at their last venue. That answered a few questions, at least.

"Well, how hurt is he?"

"Very hurt. He nearly died."

Reba wore a face of dismal acceptance. "Well, now you know. He can't keep you safe, and I'm not interested in watching my daughter get killed on his watch. You'll need to fire him."

How Glo hated it when she and her mother came to the same conclusion, even if it might be for different reasons. "I know."

Reba blinked at her. "Good. Then I'll send Sly to the hotel to gather your things and we'll head back to Tennessee."

"Tate's not even out of the hospital yet. I may be firing him, but I'm not leaving him."

"Yes, darling, you are." Reba reached out and touched her face, a whisper over her bruise. "Tate is…well, he is very handsome, but I think we both know he isn't good for you."

Glo took a breath.

"You didn't think I couldn't see right through your reasons for keeping him on staff?"

Glo's entire body turned to flame. Thanks, Mother.

"Listen. I know it's hard, but this is for the best. And I need you at home. I have a very important fundraising event in three weeks, and I need you there."

"Mother."

"Your father is attending."

Glo stared at her. "Really?"

Reba smiled, and it seemed touched with an authentic hint of warmth.

"I told you. We're all in this together, right?"

Glo nodded, the old mantra fueled more by desire than truth. But it had held them together during countless campaign victories.

And one very painful loss.

"It's just for a few weeks, honey. You and the Belles need a break anyway."

"We're up for an award at the CMGs," Glo said and instantly felt thirteen. She wasn't the girl who needed her mother's approval anymore.

Still, the cracks of the past twelve hours healed, just a little with her mother's congratulations. "You ladies can do anything you put your minds to." She grinned at Kelsey.

Glo didn't know why, but Reba had always held a special place for Kelsey in her heart. Maybe because she reminded her mother of Joy.

After all, both Kelsey and Joy had been fighters, even if one of them had lost her battle.

"We are thinking of postponing our contract with NBR-X," Kelsey said. The traitor.

"Then it's settled."

Glo drew in a breath. Yes. Settled. She didn't have the energy to argue.

And Tate would be safe on his ranch.

She tightened her mouth but nodded.

The doctor came out of the room. "He's awake and asking for you all."

"Is he going to be okay, doc?" This from Knox, who'd been standing away, texting on his cell phone.

"Yeah. He's tough. I didn't know he was an ex-Ranger."

It was news to her, too. Which showed her just how little she actually knew about Tate.

Knox nodded. "He's been out for about five years."

"I served with a number of Rangers during Operation Desert Shield. Those guys don't know how to fail."

"Let me talk to him alone," she said to Knox.

He gave her a grim nod.

She pushed into the room, her throat thick.

Tate sat up in the bed, sipping on water. He set the cup on the tray when he saw her. His mouth cracked up into a wry smile. "How you doing, Fight Club?"

His tease bounced off her. She slid onto the bed, this time near his free hand. Took it in both hands and pulled it to her chest. "Tate, I…" She drew a breath, not sure how to tell him—

His smile vanished. "Glo, first—I know I scared you. I'm sorry—I'm so sorry. I don't know how Slava found me. I thought we'd be okay. That I could slip away without the Bratva knowing I'd been in town. I made a mistake. It won't happen again, I promise."

Her eyes were filling, and he let her hand go, reached up and touched her cheek. "I hate seeing this bruise on you."

She nodded. "Tate…this is bad."

"I know, babe. But I'll be okay and back to work in no time. I know we probably need to talk about that kiss…" And now he offered a dangerous, rakish smile, despite his injuries.

That kiss. Her gaze flickered down to his mouth, back to his eyes. No, no, *no*…

"Tate—"

"Okay, wait. Listen. I need to tell you—thanks for not leaving me. I know I kept yelling at you to run, but…you saved my life. Thank you for staying."

She might be ill. Because she was going to run. Far and away.

Glo closed her eyes, tears cutting down her cheeks, and of course he wrapped his arm around her and pulled her into the well of his chest, pocketing her right next to his beating heart.

Probably in the only place that wasn't bruised.

Yet.

Tate was never letting Glo out of his arms again.

No, he was going to stay right here, clinging to her, holding her as she quietly fell apart on his chest.

He'd really scared her.

No, he'd scared them both, because everything inside him screamed when Slava slammed his fist into her face, and all Tate could think in that moment was what if Slava, after killing him, turned his fists on Glo?

What if he did to her what he'd done to Raquel?

Tate had lost his calm then, the ability to think through the scenario, find the advantage.

The panic had turned him desperate and helpless. He'd tossed the fight over in his head a thousand times on the way to the hospital, as he waited for surgery. Conjured up moves and angles and ways to take Slava down.

None of them included Knox intervening, but yeah, he'd never been so glad to see his brother than when Knox saved his life.

Of course Knox saved his life. Because that's what Knox did. Showed up.

The guy was such a freakin' hero.

But it seemed that Tate had gotten the girl anyway, because Glo lifted her head, her eyes reddened, her cheeks wet, and met his gaze.

He searched her face, longing to lean up and kiss her.

Second chances, right here in his arms.

Now she searched his face, as if trying to sort out what had happened. "I'll be okay, Glo…"

But she was shaking her head, so much pain on her face he could weep— "What is it?"

She leaned away and whisked her hands across her cheeks. "I just…" She sighed then, sadness in her eyes that…

Wait.

No…

"Glo…," he started, a fist closing in his chest. He reached out for her, but she slid away, out of his reach, and now his breathing started to cut off. "Babe—"

"I'm going back to Nashville with my mother."

37

Oh. He blinked at that. Well, probably that wasn't a terrible idea, because Senator Jackson had a small militia of security. They could watch the grounds, the events, and Tate would watch Glo.

Well, at least when he was able to get out of the bed. So yeah, he could use a little help maybe.

What he really wanted, however, was to lock her inside this room until he could move without his eyes rolling back into his head.

But that wasn't fair to Glo—she had a career, commitments, and—

"The Belles are going off the road for a few months, and my mother is ramping up her presidential campaign, so…"

He was nodding, all good here. "It'll just take me a couple weeks to get up to speed here, Glo. It's not a problem—"

"You're fired, Tate." She backed away and clasped her hands over her chest, as if to hold herself together, and he nearly scrambled out of bed, thin hospital gown and all, to reach her. "You need to go home."

Only after a second did her words land on him, settle in. Huh?

His expression must have betrayed the craziness of her words, because she nodded. "It's too dangerous for you to stay with me."

"I agree! The Bryant League means business, and even if they didn't show up last night at your event doesn't mean they're not going to make good on their threats."

"And I don't want you in the middle of that."

He blinked at her. "It's…I'm *paid* to be in the middle of that. It's my job."

"Which is why I'm firing you."

He drew in a breath. *Slow down.* This didn't have to be a disaster. "Fine. I'll come with you to Nashville—"

"No. Knox wants you to go home. You need to be somewhere where people can take care of you—"

"I don't need anyone to take care of me!" He was shouting and didn't care. "I'm fine—trust me, I've been hurt worse than this, and I got out of it just fine."

He hadn't told her much about his past, and for a second, she flinched. "When you were a Ranger?"

He drew in a breath, then nodded. "My leg was broken, I was trapped in a village surrounded by insurgents, and I still managed to fight my way out. I'm not going back to Montana while you're in danger in Nashville, for Pete's sake."

"I won't be in danger. I'll be at home. Attending fundraisers that are well protected."

Fundraisers? He must have worn an incredulous expression, because she drew in a breath. "My mother is running for president, Tate. That's a family project."

"You can't stand your mother."

Oh, not the right thing to say, because her lips pursed. "She needs me."

He knew very little, really, of the bad blood between Glo and her mother, but he knew it involved the death of her sister, Joy. And a separation of her parents when she was in her teens. But Glo was loyal to the bone, and if her mother needed her, then Glo showed up.

Just like she didn't run to save her own life.

But, "Glo. Don't fire me. Please. I..." He sighed, swallowed, and didn't care that he might be pleading. "I know I scared you, but I promise I'll be as good as new in a few days, and...listen, I have connections. Ways to know if the Bryant League is targeting you, and where."

But he was losing her, tears raking down her face, and he sort of wanted to cry too. "Glo—c'mon. We have something. It's good between us. And..." But his words only seemed to make it worse, because she was backing away, shaking her head.

"I'm sorry, Tate. I already lost one man I loved to war. And I know this is domestic terrorism, not war, but it feels the same. I'll still lose you, and I can't do this again. I can't...I'm sorry."

Then she turned and nearly fled the room, leaving him chained by an IV and his blood pressure cuff to the bed.

"Glo!"

He bit back a curse and ripped the cuff from his arm. The nurse had doped him up again, and the meds had already kicked in because he knew his movements would have really hurt. But not worse than losing Glo.

He was peeling off the tape of the IV when—

"What kind of connections?"

He looked up. Reba Jackson had come in and closed the door behind her.

He frowned.

"Ways to know where the Bryant League might be targeting us next?"

"My sister. She's in the CIA. She can help me track them down, chart their movements. We can get ahead of these guys, stop them before another bomb goes off."

She drew in a breath, as if considering his words.

"I've seen up close what these guys do. I know what to look for." And if he had to, he'd pull out his final card—his brother Ford, active duty Navy SEAL. Not that Ford could probably help, but it added some *oomph* to the Marshall family résumé.

And yeah, Tate would call him if he had to.

Reba stepped up to the bed. "It's plain that you have feelings for my daughter, Tate."

He didn't move, because she looked none too happy with that statement, her mouth pursed.

"But I will admit that perhaps you can help my team keep us safe."

He made to add to his case, but she held up her hand. "But my daughter fired you, I believe."

Oh, what was she—

"So if you join our protection team, it will be under my purview."

Yeah, he knew what was coming next.

"Which means you need to keep your…affections for Gloria to yourself."

Yeah, well, she had *affections* for him too.

But he nodded. No problem, ma'am. Because they just had to get clear of this threat and maybe Glo would see that she didn't need to be afraid.

He wasn't going to die.

Senator Jackson seemed unconvinced, so he held out his hand to her. "I promise to keep my distance from Glo. As long as I get to make sure she's safe."

Reba raised one sculpted eyebrow. "You can do that? Stand on the sidelines, watching her back as she attends parties, speeches, and events?"

"Ma'am, I can do anything if it means keeping Glo safe." His hand remained outstretched.

"Even if she's on someone else's arm?"

He frowned but forced it away. Hardly. Glo wouldn't...

Something about Reba's expression slid a cold trickle through him.

Still, he nodded slowly. "I'll keep her alive. No matter what."

"And use your CIA connections to find out about the Bryant League."

"That too." Please, Ruby Jane, don't kill him. But she had been the one to offer help when she discovered the domestic terrorist group was targeting Senator Jackson.

"You even look at my daughter with anything more than a professional gleam in your eye, Mr. Marshall, and I'll not only fire you but make sure your professional security career goes down in flames."

Now he raised an eyebrow. But gave another slow nod.

She took his hand. "Get better. I'll see you in Nashville."

He let her go, then leaned back into the pillow as she left.

The door opened again, and this time Knox came in, glancing back at the retreating senator. "You all right?"

Tate frowned at him, and Knox lifted a shoulder. "I heard what was going to go down in the hallway. If it makes you feel any better, Glo's a mess. She came out of the room crying, and now she and Kelsey are going back to the hotel to pack."

"It doesn't, thanks."

"Sorry, Tate. But maybe Senator Jackson is right. Glo is…she's in the public eye, and…" Knox made a face. "And you're…"

"What—?" Tate snarled.

"A mess, bro."

That shut Tate down. At least for a moment. Because yeah, Knox had to bring up the fact that he'd nearly gotten Glo killed.

Just like Raquel.

And Jammas.

And okay, maybe this *was* a bad idea.

But Slava and his ilk weren't going to follow him to Nashville. And Tate did know what he was doing.

Most of the time, at least, when his brain wasn't suffering from the aftereffects of kissing Glo. He'd simply been off his guard.

So yeah, he meant every one of his words to Senator Jackson. He'd keep his hands, his mind, and his heart away from Glo.

If that's what it cost to keep her alive, he'd gladly pay it.

"I know I'm a mess. So get me out of here, so I can get home, get better, and get to Nashville and back to work. Glo might have fired me, but her mother just rehired me."

Knox frowned.

"C'mon. Have you not met me?" Tate gave a smile and pulled down the neck of his hospital gown, revealing the ink across his chest. *Surrender is not a Ranger word.* "This is far from over."

Knox shook his head. But a slight smile tipped his lips. "Senator Jackson doesn't know what kind of trouble she's hired on."

"She's about to find out."

"There is movement in the compound, Charlie Three."

The voice in Ford Marshall's ear could save his life.

Steady, soft, the kind of voice that crept through him and found his bones, settled a steel surety in him that calmed his heartbeat, even here in the desolation of South Yemen.

"Confirmed, Operations."

Sweat bathed his entire body, but he was fully kitted up in battle rattle, sweat pouring into his ears, and he smelled like the local wildlife. He'd been dug into his position under a fig tree, surrounded by scrub brush and thorn trees, for nearly two hours.

They were all waiting for the terrorists in the Yemeni compound below to go to bed. For the go-word from Ops sitting at their FOB—forward operation base—on the USS *San Antonio* out in the Gulf of Aden.

Their Black Hawk hidden in the valley not far away.

They'd sat on their hands, waiting on a dusty, rocky hillside while the night deepened around them with the smells of lamb cooking in tandoors, saltah stewing on open fires, and saluf—flatbread—baking in a clay oven.

"I'm so hungry I could eat a goat," said Cruz. Their sniper's voice came through the earphones built into Ford's helmet.

Not the voice he wanted to hear, but Scarlett—or rather, Petty Officer Second Class Hathaway, assigned as combat services support to their unit—was monitoring the drone that scoped the area, as well as keeping the Black Hawk waiting to swoop in for exfil updated.

And now he had her in his brain, thanks. The last thing he should be thinking about was Scarlett's short brown hair with those red highlights gleaming like copper when the hot Middle Eastern sun hit it, and those big brown eyes that never missed anything, including tangos—terrorists—who might creep up and kill him or any of the other operators on his team.

No, not the kind of thoughts he should be having anytime about a fellow sailor. Especially one who he outranked.

His eyes burned, so dry his eyelids were nearly glued open, although that could also be from fatigue. And the frustration of watching Martha Garrety, American nurse and current kidnap victim, being dragged from the main house by the three young Yemeni men who'd decided not to kill the missionary nurse but take her captive and do—yeah, he couldn't let his brain go there.

He watched them emerge into the compound through his helmet-mounted NVGs—night vision goggles—and with everything inside him wanted to squeeze off a round into their black-and-white keffiyehs. But orders were to not awaken the entire compound.

Not start an international incident.

Just to extract Martha alive.

Apparently, it didn't matter that the militant group AQAP, an offshoot of Al-Qaeda, was headed by Nasir al-Rimi. Whoever had taken her had also gunned down her husband—probably right in front of her eyes—and another nurse serving with Medical Mission International. This was the second attack on the MMI organization—the first had been a Lebanese militant who carried a gun into a Baptist hospital like it might be an infant and opened fire.

Every other mission organization in this part of the world—and especially Yemen—had bugged out when the US government issued a warning.

Not Martha and her cohorts.

Now Martha was paying the price for her dedication. Helpless, probably violated—although he'd heard that the ultrazealous left the infidel women alone—and definitely terrified.

The team went quiet around him as Martha was dragged into the open, fell, and was kicked.

Ford heard a curse from Nez, their master chief. "Give me a good word here, Marsh."

"Still waiting on the order, boss."

"Please," Cruz said.

"Anytime," hissed Sonny, their explosives expert from Chicago, in position outside the back wall of the compound with Kenny C, their weapons specialist, poised to scale the wall for the snatch and grab.

Twenty feet above Ford to the west, Levi—from Minnesota—made a strangled, odd sound as one of the men hauled Martha up and slapped her.

"Operations, we need something, now," Ford said softly into his mic.

Yeah, time to finish this, bring Martha home.

Bring *him* home. Because he was so close to the end of his deployment, he could nearly taste the chalupa that Cruz had promised them from his backyard smoker in Coronado.

Ford had one of the tangos between the grids of his MK11, Leupold Vari-X Mil Dot rifle scope.

"Hold, Charlie Three," Scarlett said.

Only her voice kept him from lining up his MK11 for a head shot.

"According to our drone, they're leading her to an outside hut near the compound wall."

"We don't need a drone to see that," he whispered.

Maybe Scarlett heard him because she responded with, "Just relaying information, Marsh."

"They probably don't want her inside with the family," Trini—maps and logistics—said.

"Yeah or maybe they simply didn't want to hear her cry," Nez growled.

Ford didn't relay any of the team's ire to Scarlett. It simply settled in his gut.

Later, he might find her at their FOB, sit outside under the stars as the massive ship parted the black water, and let out his frustration. Like the fact that every time they chopped off one snake head in this militant-infested world, another popped up. And it was women and children who paid the price.

Scarlett would just sit, drinking a bottle of lemonade, and listen.

She'd almost become the closest thing to a best friend that a logistical teammate could get in the Navy.

Any closer and he'd be breaking the kind of rules that

could get him kicked out.

Off SEAL Team Three and back to Montana to herd cattle.

Yippee ki yay. No thank you.

Down in the compound, they'd dragged Martha to a hut ten feet from the wall. He didn't want to imagine the smells, the heat, or what it might feel like to be Martha, alone, bruised, grief-stricken, terrified.

Frankly, he already knew.

"You're a go, Team Three." Precious words, spoken with verve, the slightest hint of caution.

"Roger." Ford relayed the info to the team.

It happened fast, just as they'd planned, practiced, and run over in their minds.

Sonny and Kenny C threw a Yates climbing hook over the wide wall, yanked down on the folding hook to extend the ladder, and were up and over the wall so fast they could have bounced.

Cruz took out Tango one with a quiet shot to the head, silenced by his QD sound suppressor.

Leviticus ghosted the second man, but the third took off running.

Meanwhile, Nez headed for the entrance of the compound, where they'd extract Martha.

"Do you have her?" Ford asked as he headed toward the back entrance, just in case their plan went south and Sonny and Kenny C needed support.

"We have the package. Headed toward the entrance."

Tango three—where had the bugger gone? Ford hadn't heard shouts rising from the compound where Nasir al-Rimi probably slept, armed to the teeth with militants.

He stood in the darkness outside the back entrance, watching the gate when Nez came over the headset. "We have the package. Exfil, exfil."

"Roger." Ford toggled the mic. "Operations, we have the package. Exfiling to the extraction point."

"Roger."

He turned, but Scarlett's voice came back through the pipe. "We have movement. Three—no, maybe four—bodies headed out the back."

He hunkered down, his heart thundering hard.

Their extraction point was a half mile back into the hills, the closest they could get without alerting the village.

Apparently, HQ didn't want a full-out war with these guys, *yet.*

Carrying Martha would slow them down. A little.

Shouts, and although he could speak Arabic, he couldn't make it out. If he were to hazard a guess, he would bet it was something along the lines of "Run faster, kill them before they get away with the goods." That was his G-rated, simplified version.

Because Martha was young, pretty, and these guys weren't above a little slave trade.

He could break away, exfil through a contingency route, and meet his team at the chopper. Follow the plan.

Or…

He stood up. Squeezed off a shot, and the leader dropped.

Ford dusted the one behind him, too, before the two in back littered him with shots.

He leaped into a wadi, rolled, and came up with his HK45 and pumped two shots into the chest of the man lipping his foxhole.

The man dropped like an anvil on top of him.

The action screwed with his NVGs and he went blind, the glasses breaking free from his helmet.

Shoot!

He wrenched them up, but he couldn't see his hand in front of his face.

He pushed the assailant off him and rounded up to his knees, blinking.

C'mon, adjust. Shooter four was out here, somewhere—

Scarlett's unsanctioned scream shrilled through his comms headset. Piercing, bright, and he scrambled to his feet, every nerve on alert.

"Behind you!"

He whirled and shot, still blind.

An explosion slammed into his armor, a punch that caught him center mass, right in his chest plate, blowing him back, the air whooshing out of his lungs.

He landed hard into a pile of sandstone and rubble, the world gray and formless.

"Get up!"

Scarlett.

Yes. Get up! But the shot had shaken his .45 from his grip.

"He's on top of you!"

He brought his knees up, ready to defend, his hand on the straight blade Winkler on his war belt.

A shot sounded, but the shadowy form in front of him kept coming.

Ford's chest was on fire, but he shouted it away, rolled to his feet, yanked out his blade, and leaped for the target.

Moments later, Cruz ran up, breathing hard. "I missed him. Sorry."

"I didn't." Ford cleaned his knife, his eyesight adjusting, finally, and resheathed it. "Let's go."

Shouts now from the compound, thanks to his unsuppressed shots, but he didn't turn around, just hoofed it behind Cruz up the hillside.

They ran silently, Nez checking in when they reached the Black Hawk, now cycling up. The sound thundered across the canyon and the helicopter lifted.

"We're picking you up," Nez said.

Scarlett's voice came again, calmer. "You have two trucks on your six, gaining fast."

Ford affirmed and conveyed her sit-rep to Nez, but he didn't slow, and next to him, despite nearly a decade of wear on him, Cruz was outrunning him.

Yeah, well, Cruz didn't nearly have a hole blown through him.

The beautiful black bird rose just ahead of them, and in

moments it hovered low enough for Cruz to throw himself onto the deck. Nez raked him in.

Shots dinged off the wheel struts.

Nez held out his hand and Ford leaped for it. Sonny grabbed his body wrap, and even Kenny gave him a hand as they lugged him aboard.

The chopper lifted, the desert dropping under them.

More shots, and Levi returned fire as Ford strapped himself onto a bench.

"What happened back there?" Nez shouted over the engine, his dark eyes blazing. More shots arced into the night, like fireflies. "You don't usually go Lone Ranger on us. That's going to get you killed. Stick to the mission specs—you had orders to exfil!"

"Marsh got ambushed," Cruz said.

That wasn't—except, it might have looked that way, especially since only he had direct communication with Scarlett.

"I'm sorry, Chief. Squirters came out the back, in hard pursuit," he said, still catching his breath. His entire chest felt aflame, and suddenly he was having a hard time breathing.

His master chief must have seen him grab for the collar of his body wrap because he leaned over and examined the hole in his armor. "You've been shot."

"No lie." He closed his eyes. "But I'd be dead if Scarlett—Lt. Hathaway hadn't warned me."

Nez gave him a hard, dark look. "No more rogue ops. Good thing Cruz saw you, or we'd be circling back." He glanced over at Martha. "With a possible negative outcome."

The young woman hugged herself, her arms tight, her face bruised. She looked out onto the Yemen hillsides, the villages tucked into the crannies of bald, dusty mountains, lit here and there with courtyard fires and in some places, lights.

She appeared utterly stripped. As if she hadn't a clue where she was or what had happened.

Yeah, he got that.

He pressed his hand to his chest, aware that he'd started to feel woozy, every breath a blinding shot of agony.

He might have broken a rib.

Weirdly, Martha turned and looked straight at him, her jaw tight, her eyes hard. Almost angry. The sudden change drew in his breath past his aching chest.

But he got that too.

He could almost see the personal, emotional armor forming. After a trauma like this, it would take her years to break it down, to feel safe enough to let someone inside, to not feel as if she had to control every moment, wrestle her fears into a hard, forbidding ball.

It would also take years before someone might come along who could earn her trust, help her open her heart to hope and maybe even love.

Years before she'd be able to silence the voices of fear. Maybe even guilt and shame.

But when she did, maybe she'd find another voice. The kind of voice that told her she wasn't broken. Not wounded, but strong.

Even brave.

And someday that voice would tell her it was okay to take a chance and live again.

That voice just might save her life.

He looked out the window. They'd crossed the jagged mountains, were heading toward the coastline, and beyond was their transport ship.

The moonlight dragged a golden trail across the ocean to the deep blue horizon.

Ford put his hand on his chest, felt the hole, the ache. But underneath his palm, his heart was still beating.

Thank you, Scarlett.

3

N ever in a thousand years would I guess you'd join your mother's campaign."

Glo made a face at Cher as her red-headed former roommate set a wide-mouthed mug in front of Glo, a heart-shaped leaf drawn into the foam of her vanilla latte. She slid onto the wooden bench across the table from Glo, armed with an Americano and a gleam in her eye. "So, how did the Senator rope you in?"

Glo picked up the coffee. "I'm not really sure. It happened so fast..." She blew on the rising steam. "One minute I had a thriving career, the next I'm sleeping in the guest room."

"Still haven't moved back into your old room, huh?" Cher wore her long red hair gathered back, low and to the side. Only Glo's long-legged friend could rock the over-the-knee boots, the short black dress, and oversized gauzy shirt. She looked professional, put together, and fit, and Glo felt a little underdressed in her boyfriend jeans, striped T-shirt, and leather jacket.

Glo set her cup down. "Do you know that my mother still hasn't cleaned out Joy's things from our room? And she won't let me touch them. It's been ten years, and she still has it dusted and vacuumed every week."

"Grief does that—holds us hostage. It took my father three years to clean out my mother's closet." Cher broke off a piece of her late afternoon treat—a morning glory muffin.

"What, are you charging by the hour now?"

Cher laughed. "No. You're the one with the psychology degree. I just know that grief makes us do crazy things. Like hike across America or climb mountains—"

"Or push incredibly hot, brave, and amazing men out of our lives?"

"That too," Cher said, taking another bite of her muffin. "Listen, I'm not judging, just jealous. I haven't had a date in months."

Which was crazy. Cher was not only beautiful, but smart too. Glo always knew her small-town friend from East Tennessee was destined for greatness, starting when she'd helmed the *Vanderbilt Hustler* as editor in chief. Now she worked as a fiction acquisitions editor for a national publisher.

Maybe Glo should have gotten a "real" job, like her mother had suggested, with her psychology degree. Gone on to be a counselor, like she'd planned. But she had more than enough problems than to spend hours listening to others.

Although, maybe listening to others would help her figure out how to unsnarl the mess inside.

"Maybe you should try online dating?"

"Oh no. Most of those guys are looking for a booty call. I have a strict IRL policy for dating."

"IRL?"

"In Real Life."

Glo laughed, and it eased the fist that seemed to grip her heart since she'd flown home in the Jackson private jet nearly three weeks ago. Since she'd moved her meager belongings into the grand guest room suite of the Jackson estate.

Since she realized one bright morning that she'd been sucked, ever so surreptitiously, back into her mother's world. Listening to briefings at the dining room table over poached eggs and wheat toast. Sure, she'd done a few interviews online and over the phone for CMG, thanks to Carter's press release of their award nomination. But it felt like her world had become a rerun of…will her mother win? All hands on deck to get the job done.

Never mind her own life.

"I caught your interview on *The Highway*, by the way. And that video of you singing 'One True Heart' is trending on YouTube." Cher thumbed open her phone, and the YouTube app popped up as she handed it to Glo. "Is that Tate in the background?"

Glo nodded without looking at it.

"Yeah, I can see why you're moping."

"We really didn't have anything…I mean…he was my bodyguard, nothing more."

"*Right*," Cher said, turning off the screen. She leaned forward. "Catch me up. I want more than the high points. All the delicious details, please."

Oh, Cher was good medicine. Glo had missed her when she hit the road with the Belles. "Where to start? You heard about the bombing in San Antonio, right?"

"After one of your NBR-X shows?"

"Yeah. We were auditioning for the permanent gig, and the bomb went off in the backstage area. It trapped Kelsey, a little girl, and Knox Marshall—"

"Tate's brother?"

"Yeah. He runs the family ranch in Montana. Tate has two older brothers—Reuben, the oldest, is a smokejumper—and two younger brothers. Wyatt is a hockey player, and Ford is a Navy SEAL."

"Oh…my. So enough alpha male to go around, then."

"You're not helping."

Cher laughed.

"He also has a younger sister, Ford's twin, Ruby Jane. I met all of them but Ford a month ago at a family gathering for their mother's sixtieth birthday."

"You were at their ranch?"

Outside, the sky drizzled down a cool, late-April rainfall, reaping the fragrance of the lilacs shading the front porch and mixing with the scent of fresh-brewed coffee. A few cars splashed by.

"We hunkered down there for a couple weeks after

the bombing. It was Tate's idea. We hired him mostly for emotional well-being. None of us really thought we were in danger, but Kelsey started having panic attacks."

"Are they related to her attack in Central Park?"

"Yeah. It's been over a decade, but she still has wounds, especially since her attacker got paroled right about the time of the bombing."

Cher raised an eyebrow.

"Mmmhmm. So, Kelsey wasn't sleeping, and I thought having a bodyguard around might help her feel safe. When Tate found out about her past, he made the call to bring us to his ranch while he tracked down her attacker, just to make sure she wasn't being stalked."

Cher finished off her muffin. "And, was she?"

Glo nodded. "Actually, yes. And Tate and his brother found him, but…well, that wasn't the biggest problem."

"The biggest being that Tate has manly muscles and a killer smile?"

"I mentioned you're making it worse."

"I just don't see what the big deal is here, Glo. He's a bodyguard—he's *made* for trouble. And it sounds like he's pretty good at shutting it down."

"He got the stuffing kicked out of him by a Russian mobster and nearly died."

Cher frowned. "But he didn't. Crisis averted."

Glo ran her finger along the handle of her mug. "We got the gig from NBR-X and decided to take it. Our debut was in Las Vegas. I didn't know it then, but Tate has some sort of dark past in Las Vegas that involves the mob. They found out he was in town, and one of their thugs came looking for him."

"And you, given the bruise you're trying to cover up. And what's with the bandage on your shoulder?"

"I was shot, but that was before."

Cher's eyes widened. "Shot? You were *shot?*"

"Just a nick, but…yeah."

"You're leaving a lot out."

"Okay, back to the bombers…one of them tracked us down at Tate's ranch and winged me."

"You make it sound like you're in an action thriller."

Huh. Maybe she was. Complete with hunky hero.

Except in this version, the hero went down with the plane, so to speak.

Not the ending she was after, thanks.

"Here's the bottom line. The bombers are with the Bryant League, a leftist group who wants the United States out of all international ties. They hate my mother because she's a moderate and is on the National Security Council and has diplomatic ties with Russia and General Boris Stanislov. I've even met him. Anyway, they're trying to scare my mother into not running by threatening her—and apparently, me."

Cher's face had lost its color. "Seriously?"

"Yeah. And that means Tate would be right in the middle of it all."

"Keeping you *alive*. I'm a fan."

"And possibly *dying*. No thank you. I still have nightmares of David driving over that IED, or whatever happened—believe me, my imagination has conjured up plenty of scenarios. No…I was right when I said once is enough. You're right, grief does make you do crazy things…and I…I'm tired of losing people I love."

Cher reached across the table to touch her arm. Squeezed. "Right. First Joy, then David."

Glo shook her head. "And seeing Tate in that hospital bed. No—seeing him losing his life right before my eyes…I can't sleep. And I certainly can't live with it."

Cher's mouth tightened into a grim line. "I get it, despite the muscles and the hotness and the fact that the man would throw his body in front of a bullet for you."

"I don't want anyone to throw their body in front of me for a bullet, but especially not someone I…could…"

"Love?"

Glo raised a shoulder. "It doesn't matter. I'll never see him again."

Cher let a beat pass, then, "Okay. We need to get you back on the horse. Forget about Tate. Move on."

Glo held up her hand. "Thanks, but no. The last thing I need is a fresh horse."

"Then what are you going to do? Hold campaign signs? Give speeches?"

"Please, no. I sing, and frankly, I hate doing solos. I'm not going to give a speech. I'd rather go onstage naked with a harmonica."

Cher grinned. "That would certainly trend."

Glo shook her head, and her glance fell on a couple who sat down next to the brick fireplace. Young, so much of their lives ahead.

The last month had left her wrung out and exhausted. "Mother has a fundraising event this weekend and she wants me to attend."

"Oh, canapes and men in tuxes. Are you sure you're not interested in trading up, cowgirl?"

"Yes. And to prove it, how about you come with me, as my plus-one."

"And meet rich, eligible men IRL? Who, me?" Cher's gaze drifted past Glo a moment and she nodded a greeting.

"Who—"

"Don't turn around, but Sloan Anderson just walked in."

Glo ducked her head. "I thought he worked in DC—isn't he a lobbyist?"

"I don't know, but he's getting coffee, so you can stop turtling. But what's the deal? Didn't you two date?"

"No! He…we were just childhood friends. We played together as kids, and then in college, he sort of became a groupie."

"Back when you were playing open mics…yes, I remember now. He would sit in the front row."

"He mouthed my songs as I sang them. It was creepy."

"Or dedicated. But hey—that's what you should do. Write some songs and go solo."

"What?" She glanced over her shoulder, and sure enough,

Sloan stood at the counter. He wore a messenger bag over his shoulders and seemed to have filled out in the past couple years. Dark hair, lean body, wide, ropy shoulders as if he worked out. He wore a pair of dark gray jeans and a light gray long-sleeved shirt pushed up to the elbows.

She turned back to Cher. "I'm not a solo act."

"You used to be."

"I hated the limelight. I just wanted to sing my songs. Kelsey is our lead singer, and I'm perfectly happy with that."

"Except the Yankee Belles are on hiatus, right? Are you sure you're getting back together?"

"Uh. Yeah. I mean…" Except Kelsey had returned to the Marshall ranch with Knox and…well, she knew her friend. She'd been looking for a real home all her life after her parents had been killed. Glo wouldn't blame Kelsey if she wanted to stay.

And Dixie definitely had something brewing with Elijah Blue, their drummer. She'd seen an Instagram picture of them in Florida at some theme park.

Her realization must have played on her face, because Cher leaned back, folded her arms. "I always said you had enough of your own 'glow' to be center stage. Maybe it's time."

"It's not time. I'm not—"

"Ever since I've known you, Glo, you've had a guitar or a banjo or a Dobro on your lap, penning songs, singing to yourself. You are totally a solo act."

Glo drew in a breath. "I don't know. Maybe I'm a one-hit wonder."

"No. You're not. But I know it feels that way right now. You're caught in the post-breakup noise of *why not me* and *what if?* You're looking ahead into the future, and it feels gray and dismal."

"Are you sure you weren't a psychology minor?"

"The school of experience. You just need to regroup. Figure out what you want."

"I don't know what I want…"

"How about a happy ending to that action thriller?"

"No. Just one I can live with, I guess. One that won't leave me alone and brokenhearted. I don't know that I deserve more than that."

Cher raised an eyebrow. "Oh no. You're listening to the ghosts again. What is it they say about the dead? They always have the last word?"

Glo looked away. "Maybe they're right."

"Please. So you're the twin who lived. And the girlfriend who loved a fallen soldier. It doesn't mean you don't deserve to be happy."

Sometimes it felt that way.

"Heads up. Ex-groupie ten o'clock— Hey, Sloan."

Glo found her politician smile.

Except, *hello*. Sloan Anderson had grown up. Way up—height, shoulders, and presence. No longer the skinny, wide-eyed fan who showed up to carry her gear and offer her rides after her gigs. Which had been sweet, really.

This Sloan had a seasoned, almost streetwise aura about him, maybe gleaned from years negotiating on Capitol Hill. He wore his dark brown hair short, but with a styled rumple of curl at the front. A smattering of a five-o'clock shadow hinted at the after-work hour. And he smelled good, as if he'd just showered after a workout. "Hey, Glo. I heard you were back in town."

Even his voice had grown up. Deeper, a husk to it she'd never noticed before. It left a little unsettled trail inside her. Huh.

"Sloan." She slid out of the booth and gave him a one-armed hug, leaning away from her shoulder wound. He hugged her back, and she noticed, despite herself, the lean planes of his body. "You look good."

"You too." But his gaze fell on the yellow-red speckles of her remaining bruise. It seemed he wanted to say something, but instead he smiled and glanced at her friend. "Hey, Cher."

Glo noticed Cher's gaze run over him, a little interest in her eyes.

Sloan turned back to Glo. "You in town for your mother's big party this weekend?"

She frowned but nodded. "How did you know—"

"My father's throwing it. He's a huge supporter of your mother's campaign. Thinks she'd make a great president."

"She would. She's dedicated and strong and smart—"

"Not unlike her daughter."

Oh. Um.

But he winked. "Sorry. I guess I'm still a little starstruck. I saw your video on YouTube. You've come a long way since singing for tips at the Bluebird."

For some reason, his words found her sore, jagged edges and soothed them. "Thanks."

"So, I guess I'll see you this weekend at the fundraiser?"

She nodded, maybe a little too enthusiastically, because when she sat back down, Cher was grinning.

"What?"

"Yee-haw, honey."

"No. Cher. C'mon."

"You want to get over Tate?"

Not especially. But Glo didn't say anything. She just watched Sloan pull out a chair, put his order number on a table, and grab his iPad.

The rain had stopped, and a stream of light broke through the clouds.

Cher picked up her mug, lifted it to Glo. "Giddyup."

"Not funny."

"We'll see. Because yes, I'll be your date to the party. Let the campaign begin."

———— ◆ ————

Tate hadn't woken in a cold sweat for nearly five years. That sense that the enemy had crept up, got a bead on him, and was taking apart his position.

With a shout, he sat straight up in bed, his heart a fist banging against his ribs. The cry echoed against the whitewashed ceiling of his childhood bedroom, dissolving in the wan, early morning light filtering in through the blinds and striping the floor.

The sudden movement had brought another shout to his lips, this time from the deep-seated pain in his ribs. But he bit it back.

No need to bring his mother running down the hall like he might be six years old and broken up after a fall from his horse.

He'd come a long way since those days.

Tate eased back, listening to the screams of his nightmare dying. The shouts of his fellow Rangers, the gunfire pinging against the cement walls of a mosque, the taste of dust and blood in his mouth.

He could still feel Jammas's body in his arms, his hot blood coating his skin, his breaths shallow as he—

Tate flung the covers off, letting the chill of the late-April morning raise gooseflesh and yank him out of his memory, back to the present.

The one where his body still ached, the pain deep in his bones. Where his cut had healed to a fine, still reddened line. His broken nose had also healed, although darkness hung under his eyes, the bruises fading. He'd ditched the sling from his dislocated shoulder but still favored it, his arm held close to his body.

But he could move it just fine, thank you.

And it was time to get back to work.

Because those screams could just as easily have been Glo's as she tried to keep Slava from killing him, and if he let them sit one more day in his brain without seeing that she was safe, he might lose his mind.

He pulled on a pair of faded jeans and a white T-shirt, stopped by the bathroom to brush his teeth and splash water on his face, bypassing the shave, and headed downstairs.

The early morning light turned the two-story ranch lodge into a fairytale, complete with gleaming hand-hewn logs, a towering stone fireplace, and leather sofas made for lounging.

The recently remodeled kitchen was quiet, and he opened the fridge, letting the cool wash over him as he reached for a pitcher of orange juice.

"Coffee?"

He nearly dropped the juice at his mother's voice.

He closed the fridge and set the OJ on the counter. "Sheesh, Ma, you should work for the CIA."

"Thanks, but we already have one person in this family in the spy business."

Oh, so Ruby Jane had told her about her so-called analyst position. Well, he supposed that was better than continuing the "travel agent" lie.

His mother wore her curly brown hair up in a ponytail and looked about twenty-three in her oversized jean shirt and a pair of leggings. She'd clearly been painting, watercolor staining her hands. She set her own cup of coffee on the granite countertop. "Can't sleep?"

He retrieved a glass from the cupboard and opened the lid to the juice. "Why?"

"You haven't been up this early since…well…let's just say we had to drag you out of bed to do chores."

He poured the juice. "No. No one woke me up. I'd get up and Dad would have taken off with Knox and Reuben and left me behind." He capped the juice, then replaced it in the fridge. "He already had his mini-ranchers. He didn't need me."

He didn't mean for the words to come out as a pity party. Maybe he was just in that place, frustrated, edgy, and dark. But frankly, the ranching gene had skipped over Tate—and maybe Wyatt too, and settled on Ford.

Although Ford hadn't exactly stuck around, had he?

"That's not true, Tate. He just knew how much you hated horses."

Hated might have been a tame word.

"Horses hated *me*. I have the scars to prove it."

She shook her head. "I should have never let your father put you on a horse when you were that young."

"Reuben started riding alone when he was five. I was six. I wasn't too young." No, he was just a coward. And horses could smell fear. Especially on a child who panicked.

"Listen, Ma, it's no big deal. But I got up plenty early when I was in the military."

Her mouth tightened into a grim line and oh yeah, she didn't like to talk about his years in the service. Or the months afterward when he'd returned home broken.

"Knox is already up and outside, getting ready to ride fence."

Of course he was. Because that was Knox. A. True. Cowboy.

Tate just looked like one.

"He'd probably like some company."

"I'm going to go pack, Ma. I gotta get to Nashville and back to work."

He might as well have said he was going to reenlist for the dismay that crested her face.

"You knew I wasn't sticking around."

"Reuben and Gilly get married in two weeks. You can't stay?"

"I'll come back for the weekend. I promise."

He took a drink of his OJ as his mother went to the counter and took the lid off a plate of freshly made muffins. She grabbed a napkin and loaded it with one of her gourmet apple cinnamon muffins.

"What's this, a bribe?"

"If it works." She winked.

He leaned over and kissed her cheek. "Always."

She caught his neck and pulled him close, just for a moment. "Take care of yourself, tough guy. No more fights. You're scaring your mother."

His arm came around her and he pulled her close, just enough to feel her sigh. Then he let her go and nodded. He took his muffin and his juice and went back upstairs.

It wouldn't take him long to pack—he owned precious little after his escape from Vegas two years ago and hadn't accumulated much working odd security jobs around the country. He'd left a few belongings—a couple books, his favorite work boots, a sleeping bag, and his dog tags—in his truck, which he was storing in San Antonio. He'd hopped the Yankee Belles' bus there without a glance over his shoulder.

Now, as he finished off the muffin, he shoved a couple pairs of jeans, a white button-down that still fit him, and a few clean pullovers into his duffel bag. Added his toiletries, his chargers, and on impulse grabbed his black Stetson. Then he headed back downstairs, empty glass in hand and duffel over his good shoulder.

Kelsey sat at the counter, peeling the wrapper off her own muffin.

He set the duffel on the floor and slid onto the stool beside her.

"Does she know you're going to Nashville?"

He glanced at Kelsey, then to his mother, who sat outside, her easel set up.

"Glo."

Oh. He shook his head. "She fired me. Although I don't know why."

"Really? Not a clue, there, Rambo?"

He frowned. Kelsey wasn't pulling any punches today. "I guess it has something to do with David, the guy she wrote her song about?"

"I told you he was a soldier, right? What I failed to mention was that she was wickedly in love with him. But her mother forbade her to marry him. Said he wasn't 'right for the family.'" She finger quoted the last part. "There's a lot of complicated history between Glo and her mother. Her mother never really got over losing her other daughter, Joy. With Glo the only one left, this could be another power play on her mother's part."

"Power play?"

Kelsey brushed off her fingers. "Glo's mother has an agenda for her daughter. One that includes marrying the right man, taking over the family business—"

"Politics?"

"No. The Jackson family has a massive nonprofit organization whose stated goal is to strengthen people to meet the challenges and opportunities for global freedom. Glo is the vice-chair, although she never shows up to board meetings. I think her father is the chair. Reba isn't allowed to be associated with it since she's a political figure. But she'd like nothing more than for Glo to settle down with some rich lawyer and take over the foundation."

"How big is this foundation?"

"Glo said that last year they raised over two billion from US corporations, political donors, foreign entities. It's a huge operation."

"No wonder Reba has her own security team."

"You thought it was just because she was running? Hardly. Reba Jackson is worth a cool billion, at least. And as her only heiress, Glo is…well, we probably should have hired you long ago."

He nodded. "It's strange that Reba didn't take her death threats seriously until the bombing."

"Any more information about the Bryant League?"

"I called Ruby Jane but only got her voicemail."

Kelsey drew in a breath. "I'm all for you hunting these guys down and keeping my girl safe, Tate. But tread carefully. Glo's heart's been broken before, and I don't want to see it broken again. You may be who Glo wants, but make sure you're who she needs too. And that means not making trouble for her with her mother."

Those words hung on as he hugged her goodbye, then his mother, and finally trekked out to the barn.

Knox was inside, unsaddling his quarter horse. He threw the saddle on a mount, then unclipped his chaps and draped them over a stall. "You look like you're fixin' to leave." He took the mare's reins and led her out to the corral. Tate opened the gate, and Knox took off her bridle, then released her.

He hung the bridle on a hook. "I suppose you want a ride

to the airport in Helena."

"Truck or plane, I'm open, but yeah, I need to get back to Glo."

Knox shook his head, but a smile ghosted up his face. "You don't know when to quit, do you?"

"It's tattooed on my chest."

Knox laughed. "Yeah. In case we all forget. Let's take the ranch Cessna."

He headed into the house for the keys, and Tate threw his duffel into the back of the truck.

Leaned against it, lifting his face to the heat of the day.

No, he didn't know the word quit.

But that's exactly how Jammas had gotten killed. Because Tate had been stubborn, acting on his gut. Leading his team, on a tip, from house after house in the tiny village to find the Taliban barricaded there.

He'd found them. Oh, he'd found them.

He lifted his leg, stretching out his knee, almost an unconscious reaction.

Stubborn and stupid. Seemed like a thin line between them.

Knox returned carrying a briefcase. He put it in the cab of the truck, and Tate went around to get in.

Silence, then Knox got in and glanced at him. "Don't forget Rube's wedding."

"Nope."

"Stay out of trouble."

"Yep."

"You're doing the right thing."

Tate looked at him. Knox was driving with one hand on the wheel and raised his shoulder.

"If it was me, I wouldn't let her go either. I learned that with Kelsey."

Huh.

"This is everything I have on the bombing in San Antonio." Knox gestured to the briefcase. "Kelsey won't talk about it, won't look at it, and I think I need to get the memories out of the house, so…it's on you now, bro."

Tate reached for the briefcase and opened it. Knox's pictures, newspaper reports, emails, and every detail he'd researched about the near tragedy in San Antonio were neatly piled together. "Thanks."

Knox pulled up to the Cessna. "Stop these guys, Tate." He met Tate's eyes, his mouth a grim line. "And don't get killed."

The memory of Knox tackling Slava off his body as his last breath leaked out flashed across his brain. His throat tightened, and he wasn't sure how to pinpoint the emotion.

Knox got out, did his walk-around and final checks, and soon they were airborne.

Their land undulated below them, their herd of beef cattle lounging on the greening table. Knox kept the bucking bulls—four of them, along with their star bull, Gordo—in their own separate fields.

The hum of the plane was too loud to talk, so Tate let thoughts of Glo take over.

Glo, when he'd first met her, dirty from the bombing, standing sentry outside Kelsey's ambulance.

Glo, desperate as she searched for Kelsey when she discovered her friend missing.

Glo, sweet as she coaxed Kelsey out of a panic attack.

Glo, onstage, singing her heart out, her fingers flying on her banjo.

Glo, after a gig, sharing a pizza with him, beating him in a game of gin rummy.

Glo, dancing in his arms at the Bulldog Saloon, grinning, laughing.

Glo, calling him Tater, Rambo, and every other nickname she could think of.

Glo, bleeding from a gunshot wound, her face pale.

Glo, hanging onto him as he carried her to help.

Glo, her eyes in his after she'd sung her song about second chances.

Glo, tugging him down to kiss him, her lips warm, her

body molding to his.

Glo, weeping as she walked out of his life.

His chest ached, and he reached up and pressed a hand against it as Knox touched down at the Helena airport.

Tate climbed out, grabbed the briefcase and the duffel bag.

Knox got out too. Stood in front of him, a look of unmasked worry on his face. "Okay, so…."

"I'll be fine. See you in a few." He held out his hand to Knox.

Knox pulled him in quick, slapped his back. "Stay out of trouble."

Tate gave him a grin, then headed inside.

He booked his flight at the desk, not even blinking at the price. On his flight, he squeezed himself into a window seat, changed planes in Salt Lake City, then northern Kentucky, and finally landed in Nashville just as the sun hit the back side of the day.

He rented a car and drove out of Nashville to the Jackson family estate, listening to the radio. A Brett Young song lit up the speakers.

I can't count the times
I almost said what's on my mind
But I didn't…

Not anymore. Yes, his promise to Reba thrummed in his brain, but he'd keep the commitment.

He would keep his distance.

But it didn't mean he couldn't fall for Glo all over again.

And when this mess was over…

Yeah, no promises there, Senator.

He followed his map to Brentwood and slowed as he drove up to the gated— Oh. My.

He could barely see the house from the road. It sat back nearly a quarter mile, past a pond and rolling hills and a scant forest of maples and oaks. Beautiful chestnut thoroughbreds ran in a large field of emerald green grass.

He stopped at the gate, spotted the cameras, and a voice came over a speaker. "Hello?"

"Tate Marshall, for Senator Jackson. She's expecting me."

The gate opened, and he drove along the paved, land-scaped road to the big house.

The Jackson estate was exactly that—a sprawling, pristine white Southern plantation-style home, with black shutters at the windows and tall columns that held up a front porch.

He pulled into the brick paved driveway and got out. Sprinklers bathed the front lawn, groomed like a golf course, and as he'd driven up, he'd spotted an expansive pool area behind the house.

A man dressed in a suit—dark skinned, dark eyes, middle aged, and fit enough to be called security—walked from an outbuilding. "Tate."

He'd met Sylvester Roberts, head of Ms. Jackson's security, in Vegas. The man extended his hand to Tate.

Tate nodded, met his handshake. "Is she here?"

"The Senator?"

"Actually, no, I'd like to see Glo—"

"Sorry, Tate, no can do."

"Mr. Roberts—"

"It's Sly, now that you're on my staff, but don't get cocky." Tate frowned.

"You work for me, Tate. You follow my orders. And you work the detail I assign you. Do you think you can manage that?"

Tate drew in a breath. *And that means not making trouble for her…*

"Yes, sir."

He pointed to Tate's rental. "The Senator is unavailable, and you can see Gloria if she decides to summon you. She, however, is not here at the moment. And we've been given directives to make sure you follow protocol."

"Which is?"

"Which means you keep your distance." He pointed away

from the house. "You can park that out back, near the employee housing. We don't stay in the big house."

Tate was experiencing some sort of weird throwback to the pre–Civil War era.

"I…okay." He drew in a breath. "I'm hoping to be on Glo's detail."

Sly shoved his hands into his pockets. "Oh, you're on her detail. The Senator made sure of that. Get parked, and then we'll give you an orientation and brief you on tomorrow's event."

Tomorrow's event? His face must have betrayed his question because Sly added, "It's a fundraiser at a nearby estate. Senator Jackson and Gloria will be attending. Mr. Beckett will be joining them, and I believe Gloria has a date."

Tate just stared at him as Sly turned and walked back to the security building.

And a fine sweat started on the top of his spine and slid down his back.

Surrender is not a Ranger word.

Fine. Let the battle begin.

***

Scarlett loved her team. Which was the problem.

She could get every one of them killed, with just the wrong word.

Of course, she was safe and sound, usually tucked away in some stuffy office in the FOB, her eyes glued to a drone screen, relaying orders from Commander Hawkins, a short, powerfully built former SEAL who'd gone on to become one of SEAL Team Three's best leaders.

Calm. Collected.

Not the kind to scream through a headset.

Yeah, that had raised an eyebrow.

But she'd seen, in a horrifying split second, Ford's death played out right there on the green screen and—

Well, she'd screamed.

And he'd lived.

But once again her emotions did an end run around her sanity and took her out at her knees.

She just had to stop caring so much.

Thankfully, her CO had said nothing, even after Ford landed safely on the chopper. Even after she'd slipped off the headset and left the command center, walking through the gangways to the nearest head.

And quietly, violently lost it. Braced her hands against the stall.

Oh, she was pitiful. Because she cared for them all—Nez, the brooding, dark Navajo Master Chief who had tossed his law degree to become a SEAL, following in the heroic military tradition of his great-grandfather Charlie Nez, a code talker.

Sonny, the Italian from Chicago whose real name was Roger or something ordinary. But he'd earned the mafioso moniker with his dark looks and charming ways, and apparently, he'd done a tour in Sicily when he'd been a corpsman, before trying for the SEALs. Which put him as one of the oldest tadpoles in BUD/S but earned him the respect of the team.

Sometimes it just took time to stir up the courage to reach for something else. Or maybe just stand up for what you wanted.

Like Leviticus. Levi. The Rabbi, although the guy didn't have a hint of Jewish ancestry. A blond Viking, he'd grown up in some religious pocket of conservative Minnesota. But he knew what he believed and managed not to adopt the rather colorful language of the teams. Usually. But maybe that didn't matter as much as the fact he didn't hang out at any of the hot spots to pick up frog hogs.

Although, as far as she knew, Ford also opted out of the late-night adventures of some of the other frogmen from the base, from Teams One, Five, and Seven. No, Ford was quiet and most likely to be found working out or competing in some iron man event or on a forty-mile bike ride.

And then there was Trini. As in Trinidad. As in the big

Trinidadian from east Texas who came from a family so large they'd taken up their own section of bleachers when he'd earned his Budweiser. That kind of family love sent her into hives. She'd politely declined the offer to attend their family celebration.

Kenny C was actually named Colton. He hailed from East Tennessee, and about a year after she'd attached to the team, she screwed up the courage to ask.

Kenny Chesney. Right. Because that made sense.

And finally Cruz, aka Fiesta, a name he rightly earned for his love of hosting all the post-deployment bashes, as well as every other team gig.

Like the one tonight, a week after they'd arrived home.

The one she was apparently going to miss because of her stupid rattletrap car, stuck with a flat tire in the driveway of her bungalow in sunny San Diego.

Scarlett stepped on the lug wrench, putting her entire weight on it, bouncing in hopes it would work the nut free.

The wrench jerked away from the nut, spinning out, and of course, she fell, stumbled back, and like the not-Navy-SEAL that she was, she landed in the grass.

Her stiff, dying grass, thanks to the water shortage. Even her palm tree in the front yard drooped, and it was only late April. Overhead, the blue sky was cloudless, and her American flag hung limp and listless.

She lay back in the grass of her tiny, almost ten-by-ten yard and shaded her eyes. Maybe she should stay right here. It wasn't like she was really on the team. She was an Operations Specialist. Technically, an operations com technician, although she'd trained for her communications position and was one of the few women who was attached to CSST—a Combat Service Support Team.

But the Navy had opened up spec ops positions in the last year, and sure, women had failed BUD/S, but what if she didn't try out to be a SEAL but Combat-SAR as a rescue swimmer?

She'd go in after the team if and when they ended up in

the drink.

Then she wouldn't have to sit two hundred or more miles away watching through a green screen as her team risked their lives.

She could be the one bringing them home. Actually *be* on their team.

She liked the sound of that.

Anything to stop herself from screaming through the radio.

Liked it so much, she'd put her package in to cross rate. Now she just had to take her PRT—Physical Readiness Test— and qualify.

Fifty push-ups, sixty sit-ups, five pull-ups, five-hundred-yard swim, four twenty-five-yard underwater swims, and a two-hundred-yard buddy tow.

She hadn't quite figured out how to train for that one. Not without alerting the team to her aspirations.

Maybe she'd tell them *after* she passed her PRT next week.

But she wasn't going anywhere anytime if she didn't get the lug nut off.

She rolled over and got up, looked at her stupid car parked in the hot, cracked driveway, the ten-year-old Ford Escape she'd purchased for two grand. She didn't drive it often—mostly biked the 2.3 miles to the San Diego naval base. But she needed it for days like this when she had to drive all the way out to Coronado.

Well, she didn't have to. Probably, they wouldn't even miss her.

Ford might, but he'd barely talked to her since arriving back to the *San Antonio*. He had a cracked rib from the force of the shot and spent a couple days in sick bay, vomiting up blood.

He'd slept nearly the entire flight home in the C-130. And at the base, while others had family waiting for them, he'd gotten on his motorcycle, still parked in the lot near the cage where the team stored their gear.

She knew because she took an Uber home, no one to

greet her either.

In fact, she still hadn't received a return call from her mother.

She glanced at the flattened tire of the Escape, squashed right down to the rim. And that wasn't the only issue—when she'd tried to turn the car over, the battery didn't even tick.

Dead battery, blown tire, and who knew if those were the last of the problems.

She opened up the back hatch and pulled out the taco salad she'd made—silly her. Cruz always had a spread that rivaled the best Mexican food joint, only his fajitas, chalupas, and especially the margaritas were authentic—and he even made her a virgin variety. The man was a Hispanic Gordon Ramsay.

She tucked the salad under her arm and headed toward the house, pulling out her cell phone. She let herself inside, thankful for the air conditioning. When she toed off her flip-flops, her feet cooled against the Saltillo tile flooring that covered the entire house.

Her house.

Tiny—a minuscule seven hundred fifty square foot, one bedroom—but she'd bought it at a steal and fixed it up with her own two hands. She'd personally not only laid the tile but painted the ancient 1968 original-to-the-house cupboards, added hardware, and even remodeled the bathroom. She could turn a wrench with the best of them.

Just not, apparently, unscrew a rusty lug nut to save her life.

The call rang once, twice, and she was about to hang up when someone—not her mother—picked up.

"What?"

"Why are you answering my mother's phone?" Oh, she didn't mean it quite that way, it was just…well, she'd never liked her mother's current boyfriend, even if he had been around for nearly six years. Or was Gunnar already seven? She should have brought her half brother something from her deployment, but what could she get from Bahrain for a little boy?

Yeah, nothing she could think of.

"Sorry, Axel," she said quickly after he paused. The last thing she needed was him hanging up.

Maybe rounding on her mother.

"Is she around?"

"When did you get back?"

She could imagine him. Long, greasy hair, indistinguishable prison tats up his arms, the smell of beer on his breath. Yeah, her mother knew how to pick them. "A week ago."

He made a noise she couldn't interpret. "She's not...uh... well, you talk to her."

Scarlett frowned, but headed to the fridge to put the salad away, turning the call on speaker. "Mom?"

A sigh, then, "Scar? Is that you, baby?"

Oh no. Slurred voice. High pitched. And her mother hadn't called her Scar since...well, since she was ten, maybe. "Yeah, Mom, it's me. We got back from our deployment and I wanted to see if you were...well, how are you?"

"Where did you go?"

"My deployment. Remember—eight months on a ship?" She, like the rest of Team Three, wasn't allowed to tell where she'd been exactly, but, "I was in the Middle East."

"The Middle East. Why would anyone go there?"

Huh. "Because I'm in the Navy. And that's where... Mom, are you okay?"

"Oh, I'm fabulous. Gary and I are going dancing tonight over at the Oakhill Supper Club."

Scarlett stilled. Gary? "Mom...Gary—he...is he with you? Now?"

"No. He said...he'll be back. Axel...find my shoes. We're going for a drive. For ice cream!"

Scarlett's throat tightened. "Mom, where is Gunnar?"

Silence. "Who?"

"Mom? Gunnar. My little brother?"

A funny laugh emerged through the phone, one that reached into Scarlett's gut and twisted.

"Can I talk to Axel?" She pressed her hand to her chest.

The sound turned muffled, and Axel apparently regained the phone.

"What's going on?"

"It's not a good day, Scarlett. She's...she's been in a lot of pain since the car accident—"

"The *car* accident?"

"Yeah. Totaled the wagon five months ago and twisted her back. The doc gave her some pain meds—"

"And you let her take them? Have you lost your mind?" Scarlett slid onto a chair. "She's an addict—and she was... she was doing so well..." She cupped her hand over her face. "Where's Gunnar?"

"He's fine. At school."

Scarlett tried to picture it—Axel as the only semi-sober adult in the house—and went a little cold.

"Call back tomorrow. It might be a better day." He hung up.

She sat there, struggling to breathe.

Oh. Help.

She covered her face with both hands now. No, she and Sammy-Jo Hathaway weren't exactly close—hadn't been since Scarlett left home at seventeen. But she still cared what happened to her.

Still sent checks home every month.

Which clearly Axel was cashing. And probably using for his own fix.

Scarlett stood up, not sure where to start sorting through her options, when the doorbell rang.

Her doorbell?

She had neighbors, sure, but hadn't met even one of them.

It was Girl Scout Cookie season, however, so—

Ford stood at her door.

She just blinked at him, not sure the heat hadn't gone to her head.

He wore a plain black T-shirt, a pair of cargo shorts,

and flip-flops. Without his tactical gear on, he seemed less overwhelming, but not much, that shirt outlining his off-hour activities. He hadn't shaved today—but clearly had whisked off the beard he'd grown during deployment, his whiskers short and dark. And he'd gotten a haircut. High and tight, dark and precise. A pair of sunglasses sat upside down behind his neck and he looked at her with those pale green eyes, and oh my, even out of his uniform, in person, the man could reduce her to babbles and incoherent stammering.

This was why she did better over comms. She averted her eyes and spotted his motorcycle sitting on the driveway. She opened the screen door, still not looking quite at him.

"Hey, Ford. Uh—"

"The guys sent me looking for you."

This brought her gaze up to his, and yeah, bad idea. Because here he was in the flesh, his voice rumbling through her, making it worse. Her mouth dried, and she forced a clumsy smile.

"The…guys?"

One would think she'd never learned how to talk.

"Yes. The SEAL team you work with?" His mouth tweaked up one side. "Apparently, there are some virgin margaritas sweating in the sun for you."

Sweet. And yet, she couldn't move.

Ford glanced at her car. "I see you have a little tire issue there."

She nodded.

"So…" He ran a hand behind his neck, as if not sure what to say. Glanced back at her. "I could…give you a ride?" He smiled, something sweet and friendly and—

She burst into tears.

What the—? "I'm sorry!" She turned away, pressing her hands to her face. What was her *problem*?

"Scarlett?"

The door bumped open behind her and she knew he was walking into her house now, but she just kept walking, not sure where she was going, so she ended up facing the wall next to her mounted flat-screen. Like she might be eight years old, hiding with her hand over her eyes.

Make it go away.

"Um." He blew out a breath. "I really don't know what I did, but…I'm sorry. And…can I…is there—"

"No." She sighed, leaned her forehead on the wall. "I'm sorry. I'm having a very bad day."

She heard a jangle of keys falling on the counter.

"I understand bad days. Like when a militant terrorist lands on you and takes out your NVGs, then another shoots you in the chest, yeah, that's a bad day. And it would have been worse if it weren't for you, Red."

Oh. She looked over at him, and he was sitting on a stool, sort of parked there, like he belonged.

"I volunteered to track you down because…well, I needed to say that to you." Then he lifted the edge of his shirt, all the way up past his pectoral muscle to show her the still reddened but also greening-and-purple bruise. "This could have been a giant hole in my head if it weren't for you. If I hadn't turned around, gotten in a shot or two—probably rattled his aim." He dropped the shirt, gave her a half-hitched smile. "I felt a little like crying too."

He winked.

And oh, there they went, straight out of her head—all the reasons she'd been telling herself not to fall for Ford. Only one remained—the Very Obvious Reason. They worked together. And he was a higher rank. And they were a team.

But he had that very sexy western drawl and those eyes that settled on her, turned her entire body to a temperature that rivaled Southern California.

And when he laughed, she could feel it to her bones.

"What's the matter, Red?"

She sighed then, because they had this thing. He talked and she listened, and then she talked…and he listened, and maybe they were friends too.

And she needed a friend, if not someone to help her figure out what to do.

"I just called my mother. She's…not well. She hardly knew who I was on the phone."

He frowned.

"She's an addict, and it sounds like she's using again. And I wouldn't be worried if it wasn't for Gunnar and the fact that his dad is probably using too." She looked away, out the window, and blinked hard. No more crying. "She was in AA and doing well when I left."

"That's horrible," he said, coming over to her. "I'm so sorry."

Then, the man completely dismantled her and pulled her into his arms. A polite, friendly, I'm-here-for-you hug, and she just, well, for a long moment, surrendered.

Because she didn't have the strength to do anything else. And he smelled good.

Oh boy.

He held her against that amazing chest, his heart beating a steady, calming thrum.

She pushed away, offered a smile. "Thanks. I think…I'll be okay." She stepped backed. Gave herself some room to think, away from all those muscles.

"We all have a week of post-deployment leave—take it and go home."

She looked at him, lifted a shoulder. "My mother lives in Rockland, Idaho, nowhere near an airport. And my car…it's trashed. And…" Oh, she hated to say this. "I don't have the money. I send everything but my mortgage payment home to my mother while I'm deployed."

He shoved his hands into his pocket. "Okay, so I'll give you a ride."

She just blinked at him. "A ride? To *Idaho*?"

"Why not? I'm headed home this weekend. My brother's getting married in a week, and I have leave so…but, I could drop you off. And pick you up on the way home."

He said it like he might be going into town for groceries, was going to leave her off at the laundromat.

"You'll just…drive me home? What—on your

motorcycle?" She glanced out the front window. He had a Kawasaki Ninja—a rice rocket. Hot for driving around the city, but... "Fourteen hours on a bike...I dunno—"

He laughed. "No, Red. I have a truck. We'll take that."

Oh. And not that she wasn't exactly disappointed, but—

"I will, however, give you a ride to the barbecue." He picked up his keys. "C'mon. We all lived. It's time to party. Fiesta is making nachos. We'll leave first thing in the morning."

He walked past her and opened the door, holding it, beckoning her, the sun turning his skin golden.

And she couldn't stop herself from following him right out into the light.

4

With one article of clothing, Glo became a new woman.

A woman who fit into her mother's world of politics, glad-handing, glamour, and power.

Glo barely recognized herself in the mirror, and even if she looked closely, she couldn't make out the dark circles under her eyes or any remnants of her bruise.

Apparently, her mother had magicians for makeup artists.

Although, they could do little for the red streaking her eyes, despite the Visine she'd added. She was getting better—last night she hadn't woken in the middle of the night, gasping, the memory of Tate clawing for breath haunting her.

No, she'd simply kept replaying the look on his face as she broke both their hearts.

Maybe, someday in the future, she'd be able to piece hers back together. Get a decent night's sleep.

Until then, she'd fake it. Paste on a smile and slide into the black Versace gown. And sure, the slit up her thigh felt a little high, the neckline a little low, but she wasn't herself in so many ways these days, it felt like another layer of pretense.

Her mother, making her over into the woman she needed Gloria Jackson to be.

Aka, the daughter who should have lived.

Yes, Joy would have been the perfect fit for their mother's world. Even with her physical limitations, she was the life of the party, her love of life drawing people to herself.

Glo, more than often at these events, stood in the quiet shadows, plotting her escape.

But she was the only one left, so apparently, Reba was throwing all she had at her remaining daughter. Including a velvet jewelry box that held diamond earrings and a matching diamond choker.

Sort of like a dog collar.

Glo put it on and gave herself a final look. The broad dressing room mirror reflected the elegance of the guest bedroom—the tray ceiling, the dripping gold chandelier, the king-sized bed with a brocade white cover, the antique side tables. And outside, the stretch of lawn that bordered the pool area, all the way to the horse barn.

And if she forgot she was back on the Jackson family estate, her grandparents' portrait hung over the bed—Bishop and Alma watching over her as she slept. If that didn't give someone the urge to run...

Oh, she shouldn't be so cynical. Even if they possessed the warmth of an Eminem rap song, it didn't mean they hadn't made a positive impact on the world. They had founded the Jackson Family Foundation, had supplied antimalarial drugs to Africa, and funded hundreds of scholarships for low-income students in Tennessee. The foundation had started a twenty-million-dollar clean-water project that provided hundreds of wells all over Africa and the Middle East and subsidized schools and orphanages in war-torn Sudan, Uganda, and even Croatia and Slovenia.

They even had a disaster relief fund that distributed help all over the world.

So yeah, Grandfather Bishop hadn't been exactly cold. He'd just been driven.

Apparently, like father, like daughter.

Glo cast a look at her cowboy boots, then slid into the black heels, pulling on the back straps as she leaned on the doorframe. Grabbing her clutch, she headed toward the hallway. It curved around the two-story entry on one side, the massive family room on the other. Below, she spotted Cher talking with—Dad?

He must have heard her steps on the wood floor because he looked up and smiled at her. "Hey Glo-light. How you doing?"

She wanted to run down the stairs like a ten-year-old. Instead, she navigated it in her five-inch heels and glided over to him.

He wore a tuxedo, his hair graying at the edges. Shorter-than-average, but well-built and fit, Michael Beckett, her father, was an odd mix between history teacher and poet, preferring to keep his hair long, caught in a man bun, donning gold-tinted sunglasses, and wearing jeans, T-shirts, and Converse tennis shoes.

Glo wasn't sure how her mother fell for him, or why she didn't take his last name—inserting it into her own in the middle. Or why she'd insisted on Glo being a Jackson. Still, her mother changed around her father. Turned into a gentler version of herself.

And, Michael Beckett could clean up when he wanted to.

"You got a haircut," she said as she hugged him.

"Spiffing up for your mother's big day." He held her at arm's length. She'd covered her healing gunshot wound with the strap of her dress, and the bruising had dissolved.

"You flew in just for this event?"

"Got here a couple hours ago. Nearly got stopped at the gate by the new security crew—your mother's surely amped up the detail."

"She's freaking out about this Bryant League stuff."

"She briefed me. Said you were attacked?" Concern filled his gray-green eyes. "Maybe I should stick around and keep an eye on my girl."

Dad. Warmth flooded through her, and she caught his hand. "Maybe I should go home with you, back to Winona."

"I'd love that. But I think you have other things to do... like attend the CMGs? Maybe win an award? I'm so proud of you."

Sometimes her dad could make her feel like the only one, and her eyes heated. She blinked back moisture before she destroyed her makeup.

Cher, of course, looked like she might be a runway model in a pair of silk shorts and a glittery silver top, a pair of five-inch heels that made her legs appear a mile long. She wore her red hair down and curly.

"IRL works for you," Glo said, giving her an air-kiss.

"Are we ready?" Senator Jackson's voice echoed down from the hallway above and Glo turned, spotted her mother descending the stairs.

The senator wore a simple body-hugging dress that accentuated her height as well as her trim shape. A high collar and no thigh slit for her, but diamonds at her ears and a thick diamond bracelet on her wrist.

Elegant, in command, and the future president, if her mother got her wish. And frankly, she deserved it. No one got the job done like Reba Beckett Jackson.

"You two ladies look breathtaking." Her mother came over and gave her husband an air-kiss, then slid her hand into his. "Thank you for being here for this."

"I always knew you had it in you, RB."

"Thanks, Mickey." She blew out a breath, her only hint at nervousness, nodded to them and headed to the front door.

"What's the big deal?" Cher said as she followed them out.

"She needs funds, and tonight there are a number of big donors as well as the other senator from Tennessee and a few congressmen. She's hoping for their endorsement and the funding to give her the push to beat Senator Isaac White in the polls."

"The conservative from Montana?"

"That's the one. He's Mother's biggest contender."

They followed Reba out of the house where two limousines waited. Glo headed for the second one while her father joined the senator in the first one.

"Why aren't we riding together?"

Glo gave her a look. "Because my mother likes to arrive alone. I'm not sure why she's letting Dad ride with her—maybe it plays well with the conservative audience. No one is supposed to know, maybe, that my parents have lived apart since I was sixteen."

The limos were flanked on either side by their security detail, men dressed in tuxedos, wired up for communication, watching as she and Cher climbed into their transport.

They all looked alike. Clipped close haircuts, wide shoulders, sleek and powerful, and distant, and she couldn't help but wonder what Tate would have looked like in a tailored tux.

Handsome to the bone, no doubt.

She slid into the car and scooted over for Cher.

Their driver closed the door behind them, and the parade set off.

"Where are we going?"

"You've never been to the Anderson estate?"

Cher shook her head.

"If our place is Southern plantation, the Andersons are all Edwardian pomp and glamour. I used to think it was the white house my mother kept referring to—it's all white, with Palladian windows and a flat-roofed portico over the door. Inside, well, think massive chandeliers, Turkish carpets, so many rooms you can play hide-and-seek for hours."

"You and Sloan?"

"We were ten. We also Rollerbladed down the main hallway. And their pool could host the Olympics."

And since Cher had grown up in East Tennessee, in a tiny two-bedroom mobile home, her quiet *Wow* seemed understated.

But even with all the glamour of her mother's world, Glo would still trade all of it for her breezy attic bedroom in the old Victorian her dad owned in Winona, Minnesota.

Three blocks from the Catholic university where he taught.

Maybe she should go home with him. Run from the

ghosts that had followed her to Nashville.

Not to mention the ones that still prowled the estate.

Cher was quiet as they pulled into the long drive that led to the Anderson fortress. The sun was falling, the dinner slated for twilight on the massive patio that surrounded the pool.

White-gloved valets met their caravan, and while the security detail headed for the employee area, their personal detachment pulled up ahead of them.

She got out and noticed Sly, the head of security, stepping up beside her mother. She didn't know who was assigned to her—probably one of the new guys he'd hired when she returned home. She didn't bother to look as she and Cher headed inside.

The sounds of a string ensemble filtered down the tile entry as they were greeted by her mother's campaign manager, an African-American woman named Nicole, who'd been with her for eons, since her first campaign. "I'm so sorry, Senator. I know how you like a mic at these events. I could only secure a lapel mic."

"No. I hate those things," her mother said. "I'll just have to talk loud and hope that people want to listen to me."

Glo followed her mother through the house and emerged to the applause of the crowd already gathered in the twilit backyard.

Oh. She hadn't expected…her stomach clenched as they stood under the long roof of the patio, her gaze panning over the guests. Sure, she'd stepped into the limelight plenty of times onstage, but so often the crowd remained shrouded in darkness.

Not these people. Dressed to the nines, the finest of Nashville society had gathered to show her mother that they believed in her. Believed in her earnestness, her ideals, her family. A strange pride swelled inside Glo as she directed her attention to her mother, who gripped her husband's hand in what looked like authentic unity. And maybe so, because he hadn't left out of irreconcilable differences.

He'd left for Glo. Because she'd needed a fresh start. A

home outside the glare of the press.

As if she could feel Glo's gaze on her, her mother turned and met her eyes. Smiled. Winked.

An unfamiliar warmth flooded through Glo. As if…as if maybe she was supposed to be here.

She'd finally done something *right*.

She lifted her hand and waved. Then Liam Anderson stepped forward and gave her mother a kiss on the cheek, welcomed her and Michael, and the applause died to chatter.

"I've never been to a political shindig. They really go all out," Cher said.

Yeah, well, spend money to get money, and Liam Anderson had dropped a bundle on tonight's event. White-skirted round tables with vases filled with white roses. Gold-rimmed chargers and wine glasses, and white-gloved waiters carrying trays of champagne and fruited sangria. Candles lined the pool, flickering romance and glamour into the evening.

Glo snagged a flute of champagne to carry and wandered toward the pool. Ornamented on four sides with mermaids, she had the crazy urge to climb on the slide and plunge down into the deep end. Cher had spotted her publisher and moved off to say hello.

"Up for a game of hide-and-seek?"

Glo turned, and Sloan stood behind her, grinning. He wore a white shirt, open at the neck—the rebel—a pair of dress pants, and a suitcoat.

"How about a dip in the pool instead?" Already the evening heat had trickled a line of sweat down her spine.

"Don't tempt me." Sloan leaned close. "But it would be terrible to ruin that dress."

She hated that his words ran a sort of warmth through her. She was simply tired and sad, and his friendship hit all the right places.

He gestured to a nearby table, and they sat in the empty chairs. "You're a good daughter to come off the road for your mother's campaign."

"Not that good. There were extenuating circumstances."

"Like the bombing in San Antonio?" He had nabbed a gin and tonic from the bar and now sipped it. "Yeah, when I heard you were performing, that shook me up."

Oh.

He shrugged. "So I'm still a fan. Can't help it. But, are you okay?"

She nodded. "Thanks. We'll be back on the road in a few months. We're trying to write and get some in-studio time be fore then." A wish more than a plan, but it had been forming since Cher threw out the idea of a solo act. She didn't want to go it alone.

Hated the silence of her own thoughts, if she were honest. Because inevitably it was filled by the voices.

So, she needed to galvanize the Belles, start putting pen to paper.

Except right now her mother's world felt pretty good, with the evening glow on her shoulders, a bubbly drink on her tongue, and way-too-handsome Sloan Anderson grinning at her.

Maybe she could fill Joy's shoes.

"Listen. I'm starved, but dinner's going to be late. And unless you like octopus and fresh anchovies, I know where we can get a decent snack. How do frozen Ho Hos sound?"

"Oh, you are diabolical. I can't believe you remembered."

His eyes twinkled when he smiled, and how had she not noticed that before? Maybe the glitter of the spotlights had blinded her.

She glanced at her mother, wound up in a conversation with some general dressed in his Army Service Uniform, and nodded.

Sloan took her hand and they threaded through the crowd, around the side of the house, and up the stairs to the balcony. He led her into a side entrance.

The air conditioning raised gooseflesh, and she dropped his hand, rubbing hers on her arms.

"Sorry. I keep it pretty cool in here." He went over to a kitchen area. A long granite bar top separated the kitchen area from the pool table and the lounge area. A giant flat-screen covered one wall, flanked by built-in speakers. He opened the freezer and pulled out a box of Ho Hos. Set them on the counter. "Dad let me take this over when I moved home."

She guessed one of the closed doors might be a bedroom. "Where did you move from? I thought you were living in DC."

"I was. Worked for the NRA as a lobbyist, but...I got a better job."

She slid onto a counter stool and reached for a Ho Ho. "As?"

"Assistant campaign manager."

She stopped her movements, the unwrapped Ho Ho in her hand. "For...Senator Reba Jackson."

He pointed at her.

"Seriously?"

"Your mother represents all I believe in. She's a moderate, votes conservative on freedoms, progressive on social issues, and represents the ideals of the majority of Americans. Besides, I think it's time for a woman president, don't you?"

He seemed so sincere she just had to nod.

"And I'm not campaigning here, but your mother always... well, not having a mother, she was sort of a fill-in. She'd show up at your events, and somehow I'd end up hanging out with you guys. Going for ice cream after school award ceremonies. Your mother always took care of me."

It was good to see her mother through Sloan's eyes. Because even if it had been her sister her mother had shown up to watch, she had been in the audience.

Every time.

"I'm sure you know this, but she got into politics because of Joy. She didn't want Joy to miss out on any opportunities because of her physical challenges, so Mother ran for the school board. Made sure they were up to code, opened the door for personal help for the physically challenged, and pretty much transformed not only our school but brought changes to schools across Nashville."

"It became her platform when she ran for mayor and won. I did my homework." He winked at her. "Her law degree didn't hold her back, either."

He came around the counter. "Let's go back outside. You're freezing."

She was cold and followed him out onto the balcony, now draped in the twilight hues of the setting sun. Behind them, the crowd had begun to take their seats at the tables, but Glo stayed at the railing, her gaze out on the rolling hills, the horses grazing in the pastures.

Maybe she could fit into this world, embrace her mother's dreams. Be the daughter she needed.

Maybe she owed her mother that much.

Sloan pressed his hand to the small of her back. "I was hoping you'd come back, Glo. I..." He drew in a breath. "I missed you."

She turned to him, very aware that her childhood friend had grown up, become the sort of man any woman would want.

Any woman but one still bleeding from the broken edges of her heart.

But maybe he was the distraction she needed. The perfect way to forget Tate.

What had Cher said—giddyup?

She smiled, mostly at Cher's word, but he read it as something more maybe, because his hand came up to caress her cheek.

A feather touch, and she stilled.

No, she wasn't ready. Not yet. So she leaned away.

A shout erupted behind her. Sloan looked up, his eyes widening a second before something—or someone—hit her from behind. Slammed her into Sloan, and they all went down in a tumble.

A shot cracked, and it hit the house, chipping off mortar and brick.

Glo lay atop Sloan, who'd broken her fall in his embrace, but over the top of both of them, one of the security personnel covered their bodies.

Where had he come from?

"Stay down!" he hissed.

She felt his body over her, solid, warm, protective.

She froze. No—

But she couldn't look as more shots barked.

Then feet hammered the veranda, shouts and return gunfire.

The man protecting her was breathing hard, a tiny groan to his voice, and she deduced he might be in pain.

Shot?

Please—no—

"Let's get them inside!"

She recognized Sly's terse voice, and the man protecting them rolled away.

Sly grabbed her arm, helped her to her feet, and wasted no time hustling her back inside, Sloan on her tail.

Sly led her behind the bar and instructed them both to get down, but she wasn't moving until—

Yes. Oh no, she *knew* it. But what on earth—?

Tate came into the room, a gun drawn, his face whitened with pain.

He turned his back to the wall, leaned his head back, and met her eyes.

And incredibly, offered her a rogue, one-sided smile. "Hey, babe. Miss me?"

———◆———

Glo had nearly gotten shot on Tate's watch.

No, while he'd been watching Slick Sloan hit on her, reeling her in for a kiss.

Tate might be ill, right here in the corner of Liam Anderson's dark-paneled office. If not from the memory of Glo looking up at Sloan like…

Like she'd looked at Tate two short weeks ago. Might have been a decade for the way she acted. Apparently, it took exactly two weeks for her to forget he existed.

And while he'd been standing there, corralling the Neanderthal desire to throw Sloan off the balcony—definitely not a part of his job description—a sniper had adjusted his gun just enough for the setting sun to glint off the barrel.

A smart sniper would have wrapped his weapon, to protect it from betraying tells.

Tate's instincts had simply kicked in and he'd leapt at Glo, taking Sloan down too.

A sort of collateral save, really, but it made him look good.

Even if his shoulder felt like he'd torn something and threatened to send him to his knees. The pain radiated down his arm and across his back. He'd barely held in a shrick of pain as he landed on it, sweat beading on his forehead as he held Glo and Sloan down long enough for his crew to arrive for backup.

So, yeah, if the sight of Glo standing next to Sloan, his arm on her shoulder, wasn't enough to make him ill, Tate could easily drop into the fetal position and lose his guts over the agony coursing through him.

But he couldn't do either. No, his job was to stay quiet and resolute in the corner while Reba unloaded on Sly and her security team.

"How could this even happen? We've been prepping for weeks, even months!"

Poor Sly took her onslaught like the former SEAL he'd been. Quiet. Resolute and not without a grim look of frustration. No doubt mentally recapping his preparations. "I'm sorry, Senator," he said, his voice tight. "We have men patrolling the perimeter of the property, and all the catering staff was vetted. We're not sure how he got in…or got away."

It reminded Tate oh-so-vividly of the attack at the Marshall family ranch a month ago. Someone had fired at the barn and shot Glo.

Shot. Glo.

A fresh chill went through Tate, and his gaze landed on

her.

She must have felt his eyes on her because she glanced at him, ever so briefly. Her mouth tightened, and she blinked fast, as if trying not to cry.

Sloan pulled her close, and she drew in a breath.

Nice.

Somehow in Tate's romance-soaked brain he'd thought she'd be glad to see him. The thought of their reunion had kept him focused on yesterday's orientation, the prep for this event, the run-through of scenarios like this one—probably the reason they were all still alive and relatively uninjured—and most of all kept him from finding her last night after the lights went out, as he patrolled the perimeter of the house on his first shift.

Because he had given his word to the senator. And the last thing he wanted was to get fired on day one.

But he'd longed to see Glo with every cell in his body.

"And now?" the senator said, her voice a whisper of fury. "I have guests gathered in the hall wondering why we asked them to forgo their *two-thousand-dollar plated dinner* for dance music."

"He's gone, ma'am. And the area is secure. You can resume your festivities."

But Reba marched right up to Sly and met his eyes. In her heels, she was nearly as tall as her head of security, and the look on her face reminded Tate a little of his instructor at Ranger school.

Raised the little hairs on the back of his neck.

"I put my life—my *daughter's* life—in your hands, Sly…" She shot a look in Tate's direction, her mouth pinched. "And apparently yours, Mr. Marshall. Don't either of you let us down."

He swallowed. Nodded. Let his gaze fall again on Glo.

For a very long minute, after Tate had followed Glo up the balcony stairs, watched her laugh with Sloan inside his private suite, as she emerged onto the balcony and Sloan charmed her, Tate had wanted to leave. Because just seeing her leaning into Sloan in that body-hugging dress, her skin tan, her hair a white-gold halo, could drive a knife clear through his heart.

He hadn't seen that coming.

But now he was in it, up to his ears. Because he'd been *right*.

This wasn't over.

Apparently, the only thing dead was his hope of a future with Glo.

He looked outside at the darkness, lethal if the team hadn't swept the area again.

Deep in his gut, he just wanted to grab Glo and run.

Footsteps sounded, and Reba approached him. She stopped in front of him. "Thank you, Tate. You did your job." She held out her hand, her eyes in his, cut her voice low. "But don't forget our deal."

He drew in a breath, managed not to moan around the rush of pain—he might have freshly bruised a rib too—and shook her hand. Nodded.

She offered the tiniest smile, something honest, ripe with relief, and maybe, someday, he had a hope of earning her respect.

Not that it mattered anymore.

"In case you're wondering, you're staying. So, get yourself some medical help."

He frowned.

"I can tell when a man is in pain." She let go of his hand. "Then, call your CIA contact. We need to track down these guys before they kill me—or my daughter."

"Yes, ma'am."

She reached out for her husband, who had gone over to hug Glo. He took her hand, glanced at Tate, and gave him a grim smile.

Then, from the senator, "Sloan, we may need your help calming these masses."

Sloan headed out after her.

Glo looked like she might follow, and Tate didn't move, didn't watch her go. But he was bracing himself to turn, to force himself to trail the happy couple for the rest of the evening.

"Tate."

Glo stopped in front of him, and he sighed, looked down.

Wow, she was pretty. It could knock him flat, the way she became prettier the longer he knew her. Silky blonde hair in curls he longed to wrap his fingers around, her face a little flushed, those hazel-green eyes.

Except, oh, she had fire in her eyes, and he braced himself.

"Really? *Really*? You work for my mother?"

"Glo—"

Now tears filled her eyes. "Don't you think it was hard enough to say goodbye to you? Now I have to watch you watch me everywhere I go?"

"Don't worry, sweetheart, I won't get in the way of you and Slick." Oh, he hadn't meant for any of that to emerge and immediately swallowed, ground his jaw, and looked away.

He still felt her gaze on him, and after a moment, he hazarded a glance back at her.

Oh, she was lit, nearly a firecracker ready to blow for the way she looked at him. "For your information, Sloan and I are childhood friends. Nothing more."

"That's not what it looked like." And oh, he should just shut up.

She planted her hands on her hips. "Really? Because I thought security is supposed to be invisible and impartial. Be seen and not heard—"

"Unless we're saving you and your boyfriend from a bullet." Sheesh, he might as well give it up.

Her mouth pinched, and she considered him. "You know, you should quit before this gets ugly."

"Oh, it's already a train wreck. But I'm staying, sweetheart. Because someone has to keep you alive."

"Then avert your eyes," she snapped. "Because guess what, you're going to be seeing a lot more of Sloan Anderson in my life."

"Perfect. I can't wait."

She wore tears now and angrily swept them away. And he was a royal, tier one jerk. "Glo—"

"That's Miss Jackson to you, Mr. Marshall. Remember your place."

Then she brushed by him, slamming the door behind her.

Tate hung his head, unmoving. Only then did he remember Sly still stood in the room.

"So, I was right. You two are a thing."

Tate's head shot up. "*Were* a thing. Sort of. I don't know, now. Maybe…at any rate, it's over."

But Sly's mouth tipped up one side. "For now. But Gloria is a peacemaker, always looking out for others. You must have gotten under her skin."

He walked over to Tate. "And clearly, she got under yours or you wouldn't have rushed back to work, injured."

"I'm not—"

"Let me see it."

Tate frowned, but the big man stood in front of him, and he seemed to have no choice but to shake off his jacket and unbutton his shirt. Sly reached inside it and felt the bones, the muscles of his shoulder.

Tate gritted his teeth, but a small moan emerged.

"It's not dislocated, but it's definitely still swollen. You need ice on it and immobilization. Go back to the estate, get rested—"

"No." He jerked away from Sly. "I have a job to do."

"Someone else can do your job."

He met Sly's eyes as he buttoned his shirt. "And let's, for one moment, say it wasn't me standing there. Wasn't me who spent months training in every kind of terrain, learning how to spot threats. What if it was one of your rent-a-cops with guns who you'd assigned to protect Glo?" His jaw went hard. "You have some good guys on this team—I got that part already. But no one knows Glo like I do. No one can protect her like I can."

Sly's mouth tightened. He stepped back to sit against the desk. "I did my homework on you. I know about what happened in Afghanistan, to you and your unit."

Tate's fingers stopped buttoning his shirt.

"That's tough—to lose everyone like you did."

Tate didn't move. Took a breath. Resumed buttoning.

"The report didn't say how you survived."

Tate reached for his jacket. Held it for a moment. "I hid under the bodies of my buddies as the Taliban went house to house looking for me." For three long, horrifying days. "Then I sneaked out under cover of darkness."

"And escaped to the wilderness with a busted knee, contacted help, and survived."

The short story, yes. And the entire time, hearing shame in his ears.

He'd left his men behind. After walking them right into an ambush.

"I've met your type before. Heroes—"

"I'm no hero, sir."

"Well, you clearly don't have anything to prove to anyone, so are you sure you want to stay?"

He did have something to prove. If not to Glo, then himself.

Maybe especially to himself.

"You may or may not have noticed the black eye Glo was sprouting when she returned from Vegas," Tate said quietly. "Or even the *gunshot wound* that's still healing on her shoulder?" He took a step toward Sly. "That was on me. I failed her. Twice. It's not going to happen a third time."

Sly folded his arms over his chest. Considered Tate. "'Never shall I fail my comrades.'"

Tate's mouth tightened. He nodded. "I remember the Ranger creed, thanks."

"'Surrender is not a Ranger word.'"

"No, sir, it's not."

Finally, he nodded. "Go to the kitchen. Get some ice. I'll pick up Gloria's detail until you get back." He stood up as Tate turned.

"Tate?"

He stopped, glanced at Sly.

"We're a team here. My team. And you're not the only one who made promises to people. Good job today…but next time you show up hurt to work, I'm sidelining you. You're not the only one who can keep Gloria safe."

Tate nodded, but as he pushed out the door into the hallway, cast a look into the crowd and spotted Glo, he wanted to respectfully disagree.

Go ahead and date Slick, honey.

Because he may have lost the battle, but he wasn't about to concede the war.

Tate was out there, and she was in here and—

"Sit down, already, Glo. Or go out to the bunkhouse and find him. But you're making me dizzy."

Glo wore her pajama pants and a *Belles Are Made for Singing* T-shirt, having taken a shower after tonight's fundraising fiasco, her hair still wet. Cher sat on the bed, finger combing her wet hair. Her friend was staying over in one of the other guest rooms and had also showered, changed into a pair of yoga pants and a T-shirt.

"I can't go out there. It'll just encourage him."

"I think we're beyond the need for encouragement here, sister. The man saved your life tonight. I'd say he's all in."

All in.

She could still feel Tate's body pressing over her, feel his heartbeat thumping through his chest.

Hear the tiny grunts of pain he tried to hold in.

Stupid, heroic man. Her eyes burned at the memory of watching him in the office, the muscles in his jaw so tight she could strum them. He'd been in pain.

And not just from his shoulder.

Don't worry, sweetheart, I won't get in the way of you and Slick.

So much hurt in his voice, it put a fist in her gut.

Glo stood at the window. She'd darkened her room so

she could look out and now spied at least two security staff prowling the exterior of her mother's house, one down by the semi-lit pool area. The darkness wouldn't allow her to make out his features.

It could be Tate.

Or maybe he was inside, still icing his shoulder. The man had worn the ice pack all night, on top of his dress shirt, like the hunchback of Notre Dame.

But he was never more than ten feet from her, even when she pulled Sloan out to the far end of the pool, after the guests started to leave, and told him that yes, she'd accept those dinner plans.

Every word out of her mouth tasted sour.

Especially with Tate standing in the shadows.

Her plan, even to her own mind, sounded desperate, a scene out of a soap opera. But with her mother holding the reins of his employment—and heaven help her, she'd like to know what "deal" they'd struck—her only hope was to make him quit.

So yeah, she'd date Sloan. Hold his hand. She'd draw the line at kissing him, but…the whole idea of hurting Tate still made her ill.

"I'm a terrible person." Glo ran her hands up her arms and came over to flop on the bed beside Cher. The ceiling fan ran overhead, catching the light of the pool on its gilded blades, cascading it around the room.

"Okay, maybe a little."

She looked at Cher, who raised a shoulder. "That perfectly handsome, wounded man saved your life tonight. You should be sneaking out in a romantic Romeo and Juliet moment to thank him."

"They both died."

"Okay, bad comparison, but certainly the man deserves a little love from the woman he can't seem to stop chasing."

"The woman who is going to get him killed if he sticks around. He was inches from getting shot tonight—and not just once. He wasn't even wearing protective gear—and hello,

I'm changing that. Tomorrow, all my security details wear armor. He just hovered over me like a human shield—"

"Um—"

"If you say that's his job, I'm kicking you out."

"Of your life, or just the room? Because I'm hungry and need a kitchen raid."

Glo rolled her eyes. "C'mon."

They got up and Glo led the way down the hallway, down the stairs, and across the tile to the massive chef's kitchen. She left sweaty footprints on the cool tile and stood in the darkness as Cher opened the Sub-Zero fridge, the light cascading over her.

"Did you know Sloan is my mother's assistant campaign manager?"

Cher pulled out a container of yogurt. "Who's her manager?"

"The same woman she always uses, Nicole Stevens. She was the one who rounded everyone up and brought in the ensemble to play."

"The pretty African-American woman—"

"With the awesome hair, yes. They met in college. Nicole worked as a speechwriter, then as communications director for the governor before she helmed my mother's mayoral campaign."

Cher peeled the cover off the yogurt. "So, Sloan is back to stay."

"We're going out for dinner tomorrow night."

Cher licked the wrapper. "Really. So, we *are* getting back on the horse."

"No. We're trying to drive the Lone Ranger away. I'm hoping that the more Tate sees me with Sloan, the angrier he'll get and quit."

"Oh, I see. We're living out country songs IRL. That's a twist." She dug the spoon in. "How long before Sloan is on to your evil plan?"

She frowned. "No...it's not an evil plan. I like Sloan—"

"Yee-haw."

"Stop talking about horses!" Glo went to the pantry and opened it. What she wouldn't do for a box of frozen Ho Hos.

Or better yet, chocolate chip cookies, like Gerri Marshall made on the ranch.

And of course her brain—and stomach—had to go there. Back to the Marshall Triple M, where Tate had taken her dancing and charmed her with games of gin rummy and carried her in his amazing arms after she'd been wounded.

Forget the chocolate chip cookies. She grabbed some Fig Newtons—her mother's version of comfort food—and returned to the granite island. "Listen. I'm not saying my brilliant plan is *Ocean's Eleven*. It's a simple plot. Annoy him enough that he'll leave."

"And in the meantime, break more hearts." Cher took another spoonful of yogurt, let it slide onto her tongue.

"I won't break…cut me some slack. I'm trying to save lives here."

"So is Tate, it seems."

"Maybe you *should* leave."

Cher grinned. But she put the yogurt down and took Glo's hand. "Sweetie. Why are you trying so hard to push away a man who clearly cares for you? In fact, he would give his life for you. Don't you get to be happy…oh honey, why are you crying?"

Glo pressed her hand to her mouth, shook her head. "Because I…I'm so scared that I already love him, and…it's just going to end in disaster."

"What are you talking about?"

"I don't…nothing ever works out for me. Maybe I'm one of those people who don't get to be happy."

"Of course you get to be happy. That's crazy—"

"Is it?" Her mouth tightened. "Take a good look at the debris in my life. Joy. David. Even the Yankee Belles have disbanded."

"You're not disbanded—"

"We could be. It always happens. I dream big, put my heart into something, and it turns to sand in my hands." She drew in a deep breath. "I just wish…I wish I could just know that everything will be all right." She stared at her half-eaten Fig Newton. "I'm not a fan."

"They're certainly not frozen Ho Hos." Cher gave her a sad smile. "There's nothing wrong with dreaming big, Glo. Longing for true love."

"I found true love once. I don't know that I can lose it again."

"You do have a lot of wreckage in your past."

"Tate can't be the next casualty."

Cher blew out a breath. "Okay. So what's the plan, Danny Ocean?"

"Commence Operation Angry Tate?"

"Can I just say, this is a suicide mission?"

Glo raised an eyebrow. "Why?"

Cher nodded toward the sliding glass door, and Glo turned.

The man had the ability to stop her heart in its tracks. He'd entered the patio area and slid onto a deck chair, bathed in the wan glow of the pool. He'd changed out of his suit— so, clearly off duty—and wore a pair of jeans, flip-flops, and a black T-shirt. And another ice pack affixed to his shoulder.

He positioned his chair to angle toward her window. And wore such a dark, fierce expression, it went right through her, to her core.

Steeled her.

The very thought of him sitting out there…all night long…

If she didn't stay up all night watching him, she might actually sleep.

"'But soft! What light through yonder window breaks?'" Cher said, almost breathlessly.

"Stop it."

"'It is my lady. Oh, it is my love….'"

Glo slid off the stool, shoved the bag of Fig Newtons back in the pantry, and headed toward the stairs to her bedroom.

But not before she turned for one more look at Tate. He sat with his arms folded, his shoulders bunching, as if he refused to move out of her life.

Yes, this was a suicide mission, at best.

5

H e would get the next fourteen hours with Scarlett.
Ford's only goal was not to say something stupid, not to let her in on the fact that when he'd seen her crying, when he'd pulled her to himself, when she'd actually held onto him, something dangerous had shifted inside him.

He'd gone from wanting her in his ear to wanting her in his arms and, hello, no.

Just teammates.

But she was making it a little difficult for him to think.

"I pegged you wrong. I totally thought you'd be a country music fan." Scarlett sat on the passenger side in the cab of his truck. Dressed in a pair of shorts, a T-shirt, and a baseball cap, she looked about nineteen, her face and arms tan from yesterday's picnic in Cruz's backyard, her legs crisscrossed on the seat. She wore a pair of aviator sunglasses, the morning sun reflected in the amber glare, and ate Cap'n Crunch out of the box.

He had this weird, eerie civilian throwback memory to one of his rare dates in high school, the ebullient feeling of youth, freedom, and summer nights.

Not that he'd ever sown any wild oats, but if he had, it might feel like this—a pretty girl beside him on the bench seat, the window open, one hand occasionally riding the breeze like a dolphin through the air. She pulled her arm in and rolled up the window.

"What's wrong with the Ting Tings?" he said. "Can't a country boy listen to British girl bands?"

He glanced at her, cocked his head, and sang the chorus in a falsetto—"*That's not my name... That's not my name...*"

She laughed, and it turned his heart buoyant. He'd picked her up before sunrise, in the cool darkness of the dawn, and by the time they turned eastward at Barstow, rose gold was peaking over the mountains in the Mojave National Preserve.

"I don't know why you're so surprised. Cruz listens to Italian opera, and Nez is a wreck for books on tape. He listens to them on high speed as he works out."

"Yeah, well, Nez also owns a Prius. You're driving an F-150. If this doesn't scream Montana, I'm not sure what does. Except for maybe the cowboy boots."

"Cowboy boots are more comfortable than you'd think. But no, I grew up with Johnny Cash, Waylon Jennings, and Merle Haggard crooning in the barn. Sad songs about broken hearts and life gone wrong. I much prefer this—" He flashed into falsetto again. *"Are you calling me darling? Are you calling me bird?"*

"Never." She folded up the cereal bag, grinned, and picked up her cup from McDonald's, a large Diet Coke. The third she'd sucked down over the past four hours. She hit ice, and the sound garbled in the straw.

He had finished off his bullet coffee an hour ago, but still had some in the Thermos. His stomach growled.

"You want some of my Cap'n Crunch?" She made to hand him the box.

"Seriously? I made some grub for the road. I'll grab it at the next rest stop."

"What kind of grub? PB and J?"

"Oats, soaked in almond milk, blueberries, a little baobab powder."

She made a face. "I'll keep my sugared cereal."

"What? So I don't eat like a twelve-year-old."

"Road trips are for junk food. Haven't you ever road-tripped before?"

"Once. To Disneyland."

And that shut him down briefly, because oh, how he hated talking about it.

So, "But no, we spent summer vacations working. My father had us working on irrigation pipes, moving cattle from pasture to pasture, fixing equipment, and mowing hay. Except for Sundays, we worked from sunup to sundown."

"You and your dad?"

"And my brothers and sister. Reuben, my oldest brother, is seven years older than me, so by the time he left home, I started pitching in more, but we all started riding when we were old enough to sit in the saddle."

"Even your sister?"

"Of course. My mother too—we all worked. My mother also ran a big kitchen garden, which we were required to dig up in the spring, hoe, and pull weeds."

"How big is your ranch?"

"Now? I don't know. About nine thousand acres when Dad ran it. Knox took it over when Dad died, about five years ago, and he started breeding bucking bulls. Bought a champion headed into retirement to seed the line. He was a bull rider, and the guy just has this knack. He bred Gordo with one of our cows and produced this champion bucker named Hot Pete. He was killed recently—some sort of fire I guess. My mother mentioned it in a letter. Anyway, no road trips for us. Just hard work."

"No fun at all?"

"Oh, we had fun. We have a river near our place, and we'd go down to this pocket in the river after work, swim there. Reuben would chase us around, try and drown us."

She glanced at him.

"It was all in fun. I really looked up to him. It killed me when he left home to be a smokejumper."

"Wow."

"Yeah. My dad was a wildland firefighter, and he probably gave Reuben the bug. We had a fire on our ranch once, and a bunch of hotshots and smokejumpers came in to put it

down, so my guess is that's where it all started. But my Dad...
well, he was sort of a bigger than life guy. Rode bulls and
fought fires and worked as a range cop at one time and was a
football star in college. Hard to live up to."

"I don't think you have any problems there, Navy."

Her words found his bones and settled there. "My brother Tate was actually the first to enlist. He joined the Army
right out of high school—I still remember the fight with my
dad. Tate landed a football scholarship to Montana State, but
he turned it down. Just walked away, and Dad was so lit about
it."

"Why did he turn it down?"

"Dunno. Tate was always the guy who got into trouble—
in school, and he hated working the ranch. Has this fear of
horses from when he was thrown off as a kid. I think he just
wanted to leave it as far behind as he could. So he became a
Ranger."

"Wow."

"Yeah. Was in Afghanistan too. But he was Purple Hearted out when his squad got ambushed. I don't know the whole
story—when he got back, I was already in SQT—SEAL
Qualification Training—so I'm not sure what happened. He's
fine now, though. Working in personal security, I think for
some girl band."

"And your other brother?"

"Wyatt? He plays goalie for the Minnesota Blue Ox hockey team."

"Professional?"

"Yeah. He travels a lot—we don't see him much. But he'll
probably be home this weekend for Rube's wedding."

"And is your sister coming home?"

"RJ? I don't know. I called her a few days ago and left a
message. Told her I'd be at the wedding." He looked at her.
"She's my twin."

"Oh my, a female version of Ford Marshall. What does
that look like?"

"Tough. Smart. Pretty. She works as a travel agent for

some company in DC."

Outside, the landscape had slowly turned from rugged mountains to the mesas of the desert. The road was bordered to the south by Joshua trees, white yuccas, and valleys of purple and white wildflowers.

Adele came over the radio. *Hello, it's me... I was wondering if after all these years you'd like to meet...*

"This is such a sad song," Scarlett said. "About a woman who regrets breaking up with a guy, but when she tries to go back to him, he's already moved on."

"Too much like a country music song." He turned down the volume. "I prefer songs without any emotional commitment." They passed a state road sign. "Welcome to Nevada."

"I hate Nevada," she said quietly.

He frowned. "Why?"

"Oh. Bad memories." She turned to him. "No rest areas. Want that oatmeal now?"

"We need gas. We'll stop in a bit. What kind of bad memories?"

She made a face. "My mom left me at a diner once, overnight in some Podunk town in Nevada."

"What?"

She lifted a shoulder, drew up one knee up, and hooked her hands around it. "I was seven at the time. Not a big deal—the owner found me. Her name was Peggy, and she gave me a chocolate shake, then let me sleep in her silver Airstream she had parked out back. But it's my first real memory of being left behind, and it still makes me a little sick."

"I don't understand—did she do this a lot?"

"Unfortunately, yes. She was a California girl who had big dreams of being an actress, but she fell for all the wrong men. Mostly musicians, but a few hippies, and plenty of low-level criminals. She started using, although I'm lucky—she never used when she was pregnant. She was eighteen when she had me and followed my dad—a folk singer—around California until he dumped her. She was always trying out for bit parts, practicing her auditions in the living room. I think she was an extra in a couple movies. We lived in Vegas for a while, and she worked a couple small shows as a dancer. Then she hooked up with Terry, who took her up to Salt Lake City. I think the diner incident happened when they were together—I have a vague memory of them having a fight. Maybe him leaving her there and her trying to hitchhike to go after him. I don't know. But we ended up in Salt Lake for a couple years. Then he kicked her out, and we lived in a Monte Carlo for a while—"

"You lived in your car?"

"Mom got a job working second shift at a warehouse—I think it might have been a shipping company—so she'd lock me in the car in the parking lot. She tucked me in, and I felt safe enough." But she looked out the window, her jaw tight.

He had a feeling she might be skimming over the truth.

He touched the brakes as they came up on a semi, pulled out, and passed it.

"We got our own apartment for a while there. It was a good time. Mom was in recovery and doing well, and she was auditioning again. We'd run lines together—she taught me how to do accents."

"Like—?" Ford asked.

She affected a French accent. "'Yes, well, life is not all shoot-shoot, bang-bang, you know.'"

He gave her a blank look.

"Really? Inspector Clouseau. *The Pink Panther?*"

"Sorry. We were *Gunsmoke* and *Bonanza* people."

"Sad. I don't know if she ever got the part, but I loved that apartment. I remember this tiny Christmas tree my mother put up. It was the first real Christmas tree we'd ever had, and we made paper ornaments to decorate it. It even had lights. I begged her to let me sleep out under it, and I'd lie on the floor in my Little Mermaid sleeping bag, watching them glitter against the ceiling. It was perfect. We lived in this two-story walk-up with a pool, so during the summer, I'd lie out by the pool and pretend I was a movie star. That was when we met Gary."

She drew in a breath.

And he tensed. "Gary?"

"There's a truck stop," she said.

He took the off-ramp and pulled up to a pump.

While she was gone, he found his morning rations and ate them out of his Thermos.

Gary. The name had lodged a fist into his gut.

When she got back in the truck—carrying a bag of mini donuts, a Diet Coke, and a bag of Cheetos—she didn't bring it back up.

And really, although they'd talked before, it was mostly about football teams and local cuisine and even fellow teammates, so maybe he didn't know her at all. But he wanted to.

He glanced at her, pained by a little girl in brown pigtails sitting at a diner table drinking a chocolate shake, hoping her mother would return. His stomach clenched, the oatmeal not quite sitting right.

"Want a donut?" She held out the open bag.

He hesitated, then, "Okay," and reached in the bag.

That tasted pretty good.

They drove through Vegas, commented on a few of the buildings, and came out the other side, the road winding through desolation. Tumbleweeds littered the highway, the earth barren, dotted with scrub brush and cacti. Occasionally, a mobile home park would pop up, with rusty, small units hunkering down to survive what felt like the Apocalypse.

He'd been a little—no, *a lot*—spoiled growing up in Montana, with the rugged mountains, the lush valleys, the waterfalls, and big blue open sky.

They finally hit Zion National Park, the pink and orange sandstone cliffs rising to greet them as the sun climbed high.

"Want me to drive?" Scarlett said into the quiet. He hadn't realized how long they'd driven without talking, hadn't realized they'd found a comfortable silence.

"I'm okay."

"What are you thinking about?"

Actually, his brain had been on the op, the one where

he'd nearly gotten killed, and the conversation with Nez twenty-four hours later, after Ford had thrown up some congealed blood in his stomach. *Never again, hotshot. You don't go rogue on your team.*

"Martha, that woman we saved. And the fact that if you hadn't told me about those squirters, they might have run us down, taken her back."

"Taken you guys too."

He shook his head. "No. I'd never let myself be taken."

She stared at him through her sunglasses a long time. "You'd die first?"

"No, I'd just…I wouldn't let myself be taken."

She drew in a breath. "That's the part I don't like—knowing you guys are out there and really, I can't do anything about it."

"What are you talking about? You were my eyes out there. I went totally blind when my NVGs kicked off. You saved my life."

"Or, I could have watched you die, right there. I just…I want to do more, you know?"

"I don't know what more you could do without becoming a SEAL. You can't deploy with us into the field."

"I could," she said quietly. "They opened up SEAL training to women."

He knew better than to react. "Mmmhmm."

"I can tell by your smirk. You don't think we can do it—pass the requirements."

"Them are fightin' words, Red. Let's just say that three women have tried and not made it."

She went quiet, and he finally looked at her, the silence no longer peaceful.

She wasn't actually thinking of trying to be a SEAL, was she? He could see her then, all kitted up in body armor, face paint, camo, waiting for her at their drop or exfil point, and a coldness poured through him.

Sure, she could pass the training. Probably. Maybe.

Huh.

Even if she did…uh, no. He didn't want her anywhere near the militants who wouldn't think twice about not just shooting her but taking her captive. And leaving the wounds on Scarlett he'd seen in Martha's eyes.

Yes, it felt selfish to keep her from something she wanted. But they were a good team. They worked.

However, he couldn't turn into some sap and tell her that.

"Let's get some grub," she said then, clearly evading. Like the soldier she was—survive, evade, resist, and escape.

He suddenly wanted to do the same.

"I think I need a burger." She pointed to a green building coming up on the side of the road.

Dusty's Roadhouse. He spied a few Harleys in the dirt drive as they pulled up, and he wondered what they might be getting themselves into. But they'd been on the road for nearly ten hours, and his body was stiffening up.

He parked, and they got out. She strode toward the door without waiting for him.

He followed her in.

The place smelled like a roadhouse, the scent of fried foods in old oil saturating the worn wood planking on the walls. Neon signs listed the beer available on tap or in bottles, and at the back of the room, a stage painted black hosted a few empty mics.

She headed toward a red vinyl booth, but his gaze landed on a lineup of big guys dressed in cutoff shirts and leather pants, at the bar. He didn't love the way their gazes latched onto Scarlett.

He took off his sunglasses, gave one of the guys a hard look, then slid into the booth seat opposite Scarlett.

She grabbed a menu propped near the napkin holder and handed it to him. "Best thing in these places—the house burger and probably the fries. Order for me—I'm going to use the bathroom."

He watched her as she slid out of the booth and headed toward the back.

A Garth Brooks song came on, apropos for the

environment. *I've got friends in low places...*

Ford scanned the menu, his gaze traitorously falling on the O-rings and ribs.

He nearly missed the movement from the bar. One of the bigger guys—sporting a short beard, a bandanna on his head, and a bare chest under a leather vest—headed toward the bathrooms.

Ford put the menu down, watching.

Scarlett came out of the bathroom just as the man met her in the hallway.

He stood in her way.

Ford started moving out of the booth.

Then, suddenly, she laughed and patted the man on his muscled arm and moved past him.

Ford stilled, and her gaze landed on his, her smile fixed.

So maybe he'd sort of overreacted there. He slid back into the booth, and she joined him.

Her neck was a little flushed.

"You okay?"

"Mmmhmm." She picked up her purse. "But we're leaving. Now."

He raised an eyebrow but followed her back out into the sunshine. She climbed into the truck, and only then did her breath blow out. "Right. Okay. So yeah, he sort of mentioned a suggestion of what we might do in that bathroom together."

Ford froze. She put her hand on his arm. "I made a comment about the likelihood of that and laughed. He might have been a bit surprised at my frankness. We should probably go before he tells his friends."

Ford just stared at her.

"Unless you want to grab that steak? Might need to bring your Winkler in with you."

He put the truck in reverse. Pulled out. "You're not boring, are you, Red?"

"Just trying to keep you out of trouble, Navy." She leaned back, put her bare feet on the dash, and closed her eyes.

They hit another McDonald's in Salt Lake City, and he

retrieved his salad out of the cooler while eying her fries and chocolate shake.

They hit construction just north of Ogden on I-15, and a line of traffic slowed to a crawl. The sun hung low, casting the mountains to the east in an amber glow. She checked the GPS on her phone. "We're getting close. Get off at 13, toward Corinne." She pointed to an upcoming exit.

He took it, and they found themselves wandering along country roads, past ranches and farmland, through a small town.

They came out the other side and went under a highway with no on-ramp.

"Oops, I think that was our road." She waved him forward. "Keep going."

Well, he always obeyed her voice. He went past a Texaco, a diner, more farmland, a tiny town with a Dairy Queen, and finally noticed she'd gotten very quiet. He glanced over at her.

"Turn right at the next road."

He raised an eyebrow but turned onto a road named W 2000 S, which felt way off the grid.

They drove for five miles, as she fiddled with her GPS. Finally, she gave him a grim look.

"What?"

"We lost cell phone coverage a ways back. I…I think we're lost."

He slowed and pulled over to the gravel. Turned to her. She gave him a chagrinned smile. "Sorry."

"Okay, let me take a look."

The map was loading.

He handed it back. "We'll find directions somewhere."

He pulled back on the road, and they kept driving, but his gaze went to the fuel gauge. They'd dropped below a quarter tank going through Salt Lake City, and now the gauge hovered just above E.

And that's when the gas empty light flickered on. Forty miles to them standing on the side of the road with a gas canister, him hitching to the nearest Sinclair.

"I'm turning around."

She spotted a sign as he turned around. "Ten miles to Malad."

"That's…we were just there, Red. We passed the Welcome to Idaho sign miles ago. You're sort of useless without a drone."

"Wait—" She sat up, turned around to read the sign they'd passed. "Sixteen miles to Holbrook. I recognize that—it's on the way."

"Red—we're getting close to fumes here."

"Trust me."

He turned around and kept heading west.

They passed a vast area of grassland and a national forest sign. A weathered house looked just about ready to fall in the wind.

They entered the town of Holbrook, designated by a wooden sign and a silo. "I don't see a gas station."

"Yeah, but Rockland isn't far."

He took a right and headed north.

Mountains rose to the west, green peaks still covered in places with snow. A lone red farmhouse sat off the road, a gate sagging, clearly abandoned. Purple sage blew in the wind.

He glanced at his gauge. Twenty-eight miles to E.

Scarlett had fallen into a pensive silence.

"You okay?"

She took a breath and gathered herself. Nodded. "Yeah. Yep. All good."

"Yeah, you're lying."

She glanced over at him. "I don't like my mother's latest boyfriend too much. His name is Axel. He's an ex-con, which doesn't make him a bad guy, it's just…he doesn't work, and he doesn't treat her very well and…I just wish better for her."

"This guy isn't…well, he's not like Gary, right?" He wasn't sure why he'd brought that up again, but something about the way she'd handled the guy in the roadhouse, an understanding of how to evade and escape—he'd begun to wonder if it didn't come from the military but personal experience.

"No," she said quietly. "He's not like Gary."

Ford's hands tightened on the steering wheel.

"It's up here." She sat up. He spotted a tiny community nestled into the draws and foothills of a nearby mountainous rise. A tiny white church rose from the main street. Another one, bigger, sat at the edge of town. "The Mormon church." Scarlett pointed it out. "Take a left at the café."

The word Café in red lettering jutted out from the door of a nondescript white house. Yeah, he'd bet there was a lineup.

Across from an ancient Amoco, rusty and permanently closed, the tiny building had been converted to an outdoor eatery. It looked more like an auto parts store than a café.

"Right on South Willow."

Surprisingly, the community was clean, the yards trimmed, the houses kept up. He drove past a row of double-wides with front porches and hanging flowers.

"There."

He wasn't sure what he might be expecting, but something inside him unclenched a little as he pulled up to a tiny green house with a white painted front porch. A potted geranium had breathed its last on the front stoop, but he spotted a trampoline in the side yard and a bike leaning against a mature oak tree.

He pulled onto the gravel drive, and Scarlett reached for the handle. "I'll grab my stuff."

Wait. He felt the pulse inside him as she let herself out.

Wait. Another tharrumph as a man came out onto the porch. He was tall and muscled, his shoulders thick. Maybe early forties, his long hair pulled back into a ponytail, and a layer of whiskers, more lazy than GQ, on his face. He wore a black muscle shirt and a pair of loose-fitting gym shorts, flip-flops. And his gaze settled on Scarlett with a slight uptick to his mouth.

Axel?

Ford didn't know why he'd expected someone in his

sixties. Maybe because his mother had just turned sixty and he thought Scarlett might be a year or two older than him. But this guy...

The man came off the porch toward Scarlett, swagger in his steps, like...well, a little like the biker at Dusty's.

Ford got out of the truck. Clearly this ride wasn't quite over.

6

The woman was on a mission to make him lose his mind. And it just might work.

Tate didn't move a muscle, his gaze on everything but Glo as she walked along the Japanese gardens of Cheekwood Estate, hand in hand with Sloan Anderson. A slight May breeze bullied the white Japanese lilacs that bordered the meandering paths dappled in purples and reds from the lingering twilight.

The perfect romantic stroll for a couple in love.

He glanced at Glo, just a check-in, then surveyed the area beyond her, the pavilion and stunted pines on the horizon ahead.

An impulsive stroll after an early dinner at the Watermark, just off Music Row.

At least he didn't have to try to keep her in his sights at one of the blues joints on Bourbon Street or on the packed dance floor of the Wildhorse Saloon, venues he thought might be more the taste of the woman he knew.

Once knew.

But apparently that woman had vanished, replaced by this upper-crust society woman who preferred dinner and jazz at Sambuca, and Brahms at the Nashville Symphony. Gone were her red cowboy boots, her daring painted-on tattoos, and the twinkle in her eye as she glanced at him standing in the wings.

No, all her glances and even sweet smiles she reserved for Sloan. Tonight she wore a high-collared pink dress, black heels that had to be killing her, and twined her fingers through Sloan's as she listened to him drone on about the exploits of a senator during his season as a lobbyist.

A voice came through his earpiece—the driver, one of the security staff, waiting at the gate.

"Rango, it's Swamp. ETA?"

Swamp, aka Baker Flemming from Florida. All the guys had nicknames beyond their formal names. Tate had been dubbed Rango after some cartoon Swamp had seen.

On his shift he worked with Rags—Art Ragsdale; Petey-Boy—Bobby Peterson; and Mitty—Walter Jenkins. Good guys who had stayed out of his business with Glo but knew something might be up after he'd come in one night a few days ago after a shift of watching Glo swoon over Sloan, taped up, and attacked the hanging bag in the weight room. Nearly threw out his shoulder again but felt the muscles start to knit together, and by the end, the adrenaline and heat of his frustration had worked into his bones, settled them, and spread out into determination.

Glo couldn't possibly *really* like this schmuck. He was smooth and manipulative. And he wanted his own limelight.

Glo needed someone willing to stand on the sidelines and watch her shine.

The bunk room, for the guys who worked full time and didn't have digs in town, hosted a weight room, sauna, pool table, darts, a kitchenette, laundry, and a communications room that rivaled NASA.

He'd spent more than a few hours doing homework on the Bryant League. Had a call—or few—in to his sister, who seemed to be ignoring him.

The sooner he caught the sniper and the guys who bombed the arena, the sooner he knew the immediate threat had been neutralized, the sooner he could ditch his agreement with the senator, turn his attention on Glo, and make this a fair fight.

The couple stopped in the cool shade of the pavilion, and

Glo leaned against one of the corner poles, turning to Sloan. She touched his chest, a playful gesture as she laughed.

The flirting slipped under Tate's skin, buzzed. He gritted his jaw as he stopped and stood at a distance, his body turned away, searching for threats, although honestly, the unscheduled stop was probably one of the safest moves.

Still, they couldn't completely shut down the garden without prior notice, so it was on him to keep a heads-up.

His scan brushed over Glo and just as it did, she looked up.

She had the most amazing hazel-green eyes, with glints of gold in the sunshine, darkening as twilight dipped into them, and now they held on to him, just a moment.

Testing?

He didn't know what to think. And of course, Sloan picked right then to lean in, to cup her cheek and go in for a kiss.

She turned her head, laughing, but Tate couldn't move, caught in the horror of watching the woman he loved—okay, maybe not loved, but—well, he didn't know what else it might be called when it felt like his freakin' heart was being ripped through his ribs, his breath serrated in his chest. He held in the nearly uncontrollable urge to close the gap and yank Sloan away from her—

And right then Kelsey's voice ripped through him. Steeling him. *You may be who Glo wants, but make sure you're who she needs too.*

He may not be who Glo wanted anymore, but yes, he was who she needed.

Which meant he stood there, a stone falling through his chest as he watched Sloan pull away and kiss her forehead. So far, she'd dodged him, but it would only be a matter of time before Sloan actually landed one on Glo and then Tate's head just might pop off.

Tate swallowed, anything to loosen his dry throat, and turned away.

Shoot, all the moisture in his throat had gone to his eyes.

This was stupid. Maybe even fatal.

"You okay, Rango? You were making some funny sounds through the comms."

"I'm fine." Movement out of his periphery had him looking back at Glo. She'd taken Sloan's hand again and now they were headed back up the path.

Hopefully home.

Please.

He followed her out and met Swamp's gaze when he spotted him standing next to the car. The man wore his blond hair longer than most, had a surfer vibe, despite his suit and tie. He opened the door for Sloan and Glo, tucked them inside, and Tate went around to the passenger side, front seat.

The partition was up, and he turned the AC on full blast.

Swamp said nothing as he slid into the driver's seat and headed back to the Jackson estate. Except, when they pulled up, Glo slid down the partition. "Tate can get out here. Then we'd like to continue on to Sloan's place. Baker, you can take over from there."

Tate closed his eyes in pain, argument broaching his lips just as Glo slid the partition closed.

Swamp glanced at him. "I got this. Get outta here."

Yeah. And maybe Baker was right on the nose.

He should leave. At the very least, Tate needed fresh air.

He got out, and Swamp pulled away, leaving Tate standing in driveway as the night dipped around him, his hands in fists.

Wow.

He pulled off his tie as he headed back to the bunkhouse. Slammed the door open. It banged on the wall, and from his twin bed, Rags looked up. He was tall, lean, and built like a wide receiver. In fact, he'd been an All-American, Division III, a star, but not NFL material. Rumor had it that he'd played Arena ball before joining the military and going to sniper school for the Army. He had blond-brown hair, a white smile, and a country-boy aura that probably worked well for him down at the Wildhorse Saloon on his days off.

He popped out his earbuds, put down his phone, and

leaned up. "'Sup?"

"Nothing." Tate shrugged out of his jacket and hung it in the closet near his bed. He'd taken the one by the far wall which also allowed him space to empty Knox's briefcase of evidence, tape it to the wall, and start his own obsession. Now he sat on his bunk as he toed off his dress shoes, then unbuttoned his cuffs and shirt.

Rags came over, the earbuds hanging around his neck. "Why don't you quit, dude? We all know you have it bad for Glo. It's written all over your face—you sort of turn shades of purple every time you see Glo and Sloan together, which lately has been, um, always."

Well, not always. Today she'd spent at least three hours reading a magazine in her bikini near the pool. Yeah, that had been fun—him, trying not to stare at her legs, those curves as he patrolled the pool area, sweating in his suit pants and white oxford.

He missed his days guarding the Belles.

"I can't quit," he said as he stripped off his shirt. Sly made him wear an undershirt, too, and now he untucked it from his pants. "I don't have anywhere else to go."

"What about your ranch? Sounds like a sweet gig—Montana, right?"

"It's not my ranch. It belongs to my brothers Reuben and Knox. I'm not a cowboy—I hate horses. Got bucked off when I was six and never took to them after that." He slid his belt from his loops. "No, I left the cowboying to my brothers and enlisted when I was eighteen. Went to Ranger school right after boot camp. It's who I was." Until he wasn't.

"How did you get into the security field?"

A fight. Words with his father after he'd returned from Afghanistan. Anger. The story could undo him, so, "Sort of fell into it after I left the military. I met Glo and the band while I was working security for the San Antonio arena."

"You were on the bus with them?" Rags wore a smile.

"So was their drummer, Elijah Blue. Don't get any ideas."

"But that's how she got under your skin, right?"

And into his brain flashed the memory of Glo sitting on one of the couches, leaning over her guitar, picking out a new tune. Scribbling in her journal, her bottom lip caught in her teeth.

Where was that girl?

"Listen. We got this, bro. Sly filled us in—told us about the shooting and some sort of fight in Vegas Glo was involved in. We understand your commitment, but really…it's like watching *Rocky IV*, and Apollo is going down against Ivan Drago. It's not pretty."

That eked a smile from him. "Yeah, well, maybe I'm Rocky. I'll win in the end."

"Still not sure it's worth it."

Rags walked over to the wall. "This must be your art wall from the bombing?"

"Yeah. Everything my brother collected." Tate stood up and pointed to two hand-drawn pictures of the suspects. "The local officials identified the bomber as a rodeo clown, but my brother saw a picture of him with these two guys. One has a tattoo of bright orange flames circling his neck, the other had gauged ears and a port-wine stain. Apparently the one with the port-wine stain is the mayor's son, so I don't think they leaned too hard on him. His name is Alan Kobie, but he didn't give up his friend's name. My sister works for the CIA, and she's trying to dig up the identity, but the Senator thinks the bombing is the work of a rogue leftist group trying to thwart her campaign."

"Was one of these guys responsible for the attack at your ranch?"

Wow, Sly really had opened up his file. "We think so. Kelsey, Glo's bandmate who was with her that night, identified a guy with gauged ears, so…maybe…" He tapped the drawings. "Could be Kobie, but he's gone to ground." He turned to Rags. "Did you find anything at the Anderson place?"

"Sly turned a team loose there, but so far, they only found a couple spent shells."

This perked Tate up. "What kind of shells?"

"Brass, 7.62x51mm NATO."

"For a M40A5 sniper rifle."

"That's what I was thinking too."

"You ever shoot one of those?"

"I wasn't a Marine. Straight up Army."

"The Rangers used MK11s." Tate turned back to the wall. "Which means our man could be a former Marine. That helps. Maybe RJ can cross-reference known members of the Bryant League with former Marines." He picked up his phone, sent a speed dial, but the call went directly to voicemail.

He bit back a word and tossed the phone on his bed. Considered it for a moment. "Maybe I need to get on a plane. She hasn't called me back for over a week. It's weird. And we're supposed to be together this weekend for my brother's wedding."

"Oh, leaving the ship in the hands of the crew, huh?" Rags leaned against the wall. "Good. Go to a wedding, find a cute girl, try and forget Glo."

"Every girl there will be either my sister or future sister-in-law, so…probably not." But maybe he could go down to the Bulldog Saloon…

No. The very thought tightened his gut. He hated the man he'd been during the two years since Vegas, trying to forget Raquel.

In fact, he liked the person he was now, or at least the one he was turning into since he'd signed on with the Belles.

The guy who refused to stay down. Steady. Reliable.

It might be the first time he wasn't ashamed of himself.

"Naw," he said to Rags. "I'm in it for the long game. Even if she breaks my heart, I'm sticking around. But yeah, I need to get some headspace. Glo is desperately trying to push me away—I get it. I get her. She's got some baggage in her past that makes her terrified that I'm going to get killed. But there's only so much pummeling a man can take."

"Right?" Rags said.

Tate picked up his phone, pocketed it. "How about a

game of eight ball?"

"Instead of camping out by the pool staring up at her room?"

He let himself smile, lifted a shoulder. "That'll come later. After she gets home."

"Rango, you're in such trouble."

Yeah. Well, maybe for the first time it was the kind of trouble he wanted.

Glo stood at her window, the morning light sliding across the creamy white carpet, and noticed that his deck chair was empty.

In fact, when she'd returned home last night, it was empty too.

And although she'd checked, he never showed up.

Glo had made a real mess of everything, just as Tate predicted. What had he said...a train wreck?

Because Sloan Anderson just might be in love with her.

And Tate wasn't going down for the count. She'd thought two moonlit walks, maximum. Thought after the first night when she'd let Sloan kiss her—just a quick good-night peck on the cheek—that Tate would charge into her mother's office and tender his resignation.

Instead, after she'd gone inside, she'd seen him appear poolside in his off-duty attire of a pair of faded jeans, a white T-shirt, and flip-flops—not exactly the most utilitarian of footwear if he wanted to run down an assailant. But maybe he wasn't sitting out there because he feared for her life.

Maybe he simply wanted to remind her that she still had his heart.

O Romeo, Romeo.

She turned away. Maybe she'd finally driven him away, and that thought hollowed her out, just a little. But, good.

Right?

Maybe it had been impulsive—and frankly, cruel—to

order him from the car last night. But when she'd looked over and seen him watching as Sloan put the moves on her, as his jaw tightened, she just knew the man wasn't quitting.

She had to get drastic. So she'd made him think she was going back to Sloan's place. Alone. With Sloan. Wanted to drive home the point that she could do what she wanted, and no amount of his glares, pursed lips, and tight shoulders could stop her.

Except, well, it had stopped her. Because she'd also managed to give Sloan the wrong idea and had to convince him to sit with her by his pool, cocooned in his embrace, watching the stars.

He'd traced his finger up her arm and told her that maybe they had a future after the campaign. After her mother made him press secretary in the new White House administration. She'd love DC, by the way. His favorite bagel place was only two blocks from the Capitol.

Yeah, she had a Sloan problem. Or maybe not a problem, because Sloan was everything a girl could want, really. Smart, wickedly handsome, and he nearly worshiped her.

But every time the man took her in his arms, every time he tried to kiss her, all she could remember was the amazing kiss with Tate, the way he had set her entire body on fire.

No one had kissed her, ever, like Tate Marshall. Like she might be a drink of water to a parched man. Needing her.

She couldn't bear the thought of kissing anyone else.

Eventually, she'd left Sloan alone under the Milky Way and headed home.

Felt the smallest—okay, a pretty large—twinge of disappointment at the empty deck chair.

She swallowed away the memory of Tate's lips on hers and grabbed her iPad, a towel, and her sunglasses. She had a slew of emails to answer.

Her father was in the kitchen, sitting on a bar stool, eating a half grapefruit, drinking coffee, and reading something on his iPad, his reading glasses low on his nose. "There's my Glo-light."

"Hey, Dad." She opened the fridge and grabbed a yogurt. Then poured a cup of coffee and sat on a stool next to him.

"Nice picture of you." He flashed her his iPad. Kelsey stood in the middle, a cowboy hat pulled down over her eyes. Glo stood on the left, a painted rose tattoo down the arm that held her Dobro, dressed all in black.

Dixie flanked them on the other side, wearing a short, sequined dress, her legs about a mile long, her blonde hair down, her violin propped against her shoulder.

"It's a few weeks old from when the nominations were announced. Carter sent it out."

"Are you going to the CMGs?"

"Of course. It's a huge honor even to be nominated." She opened her yogurt.

"Are you taking Sloan?"

She set the cover on the counter, picked up her spoon. "I...I don't know. I hadn't thought about it."

"You get to bring someone, right?"

She hadn't gotten that far.

Or, rather, yes she had. She pictured Tate beside her. As her bodyguard, maybe, but still.

Tate was the Belles' bodyguard. He deserved to participate in the fun.

"You and Sloan are spending a lot of time together."

"Mmmhmm." She took a bite of her yogurt.

"Reminds me a little of your mother and me, back in the day. She had political aspirations...I just went along for the wild ride."

"I don't think Sloan has political aspirations."

Her dad took off his glasses. "You can't be serious."

She took a sip of coffee. "Okay. Yes. He wants to be a speechwriter, but run for office?"

"He's an idealist, like your mother. They see a world that is fairer, kinder, and safer."

"So do I."

"They want to do something about it."

She made a face. "So do I..."

"Of course you do. But this…political life is challenging. And consuming. Some of us have to stay behind and support those who are changing the world. Your mother is a fireball. I'm not. But I do know how to keep the fire going." He winked.

She didn't want to know what he meant. Except, "Then why did you leave her? You two have lived apart for…well, nearly ten years."

He frowned, something quick. "It was because of you, Glo. You needed to get away. After Joy died, you were so withdrawn and scared and—"

"I was withdrawn and scared because Mother blamed me for her death." Oh, and she didn't mean for that to come out, but…well, "When I woke up after the surgery, Mother wasn't there. She was with Joy, waiting for her wake up. And I got it…she was always with Joy. Joy was her favorite. Joy needed her, and Mother likes to be needed. But…I needed her, too, and…"

"And she didn't show up, even after Joy passed." Her father touched her arm. "And then we brought you home to the room you shared with your sister."

"I couldn't sleep there, Dad. I just kept staring at her empty bed."

"I know. That's when you started sleeping in the guest room. Maybe I shouldn't have taken that job in Minnesota, but we thought it was best to get you into a new environment. And your mother was busy with her life in DC. Still is. She's always had a free spirit—and I didn't want to get in the way."

"Me either. I guess that's why I feel like a guest in my mother's life." She stirred her yogurt. "And frankly, that's okay. I don't like the things she likes. I'm…"

"A poet like your old man." He laughed and gave her arm a squeeze. "You are so much like me, Glo. Thoughtful. You see the needs of others and jump in. But you're like your mother too…a fireball in your own right. Creative, bold, smart. And you need a man who will tend your fires. Is Sloan that guy? Can he put his dreams aside to keep yours alive?"

She considered him. "What are you saying?"

He ran his thumb down the side of his coffee cup. "I keep seeing a man sitting out by the pool every night. Sleeping on a deck chair."

She shook her head, turned away. "I'm not...I don't deserve him, Dad."

"What?"

"No, really. I've been a total jerk to him this week. I've deliberately thrown myself at Sloan just to make him jealous."

"Why?" Her father's tone betrayed the shame she felt.

"Because...well, why should someone put their life on the line for me? I...I'm not...I'm just a regular person. I'm not the president, or even anyone important. I'm just...I'm just...well, you know."

"No. I don't know. My beautiful daughter?"

"Not the beautiful daughter, Dad. I'm the other one. The one who lived."

He just blinked at her, and she looked away, her throat tight.

"Glo—"

"Joy should have lived, and we all know it. And it was my fault she didn't."

"Hardly!" He turned and took her face in his hands. "She was sick. Too sick. And that wasn't on you."

"It was my kidney, my body."

"You were fraternal twins, not identical. And we knew it was a long shot. For the record, I was against the transplant from the first."

Glo shook her head, moving away from his grip. "I would have done it, even if you had said no. I loved her..." Her eyes filled. "I just don't understand God. Joy was perfect. Smart. Beautiful. And yet I was born with the healthy body. It's a terrible joke on everyone, and Mother knows it best of all."

"Your mother has her faults—she is very focused on her goals. But she loves you, Glo."

Glo drew in a breath. "I know. And I love her. I have no reason to complain, I know that."

He took her hand. "You've had a few rough starts, Glo-light, so I think you have reason to complain. But that doesn't mean you don't deserve to be safe. Or happy. Or to have someone protect you. You have your own light, Glo, separate from Joy's. It's time to let it shine."

"I don't know, Dad. All I've done this week is push Tate away. If I were him, I wouldn't stick around."

"Yes, you would."

She smiled.

"Listen. You spend all your life helping others. I've always thought of you as a lioness—you'll protect everyone else, but you won't protect yourself. Or let others protect you."

She drew in a breath, the words stinging.

"I..."

"I get it. What if you ask, and they don't show up? They say no?"

She looked away, her jaw tight.

"No one is going to say no, Glo. You are worthy of help. Of protection. Of sitting night by night by the pool in a lounge chair, pining."

"Tate is not pining."

"That's *exactly* what he's doing. And for what it's worth, I liked David. And if Tate is anything like David—"

"He's not as young and naive. But he is brave and sacrificial and..."

"You love him."

She looked at her dad, his words congealing. "I don't know if I love him, but...well, he keeps my fire lit."

"Okay, enough with that metaphor." Her father laughed. "So...maybe tell him that. Poor man is suffering."

She leaned over and kissed her father. "You should come around more often."

"I'm moving back, at least for the campaign. We'll see if I make it all the way to the White House. First Gentleman...I'm not sure what that looks like."

"I think the world will be a better place because of it." She grabbed her yogurt and slid off the stool.

The sun had already bathed the pool area in white light. She put on her sunglasses and found a deck lounger in the shade of an umbrella. Hopefully it wouldn't be long before Tate would stroll by, trying not to look...

And she'd do what?

She thumbed open her iPad.

Maybe she'd start with an apology.

A text message flashed on her screen from Kelsey. *Found the perfect dress for the CMGs.* The message contained a link.

Glo opened it, then scrolled through the also-boughts. Found one she liked and sent the link in a group message to Dixie and Kelsey.

The maintenance crew was on today, and in the distance the sound of the mower bit at the air. The fragrance of fresh-cut lawn seasoned the morning. She glanced around for Tate, but he was nowhere to be seen.

A text came back with shoe options from Dixie. *I can't believe we might get onstage!*

Glo would let Kelsey accept the award. Maybe she'd even stay in the audience. But she did have her own fire, the kind that stirred tunes inside her. Even made her take a mic, sing her heart out to a man in the wings.

Boy howdy, Tate knew how to keep the fire going, and she was a jerk for hurting him. At the very least she needed to apologize. And frankly, not just to Tate.

Sloan deserved the same. Yeah, train wreck of epic proportions.

The French doors opened, and she looked over to see her mother walking over to her. She wore her white linen pants and a bold orange shirt that set off her tan, her amber hair caught back in a loose bun.

"I hope you're using sunscreen," she said as she sat down on the edge of Glo's lounger. "A little tan is fine, but you're not like me. You burn so easily..."

"I'm in the shade, Mother."

"I know, I just..." She drew in a breath. "I just want you to be happy."

Oh. Uh.

"And, I have a campaign problem that I don't know what to do about. I need your help."

Her. Help? Glo set down the iPad.

"Nicole got an email from Carter, hoping to coordinate security for the CMGs and…she looked at the calendar. I have an event that day in Atlanta and trying to coordinate the security staff to get back for the awards show…maybe I should cancel the event."

Glo stared at her. "You'd do that for me?"

"Of course. You're my daughter. And you're getting a big award. And I couldn't bear it if anything happened to you. Security is essential, and you need the entire team. Nicole says the venue is a nightmare, even if she coordinates with the CMG security people. We could hire more people, but to get them trained and up to speed before both events… it's a logistical nightmare." She paused. "No, of course I will cancel. I'll call Nicole and tell her to halt the preparations for Atlanta."

Glo considered her mother, measuring her, but she had picked up her phone—

"No, Mother, don't be silly."

Her mother looked up, her thumb hovering over the Send button.

"I don't even know if we're going to win, and if we do, the last thing I want to do is go onstage. No. I don't need to go. Besides, it's just going to cause chaos for everyone. It's just selfish." She touched her mother's hand. "Go to Atlanta. Maybe I'll even go with you. Hold a sign or something."

Her mother stilled, met her eyes with so much surprise, even warmth in them, it coursed right through Glo, hit her heart, left it a little unwieldy.

"Really?"

"Yeah." Glo's voice emerged embarrassingly wrecked. "I'm here to support you, Mother."

"Oh, thank you, Gloria. The folks in Atlanta have worked so hard." She squeezed Glo's hand and got up. "I'm so glad you've joined our team. We could use your help if we're going to make it all the way to the White House."

She went inside and Glo leaned back in the chair, feeling strangely unsettled. But of course it was the right thing to do.

"Apparently, there's an epidemic going around."

She turned at the voice and startled to see one of her security standing nearby, quiet, unobtrusive. But he'd spoken, so she pulled down her glasses. "I'm sorry, what?"

"People not getting what they really want."

"I'm sorry, which one are you?"

"Rags—Art Ragsdale, ma'am. And I know it's none of my business, but I think you should go to that awards show. Get your award."

"You're right, it is none of your business."

He lifted a shoulder. "Just seems that it's not selfish to enjoy the fruits of your labor, so to speak. But apparently, suffering in silence is epidemic around here."

She opened her mouth to retort, had nothing, and closed it. Then, "Are you…I was expecting—"

"Rango, right?"

She raised an eyebrow. "No. Mr. Marshall."

"Yes, ma'am. I'm sorry, but he's not here. He left this morning."

Left? *Left*…?

"What do you mean?"

"I mean, when I got up this morning, he was gone. And Sly assigned me to your detail."

She turned away from him, her throat tightening.

Gone.

Because she'd made him suffer in silence.

Brilliant plan, Glo. Just brilliant.

Operation Angry Tate: mission accomplished.

———————◆———————

Ford wasn't leaving. Not the baseball game, despite the hot sun, and clearly not her life.

Or at least he hadn't left yet, and going on day five, with him cheering for Gunnar as her brother squinted into the sun in the outfield, Scarlett was starting to get the message.

One she should have spotted on the horizon when thirty seconds after they pulled up, as she'd been retrieving her gear from the back seat, Ford got out.

Then he'd walked around the truck to intercept her mother's burly boyfriend with a hand out, all gentlemanly, introducing himself as Petty Officer First Class Ford Marshall. With the US Navy SEALs. And yes, he was a teammate of Scarlett.

Sort of like a throwdown, right in her mother's grassless front yard.

Axel shook his hand, tight-lipped, trying to turn Ford to ash, and although he stood about an inch taller than Ford, maybe six-one, and had the shoulders of a small buffalo, he didn't possess Ford's confidence, the buzz under his skin that tremored the very air around him that said: Be. Careful.

Not that Ford emanated that on purpose, but it simply oozed out of him, a product of thousands of hours jumping out of planes and swimming through dark waters and scaling rough terrain and surviving active shooters, people who wanted to kill him.

So no, Axel Montrose hadn't a prayer of intimidating Ford.

Ford had let him go then and turned to help her with her duffel bag.

That was a first.

Mostly because she was usually the one helping them with gear, thanks to her job as a supply officer and communications liaison.

He took her big bag from her, not meeting her eyes, and walked it to the front porch, setting it there. And that might have been the end—he might have gotten into his truck and driven away—if her mother hadn't come outside to greet them.

She still looked like a California beach song. Sure, she had a few years on Scarlett, but Sammy-Jo Hathaway had a body made for sunshine and bikinis. Scarlett had long ago realized she'd gotten her curves, including the hips she couldn't quite get rid of, from the father she couldn't remember, because Sammy-Jo still sported a size four frame, legs that didn't quit, and a bustline that most twenty-year-olds would be jealous of. She came out wearing a sports bra, a pair of leggings, and an off-the-shoulder sweatshirt, as if she might be caught in the eighties. Her blonde hair was up in a high ponytail and frankly, her mother looked about twenty-five.

Not forty-three.

And maybe not even high.

Her eyes had lit up. "Scarlett?" She came down the stairs in her flip-flops and threw her arms around her daughter.

Scarlett couldn't move, just holding on, painfully aware that maybe she'd dreamed up her panic. Sorry, Ford.

But he stood back, his hands in his pockets, smiling.

Her mother backed away, caught Scarlett's face in her hands. "You're so beautiful!"

Huh.

Then she turned and looked at Ford. "And this must that boyfriend you told me about."

Oh. No. No—uh, her mother was clearly remembering back to the brief romance she'd had almost five years ago. She glanced at Ford, not sure what to say, but he simply held out his hand.

"Yes, ma'am. My name is Ford."

Then he leaned forward and gave her mother a kiss on the cheek.

Scarlett had to close her mouth before something flew in.

Her mother giggled, Ford grinned, and suddenly he'd been invited for dinner.

To Scarlett's shock, he stayed. So long that he helped with the dishes, then went outside and played catch with Gunnar, who had come home from practice shortly after they arrived.

The kid had grown up into a rascal with an impossible mop of blond curls, cheeky blue eyes, and a savviness that probably came from having to fend for himself. She recognized a lot of herself in him.

Still, he was young enough to give her a hug. And be impressed by Ford and his wicked bruise.

Because apparently, it was cool to nearly get shot.

It was right after dinner, as night fell, as the dusty winds whipped up, and the stars dripped from overhead, that she'd lost control of her week. Not that she had any real plans, but she'd seen herself alone, trying to unravel her snarled fears about the future.

Ford had gotten up, looked at her mother, and asked a question about a gas station. Axel was lying on the sofa, watching some horror flick, and grunted laughter.

"I think they're all closed this time of night," Scarlett said and made a face.

Ford had walked out onto the porch, the night deepening, and then turned to her. "I'll be right out here if you need me."

Weird, but she'd nodded because she didn't know what else to do.

The man had spread out a pad and sleeping bag in the bed of his truck.

Scarlett had expected to see him gone when she arose at first light, but there he was, in the kitchen frying up eggs while her mother, dressed in a bathrobe and hardly anything else, sat at the kitchen table drinking coffee and telling him about the time she sang onstage at the Bellagio.

Sure, Mom.

But Scarlett slid up to the table, across from her mother, and Ford appeared with a cup of coffee like he belonged there, in her mother's tiny kitchen.

It was clean—maybe Ford's touch—and Scarlett might have settled into the moment, believing that everything would be all right, if her mother hadn't turned to her and said, "This nice man was sleeping outside in his truck. In our yard, Scar! How did he get there—and aren't you going to be late for school?"

Her coffee pitched in her stomach, and Ford offered her

a sad look. "She asked me if I played baseball for the local team," he whispered.

"See, I told you," Axel said from the open door. He sat on the stoop, smoking a cigarette. "She's bonkers." He rotated his finger around his ear. "Bonkers."

"I think it's called a disease," Scarlett snapped and ran a finger under her eyes. "Have you even tried to get her into a treatment center?"

Axel lifted a shoulder. "We ain't got a car. What do you want me to do—put her on the back of my bike?"

"Where's the nearest center?" Ford asked as he slid scrambled eggs onto a plate in front of her mother, then her. The man even made a plate for Axel and served him at the door before serving himself. "Gunnar already left for school," he added.

She had slept like the dead on the sofa pillows in Gunnar's room and hadn't heard a thing, apparently.

"Salt Lake City," Axel mumbled.

Ford managed to find a gas can in the garage and fed the car with enough juice to get them back to Holbrook. They spent the day driving the 156 miles to the city, waiting for an appointment to talk to the rehabilitation counselor at Pathways of Hope, then traveling back home with the dismal waiting list, Sammy-Jo's name on the bottom.

Scarlett stared out the window in silence, Ford driving grim-faced, her mother babbling on about the doctor and how she had dated a podiatrist once…

Ford had reached across the seat and touched Scarlett's hand, just once, ever so briefly, and given it a squeeze.

That night, she found him sitting on the porch and sank down next to him. "I don't know what to do. I thought last time I left that she was going to be okay."

Her leg brushed against his, and he reached out and put his arm around her. Easy. Friendly. "I don't think there's anything you can do, Red." He'd turned to her then, however, and met her eyes. "She has to make her own choices. But I'm not leaving here until you're ready."

Oh.

His gaze met her eyes. "We don't leave a teammate behind."

She didn't know why she'd experienced the tiniest sense of disappointment. Because yes, she was his teammate.

And frankly, she was starting to like having him around. Liked hearing him hum the songs on his playlist. Liked seeing the way he listened to her mother, even when she repeated herself. Liked coming out of the bedroom to see him stirring up eggs or oatmeal or even some kind of smoothie from the ingredients he'd picked up in Salt Lake City.

It made her feel that much safer around Axel. Although, maybe the little hairs that rose on the back of her neck when he walked into the room could be attributed to her mother's history with men—the kind who liked to turn their attention toward her daughter—and not actual bad behavior, because Axel barely looked at her when she was in the room.

Spent a lot of time watching television.

But if Ford wasn't leaving—and she'd attempted the slightest argument, which he shut down with a look and a shake of his head before he went to play catch with Gunnar—then she had to sort it out.

Her mother needed help—that much was clear. And that's where her brain shut down.

Or rather, the ideas that formed were too painful to consider.

Now, as she watched Gunnar run into the dugout, grab his bat and tee up, she let thoughts roll over the possibilities.

Leave the Navy, move to Rockland, and take over her mother's care.

She'd rather be taken by terrorists. Okay, not really, but living with Axel felt very much like living under oppression.

Move her mother—and Gunnar—to San Diego, enroll her mother in a treatment facility there. But Scarlett was gone so often, and Gunnar needed supervision. He'd invited Ford to watch his game, and by the excitement in his blue eyes when they showed up to the game today, he probably didn't get a lot of personal fans.

"C'mon buddy, knock it out of the park!" Ford sat next to her, wearing a baseball cap, jeans, and his cowboy boots. The man fit right into the local wildlife, a few others—fathers or uncles—cheering their boys. The tiny baseball field sat outside the long school, a creek running in the distance surrounded by scrub pine and juniper. To the east, a rumple of mountains shaded the valley, and the wind swept a cool breeze across the fading day.

"Here we go, Gunnar!" she said, clapping.

The kid swung and missed, and Ford made a face.

"He'll hit it," she said.

"I should have taught him how to hit. We've spent all week working on his catch and throw—"

She looked at him and he shrugged. "Sorry. Personality flaw. I get involved and suddenly I'm taking personal responsibility for the success and failure of the mission."

"Operation baseball star?"

A tiny smile tugged up one side of his mouth. "Something like that, maybe."

His gaze lingered on her a second longer, and the ump shouted, "Strike two!"

Ford turned back to the game. "C'mon, buddy! Only swing if it's good!"

She cheered, too, especially when the ump called the next pitch as a ball.

"I'm thinking about separating from the Navy when my contract is up."

He looked at her again, frowning. "What?"

"Ball two!"

"I can't leave my mother alone with Axel—you've seen him. He doesn't have a job—I think he lives off my paychecks, to be honest. But I'm mostly worried for Gunnar."

"Ball three! Full count."

She turned back to the game with a cheer for Gunnar.

But Ford drew in a long breath, as if he might be weeding through his words.

"What about…well, who would…" He took a breath then and nodded, as if backing up to form words. "We need you, Scarlett."

She glanced at him again. His green eyes were in hers, steady, holding them, and for a second, she couldn't breathe. *We need you?*

Or *he* needed her?

A crack, and Ford focused back on the game. Gunnar had connected with the pitch, and the ball flew up and over the backstop.

"Foul!"

Ford breathed out. "Shake it off, big Gun. Eye on the ball. Connect."

"I know. And I love my job. Well—I love being involved with what you do."

The coach from the opposite team had come out to the mound for a conversation.

"What *we* do, Red. Like save lives and take down global threats and rescue people and pretty much act as the tip of the sword in keeping this world from going to chaos."

He was sitting on his hands, as if he wanted to gesture wildly and was just holding them in place, trying to keep himself under control. "I can't imagine going out there without…" He swallowed and met her eyes.

Heat infused her entire body, and not just because of his words, so softly, earnestly spoken, but because his gaze latched on her then, and this time didn't let her go. As if he might be trying to say something else, but the words were cemented inside his head, unable to break free.

Then the bat cracked, and they turned to see the ball soar across the field into the blue and lavender of twilight.

"Run!" Ford hit his feet and she followed, screaming.

Gunnar threw the bat—somebody ducked—and scampered to first base.

Out in the field, the ball tipped off the outstretched hand of the middle fielder and kept rolling.

Gunnar rounded first and headed to second.

The outfielder took off after the ball and ten feet later, scooped it up. Threw it.

The ball fell halfway to second base, still in the outfield. The second baseman took off to fetch it as Gunnar hit second.

His coach was rounding him to third, and Gunnar slipped, fell, and scrambled back up as the second baseman picked up the ball.

"Run, Gunnar!" Ford hopped down the bleachers to the ground, running along the fencing, his arm swinging. "Go home! Home!"

The coach had the same idea, and Gunnar popped the bag and kept running.

The second baseman threw in the ball to the pitcher.

Scarlett was on the ground now, running beside Ford as they kept up with Gunnar, bouncing along the fence, screaming.

The pitcher turned.

"Slide! Hit the dirt!" Ford shouted.

Gunnar threw himself face first into the plate, diving low.

The catcher grabbed the throw just as Gunnar slid over the rubber.

A breath, and in that moment Scarlett's gaze fell on Ford.

He was just as fierce as she imagined him out in the field of operation, his expression tight, his pale green eyes on fire, almost daring the ump to call Gunnar out. But that was how Ford lived his life—all in, playing hard, and getting back up when he fell. Even if he had to fight back blindly. He never gave up. And she wanted...no, needed, that kind of man in her life.

More, he'd nearly died—would have died, maybe—if she hadn't called out the tango on his back.

So yeah, maybe this man did need her.

"Safe!"

The crowd erupted, and as Gunnar was rushed by his teammates, Ford turned.

He swept Scarlett up against him, swinging her around,

holding her tight.

Her entire body turned to fire.

He set her back down, grinning, and for a second he looked like he might kiss her, something forming in his eyes.

Then he turned away and ran toward Gunnar, getting down on his level to high-five him, then pulled him into a hug.

Gunnar beamed like she'd never seen before.

Please, Ford, don't leave.

7

When Ruby Jane had announced a little over a month ago at their mother's sixtieth birthday party that she wasn't a travel agent but worked as a CIA analyst, honestly, Tate didn't believe her.

After all, she was his kid sister. The twin of his Navy SEAL brother, sure, so that meant she definitely possessed some serious get-'er-done genes and no doubt the smarts to untangle diabolical international plots.

But for the CIA?

Really?

Except, she had tracked down information on the Bryant League when he'd asked. But he'd also done a Google search and unearthed similar information. The Bryant League, an offshoot of a group called the World Can't Wait, or WCW, was affiliated with the Revolutionary Communist Party, an isolationist group that wasn't afraid to use domestic terrorism to take down the government elites and give the "land" back to the people. Aka, socialistic reform.

Which really meant they wanted to be in power, call the shots, and dominate the people.

And people like Reba Jackson stood up to them.

So, yeah, she had his vote. And he had her back.

And the sooner he tracked down the two yahoos who probably had really planted the bomb at the San Antonio arena, not to mention fired the Marshall family barn, shot

Glo, and somehow gotten inside their security perimeter at the Anderson event, the sooner everyone could simply calm down.

He would crawl out of the senator's clutches and go back to his sweet and easy gig running security for the Belles.

If they'd take him back.

Regardless, he wouldn't have to endure for one more minute watching Glo be charmed into another man's arms.

He'd called ahead to Ruby Jane when he landed in DC, but his call went to voicemail again, so he pocketed the phone, picked up an Uber, and directed the driver to RJ's address. She lived outside the Capitol Hill area, in the northern corridor in a one-bedroom condo. He'd seen it a couple times on their FaceTime calls but had a moment of pause when he pulled up to the brick building.

Clearly, Sis made bank at whatever job she'd landed here in DC.

He got out and buzzed her apartment number. No name was listed, so he braced himself to be the pizza guy, wrong apartment, but when he recognized the voice he said, "It's Tate."

A pause, then a buzz, and he entered, walked up a flight, and knocked on 203.

She must have checked the peephole, because it took a moment for the bolts to slide back, and there she was.

Dressed in black heels, an untucked white oxford rolled to her elbows, and black dress pants, her dark hair down and mussed, she stared at Tate with a look of nonrecognition.

Or maybe simply surprise. Then, oddly, she looked past him into the hall, grabbed his jacket lapel and pulled him inside.

Slammed the door and bolted it.

"What the—"

She threw her arms around his neck, holding on. "Tate. Sheesh. Knox told me about the fight." She leaned back, glaring up at him. "Why did you let him get the jump on you?"

He blinked at her. "Uh…"

She grinned. "Kidding. But you scared the snot out of me." She kissed his cheek. "What are you doing here?"

"Don't you answer your voicemails?"

Her mouth gaped a moment before she made a face. "Oh. Right." She went into the kitchen and opened a drawer. Pulled out a smartphone and scrolled. "Seven messages?"

"I've been worried."

She set down her phone. "Aw—"

"No, seriously. I've been calling you for nearly two weeks. Where have you been?"

She slid the cell phone back into the drawer. "At work."

He made a face.

"Sorry. We've had a few things, uh, going down…"

Her gaze flickered to a satchel tossed onto the sofa. And that's when he spotted the suitcase. The Delta planeside check tag still dangled from the handle. "Work?"

She walked over and grabbed the bag. "Work travel."

He spotted her passport in the side pocket of the satchel and made a grab for it.

"Tate! That's my personal business."

"Italy. You went to Italy?" He thumbed another page over. "And the Czech Republic?"

She retrieved the passport from his hand. "Yes. I…had work there."

"RJ—"

"Have you eaten?"

"Not since this morning. A bagel in the Nashville airport."

"Nashville." She trolleyed the suitcase into the bedroom and he followed. She threw it on the bed, then pushed him out of her room and back to the living room. "What are you doing there?"

"I'm working for Senator Jackson—nice digs, by the way."

A long, gray contemporary sofa lined one wall, two armless chairs on the far side by the window, and a metal-and-glass coffee table centered the room, all on a white Persian rug over wooden floors. A flat-screen television hung from the wall.

144

"Yeah, yeah. Senator Jackson? Glo's mother? How did you get that gig?"

"Glo fired me, her mother hired me. Easy. And now I'm trying to keep Glo safe from the Bryant League."

Ruby Jane sank onto the sofa and pushed her hands into her hair. He'd forgotten her habit of messing her hair when she was thinking. Or frustrated.

"You okay, sis?" He sank down into one of the armless chairs.

She leaned back, let her head flop, closed her eyes. "Yeah. Long few days."

"At work. In Europe. Yeah, that jet lag is a beast."

Her mouth quirked into a smile. "Fine." She opened one eye. "I sometimes go out to the field to help with... situations."

"Like lost luggage?"

"Like a rogue agent who just might be tasked to kill someone very important."

He raised an eyebrow.

"Hypothetically." She looked at him. "If I were telling you the truth, I'd be in big trouble." She winked, and now he was totally confused. She reached into her satchel and pulled out a thin computer. "Okay, the Bryant League. Where were we?"

"You were trying to locate the identities of the two people seen with the suspected bomber. We thought they might be connected with the Bryant League, who had sent numerous threatening emails to the senator before the attack."

"Right. Knox's mystery men." Her computer booted up, and she seemed to be pulling up the file.

"I have new information," Tate said. "We had an attack at a fundraiser event a couple weeks ago, and we finally got ballistics back. The shells were from a M40A5. It's a sniper rifle used by the Marines. I'm hoping you can cross reference any members of the Bryant League with military service—especially the Marines."

"You came all the way here with that tiny piece of

information?"

"You weren't answering your phone."

"Desperate, anyone?" She looked up at him. "The search is running. Does this have anything to do with a certain curvy blonde?"

He just stared at her.

"Ve have vays of making you talk."

"Seriously?"

"Okay, well, actually, we do have ways—"

"Fine. Yes. Okay. I'm working for Jackson on the agreement that I don't date—or even flirt, I suppose—with Glo. Except that Glo and I shared this moment—"

"Moment? A long, naughty moment?"

"No! Who are you? A *kiss*. We shared a kiss. Right before I got jumped by the Bratva in Vegas."

Her smile dimmed. "You got jumped by the *Bratva*? The Russian mob?"

"I told you I worked in Vegas, right? Well, the guy I worked for worked for them. And…when I turned him in to the FBI—"

"You turned in a Bratva mob boss to the FBI? Have you lost your mind?"

"He killed a woman I cared for."

Her mouth tightened. "You were always the one with the soft heart. I remember you sitting outside with the goats, feeding them one by one."

"They beat her to death to get me to stay quiet."

"I'm sorry, Tate."

"Yeah, well, the important part of the story here is that they found me in Vegas, right after I kissed Glo. And she was nearly killed trying to save my life."

RJ touched his arm. "You both okay?"

"Yes. For now, but…this thing between me and her…it won't go away. But she seems to think she can save me if…I think…if she can get me to quit. At least I hope that's what is going on, because she certainly has put the like on Sloan Anderson."

"Sloan Anderson? She's dating Sloan? Oh boy, the plot thickens—"

"You know Sloan? How small is this town?"

"Smallish. But…I know Sloan because he used to work with us."

"Sloan worked for the CIA?"

"With. Like a volunteer helping the greater cause."

"Like an informant."

"Like a friend who helped us help the world. He was a lobbyist. And lobbyists are supposed to influence legislation. And sometimes the right legislation needs a nudge now and again."

"What kind of legislation?"

"Oh, things like votes on some of our government 'aid' packages overseas." She finger quoted the word "aid."

He went quiet. "Aid, as in arms?"

"Now you're getting into specifics that could get us in trouble. Let's just say that he has a lot of connections, a lot of friends, and a lot of information about people that could probably come in very useful to your senator friend."

"And he's very good at wheeling and dealing."

"He's a lobbyist. They *influence*."

He'd like to influence Sloan right out of Glo's life, and pronto.

"Your search came back empty," she said, glancing at her screen. "Want me to search wider parameters?"

"Yeah. Military in general."

Her stomach growled.

"Apparently, I'm not the only one who hasn't eaten."

She nodded to the kitchen. "There's a Chinese delivery menu in the drawer with the phone."

He got up and headed over to it. Found the drawer, the menu to Jade Fountain, and grabbed her phone.

She had seventeen unread texts and nine calls. "Why don't you answer your phone? Or your texts?"

"I will. Later. I would have eventually called you back."

He frowned. "You have a burner phone, don't you?

Because there is no way you'd leave the country without a phone."

She leaned her head against the sofa, spreading out her long dark hair. "I'll take house fried rice and cream cheese wantons."

He shook his head and ordered.

By the time the delivery arrived, they'd run searches on all branches of the military.

"Sorry, bro. And while you were unwrapping your chopsticks, I ran a general search on all Bryant League activity. There's nothing even on the radar for months. The last known event was a bombing at a recruitment station in Abilene, Texas, over a year ago.

"Could be the same guys—it's Texas…"

"Are you sure that Kelsey's stalker wasn't the same guy who shot Glo in Montana?"

"No. But Kelsey clearly saw the gauged ears that Knox described in his drawings of the bombing suspects. They're just not that common."

"Getting more so, but…okay. I'll keep looking. But you might want to start considering that the bombing in San Antonio was exactly what the police say—an act of desperation by an angry man."

"An angry rodeo clown? I don't think he's good for it, despite the evidence. I think he was the fall guy."

She picked up her carton of rice. "Yes, I see the irony. But, even the shooting at the house could have been her stalker. It was dark, and who knows what Kelsey saw."

Tate was finishing off his Kung Pao chicken. "Then who attacked us at the Anderson fundraiser?"

"Anyone have a vendetta against Senator Jackson?"

"Probably. She's a senator after all."

"Maybe you should start searching a little closer to home. But here's the good news…if the Bryant League has nothing to do with any of this, then Glo is probably relatively safe. Which means she doesn't need your protection. You can quit working for the senator and you and Glo can ride away on your shiny white horse."

She stopped mid-bite. "Oh, sorry. Your shiny black motorcycle."

"I can ride a horse, RJ."

She kept her mouth closed, but her eyes laughed.

"I was six."

"I wish I was old enough to remember. But the stories— oh, Knox and Rube were merciless."

"I broke my wrist. Of course I cried."

She looked at him, then something of kindness crested her face. "Just because you aren't a cowboy doesn't make you a failure."

He drew in his breath. "I know."

"Do you? Because you got it in your mind when you were six that you weren't cut out for ranching. And you told yourself that you had to be awesome at something else. And nearly died proving it."

"It was war—"

"Long before the war, Tate. Let's talk about that motor-cycle you fixed up and spent hours driving around the ranch. Your wall of BMX awards."

"Until I broke my shoulder and Ma forbade me to ride it."

"That's my point. Then there was your glory on the football team."

"Rube played football. He was the captain."

"He wasn't a running back. Hello, three state records and two concussions. But do you take advantage of that athletic scholarship and go to Montana State, like Knox? No. You join the military. Become a *Ranger*, for Pete's sake. Trying to prove something, again."

He looked away. "I was serving my country. And I was a good Ranger."

"You were an amazing Ranger. A decorated hero—"

"I wasn't a hero."

"Yeah, actually, you were. Your Bronze Star? Your Purple Heart?"

"All but one of my squad was killed—and I was their team leader. Heroes don't get people killed." He didn't know how the conversation landed here, in his regrets. His wounds. And now he'd lost his appetite. "Are you coming home for Rube's wedding this weekend?"

She stared at him a long moment. Then she set down her carton, wedged the chopsticks inside. "Okay, Tate. Let's not talk about your insatiable need to be better than Rube and Knox. Let's not talk about the fact you're still six years old inside and angry, hurt, and embarrassed after being bucked off a horse. Let's talk about superficial things that won't let you see that you don't have to do anything to be awesome. Or loved. We're already crazy about you, just because you're you. Hardworking, reliable, brave, and heroic. So yeah, I'll try and make it to the wedding."

He looked away.

"But we're still...working. At work. So...I probably have to *work*."

He looked back at her. "And I guess we won't talk about your need to keep up with Ford. To save the world."

Her eyes flashed. "I am saving the world."

He didn't think she was kidding, and a cold hand tightened around his chest. "In Italy or the Czech Republic?"

She looked away, took a breath. "Listen, if I don't make it, I'll try and Skype in."

"You're as bad as Ford."

"No, I'm worse. Ford is going to be there. He called me from San Diego. He's going to surprise you all." She looked back at him and offered a conciliatory smile. "Surprise."

He offered one back. "You're terrible."

"But I know all the best delivery places, right?" She gestured to his food.

"Yeah, you do." He touched her hand.

She turned hers in his and squeezed. Met his eyes with warmth in them.

We're already crazy about you, just because you're you. He looked away. "I gotta go, my Uber is five minutes away."

"What—you've been here a total of three hours." She let go of his hand as he got up.

"I'm headed back to Nashville. It's time for Glo's silly game to end."

"Go get 'er, tiger." She punctuated her words with a fist and a swing of her arm.

He rolled his eyes. "Answer your phone once in a while."

She got up and gave him a hug. "Stay out of trouble."

Oh, there probably wasn't a chance of that.

"I'll try."

———◆———

She'd always known her mother's life glittered. Glo just never realized that she might glitter with it.

Or, that she wanted to.

"You look gorgeous tonight, Gloria," Sloan said as he opened the door to her limousine. She didn't know when he'd stopped referring to her as Glo in public, but she noticed it now as she took his hand and climbed out of the car under the awning of the glorious and historical Hermitage Hotel in downtown Nashville. A top-hatted doorman stood at the ready, and a few flashes went off as Sloan led her to the door. He was dressed in a burgundy tuxedo jacket, this time with his collar buttoned, his bow tie perfectly symmetrical under his shaven chin.

The man looked every inch a millionaire's son, and for the first time she saw Sloan not as the neighbor next door, but as a man who embodied the future he'd tried to unfurl in front of her.

Apparently, one he had hopes she'd want to run into with him.

She caught a glance of her reflection in the massive glass doors. She wore a strapless, royal blue satin dress that hugged her body, all the way down to her silver stilettos, a vintage diamond broach at her neck, and diamond studs at her ears.

Yeah, she'd upped her game since joining her mother's

campaign gigs. But her feet hurt, and frankly, she just might topple over if she didn't hang onto someone.

She slid her hand over Sloan's arm as they entered the grand lobby. Marble arches and columns supported the ornate glass ceiling overhead and bounced light from the gilded chandeliers that hung from the four corners of the room. Sloan waved to a few reporters—handpicked journalists allowed to attend tonight's private art auction-slash-fundraiser—and led her to the stairs where, on the balcony above, the donated pieces from local artisans were displayed. Watercolors and oils on easels, sculptures in mixed mediums on shelves and tables, and down at the end of the hallway, a crazy-looking goat made from discarded car parts.

White-gloved waiters mingled with the guests—hobnobbers from Nashville society—and offered canapes and aperitifs.

"Where is your regular hound dog?" Sloan said, leaning over to her, and she glanced at him, frowned.

"Who?"

"Your faithful bodyguard. You have a new guy." He glanced behind him, and she followed his gaze. Rags trailed them, unobtrusively, five feet away. He met her eyes, offered a grim smile, then looked past her, on the job.

"Yeah. The other guy left."

"Good," Sloan said and slipped his hand over hers. "He made me want to punch him, the way he looked at you."

Probably Tate had felt the same way. She kept her smile but felt a tinge of guilt.

Something to go along with her openly bleeding heart.

She'd spent most of the afternoon fighting the desire to call him. Or better, hop on a plane to Montana.

But why? She'd won.

Except, it felt so very much like losing. Big.

And poor Sloan. She'd *used* him in her little game, like a regular politician. Wow, she hadn't quite realized how much her mother had rubbed off on her.

She felt sticky and dirty.

What if this was her world now?

Lies? Political games?

No. She didn't want that life. But maybe as First Daughter in the White House, she could change the world. Make it safer, healthier, fairer. It wasn't the stage, with the songs pouring out of her heart, but maybe it could be a different stage. *I'm so glad you've joined our team.*

Yes, maybe she had.

But she'd do it without the deceit. Which meant she had to tell Sloan the truth.

Probably he wouldn't want her either, after he found out what she'd done.

The thought left her stomach tightening. Because she was a stupid girl to not be diving headfirst into handsome, successful, and wealthy Sloan Anderson's arms.

Sloan led her over to an older gentleman who was surveying a massive oil painting of sailboats.

"Gloria, I'd like you to meet the other state senator, Roland McGraw." She held out her hand and he took it. A beefy man, with a few steaks under his belt, he held a whiskey in one hand and hers in the other, his touch sweaty.

"Darlin'," the man said and looked her up and down.

"Nice to meet you." She untangled her hand, even as Sloan settled his on the small of her back.

"Gloria is not only Senator Jackson's daughter, but my girlfriend, so be nice to her, Senator."

The man laughed. "Well done, my boy." He slapped Sloan on the shoulder.

Glo tried not to be weirdly offended.

The man moved away, and Sloan edged her to another man, a lawyer from one of the big firms in Nashville. Glo had never heard of it, but when he introduced her again as his girlfriend, this time he offered a wink.

Since when had she become his official girlfriend? Although, given the time they'd spent together...

She took Sloan's hand and pulled him toward a bronze sculpture of a flying horse. In her painful stilettos, she was nearly to his shoulder. But she felt tall enough to meet his gaze. "Sloan…we need to talk."

But he wasn't listening, or at least his body might be turned toward her, but his eyes were far away. "Do you hear that?"

She stilled, listening. "What? The cello? The conversation—"

"The country music." He walked to the balcony and looked over.

She joined him, and yes, she could hear it now, drifting up from the restaurant area, a half-floor below the lobby.

"Aw, I told them not to book a wedding tonight."

"Sloan, it's no big deal, you can barely hear it."

Except, yes, as the sound formed in her ear, she could almost start singing along.

She met him on a night like any other
Dressed in white, the cape of a soldier
He said you're pretty, but I can't stay
She said I know, but I could love you anyway…

The Belles' song.

He may have recognized it too because he looked over at her. "It's a great song, but it's a bad mix for our event." He kissed her hand and headed down the stairs.

Maybe *she* was a bad mix for the event. Because suddenly she just wanted to go downstairs, kick off these stupid shoes, hike up her dress, and two-step. Or better yet, take the stage and belt out the chorus.

But you don't know if you don't start
So wait…for one true heart…one true heart…

And then, strangely, her eyes were filling, burning…

She needed air. Because yes, she cared about her mother and the election and the team, but…she just needed a moment to breathe.

To catch up to where her life seemed to be careening off to.

She turned and spotted Rags standing a few feet away. Something on her face must have alerted him because he frowned and took a step toward her.

Sloan stepped between them. "Okay, I think we got it settled. They're going to wait until cocktail hour is over before they start the music. I told them we'd pay for another round of drinks for their guests."

"That's pretty expensive."

"Your mother needs a night without complications."

He might have been referring to the shots fired at her last event—Glo didn't know, but she couldn't agree more. "I don't feel well, Sloan. I'm going to go home."

He frowned, caught her elbow. "Are you sure? Your mother could sure use you tonight."

"For what...campaign candy?" She felt a little weird saying it, especially when Sloan grinned, lifted a shoulder.

Yeah, now she really was starting to feel ill. "I'll have Rags take me home."

"Who?"

She gestured to the man standing a foot away behind him.

Sloan's mouth tightened.

"But we do need to talk, Sloan. I…"

"I'll call you after the event."

"Maybe you could come over?"

He was looking over the top of her head. But his focus came back to her, briefly, with a nod. "Yeah, sure. I'll see you afterward." Then, before she could pull away, he kissed her cheek, something quick but definitely public before he let her go. "Feel better."

Yes, she would, after they talked. After she told him that they needed to slow down. As in stop. Maybe reassess.

Figure out who she was, what she wanted.

Oh, how she wished it were Tate lending her his arm down the stairs, leading her to the limo.

She climbed in, leaned her head on the seat. Closed her

eyes.

She felt her phone vibrate in her purse but didn't answer it. It was probably her mother, berating her for leaving.

Rags sat in the front seat, and now she lowered the partition. "How about some music? Any country station will do."

She closed her eyes again as a Cole Swindell song came on.

I took a few wrong turns…Down a couple back roads
But wound up where I was supposed to…Making my way making my way to you

She thumbed away a tear and sighed.

Looked out the window as the lights of the city splashed by. *You've had a few rough starts, Glo-light, so I think you have reason to complain. But that doesn't mean you don't deserve to be safe. Or happy. Or to have someone protect you.*

Her throat thickened, remembering her father's words.

She disagreed. She didn't deserve Tate. Not after how she'd treated him.

It was better that he'd left. She'd make sure her mother gave him a good reference.

She ran her hand again across her cheek.

They finally pulled up in front of the house, and Rags gave her a sad, tight-lipped smile as he helped her out.

"I'm just going to sit by the pool for a while, Rags, so… you can turn in."

He gave her a nod, although she wasn't sure he was going to obey. She let herself into the quiet house and pulled off her shoes. Dangled them between her fingers as she headed to the kitchen. She dropped them on the tile floor, then opened the Sub-Zero in search of chocolate.

Not a hope of comfort to be found. She closed the door and glanced out toward the pool. The empty lounger.

And for some reason the memory of Tate sitting there compelled her outside. The bricks scrubbed on her bare feet, and she lifted her dress to keep it off the patio.

She stood at the edge of the pool, the smell of chlorine lifting into the night. Overhead, the Milky Way spilled out in glorious repose, the air cool, carrying a touch of summer on the breeze.

You are worthy of help. Of protection. Of sitting night by night by the pool in a lounge chair, pining.

She ran her hands up her arms, a chill finding her bones. No, actually, she wasn't. Not this time.

Steps sounded behind her on the patio, and she glanced over her shoulder and spotted a figure standing in the shadows.

She turned back to the pool, her hand on her stomach. "Sloan, I'm sorry for tonight. For leaving. I know I should have stayed, but…I just…"

More steps, but she couldn't turn to face him. Not with the lies between them. "I need to tell you something, and it's going to hurt you, and I'm sorry about that, but I need you to know…when you first asked me out for dinner last week, I said yes because I was angry at someone. Very angry, and I used our time together to make him more angry. And I'm sorry for that because you're a great guy and I shouldn't have used you. You deserve better than me."

A breath drew in, and she closed her eyes. "I understand if you never want to see me again."

A hand slid over her shoulders. Warm, solid, sending a tremor through her. "If I never wanted to see you again, I wouldn't have taken the red-eye from DC back to you."

She stilled, then suddenly turned.

And he was right there. Standing in front of her, his smile a little chagrined, wearing a day's whiskers on his face, his blue eyes shining down on her. He wore a black leather jacket, dark pants, and now took her face in his hands. "I know I'm not supposed to be talking to you, and especially not… touching you. But you looked so beautiful standing out here in the glow of the pool, I couldn't stop myself."

Then, as if to add truth to his words, he leaned down and kissed her.

Something powerful and possessive and thorough, and she couldn't help but wind her hands around his body and pull him close. Kiss him back in all the ways she'd been dreaming of since the moment in Vegas. The moment when she'd decided not to let her past, her wounds tell her who she could—and couldn't—love.

Tate.

He tasted of coffee, probably from his flight, and smelled of aftershave, the fresh scent of cotton, and the deep husk of leather. And when he nudged her mouth open, when he let her have the finest taste of him, she found the world dropping away until it was simply her and Tate. Alone under the spray of moonlight.

Safe.

He made a tiny sound from deep inside and almost with violence pulled himself away from her, breathing hard. Stepped back, his hand up. "Okay, okay. I… Sorry. I—" He wore a stricken look and swallowed, and the expression made her pause, too, her throat thick.

"What—?"

"Your mother is going to kill me."

"Why, because you had a deal?"

She didn't know where the anger came from, but when he nodded, she wanted to advance on him, push him. "What kind of deal? The kind to drive me crazy? To make me insane with worry? To break both our hearts?"

"The kind to keep you safe!" He took a breath, schooled his voice. "I promised not to…well, do this. Right here. To do what every instinct has been shouting at me to do since Vegas." He stared at her, apparently okay with her seeing all his emotions—frustration, helplessness, anger, and desire. Oh, the desire. It dried her mouth. But when she took a step toward him, he kept his hand up.

"Just give me a sec, here, Glo. I have to think."

"Think?"

He lowered his hand and gave her a look. "If I do what apparently we both want right now, it involves more than just standing in the moonlight kissing you. Something along the lines of finding a car and driving us both far, far away. Away from the clutter and complications of your life, and yeah, I'm not exactly sure of the destination, but it would be with me. In my arms. Not Slick's."

Oh, Sloan.

She grinned at his name for him.

"What's so funny—?"

"It's just…nothing. I like that idea very much."

He drew in a breath, his eyes widening. "You do?"

"Yeah. Save me, Tate. I…" She looked down at her gown. "I'm not sure who I am right now."

He groaned and closed the gap between them, his hand on her face. "You're Glo Jackson. Singer, musician, rummy shark, late-night thumb battler, and the woman I would die for."

"You're such a superhero, Captain America." Her arms went around his neck as she pulled herself against him, moving his head down to capture his mouth. Tate. She could write a new song right here, right now, about love gone right and lost dreams showing up in the night, and maybe something about never giving up the fight and—

A snap sounded behind her, in the bushes that lined the pool.

Tate looked up, his entire body on alert.

"Someone's out there," he said. He shoved her behind him. "Hello?" Then he turned to her. "Who's on your detail tonight?"

"Rags. But I sent him away."

Tate's mouth tightened in a grim line. He grabbed her hand and took her into the house. "Turn the lights off and stay down, behind the island."

What—no! She caught his hand. "You're not going out there."

He gave her a look. "Yes, I am. But I'll be back, I promise." He kissed her hard.

And then she watched the man she loved step out of her

life into the darkness.

He'd let down his guard for a blinding, delirious second—
So much for coming home with the news that Glo was safe.

News that Tate hadn't quite announced before he simply took her in his arms and kissed her. Breaking his promise to her mother—stupid, frustrating promise that it was—and trampling every smidgen of honor that still remained.

Yeah, a real hero.

What had he told RJ? And Glo? Clearly, the truth.

He might not be a hero or even particularly honorable, but he certainly was going to keep Glo safe.

Tate trembled, the adrenaline buzzing through his body as he crept out into the shadows of the pool house. He wished he had his gun, but he couldn't take that on the plane, and he hadn't exactly stopped by the security building on his way in to check out a weapon.

Fine. He could handle this joker with his bare hands.

He stayed down, heading toward the shrubbery behind the pool and came across the place where the intruder had hidden.

Yep. He knew his instincts were firing correctly when he'd seen the flash of light—moonlight on a weapon? Or something else, he didn't know. But when it was followed by the sound of branches breaking he called himself an idiot for letting his guard down.

Again.

So. Easily. Distracted.

He ground his teeth as he crouched in the warm spot, the branches to the shrubbery broken and snapped. How long had the assailant sat there, watching as he'd kissed Glo?

Really, finally, kissed Glo. Two weeks of patience and pent-up agony as he watched Slick hold her hand. Kiss her. Touch her hair.

Yeah, well, he'd been watching—Glo didn't come alive in Sloan's arms like she did in his, thank you.

And maybe that was testosterone talking, but Glo was his girl. He knew it in his core.

He'd give about anything for NVGs right now. But the full moon illuminated the open fields surrounding the house, and he scanned the horizon.

Spied, in the far distance, a figure running toward the horse pasture.

He didn't have time to get keys, sort out vehicles—he took off at a full sprint.

As he ran by the bunkhouse, he gave a shout, and from the back, Rags and Swamp emerged.

"Intruder!" He kept going.

The man had disappeared behind a hill, but there was a quarter mile of pastureland between him and the road. And Tate was fast.

He kept his eyes on the place where the man had vanished, glimpsed a form, also running hard, and his chest began to hurt.

A motor thundered up behind him and he turned.

Rags held his arm out and Tate hooked it, leaped, and landed behind him on one of the estate's motorcycles.

He gripped the back of the seat, leaning with Rags as they ate up the earth.

He pointed toward the sight of their quarry, growing larger, and Rags gunned it, kicking up soil and grass.

Behind them, Tate heard another bike—probably Swamp, but he didn't turn to look.

The man grew larger. Lean, tall, but young and fit for the way he was keeping pace.

If he'd come in by car, he might have parked closer.

He came into clear view—the man wore a black shirt, and a camera bounced hard against his back as he ran. He glanced over his shoulder at them, his eyes wide.

"Stop!"

Clearly, that was a no.

"Get close to him!" Tate shouted.

Rags obeyed. Tate drew up his leg to the seat, then leaped for him.

They went down together in a rolling tackle, Tate letting him go so he could find his feet.

He'd gotten the wind bullied out of him a little but gulped back hard as he rounded on the man.

The intruder sprawled in the grass, his hands over his head, his legs brought up to protect his belly.

"Sheesh," Tate said. "Get up. I'm not going to beat you."

The man pushed himself up onto his knees, and Tate gave a start. Not a man, but a kid. But young and gaunt, and fear in his eyes. "What are you doing here?"

He was breathing hard. "I saw Miss Jackson leave the event tonight and I thought maybe I could get some pictures of her and her new boyfriend."

Rags had circled back around and now pulled up. "Who is he?" He cut the engine.

"Paparazzi."

"No, man. I'm a freelancer. I work for the Lincoln. It's a political website that discusses national issues."

"Seriously. And taking pictures of Gloria Jackson and her…friend…is political how?"

"If Sloan Anderson has the ear of the future president via her daughter, the world needs to know."

"Why?"

"Because of his ties to Russia! He has known liaisons with low-level Russian diplomats in Washington."

"Liaisons, how?"

The kid drew in a breath. "He plays golf with Russians."

"He's a lobbyist. Of course he does." Tate reached down to haul the kid up to his feet. Then he yanked the camera from his neck.

"Hey!"

Tate held his hand up in warning, and the man piped down. Tate opened the screen, scrolled through—oh my, he had shots of their kiss.

His hands in Glo's hair, his mouth practically devouring hers. And Glo's arms around his neck, equally as eager.

Delete.

He scrolled more, found the ones of Glo standing by the pool, pouring out her heart as he walked from the shadows. He looked like a freakin' wounded puppy.

Delete.

He sort of wanted to keep the one of Glo staring up into the sky, as if seeking answers from the moon, her hair glowing, her eyes soft.

Delete.

The next one was of her at some fancy hotel, getting out of her car, then going inside, then—

Wait.

He enlarged the picture.

And his heart simply stopped. There, standing in the crowd was a man with a fire tattoo licking his neck, his gaze trained on Glo.

Tate looked closer. It was definitely taken tonight because Glo wore that same gorgeous blue dress.

He ignored Sloan in the picture.

"I need your camera," he said to the kid. "It's got a picture I need."

"That's a Nikon D5. It cost me seven thousand dollars."

Tate wanted to say something like, *cry me a river, kid*, but Rags interjected, "Let's go back to the house. We can take the picture off the hard drive, grab the SD card, and wipe the camera."

Swamp had pulled up on the other motorcycle, and surprise, surprise, Sly was right behind him on one of the four wheelers. He got out and stalked over to Tate.

"I didn't expect you back until tomorrow."

"Then you should have had someone on Glo's detail tonight. She was out there alone, or this jerk wouldn't have been able to sneak in."

"I did have someone on." He looked at Rags.

Tate followed with a glare. "You left her alone?"

Rags held up a hand. "Sorry. She dismissed me. I don't have the same obsession, bro. I'm not going to sit outside on a lounge chair and watch her window all night."

Tate wanted to go for Rags's throat.

Would have, maybe, had Sly not caught his shoulder, pushed him back and away from Rags. "No. I get it, but no."

Tate drew in a breath, shot a look over to Rags, back to Sly. "She doesn't leave my sight."

Sly nodded.

"Which means that she goes with me this weekend to Montana."

Sly raised an eyebrow. "That's not how it works, Tate. You work for her, not the other way around."

"I'll go."

Tate froze, then turned, and yes, Glo appeared, seated bareback on one of those pretty thoroughbreds. She wore a pair of yoga pants and a T-shirt, diamonds at her ears, barefoot like she might be a modern-day Viking princess.

She could even ride a horse.

Then again, hello. He should have guessed that after seeing the highbrow livestock around her. And didn't she once mention that her grandfather raised thoroughbreds?

"I'll go to Montana. With Rango."

She knew his nickname? It sent a strange, not unwelcome heat through him to hear her revert back to her crazy practice of calling him by funny names.

Like something good might have reset between them.

"No," Sly said.

"Yes," Tate replied. "Listen. I know my ranch, and it's unexpected. We—me and my brothers—can keep her safe there. Trust me. She'll be safer there than here."

Sly gave him a look. "Excuse me, but last time she was there, she was *shot*."

Tate's mouth tightened.

"I'll be fine. I trust Tate. And I need to get away, just for a few days."

He hadn't expected that part, or the fact that she'd betray

that to any of them. But Sly walked over to her and grabbed the reins of her horse. "You'll do everything he says, without argument?"

Tate grinned as he looked over at her for her answer. Even added, "Without *argument.*"

She glanced from Sly to Tate. "You're not the boss of me, Tator."

"This weekend I am, honey."

She sighed, then turned back to Sly. "Fine. Yes."

Sly considered Tate. "And you'll keep her safe, no matter what."

Tate gave him a look. But since he was his boss… "With my very life."

Sly shook his head. "Okay. But don't forget your *deal,* bucko."

Right, his deal. What deal was that?

"And don't let your guard down," Sly added, his gaze flickering to Rags, then back.

His smile fell. Because yeah, Sly was right.

He glanced again at the camera, then at Glo sitting there with the slightest smile of triumph.

Oh boy.

———◆———

Ford was going to miss his brother's wedding.

He'd come to that conclusion within twenty-four hours of arriving in town, when he heard the doctor's prognosis.

When he saw Scarlett break in front of him.

And sure, Ford had stayed for Gunnar and the gleam the kid got when someone—anyone, probably, but especially Ford—showed him any attention.

And he'd stayed for Sammy-Jo, who needed someone to collect her memories with her, to care that they were fading, turning her world smaller with each day.

He'd stayed, of course, for Scarlett because he didn't exactly know how he'd cope with leaving behind a mother who might not remember him the next time he returned. Or worse, giving up the one thing he'd worked his entire life for—his career—to return home and watch his mother throw her life away. So he stayed because she needed a friend.

But mostly he stayed because of Axel.

Because the man set his teeth on edge the way he now watched Scarlett's every movement. He didn't even bother to hide it from Gunnar, from Sammy-Jo, even from Ford.

Which is why Ford kept the boyfriend card on the table. Why he put his arm around Scarlett just often enough to make it believable without going over any personal lines between them.

Why, after that first night when he'd seen Axel consume an entire six-pack, he'd carried his sleeping bag onto the porch, right under Scarlett's open window, just in case he heard anything.

Why he'd slept poorly that night, his dreams a poor place for his fears to linger.

And, why he stayed up on the porch, sometimes listening to an audiobook, watching Axel until the man turned off the glow of the television and went to bed.

Truth was, he couldn't leave her. Because he still heard her voice in his head. *Gary.*

But for a moment there, at the ball game, he'd nearly bolted. Panicked as his heart pulled a Rambo on him and went renegade, wanting to cast the truth at her feet. *I don't know how I'd do my job without you. I mean I would, but it would… it would stink.*

The words almost tipped his lips. And it would stink, but he was a pro and he'd get the job done—Hooyah—even if she wasn't on the other side, feeding him quiet information. Truth was, he could probably figure out how to do his job without Scarlett. He just didn't want to.

Worse, he knew how terrible it sounded. Because she was in a no-win situation with her mother, and of course, all he'd thought about was himself.

So, if she decided to leave, he'd suck it up. He didn't do

vulnerable and needy, and his panic belonged in some sappy television show they always got wrong about Navy SEALs. Something that might happen, but no one really wanted to admit.

Still, his brain had tangled up into a mess of catastrophes and left him with nothing but staring at her, trying to figure out what to do next.

Until Gunnar had hit that home run today and he was saved by the seven-year-old.

Ford even got a hug out of it, one that lingered rebelliously in his head.

What he'd come to, after a day of pacing it out in his brain, was…he had no right to tell her that she couldn't… well, do whatever she needed to.

In the meantime, he'd keep a keen eye on Axel, even if he had to sit on this cold porch all night, again.

He went out to the truck and retrieved his sleeping bag and self-inflating pad and settled down below Scarlett's window.

The temperature hovered in the low sixties, and her window was open to the night, no AC in the house. He lay down, folded his arms under his head, staring out at the sky, the stars so bright they fell in a cascade of diamonds.

He'd slept under skies all over the world, but none felt right until he stretched out under this part of the world. How many times had he slept out on the range with Rube, Knox, Tate, and Wyatt—and even Ruby Jane. He'd longed to be like his brothers—cowboys, tough as leather, afraid of nothing.

Wow, he missed them. And the thought of calling his mother tomorrow and telling her that he couldn't make Reuben's wedding put a knife through his ribs.

But he couldn't leave Scarlett in this mess. Not until she got her feet under her, figured out what to do.

Maybe not even then. Because this week had been a weird sort of vacation, detaching himself from his everyday routine of PT, training, lunch, more training, maybe lifting in the gym, occasionally picking up a game of basketball. A few of the guys liked to sea kayak, so he sometimes joined them.

Had taken a few surfing lessons.

But mostly, he spent his time alone, in his thoughts, reliving scenarios. Often in the gear room caring for his kit, his weapons.

His entire life was his job—he'd breathed being a SEAL since Tate became a Ranger. Had seen the pride in his father's eyes after Tate graduated from Ranger school and wanted that too.

But he'd missed out on so much. His father's death being the biggest regret. He'd gotten the news from Knox, who'd been out on the circuit trying to make a name as a professional bull rider. And Reuben had been smokejumping and Wyatt playing in the minors, Tate working as a bodyguard, Ruby Jane in college and he—he'd still been struggling through SQTs back then, trying to qualify.

His father had never seen him receive his trident.

His throat tightened at the memory. *Ford, Dad died. Heart attack while he was out moving cattle.*

Which meant he'd been alone. Not one of his sons around to help him.

Ford sighed and threw a hand over his eyes.

And that's when something crashed in the kitchen—glass breaking, then a shout. "Get away!"

Ford found his feet in a second, still not in his bag, and hit the front door.

He slowed at the sight of Axel with his arm around Scarlett, leaning over her from behind, his other hand moving over her body. He'd clamped one of her arms to her torso.

The other was free for her to use.

"Get—off—me!"

She slammed her foot into his ankle, hard, and he shouted. Then she made a fist and swung it behind her, aiming for the soft parts.

She must have hit something because he cursed and doubled over.

And she rounded out of his grasp and slammed her open

palm in his chin, reeling him back.

"You—" He called her a word and that was just it.

Ford took two steps and yanked the man into a sleeper hold, pressing hard on his carotid artery and jugular vein. "Don't struggle."

Of course, Axel struggled, slamming his elbow into Ford's chest. Ford saw a few stars, the pain of his busted rib crashing through his brain, but he held on.

Oh, the man reeked. More than beer—he'd probably graduated to one of the bottles of whiskey atop the refrigerator.

In seconds, Axel's legs started to give out.

He went down like a noodle, and Ford caught him before he hit his head on the floor.

"Wow—how did you—how—that was so cool."

Not the reaction Ford had expected from a kid watching his dad hit the floor, but, well, maybe he'd been through more than Ford wanted to guess. "He's okay, Gunnar. Just asleep."

The kid wore a pair of pajama bottoms, no shirt, and now crouched next to Axel, touching his face. "When he wakes up, will he be angry?" His voice trembled a little.

Oh. Ford looked at Scarlett, who stood next to the counter. Slowly she put down the kitchen knife she'd grabbed. She swallowed, a little white.

"You okay?" Ford said, standing up and putting his foot on Axel's chest. He would normally flip the guy and put him in flex-ties, but well, technically Ford had broken into his home.

Scarlett should do the honors.

"Call the police—" Ford said.

"What is happening—oh, Axel!"

Ford saw the horror reflected in Scarlett's face as her mother ran out of the bedroom.

He turned toward Sammy-Jo and wished he hadn't. The woman wore a low-cut, black silky nightie and a shower cap. He wanted to throw a blanket over her, but she knelt beside Axel, her hands on his chest, and started to scream.

"Mom. Mom—it's okay. Ford didn't hurt him. He's

fine—"

But Sammy-Jo began to wail, her hands over her face. "He killed him! He killed Axel!"

Oh wow.

He spotted Gunnar who had backed up, his eyes wide. Ford got up and walked over to the kid. "Gunnar. Buddy. Why don't we let your sister try and calm your mother down."

Gunnar nodded, and Ford pulled the kid close to him, headed him outside. "Why don't you sit in my truck for a bit, okay? I have a pretty sweet sound system..."

He walked him over to the truck and put the keys into the ignition, turned on the radio, queuing up his playlist.

Shut up and let me go...This hurts, I tell you so

The Ting-Tings, spot-on for once.

Gunnar smiled up at him, but tears cut down his face. Ford shoved his hands into his pockets, wishing he knew what to do. Kids weren't his thing, really. Sports, yeah, and he knew how to cook, but he was in over his head here.

The wailing had stopped, but the shouts, male and angry, turned Ford, and he sprinted back to the house.

"Scarlett!"

She stood in the family room, her mother in her arms as Axel came out of Gunnar's bedroom, heat in his eyes, carrying Scarlett's duffel bag, her belongings shoved inside, messy, trailing out. He spotted Ford, and the crazy in his expression had Ford stepping back. Holding up his hands. "Take a breath here—"

"Out. Of. My. Way!"

If Axel's hands hadn't been full, no doubt he would have taken a swing at Ford. But he kicked the door open, stalked out to the porch, and threw Scarlett's belongings into the yard.

Rounded, breathing hard. "Get out of my house."

"Dude—"

"*Now!*" He came back inside and strode toward Scarlett.

Ford moved in his direction. "Axel, step back—"

Sammy-Jo twisted out of Scarlett's arms and ran to the

man, clutching him around his waist. "Baby—don't leave me. I promise I'll be good."

Axel's arms went around her, and Ford stood stymied as the man kissed the top of her head, smoothing her hair, shushing her. "It's okay, Sam, I'm here. I'm not leaving."

Scarlett looked sickened, shaking her head.

Axel looked over at her. "Now," he growled. "Or I call the police."

"You attacked *me*!"

"I tripped. You freaked out—"

Scarlett's mouth opened. Axel took her mother's face in his big hands. "You'll be okay, sweetie. I'll take care of you."

Scarlett shook her head. "If I leave, I come back with the cops."

"Feel free. She's my wife, honey. What do you think is going to happen here? She's not going anywhere."

Ford found Scarlett's hand and squeezed because he felt very sure she might just lose the strength in her legs. Either that or pick up the knife again.

He tightened his hand on hers as she asked, "When did you get married?"

"Four months ago." He smirked at Scarlett. "Say goodbye to Scarlett, Sammy-Jo."

Her mother leaned back and looked at Scarlett, then smiled, her eyes warm, as if she might not know her. "Bye-bye, Scarlett."

Scarlett drew in a breath, her body shaking. And if it were up to him, or any of his teammates, the man's life might be in jeopardy.

Ford tugged her away. "He's not worth it."

"Send my kid back in the house."

Ford wanted to be ill, but he led Scarlett out to the yard.

She shook out of his hand and stalked over to the open door of the truck while he retrieved her belongings from the yard and packed them in the duffel. He opened his back door and caught the words Scarlett was saying to Gunnar, whose wide blue eyes were in hers.

"Listen to me, Gunnar. If you ever need me. Or you're afraid, or if Axel doesn't take care of Mom, then you call me. Day or night, I'll come for you. You're not alone, okay? Ever."

Ford closed the door and came over to the kid. "And me. You can call me. And guess what, I have an entire team of superheroes who will help you. All you have to do is call."

Gunnar nodded, his eyes red.

"Gunnar, come in the house." Axel stood on the porch. He tossed Ford's sleeping bag and mat into the yard.

Gunnar climbed down from the truck and trudged toward the house.

Ford picked up his belongings and shoved them into the back seat. Scarlett stood at his open door. He came to stand in front of her. "Get in, Red."

Her jaw tightened. She didn't even bother to swipe away the tears, and he forced himself not to do it either.

But he stayed there, his back to Axel, his eyes on her until she got in.

Then he closed her door, turned.

Stared at Axel. The man had his hands on Gunnar's shoulders.

Ford drew in a breath, crossed to the front of the truck, and got in.

He backed out. "Don't look back."

But Scarlett couldn't tear herself away, her hand on the window.

"Red." He didn't know what to do.

She looked at him. Shook her head, her eyes red.

He raised his arm.

She hesitated just a moment, then slid over, put her head on his shoulder, and as they drove north to Montana, for the second time, the toughest woman he knew wept in his arms.

8

The Marshall Triple M possessed the kind of opulence the Jackson estate didn't have a prayer of attaining. Sure, the lodge home might have been built nearly seventy years ago, with a number of upgraded additions, and the horse barn needed painting after the repairs to it following a near-catastrophic fire. But the Marshall family home sat in a pocket of mountains, in a greening valley backdropped by a lush landscape of lodgepole pine, craggy ridges, and the endless arch of famous blue sky.

The last time Glo had arrived—with the Belles in their tour bus—the place had served as a hideout, a soft place to land after the trauma of the bombing that had nearly killed Kelsey and Knox and had rattled them all. Even Glo had been shaken, although she hadn't wanted to admit it.

Knowing Kelsey had been trapped under a pile of debris, Glo could only stand back helplessly as the rescuers dug them out. It had resurrected too many sideline moments of watching medical personnel working on Joy.

Glo had needed to take a deep breath, fill her lungs with the sweet, fescue-scented air, lift her face to the sky, and let the sun bake through her bones. Remind her that she'd survived.

And to try not to feel guilty about that.

But yes, last time Tate had brought her because she was a member of the Yankee Belles.

She wasn't entirely sure why he'd insisted she accompany

him this weekend. Sure, her heart had taken rebellious flight when she'd ridden up and heard him announce that she was going with him—a strange, unfamiliar joy at his protectiveness.

Over the past twelve hours, that joy had dissipated into confusion because the man refused to touch her. Had barely spoken to her.

She wanted to blame it on her mother, who had stood at the door this morning breathing fire as she met Tate and their driver.

Her fury must have singed Tate because he'd been oddly silent during both flights—from Nashville to Salt Lake, then to Helena—then the two-hour drive in the rental car. She'd touched his hand once, and he'd closed his around hers just long enough for her to know it wasn't simply a flinch before taking it away.

A one-eighty from the way he'd touched her last night, thank you.

She must be made of poison, have some sort of contagious disease. She didn't want to ask if she had done something wrong, mostly because she couldn't bear the answer—the one that suggested that in the end, she might just be too much trouble. And why not? He was still nursing some bruised ribs, made worse by the takedown yesterday, and he'd favored his still-healing shoulder when he grabbed her suitcase from the limo.

Nice. She just loved it when the people around her got hurt because of her.

They'd arrived at the ranch just before dinner, and Glo fell easily into Gerri Marshall's arms. Tate's mother had a way of making a person feel like they belonged. Even if they knew otherwise.

Knox and Kelsey were at the house, although Knox was out on the range somewhere with his brother Reuben, the groom. Glo got settled in the upstairs bedroom that she shared with Kelsey, then changed into a pair of jeans and a clean T-shirt.

Breathe. Last time they were here, Tate had stepped back

from his crazy, over-the-top, protective persona and become the charmer she'd fallen for.

Please.

She came out of the guest room and down the wide log stairs into the main room with the soaring fireplace.

Kelsey was in the kitchen with Gerri, chopping up onions like she might be the Pioneer Woman. She wore an apron, her hair up in a ponytail, and Glo just stood in the middle of the family room, trying to get a handle on the transformation of her lead singer.

Kelsey looked…well, healed. Tanned, a freedom in her laughter—and the way she looked at Gerri turned a tiny screw into Glo's heart.

As if Kelsey had finally found a mother for the one she'd lost. Sure, Dixie's parents loved her—but Kelsey had always felt like an add-on, the orphan they'd adopted.

Frankly, it had been the thing that bonded Glo and Kelsey—the sense of being not necessarily wanted.

Until now.

Well, at least *Kelsey* was wanted. Glo wasn't quite sure what she was doing here.

"Can I help?" Glo asked.

Gerri looked up from where she was pulling a plastic container from the fridge. She'd already given Glo a rundown of the activities. Tonight, a cookout after the brief rehearsal in front of the family room fireplace. Tomorrow, the small ceremony—just the family and a few friends who were driving down in the morning.

Glo heard voices and glanced outside to where the screen door led to a porch. She spotted the bride, Gilly Priest, a petite redhead and the pilot for the Jude County Smoke Jumpers team, with another woman about her age. They were wrapping purple and gold wildflowers in twine and plunking them in mason jars.

"I think we have everything under control, Glo," Gerri said. "Gilly's sisters are preparing the cupcakes, and Kelsey's salting the onions…" Gerri glanced at Kelsey.

Glo startled when Kelsey looked up, crying, but then her friend grinned. "Onions." She wiped her face with her apron, then slid the onions into a bowl.

"I'm just going to grill this chicken for tomorrow's salad—" Gerri started.

"I'll do that." Glo reached for the container. "I can grill." Probably. Because how hard was it to put meat on a grate and watch it cook?

Gerri lifted a shoulder and handed her the container. "It's lit and warming. Just put these tenderloins on and let them cook, a few minutes on each side." She handed Glo pair of tongs.

Glo toed open the door and found the grill already steaming on the porch. She opened the lid, leaning back when steam billowed out.

"Careful. That thing is awfully close to the house," said a voice, and Glo looked over to see Gilly getting up. "I didn't see you come in, Glo. How are you?"

Oh. Gilly was referring to the fact that the last time she'd seen Glo, she'd been bleeding from a gunshot wound. Gilly had flown her to Helena.

Tate had held her hand and tried not to have a meltdown right there in the plane.

How they'd gone from hot to cold in a matter of a month, she didn't know. But he'd brought her suitcase inside, greeted his mother, and vanished.

She would have been just fine at home, sitting by the pool under Rags's watchful, albeit chagrined, eye.

"I'm good. It looked worse than it was." She lifted her T-shirt sleeve to show the still-reddened but fading scars.

Gilly made a face. "My father always says, 'Don't be ashamed of your scars. They are tattoos of triumph.'"

Huh. They mostly felt like just ugly scars to her.

Gilly's friend came up behind her. Tall and lean, she wore her auburn-gold hair in a low ponytail and carried a baby on her hip, maybe a year old, tawny curls askew as the little girl lay her head on her shoulder, her eyes closed. "I'm Kate

Ransom," she said quietly. "And this is Amber."

Kate filled her in on how she knew Gilly—the smoke-jumping team, her husband, Jed, a longtime friend of Reuben, Gilly's future husband—while Glo put the chicken on the grill and closed the lid.

"And you're one of the Yankee Belles," Kate said. "This is such a small world, because Reuben's friend Pete—he couldn't be here this weekend, sadly—knows Benjamin King. The country singer. Do you know him?"

"Yeah. He's a great guy. We played with him once."

"Tate told us that your band is up for an award."

"CMG's New Group of the Year."

"I love your song—'One True Heart,'" Gilly said. "I was sort of hoping you might sing it at the reception tomorrow."

Oh. "Uh…"

"Gilly. Let the woman relax," Kate said. "She's here to enjoy herself."

Was she?

Smoke began to billow out of the grill.

"I'm actually not sure why I'm here."

Gilly frowned. "Didn't you come with Tate?"

"Yeah, but…well, he's actually on my mother's security staff. He's my security detail."

Silence between the two ladies.

Then Gilly smiled. "So. Tate Marshall is going to keep you safe?"

What did that mean?

"Sorry. It's just…well, Tate has a reputation with his brothers for getting into trouble. I'm sure he's a fantastic bodyguard."

"He saved my life already. Twice."

"And he was a Ranger, don't forget that." The voice that emerged from the screen door as it opened belonged to a younger, darker version of Tate, someone Glo had never met before. He wore a black T-shirt, faded jeans, flip-flops, and a smattering of dark whiskers along his strong jaw. His dark hair was cut military short, and from her quick assessment, he didn't possess an ounce of body fat on his work-honed body.

"Ford!" Gilly said. "I didn't know you were going to make it home."

Ford gathered her into a hug. "Hey, future sis. Long time no see."

Something panged inside Glo as she watched the exchange, the way Gilly so easily slid into the Marshall family. Like Kelsey, she simply belonged. Glo's throat tightened.

Ford let Gilly go and was turning to Glo when his eyes widened. "Hey—the grill's on fire!"

Black smoke puffed out of the grill, flames licking under the cover. She opened it—

"No!" Kate shouted and turned, shielding the baby's face.

The flames whooshed up, engulfing the grill.

Glo screamed.

The screen door banged open and a bigger man came out—he filled the porch with presence and intensity that could only belong to the oldest Marshall—Reuben. He took two steps and slammed the cover down, then turned off the gas. "Ford—get some baking soda—"

But before Ford could obey, Tate came out of the house with a fire extinguisher. He opened the lid and sprayed down the fire still clinging to the charred chicken strips.

The hiss of the foam rose above the silence.

The fire died, the chicken coated in white.

He stepped back.

"Well. Okay then," Reuben said. "That chicken is dead."

"So is the grill," Ford added.

But Glo could only stare at the foamy mess, now dissolving and running off the grill onto the porch.

Oh no.

She hadn't even heard Gerri come out, but now the door closed behind her and every eye turned Gerri's direction. Her mouth was a thin line, and she looked first at Reuben, then Tate.

Finally, "I hope you all like tuna."

Then she turned back inside the house.

Silence. A beat. Then Gilly giggled, and Reuben smiled and closed the lid on the grill. "I'll get this cleaned up."

Glo couldn't breathe. She walked off the porch, her hand to her chest.

Nice.

Her eyes filled with the pressure in her throat, and she had no thought but to just keep walking.

Just…walk away.

She picked up speed, and in a moment she was running. A full-out sprint toward—well, she didn't know exactly where she was going.

Her eyes blurred, and she heard her name, but she couldn't stop. She ran through the grass, spied a trail along the edge of the backyard, and tripped and scraped her way up it until she reached a meadow.

Her brain caught up to her there, and she knew she must look ridiculous, but she couldn't bear to turn around, to face the catastrophe, so she slowed but kept walking.

"Glo!"

She closed her eyes, wincing at the sound of her name. "Go away, Tate."

His breathing was hard, closer. "No."

"Really, I'm just being silly."

"No, you're not." He ran up and fell into a walk beside her. He reached out to touch her, but she drew her arms to herself. "Okay, listen. You gotta calm down. It's no big deal."

She rounded on him. "I incinerated the chicken for tomorrow's reception! And nearly burned down the house. Did you not see the inferno?"

His mouth tweaked up. "It was an old grill. And it's happened before…"

She just stared at him, shook her head. "I can't believe I did this." She turned and kept walking. "I should have stayed home."

"Then I would have missed the wedding." He caught up to her. "So, thank you for coming with me."

"I would have been perfectly safe with Sly or Rags."

"But—" He touched her arm now, stopping her. "I didn't want Sly or Rags keeping an eye on you." He turned her. "Don't you know, Glo, that I would watch you every minute of every day if I could?"

"You practically do."

His eyes finally warmed. He blew out a breath and touched her face. Ran his thumb over her cheekbone. "Your bruise is gone. Finally. I could hardly look at you without feeling guilty."

"I thought it was because you didn't want to see Sloan."

His eyes darkened. "That too."

"I'm sorry about Sloan. I just…" She broke away from him. "Tate, you really don't want me. I'm…I'm so selfish—"

"What?" He caught up to her. Spun her to face him. "What are you talking about?"

She met his eyes, hers hard, despite the burn in them. "I hurt you deliberately. *Deliberately.*"

He wore pain in his eyes but didn't move. "I know."

She stared at him a moment, then shook her head. "Then I'm not sure why you're still here. I'm *not* a good person—"

"Glo—"

She pulled away from him. Held up her hands. "Really. Trust me on this—"

He was advancing on her, but she put a hand to his chest. "Listen. I'll prove it. I was born a twin—a fraternal twin to my sister, Joy—"

"I know."

"But what you *don't* know is that Joy was born with spastic diplegia cerebral palsy. It's a less traumatic CP but affects the muscles of the legs. My sister could walk on her toes, with a sort of scissor gait, but it was…frightening. She'd fall a lot, so in school she used a wheelchair. And she had seizures, which eventually led to her kidney failure."

He was just listening, frowning.

"It was my job to take care of her. I wheeled her to class. When the other kids went out for recess, we stayed inside. If my sister went to the doctor, I went too. We never did anything apart."

He raised an eyebrow.

"Don't get me wrong—I loved my sister. My mother says we were born holding hands, and maybe we were. She was… she was pure light. I had the healthy body, but she had the healthy spirit. Nothing ever got her down. It was easy to see why my mother loved her best."

Tate opened his mouth, as if to argue, but she shook her head. "It's okay. I had a healthy body, I could do anything, *everything* my sister couldn't. I couldn't begrudge her the attention she got from my mother. And it wasn't like Mother ignored me—she came in every night and read to Joy—read to both of us."

She resumed walking. The sun had dropped into the horizon, casting shadows across the meadow, a purpling hue clouding the mountains to the west. "Joy's first kidney failed when she was eleven. By the time she was thirteen, the other was dying. She went on dialysis at fifteen, and after waiting for a perfect match for a year, they finally decided to give her one of mine. It had nearly all the markers, and it was a 98 percent match."

She reached a bench, and for a moment, the place jogged the memory of being here over a month ago, hiding from the stalker who had shot her. Kelsey had pushed her into the ground, kept her silent. Her adrenaline had numbed the pain long enough for the Marshalls to find them.

For Tate to pull her into his arms.

For her to believe that maybe she even belonged there. It had given her a strength she didn't know she possessed.

"Right before she went into surgery, they gave us a moment together, and she looked at me and took my hand and…" She drew in a breath. "She said that the angels were coming for her. That she would be gone in an hour." Her throat thickened. "I told her not to be morbid and that we'd be fine and made her promise that she'd live. I was so *angry* at her. I don't know why, but here I was giving her a kidney and she was planning on dying on me—" She ran her hand across her chin.

"I went into surgery thinking she was ungrateful and selfish and…" She glanced at Tate, who watched her, his eyes soft. "And she never woke up again."

He didn't move. Just his chest, rising and falling.

"The last thing I said to her was that if she died on me, I'd never forgive her." She shook her head. "Nice. Real nice."

"Glo—" He reached out for her, but she stepped away.

"No, Tate. Listen. She's not the only one I was angry with. I know that Kelsey told you about David, about the boy I dated in high school. What you missed was that I begged him not to enlist. I gave him an ultimatum—if he loved me, he would stay. He enlisted anyway, and I was so angry with him, I didn't write to him." She closed her eyes. "He went to war and never…" She whisked her hand across her wettened cheek. "He never heard from me again. And he died, thinking I was angry with him."

He drew in a breath.

She covered her face with her hands. "See, Tate? I'm not the person you think I am. I'm selfish and angry—"

"And hurt, Glo. You're grieving. And anger is a huge part of grief." He stepped up to her and put his arms around her, turning her. "You gotta give yourself some grace."

She didn't have the strength to push him away, but instead curled into him. He was warm and solid and simply held her, the cottony, freshly showered smell of him seeping into her skin.

Oh, this man could turn her weak, as if she didn't have bones in her body. But, "I hurt you because I was angry at you, Tate. And truthfully, I'm still angry. If you get killed—"

He held her at arm's length, his blue eyes in hers. "Stop. Listen. I'm not going to get killed—"

"You can't say that—"

"When I was six years old, I got bucked off a horse and broke my arm. My brothers Reuben and Knox thought it was hilarious."

"What—why?"

"Because the horse only bucked because I screamed. It reared up and I tumbled right off, onto the ground. I lay there in the dirt crying, and my dad came and picked me up and told me I'd be okay. To stop making such a fuss. To shake it off."

"You broke your *arm.*"

"Yeah, well, people get hurt all the time on a ranch. It took two days for my mother to bring me in to the doctor. They both felt pretty bad when they discovered I'd broken my arm—but by then, I'd decided that I wasn't going to let fear land me in the dirt again. And if it did, I was going to get back up, without crying. I hated horses after that—hated ranch life, actually, but I still learned to ride, still ran cattle, still rode fence. I'm not the guy who stays in the dirt, Glo. I get back up. And if I say I'm going to do something, I do it." He took her face in his hands. "And I promise you right now—I'm not going to let anything happen to you...or me."

Oh, she wanted to believe him. And maybe her doubt showed in her eyes because, as if to reassure her, he leaned down and kissed her.

And it wasn't the kiss of possession back in Nashville or even the tentative wonder they'd shared in Vegas, but one of surety. One that said, *you are safe.*

You are wanted.

He held her face in his big hands and he slowed down the kiss, tasting her, drawing her close.

And something that had been simmering between them for over a month simply blew open and found her soul.

She didn't know why Tate liked her, but when she was around him, when his gaze turned to her, she felt whole. As if she didn't have to do anything but smile in his direction and he'd want her.

And even that smile was optional.

Because she'd done her dead-level best to push him away and he'd still followed her across the country, dragged her back to his home, and chased after her to...to...

She broke away, searching his face. "Did you bring me

here because you wanted to get me away from my mother and your 'deal'?"

His smile was slow, like the sunrise, something lighting in his eyes. "What happens in Montana stays in Montana, Glo." Then he winked.

No, she hadn't a clue why this man wanted her.

But for today, she wasn't going to argue with him.

The perfect night, the perfect place, the perfect moment and Tate never wanted it to end.

He sat on the ground, his back against a wooden bench that faced the flickering campfire. Glo sat beside him on a blanket he'd spread out, prying a gooey marshmallow from a skewer, the mess twining around her fingers as she listened to a story Reuben was telling about his smokejumping team, something that had happened this past summer in Alaska.

"Then the fire curled around the lake, right for this homestead, and apparently, Riley's girlfriend was trapped there. So the man jumped into a plane and dropped right in on top of her—"

"Even with his broken shoulder?" Kelsey asked. She sat on the ground in front of Knox, her back to his chest. She broke off a piece of chocolate and handed it to him.

"I remember Riley from rookie camp a few years ago. The kid had crazy eyes," Kate said. "I'm not surprised."

"He found her just in time but had to deploy his shelter."

Kate made a face as if she'd been there, done that. Sometimes Tate forgot how dangerous wildland firefighting was. Probably it was a good thing Reuben was hanging up his chain saw and joining Knox on the ranch.

Actually, replacing Knox, who'd decided to take the job as Director of Livestock for NBR-X, a professional bull riding show. The same show that had hired the Yankee Belles for a six-month gig.

Glo hadn't mentioned the Belles getting back together,

but the minute she did, he'd quit working for the senator and beg Carter, the Belles' manager, to take him back.

He'd even become a groupie if it meant having Glo in his life, in his arms.

Without guilt.

Because despite his best moves, he kept hearing his promise to Senator Jackson in his head, her challenge, and his own stupid words in reply. *I promise to keep my distance from Glo. As long as I get to make sure she's safe.*

You can do that? Stand on the sidelines, watching her back as she attends parties, speeches, and events?

Ma'am, I can do anything if it means keeping Glo safe.

Apparently, he was the King of Liars because if he searched his heart, he had no intention of staying away from Glo.

And yes, it had decimated him to see her with Sloan.

But he'd given his word, and once upon a time, that had meant something.

Still he wasn't so disgusted with himself that he wasn't going to pull Glo against him as the firelight crackled into the Montana darkness, pine scented the air, and the stars spilled out in brilliance overhead.

"I can't believe you're giving up jumping out of planes, Rube." Ford sat next to their mother, poking the fire with his empty skewer. "It's one of my favorite parts about being a SEAL." He turned to Tate. "You jumped out of planes when you were a Ranger, right?"

Tate didn't have to disguise his surprise at seeing Ford when his little brother had pulled up in his F-150 this afternoon. The kid had turned into a man, built to serve his country, with a calm demeanor that reminded Tate a little of Knox or even Reuben, a quiet steadiness that had bypassed Tate and Wyatt, their hockey star who'd called in with a no-go on this weekend's events. They hadn't heard from Ruby Jane.

Ford wore his hair short but had let his whiskers grow into a dark shag and bore the wizened expression of a man who'd seen things that most people shouldn't. One that Tate reluctantly recognized.

Tate nodded. "It was fun. Although really, it was only at Elgin that we conducted any airborne training."

"I had a friend who was a Ranger," said the petite brunette whom Ford had brought with him. Scarlett. Quiet, but watchful, she wore a rare smile and seemed a little buttoned up. She'd helped Ford clean up the grill mess today and later had made a taco salad for a quick dinner save, freeing Gerri to help with the casual rehearsal.

Gilly's father was marrying them, but he and his family were staying at a hotel in nearby Geraldine. Tate was thinking about taking Glo in for dancing at the Bulldog Saloon later.

Maybe write a different ending to their last date, one that finished with him nearly punching Knox. Although later that night, he had cornered Glo in the pantry and right then, he realized that the woman had gotten under his skin.

It had only gotten worse, especially the way she snuggled against him, tucked under his arm, her body warm and smelling like sunshine and wildflowers and—

"Actually, he was an interagency trainer. He did training on the reliability of local intel." She looked at Ford. "Remember that? He told us a story about the ambush of an entire Ranger squad in Afghanistan?"

Ford just looked at her, nothing on his face, and Tate drew in a breath—

Stop—

"It was a horrible story about this team leader who followed a bad tip from a local contact and led his team into an ambush. Five troops died—"

"Four. Two got out," Tate said quietly.

She looked over at him. "Oh, so you know the story?"

The family had gone quiet, and Ford looked up at him, a little pain in his eyes.

Tate swallowed, looked into the fire. Listened to it crackle.

He'd never told them—not even his father—the entire story. And if he had, maybe they'd stop looking at him like he was some kind of tragedy, some victim.

See the truth.

"It happened in the Paktia Province, in eastern Afghanistan. After the Taliban lost control of the area, it fell into chaos, and rival militias were fighting for control. There were also rumors that it was a safe haven for militants from one of the Taliban subgroups. One militant in particular—a leader—was hiding in a tiny village about twenty clicks into the mountains. The Rangers were going off the intel of a twelve-year-old boy who'd proven reliable in the past."

He leaned away from Glo, picked up his skewer, and forced it into the flames of the fire, watching the tip glow. "He was a good kid. Played soccer with some of the younger troops, spoke English like a champ, and wanted to move to America someday. We trusted him."

He felt the gazes on him but didn't look away from the flames.

"There were a lot of skirmishes in the region, and then a local governor was killed by a Taliban suicide bomber, and HQ said we needed to root out the militants. We had acted off similar intel before—sparked by this kid and confirmed by other sources. This night…"

The flames had found the skewer, burning it to a fiery red. His voice had dropped, quiet, and he saw Jammas's big brown eyes, nothing of guile in them.

"At first, I didn't think Jammas knew it was a setup. And it certainly didn't look that way—we had outside intel confirming the location of our target and had reconned the area for hours beforehand. Had seen a number of Taliban operators enter the mosque in question. So we felt secure in our assessment, and I gave the order to proceed."

No one spoke.

"It was a classic ambush—I can't believe I didn't see it coming. Worse, Jammas was right at the front. He ran into the mosque, and after a few minutes, poked his head back out, as if giving us the all clear. I figured out later that it was the signal not to us, but to the militants who were waiting for us to get into the open. Jammas was a good kid, but he didn't have the strength to stand up to his family or whatever factions controlled his life. We weren't five feet away when an RPG exploded the wall in front of us, and suddenly we were taking fire. We took cover in the mosque—which was not only empty but destroyed. Two of our guys were already wounded, and the militants were raking the building with fire. My radio man had been hit, and I was trying to get to him to call in support, but they shot in two 120mm mortar rounds and the building practically came down on top of us."

He was right there, smelling the smoke, tasting the dirt in his mouth.

His voice turned whisper thin. "Then everything went quiet. I was hurt and stunned, and all I could hear was Jammas yelling at me to get up. He was trying to get me to run—they were raking us with gunfire."

He looked away. "Jammas was shot. He died right there in my arms. And that's when I realized that only Specialist Jordan, my radio guy, and I were alive."

He felt Glo's hand on his arm but didn't move.

"I'd been shot too—my knee a complete wreck—but I knew we had to get moving if we wanted to live. I'm not sure why, but it took the Taliban a while to check on us. The walls had come down on top of us, so my men—and I—were buried. When I heard them coming, I put Jammas's body over mine and pulled the debris around me."

He just let the words land, not caring about the judgment. "I don't know how, but they didn't find me."

"Thank God," whispered his mother.

No. Maybe. He hadn't thought so for a long, long time.

He didn't look at her as he continued. "Somehow, Specialist Jordan was also overlooked. He was in bad shape—he had a gut wound, and his leg was broken. That night, I crawled out of the village with Jordan on my back. I hid him in the mountains and dragged my way back to base. I was found by a forward operator two days later. They saved Jordan, but he lost his leg to his hip. Gangrene."

He looked at Scarlett. "For that, they gave me a Bronze

Star and a Purple Heart. I wanted to give both of them back."

She met his gaze, unflinching.

"So, yeah, it's a great lesson in knowing when you're being played. How not to trust anyone." He pulled his red-hot skewer from the flames, shoved it into the dirt, and got up. "Excuse me, I need a drink."

No one said anything as he walked into the house. He stood at the kitchen sink, ran cold water, dipped both hands in, and sloshed water over his face.

He could smell the flesh burning, hear the groans of his men, dying. Taste the rubble on his lips, feel Jammas's blood seeping into his camo.

"Tate?"

He stiffened. Not the voice he'd expected, really. Because knowing Glo, she would have wanted to run in after him, help heal his wounds.

But big brother Reuben wasn't the coddling type.

"Tate—"

Tate grabbed a towel and turned, holding up his hand. "Save it, bro. I don't need your pity."

"None here. Trust me—I've been there enough to know what's going on in your gut. I nearly got Gilly killed, twice."

"Yeah, but she's here, marrying you tomorrow, so you must have done something right." He ran the towel over his face.

Reuben walked over to the cupboard and grabbed a glass. "The only thing I did right was give myself permission to have a second chance."

Tate gave a sad shake of his head. "Yeah, well, I tried that. And managed to get a girl killed."

Reuben frowned as he handed Tate the glass.

"Vegas. Back when I was working security for a mob boss. Another slick idea of mine. I turned in my boss to the FBI, but not until they killed the woman I was dating to warn me off."

Reuben leaned back against the counter, his arms folded. "How did I get so far out of your life that I never knew these things?"

Tate filled his glass with water. "It's no big deal. I was a mess. I didn't stick around long after my medical separation from the military. Dad sorta told me that if I wanted to be a hero, I needed to act like it."

Reuben frowned. "Dad said that?"

"I might have come in late from the Bulldog, a little too much beer on my breath."

Reuben gave him a nod. "It's tough when the one we worship falls hard."

"I didn't worship Dad," Tate said.

"I wasn't talking about Dad." Reuben raised an eyebrow. "The number one idol of the human race is ourselves. Or at least that's what Gilly's dad is always preaching from the pulpit. And he's right." He smirked. "It's hard not to feel like you make your own tailwind when people are in the stands screaming your name, Twenty-Two."

Tate opened his mouth. "I don't—"

"Want to impress yourself? Prove to yourself that you're not the scared kid who fell off a horse?"

"Yeah, well, *I* didn't leave home to jump out of airplanes into infernos because of my pride." Tate didn't mean for that to come out quite so darkly.

But he didn't expect Reuben to nod. "I admit, I was running from my own demons, my own broken places. Problem was that no amount of my own awesomeness could heal me. No matter how many fires I put out, I still came home to an angry Reuben."

Tate finished off his water, set the glass on the counter. "So, how did you get from there to…well…" He glanced out the window to the family campfire. To Gilly.

And of course, looked at Glo, who had drawn up her knees, clasping her arms around them. She glanced at the house, as if feeling his gaze on her.

"I had to stop trying."

Tate looked at him. "What?"

"I know. It sounds crazy, but I had to stop trying so hard

to prove that…well, that I was somebody worth loving, I guess. And just let Gilly—and God, too—love me."

Tate reached for one of the cupcakes on a plate on the counter.

"Touch that and you'll pull back a nub."

Tate glanced at his brother. Held up his hands. "Fine. Listen, I don't need to prove to anybody that…whatever. It's no big deal."

"It's the *only* deal, Tate. When you show up with nothing and discover that you're loved because of who you are—that's when you realize what it means to be a son of God. That's when you discover that you've inherited more than you could possibly imagine. It's pretty breathtaking." He grinned. "Sort of like free-falling, knowing that your chute is going to catch you."

He frowned at Reuben, but the door opened, and Gilly came in. "I'm checking on my cupcakes."

"All good here, honey," Reuben said and pulled her against him. But he looked back at Tate. "Just remember, bro. You're not the good news. Jesus is." He clamped him on the shoulder and guided Gilly back outside.

A son of God. Tate didn't know why those words settled inside him, rough-edged and itchy.

He'd never really seen himself as the son of anyone—sure, Orrin Marshall, but he was so very different from his father.

Different from his brothers.

He watched them out the window. All of them loved the ranch, knew how to throw a rope, were easy in the saddle, and sure, Ford had gone on to become a SEAL, but at the end of the day, he was a cowboy to his core.

Tate had hated the ranch.

No, he hated not measuring up.

As he watched, Ford got up and, after a glance at Scarlett, headed to the house.

Nice. Tag team brotherly counsel.

He was leaning against the counter, his arms folded when

Ford entered.

Ford gave a smirk. "Right. Okay. So I'm just adding that Scarlett didn't know it was you in that story."

"I know."

"And although I didn't know the entire story, I do know this." Ford crossed his arms to match Tate's. "We train every day, for months, hoping to get things right, and we still make mistakes. No op is perfect. You go in, stay alert, and rely on your brothers to have your back. And I'm not just talking your fellow Rangers."

"I was impulsive, and I got people killed. And I still do." He looked outside. "I can't let anything happen to Glo."

Ford nodded. "I get that." He had been looking out the window, too, and now turned back to Tate. "And sometimes you have to follow your gut. You, more than anyone, know that. It's how we stay alive out there, right?"

Tate shrugged.

Ford walked over to the pantry. "Man, if you only knew how much I wanted to be like you when I was younger. You were always doing the cool things."

"If you mean breaking bones and driving Ma crazy—"

"Like I said. And I still look at you and think…man, he's got all the luck. The jerk."

"Hardly."

"Take another look, bro. Because you have that hot girl pining for you out there. And I can't figure out how to get past the mess I've created with Scarlett."

Oh?

Ford stood in the glow of the overhead light of the pantry. "What? Ma doesn't have any health food?" He grabbed a bag of Doritos.

Tate hadn't moved, but he raised an eyebrow.

"So," Ford said, opening the bag and scoring a chip, "Scarlett is our FOB operations communicator when we're in the field, and I'm radio communicator, field ops, so…she's talking to me. And we have this rapport, see, and…we're friends."

"Mmmhmm."

Ford threw the chip in his mouth. "She needed a ride to Idaho last week, so I gave her a ride."

"Because it's on your way to Montana."

"Actually—"

Tate held up his hand. Grinned.

"Anyway, we're driving, and on the way she tells me she wants to go into SEAL training—"

"What? Seriously?"

Ford found another chip. "I know. They're letting women in, and sure, I'm game for anyone who can be a solid operator. But…yeah, the idea of Scarlett there, beside me, or even on SWCC, in the heat of things…honestly, I'm not a fan."

"We had a few women who tried to be Rangers. Brave, tough, smart. But in the end, the thought of them being captured and put through torture—it makes me sick."

"Right?" Ford leaned a hip against the counter and dug in for another chip. "And then we get to her mother's house, and she's forty-three and has early-onset Alzheimer's and can barely remember Scarlett."

"Oh no."

"Yeah, and her husband is a jerk, taking the money Scarlett sends for her mother and little brother. Now she thinks she should quit the military and help her mother."

Ford finished the Dorito he held in his hand then rolled the bag up. "And I just want her to stop talking and go back to being the woman in my ear. And it feels so selfish, I'm making myself angry. Because I also really just want to kiss her, which would screw everything up and…"

"Wow. I feel a lot better. This tag team counseling is a great tactic."

Ford just eyeballed him.

"Okay, what happens in Montana stays in Montana."

Ford frowned.

"That's all I got for you, bro."

"I really expected more."

"I told you. You don't want to be like me. I have a

couple of killers stalking Glo—or I used to think so—and meanwhile, I'm breaking promises like I'm throwing china at the wall." He glanced out the window, and now Glo was standing up, again looking this direction. "And I don't think I'm stopping anytime soon."

"A couple killers?"

"The guys who bombed the arena in Texas. But according to RJ, there's no connection. I'm back to speculation and some bad photos."

Ford frowned.

"The important part here is that I'm so beyond my instincts, I'm not sure what to do. All I know is that when I'm with Glo, all that clutter of the past seems to fade, and she makes me think that everything will be okay. That I'm not a freakin' mess and that maybe...yeah, that I could give myself permission for a second chance."

Ford let a grin slide up his face and he glanced past Tate, out the window. "Or that some ops are worth the risk."

Tate held up his fist.

"Hoo-yah." Ford bumped it. Turned to the door. "Hey, Glo. I'm tagging you in."

She stared after Ford, then turned to Tate. "You okay, tough guy?"

She looked so concerned, her hazel-green eyes searching his. He reached for her, his arms around her waist, pulling her close, meeting those beautiful eyes. "I am now." Right now.

He wouldn't think about tomorrow.

So he bent, searching her gaze for a brief moment, caught in the wonder, the sparkle, the hope that was Glo, the sense that, with her, he didn't have to be anything more... and kissed her.

Giving himself that second chance.

9

The perfect wedding, the perfect life. One she'd never have.

Not that Scarlett was made for all this happy-sappy, family reunion Hallmark movie-type emotion, but something about the simple ceremony of seeing tough Gilly Priest marry big Reuben Marshall, had tugged a cord deep inside her.

Maybe one of the romantic threads she'd inherited from her unlucky-in-love mother, the ones she'd been trying to pluck from her life.

She needed to remember that men, in general, couldn't be trusted.

Well, except for a handful. With the last name Marshall, maybe, because Ford had surely been more than a gentleman, letting her weep on his shoulder as they drove out of Idaho. Making a bed for her in the back seat of his truck while he slept in the truck bed under the stars, garbed only in his leather jacket. Even last night, after her painful gaffe where she somehow opened private family wounds, Ford had said nothing of recrimination.

The man couldn't be real. Especially looking the way he did today—he'd gussied up in his dress whites, with his rows and rows and rows of medals, including his trident. He escorted his mother down the three-row aisle to sit in the front, then stood at attention behind her.

She'd seen plenty of sailors in their dress whites. None

filled out their uniform quite like Petty Officer First Class Ford Marshall, United States Navy SEAL.

It wasn't like the rest of the family didn't clean up well—Reuben wore a black suit, and Tate and Knox both wore suitcoats, jeans, and their cowboy boots. Scarlett sat in the back row with Kelsey and Glo—never mind their crazy outfits. She knew of the Yankee Belles but meeting them in person felt surreal. Kelsey was maybe down to earth, but she wore a deep-V-necked purple dress and a pair of cowboy boots. Glo, however, wore a silvery short dress that cut out in the middle, showing off her tanned stomach, not to mention her legs, and only accentuated all her curves.

Like she might be onstage or something.

And Scarlett felt downright dowdy in her plain black dress she'd bought from a thrift store. Maybe she should have worn her uniform, but somehow those only looked good on the men.

Besides Gilly's parents and two sisters, friends of the bride and groom had driven down for the wedding, mostly coworkers who jumped fire with them. A small but sweet wedding that seemed to be over pretty quickly.

And with a very odd sermon in the middle, from some obscure text in the Old Testament. Not that she knew anything about the Bible, but even she could figure out that warnings about dry wells and broken cisterns weren't a great encouragement.

Although, maybe appropriate according to her view of marriage, something she planned to stay far, far away from.

Now she stood on the porch, the music from the reception taking place in the main room winding out into the darkening yard. Last night's fire still played in her mind as she peered out into the horizon, this safe world that Ford's family had built.

She couldn't begin to imagine this kind of legacy.

Tried to decide if it would feel suffocating.

"You okay, Red?"

She glanced over toward the voice. Ford had come out

the back door to stand beside her. He'd taken off his lid, and now it was tucked in his back pocket. And he'd shaved for the ceremony, the scent of aftershave on his skin.

She turned away before it went to her head. Just friends.

"Nice ceremony," she said. "Sweet."

"Yeah. Reuben should have married her two years ago, but he's sort of shy about things. Doesn't like to go charging in, unless it's a fire."

"Not like you, huh?" She glanced over and meant it as a joke, but some of the blood had drained from his face.

"What?"

"Nothing."

Oh no. She'd meant it as a compliment.

"I was just thinking that maybe sometimes I do that. I sort of don't think about the consequences. Like our last op. I'm thinking that maybe I should have not engaged with those militants—"

"Ford—"

"Or maybe stuck around like some kind of hero at your mother's house. I...sort of thought maybe I was helping..."

"You were helping. Gunnar loved you. And..." She lifted a shoulder. "Thanks for taking care of Axel."

"You could have handled him. And maybe not gotten thrown out of the house."

"Maybe." She looked back out at the horizon. "I've learned a few things, that's true."

"Since Gary?"

She glanced at him. "That's really bugging you, isn't it?"

His mouth opened, then he turned away, his jaw hard. "Yes. Actually. Yes, it is. I just keep imagining the worst—"

"Yes."

He looked at her, and she lifted a shoulder. "Yes. To everything you're thinking. Gary was my mother's boyfriend, but he was also 'Uncle Gary' to me." She finger quoted the words. "And Uncle Gary liked little girls."

Ford's eyes darkened.

"That's why I joined the Navy as soon as I turned

seventeen."

"Did you tell your mother?"

"No." She held up her hand to the argument forming on his face. "Listen. It wasn't like that at first. He didn't... well, nothing serious happened until I was fourteen, and after that, I figured out ways to dodge him. I slept in the car or stayed at friends' houses. And, like I said, it wasn't all the time—just when he got drunk. Or when he and my mother were fighting. And then..." She looked away. "You learn to live with things, especially if you want to be safe."

He was silent beside her and when she finally looked over, his jaw was so hard she thought he might break something.

But she started at the wetness in his eyes. She touched his arm. "It's okay, Ford."

"In what world is it okay?" His voice rose and he took a wavering breath. "It's not okay, Scarlett. *Nothing serious until you were fourteen?* It's *all* serious, Red. You shouldn't ever have to be scared, let alone learn to *live with things* to be safe."

And then he closed his eyes, as if reining in more. "I'm sorry. I don't know what life you lived, what shoes you were in. I'm not judging—"

"Yes, you are—"

He opened his eyes. "No, I'm not. I'm angry. I'm wishing that I had been there—or someone—to step in. To be the person who made it stop."

Oh, Ford. "You made it stop with Axel."

He drew in a breath then. Licked his lips, turned away, an emotion on his face she couldn't read. "Yeah, well, I got you kicked out of your home."

"It wasn't my home. I was a guest. And I...the longer I stayed the more I was freaking out, so at least now I can get some clarity." She sighed and walked off the porch. He followed her, and behind them the music faded. "I guess I'm just trying to figure out why I always have to be the one to save my mother. She abandoned *me*. But I can't abandon her, and it makes me...I'm so angry."

Her own words made her catch her breath. "Yeah, I'm

not just angry, I'm *furious*. I'm just…I don't know. But my entire life all I've wanted was to get away from her, and I still can't. I used to beg my friends to let me spend Christmas or summer vacation with them. I took every job I could so I could be out of the house, and I'd still come home and find her drunk, or gone, or…after Gary, with who knows who." She drew in a breath, cutting her voice low again. "And here I am, having to give up my career to take care of her. And of course I have to—she's my mother. But…I'm just mad. At life, maybe."

"Maybe you get home health care for her and move her down to San Diego."

"Axel will never let me do that."

Ford's eyes darkened. "You let me take care of Axel."

"Ford. C'mon. What are you going to do? You can't shoot him."

He wore a look like that might be *exactly* what he wanted to do. "Guys like Axel are just cowards at their core. Trust me, I know. You get Axel alone, and he'll fold."

She blinked at him, and he took a breath, looked away.

Huh.

But before she could chase that, he turned back to her. "Let's get out of here."

She frowned.

"I'm going to change out of this sausage casing, and I'll meet you in the barn in ten minutes. Wear jeans."

"Ford."

"Please?"

Well, when he said it like that. "Aye, aye."

He grinned at her and then took her hand and pulled her to the house, letting go as they walked inside. He didn't look back as he headed upstairs to his room. She was sleeping in the main floor den, so she went inside, changed into a pair of jeans and a T-shirt and her Converse tennis shoes.

A slow song was playing as she came out and noticed the dance floor was packed. She wanted to high-five Ford for his brilliant escape idea.

She met him in the barn. He wore a pair of faded jeans, his cowboy boots, and a hat.

He had a pretty Appaloosa bridled. "What—no, Ford. I can't ride."

"C'mon, Red. Trust me." He stood next to a bench, jumped on it and threw his leg over the horse's back. He held out his hand, and she took a breath.

"You can't be a spec ops soldier without knowing how to ride. Did you never hear of *The Horse Soldiers* or *12 Strong*?"

"You should be the team negotiator." She held up her hand, and in a second he'd pulled her on behind him.

"Arms around my waist."

"Where else am I going to hold on? The tail?"

But sure, she'd put her arms around his lean waist, tuck herself against him, breathe in the strength radiating out of him as he urged the animal forward, into the darkness.

"I've never been on a horse," she said as she moved with him, with the horse. Its body was wider than she'd imagined, but the smell of horseflesh, earthy, honest, bled into the night as the sounds of the cicadas, the occasional low of a cow rose up to fill the silence.

"Just hang on to me. You'll be fine."

The mantra of her life, maybe. Oh, she was turning into a romance heroine. What happened to the wannabe rescuer?

Maybe she could be both tough and sappy?

Ford had a wide back, strong arms, and rode easy, like the horse might be one with him. He took them down the dirt driveway, then cut up around the far pasture, and back along a coulee behind the house on a trail that both he and the horse seemed to know well.

She heard a rushing that sounded deeper than wind. "Is that a river?"

"Yep. The bottom of a falls that winds into Geraldine. It's got a few cool caves and a swimming hole."

"Just for the record, I'm not going skinny dipping."

He laughed, and his entire body rumbled. "It's also the best place around to star gaze."

He pulled up the horse, then held his arm stiff as she swung down. He landed beside her and dropped the reins.

"Will he stay?"

"She, and yes." The mare turned toward them and nudged her with her soft muzzle. Scarlett lifted her hand, a little unnerved by the teeth, but drawn in by the giant, doe eyes.

Ford took her hand and pressed it on the horse's nose.

"It's so soft."

"Mmmhmm. Their mouths are actually very tender, which is why you don't need much to give them direction. A good horse will respond with just your legs and the slightest movement of the reins." He ran his hand down the mare's face. "You remember me, don't you, Georgia?"

Oh, why did this man have to be a teammate?

He glanced at Scarlett, and she spied something in his eyes that might have been the same question. As if asking the question, he reached out for her hand.

Despite her better sense, she took it.

He walked her out to the edge of a glistening, silver river, maybe twenty feet wide, the moonlight cutting through it like a ribbon. Rocks jutted out from dark depths, and a ledge careened out over a section of froth and gentle rapids. He climbed up the ledge, pulling her up behind him, then let her hand go as he walked out to the edge.

"Farther down the river there are a number of caves. I got lost in one, once."

She came to stand by him. "Scary."

He nodded, quiet. Took a breath. "I didn't know how to get out. Eventually, I found a ledge above water and sort of climbed out and stayed there, terrified to get back in, pretty sure I was going to drown."

She tried to imagine him, a skinny kid, shivering in the darkness. With Ford standing next to her, bold and strong, she struggled to wrap her brain around the image. "The worst part was that my sister was with me. We were trapped together, and you'd think it might be easier, but it was actually worse because I kept thinking...if I left her behind to get help and couldn't find her again, she'd die in that cave."

He turned to her then. "That's a little how I felt at your mother's place, Red. I feel like I brought you into this mess— it was my idea for you to go home, and I practically dragged you there, and now...I don't want to leave you alone with it."

"No man left behind."

He didn't smirk, nothing on his face. Just silence as his chest rose and fell.

Finally, "The worst part is—I'm insanely angry. At Axel, at the idea of you leaving the team, and I know that makes me a total jerk, but..." He looked away, into the distance where the town glittered in the valley below. His voice emerged a little pained. "I like you in my ear, what can I say?"

She drew in a breath. Swallowed. But his gaze turned back, and he must have read her face because he shook his head.

"And I like you in mine," she whispered. She met his eyes and drew in a breath.

His breath shuddered out. "Aw, Red, I'm in a dangerous place here—"

"Kiss me, Navy."

He blinked at her, as if, for the first time, he didn't know what to do with her information.

She'd surprised herself, actually, but it felt honest and right and...*finally*.

"What—"

"You heard me. Kiss me. Right now."

He drew in a breath. Made a chest-deep noise of surprise, or maybe satisfaction.

And then he smiled and became the man she knew. All in. A hundred ten percent bringing it to the mission. He wrapped his hand around her neck, pulled her to himself, and dove in. Not needing her voice in his ear to tell him what she wanted.

Him. Closer. Holding her. Because for some reason when he was with her, the world didn't feel quite so out of control.

Maybe for him, too, because he was practically inhaling her, as if he had also been telling himself a thousand different ways why this shouldn't work and no longer cared.

Fact was, she'd wanted Ford Marshall in her arms since the day she'd seen him walk onto the deck of the USS *San Antonio* for his rookie op. Kitted up, looking dangerous and powerful, his mouth a grim line of determination, so much fierceness in his expression—if anyone could get it done, it was Ford Marshall.

He made her believe, all over again, in honor.

So, as he kissed her, she cast aside all the noise in her head and wound one arm around his neck, the other under his arm, molding herself to his lean, work-honed body. Warm, powerful, and everything she'd imagined.

He tasted of the champagne they'd toasted with and smelled of his aftershave, and she liked the way he had no whiskers to slow her down. Truly, there was probably no romantic finesse to the way she moved her mouth against his in a sort of desperate urgency.

Wow, she needed him. Wanted him. And she didn't care if she might be breaking rules and breaching walls and turning to shambles any hope of rebounding back to just friends.

Oh, who was she kidding? She wanted Ford's arms around her like she wanted her next breath.

Teammate.

Coworker.

She slid her arms around his back, pressing her hands against those wide shoulders.

He ran his hands into her hair, drew his thumbs down the side of her face in a soft caress, then dropped his hands to her shoulders, leaning back from her. "Scarlett." He swallowed, breathing hard. "Um, okay…"

He backed away, holding up his hands as if suddenly afraid to touch her. "You gotta know that I've been thinking about that for a very, very long time. And I'm all in…as long as you are."

Her heart was thumping, the desire to pull him back to her nearly taking possession, but somehow his words thrummed through.

All in.

Wait. What was she *doing?* She had plans. A new career waiting for her.

No, she couldn't get involved in a tug-of-war between love and career.

Career had to win, if she wanted to live a life different from her mother's.

Especially since this was Ford Marshall. Oh, this could be a very bad idea because she *knew* Ford. When he went all in, it became a get 'er done mission for him, no backing down, and the last thing she needed was him telling her how to live her life.

"I'm sorry," she whispered, backing away. "I shouldn't have—"

"Wait—Red. Listen. I get it. It could get complicated, but I can do complicated—"

She held up her hand. "No, Ford, it's not that...or only that. I...uh..." She sighed. "I put in a package to transfer rates to Rescue Swimmer. It's a five-week certification in Pensacola. If I want to, I can go on to be an Aviation SAR and deploy from a chopper."

He was such a warrior, he barely stiffened, barely drew in a breath at her words.

Barely. But she felt it.

Then, a hard swallow. "So that's what that chatter about the SEAL training was about."

He shook his head and walked away from her.

The air rushed in, chilled by his distance.

"Why?" He turned and stared down at her, so much concern in his eyes, it rattled her.

"Because I...I hate sitting on the sidelines—"

"You're hardly sitting on the sidelines! You're my eyes out there. You saved my life, Scarlett. That's hardly doing *nothing.*"

"I...want to do more. Be more. I want to..."

He blinked at her, and no, she couldn't say it because it sounded crazy.

So he said it for her. "*Protect* me?"

She looked away.

He wrapped a hand around his neck. Shook his head.

"It's not crazy—"

"It is crazy. It's..." He rounded on her. Held up his hand. "Listen, I know that plenty of female sailors are rescue swimmers. And yeah, you could do it but..." His mouth opened. Closed. And then he looked away.

"What?"

"I don't want you to!"

He looked at her, his eyes fierce. "It's a dangerous job—"

"You have a dangerous job."

"I'm a SEAL!"

She recoiled. "No, what you mean is that you're a man. And I'm a woman. And women shouldn't have dangerous jobs."

He tightened his lips. Shook his head ever so slightly.

She didn't believe him. And maybe he didn't believe himself either, because he closed his eyes and walked away from her.

Overhead, the stars spilled out, a brilliant cascade across the velvety night. He was right. This was a beautiful place to watch the stars. To hope in dreams and a future.

To find herself in the arms of a man she...okay, yes, cared about.

But not enough to lose herself.

Not enough to become her mother.

Although, maybe she didn't have to give her heart away to find happiness.

He stood there, his wide back to her, his arms folded, and she couldn't stop herself from walking up to him. Putting her hand on his back.

He didn't look at her. Finally, he said into the darkness, "Never mind how I feel about this. What do you want, Red?"

She looked up at him, and her breath caught with the answer. *You. I want you.*

In fact, she wanted the whole darn package. She wanted to be the teammate, the warrior, the protector, and the pretty girl who just wanted a hero. And to be one back, perhaps.

Maybe in the end, she was a romantic dreamer, just like her mother.

I want the happy ending.

She even wanted the sappy wedding.

If she were to face the truth, people like her never got the happy ending.

Prudence said she should probably disentangle herself from his arms, ask him to take her back to the ranch before she did something stupid like fall in love with Ford Marshall.

What *did* she want? Right now, right here? "I want this. Just this, right now."

He glanced at her, closed his eyes. "I'm not that guy, Red." Then he opened his eyes. "But, let's go back before I turn into him."

Oh. Her throat tightened.

She nodded, and as she got on the horse, as she settled her arms around his waist, her body against his, she couldn't help but wish that she might be a different girl.

"What do you mean, you're not going to the CMGs?" Kelsey held a serving plate, wiping it with a towel, and looked at Glo like she'd just suggested she might move to Canada and take up dogsledding. "We have to go—we're up for an award."

"Can't we just…you know, videotape something?" Glo set the punch bowl she'd just cleaned on the granite counter. Overhead lights spilled across the great room of the lodge, now quiet as the guests had left. Knox was flying Reuben and Gilly off to Helena to catch a plane for their honeymoon to Hawaii.

Tate folded up a chair and carried it and two others to a stack in the corner, in the process of arranging the living room back into its normal state.

Ford had left earlier with Scarlett—Glo noticed them

sneaking out of the house. She didn't blame them—she'd wanted to sneak out of the house and clear her head of all the romance in the room. Knox and Kelsey had spent the evening dancing, the man leaning down to whisper into her ear something that turned Kelsey a little pink. And of course Gilly and Reuben—to look at a man like Gilly did and know he wouldn't walk away with your heart…

Yeah, way too much romance because Glo's gaze had more than once fallen on Tate, the way he cleaned up in a suitcoat, jeans, his cowboy boots, and a fresh shave. The man could break hearts in a pair of joggers and a T-shirt, but this attire had him at his best—the aura of tough cowboy emanating off him like a country song.

Too bad it also reminded her of his regular gig—standing in the shadows, watching her throw herself at Sloan. She'd lost her appetite after that image emerged and hung around too long in her brain.

Until Tate had found her, pulled her into his arms on the dance floor, and made her believe all was forgiven.

She never wanted to leave the Marshall Triple M. Not if it meant returning to the mess she'd left in Nashville.

"My mother has a political event in Atlanta that day, and she can't spare the security staff," she said now to Kelsey, ruing the fact she'd opened her big mouth.

"The CMGs have their own security. And we have Tate."

"How much danger is there?" Gerri handed Glo a rinsed china plate. She'd insisted on washing the heirloom china by hand and Glo had offered to help. Please, give her something to do before she did something dangerous and overwhelming and walked out into the starlight with Tate and lost herself forever.

It was probably too late, anyway.

In the back of her mind, she couldn't get past the story of Tate walking into an ambush. Of him hiding under the bodies of his brothers and a twelve-year old boy. Sneaking out at night with a broken body and hiding in the wilderness. The way he'd told his story, too, so detached, his voice almost cold in the retelling…she'd been quietly weeping.

He'd been betrayed by someone he trusted, a child, and it cost him in a way she might never understand. It had made her want to fix it, to soothe away the memory. But he hadn't talked about it further when she'd finally come inside. Just taken her in his arms and kissed her like she might be nourishment.

"I don't know, really," Glo said in answer to Gerri's question. "Enough that Tate didn't want to let anyone else protect me this weekend."

Gerri laughed as she washed another plate. "Oh, honey, that's not why Tate brought you back here."

Kelsey was grinning too.

"What?" Glo asked. She put the dried plate on a stack.

"You're good for him," Gerri said, handing her another plate. "Even he knows that." She turned back to the sink. "When he came home from Afghanistan broken, healing from his wounds, he was so dark. He didn't speak for days sometimes, and then when he got better, he started going out to the shooting range on the edge of the property and he'd spend hours there. And when he wasn't shooting, he was in therapy or working out. As if he could sweat away the demons inside."

Glo looked over at him, across the room. He was stacking folding chairs, his jacket off, his sleeves rolled up past his forearms. Yes, he was a powerful man, and she had seen him fierce and focused. He glanced over at her and smiled, his eyes shining.

Maybe she *was* good for him. Huh.

"Then he started going out to the Bulldog Saloon at night. Not very often, but sometimes I'd find him on the sofa in the den the next day. Once Knox had to pick him up at the local jail for a drunk and disorderly. I think he and Knox had it out, and when Orrin found out—oh, Orrin was angry. Dressed him down like he might be thirteen. Told him that he was a hero and should start acting like it." She handed Kelsey another plate. "Tate left the ranch not long after that.

He'd call me every few weeks and let me know where he was. Bozeman, then Cheyenne, then Vegas. I think he worked as a pool boy in Vegas…" She glanced over at him. "And I'm not sure I want to know what else."

Glo didn't elaborate on the fight, the Bratva, and whatever past Tate had tucked into the dark, secret places. Even she didn't know and wasn't sure she wanted to, either.

"It just about destroyed him when Orrin died. I'm not sure they ever made up, and it breaks my heart."

Tate was shoving one of the big couches in place under the massive stone fireplace.

"And then he showed up with you, Glo. You and the Belles, and for the first time in years, I heard him laugh again. Tate was our rascal, the troublemaker, but he was also my smiler. Refused to let his pain show. He broke his arm when he was six—fell off a horse—and walked around for two days acting like it was fine."

She handed Glo another plate. "Never wants anyone to know he might be afraid or overwhelmed or hurt."

Well, who did? It was easier, safer to pretend. To be okay. Because what if you acknowledged your pain and no one cared?

"But with you, Glo, it's like I can see little glimpses of the boy I knew," Gerri said. "The one who waved to me from the end zone after scoring a touchdown. He's happy again."

Yeah, she understood that. Because loving Tate felt very much like diving into the cool waters of her pool—cool, brisk, enveloping. But it was the letting go to float in the middle, nothing to hold on to that had her struggling in the water.

She could love Tate Marshall. Probably already did. But if she gave him her heart and he walked away, she'd have nothing of herself left.

"Tate made us all feel safe on the road," Kelsey said. "And I'm sure he can keep you safe at the CMGs, Glo."

"It's not that. I know he could. It's just…my mother needs my support—"

"And you need hers!" Kelsey set down her plate on the

stack and draped the towel over her shoulder. "Listen. I understand, believe me. Your mother is a force to be reckoned with, but so are you. You have your own light, and you need to let it shine."

"I do—I am. But running for president is no small thing. She needs all the support she can get."

"No, Glo. She's trying to control you, and you're being sucked into her matrix, again."

Glo frowned at her.

"Your mother is a politician. She knows how to manipulate you."

"She doesn't—"

"You learned that if you wanted your mother's love, you had to show up and smile. You had to serve Joy and if you didn't, then you were forgotten. Rejected."

Wow, she hardly wanted this aired out in front of Gerri. She cut her voice, schooled it. "No—I loved Joy. She was my sister."

"Of course you loved her, but I remember you when you showed up in Minnesota. Angry. Wounded. Bitter. And shoving it all down inside to put on a happy face. Raise your hand if you made the cheerleading squad." She lifted an eyebrow.

Glo didn't bother raising her hand, but yeah. "What did I have to complain about—I was alive."

"And scarred. You still are. You somehow think that you have to earn your mother's love. Or maybe love in general, because our profession surely feeds that lie. But I have news for you. You don't need to do anything to be loved by the right people." She cast her gaze to Tate, who was carrying over an end table to put in place.

"And," Gerri said, "I'm going to add to this conversation I've butted into. Heaven sees you, Glo. You don't need to do anything to get God's attention. You had it before you were born."

Oh. Glo could see why Kelsey liked hanging around here. But the words settled, trying to find root.

Funny, she'd always thought that she was the extra, the

afterthought. That despite her birth defects, Joy was the one whom God loved.

Kelsey shook her head. "I just can't believe that after all we worked for, all you've been through, you're not going."

"Not going where?" Tate came over, carrying a couple dirty glasses. He set them on the counter.

Kelsey turned to him and promptly, without hesitation, threw Glo under the bus. "To the CMG awards. Glo says her mother has a big event and there isn't enough security staff."

He frowned. "I happen to know that Sly was working on the specs before I left."

Glo shot Kelsey a glare and turned to him. "Yes, and they don't work. If I go, she has to cancel an event."

"No." Tate came over to her and pulled a plate from her hand. "You're going. That's the end of it."

"But—"

"Your mother doesn't own you, Glo. Do what you want. And I'll be there. Watching." He fixed his gaze in hers. "And cheering as you win."

She drew in a breath, wanting with everything inside her to pull him close.

But not in front of his mother, who was grinning at them.

Behind them, the front door opened, and Scarlett and Ford walked inside. Scarlett glanced at them and sighed before going into the den, closing the door.

Ford hung up his hat by the door and toed off his cowboy boots, sinking down onto a bench. He leaned his head back against the wall, something of defeat on his face.

Glo looked at Tate, who made a face and headed over to his brother.

"I'll put these dishes away. You two girls head to bed." Gerri picked up the stack of plates.

"I'm finding you a dress," Kelsey said and pulled Glo away. Glo glanced at Tate who'd walked over to Ford, who had closed his eyes, as if in pain.

She knew the look of a broken heart.

Upstairs, Kelsey climbed onto her bed and pulled out her

phone. "I pinned a number of dresses."

Glo sat on the other bed. She loved this room—the two twin beds with the curved leather headboards, the western blankets, the mountain of white pillows, the watercolor pictures of white columbine and purple irises over the beds. It was an oasis in the middle of a rugged landscape.

Yeah, she'd stay forever, given a choice.

But she didn't have a choice.

She closed her eyes.

Kelsey moved over to her bed and landed next to her. "Speak."

Glo opened her eyes. "About—"

"What's going on between you and Tate? The man is crazy about you. And you…you act like this is a bad thing."

"He's…" She drew in a breath. "Confusing. I don't know why he wants me. I'm a complicated package, Kelsey. And yet he makes me feel like I'm easy, simple. Like I don't have to do anything but…"

"Receive?"

"I guess. And that's what is so, well, terrifying."

"Because you can't control his love for you. You can't make him stay any more than you could make David or Joy stay."

Glo drew in a breath.

"You'll just have to trust him." Kelsey smiled. "Knox and his mother read the Bible a lot. And I've been learning some things. Like, did you know there's a verse that says, 'We love because he first loved us'?"

Glo nodded. "Didn't you pay attention at all in church?"

"I was tired. A lot. But…what if that's the key? We love simply because we're loved. God's love comes first, and ours is just a response. We didn't trigger it—He did. And maybe that's what you get with Tate—just love. Not because of anything. Just…love."

"It feels like a terrible gamble."

"Or overwhelming grace."

"You're never leaving the ranch, are you?" Glo asked.

"I am. In three days. With Knox. And I expect you to be there." She held up her phone. "Take a look at my pins. We can have any of these dresses sent to Nashville."

Glo took the phone. Began to scroll through the pictures.

"It's time for you to live your own life, Glo."

She found a teal-green sleeveless dress, short in the front, with a long sheath overlay over the back. "This one."

"That's my Glo."

She could almost hear her father. *There's my Glo-light.*

"Okay. I'll go."

"With Tate as your date?"

She smiled, turned to Kelsey. "He did say he'd be there to keep me safe."

"If that's what you want to call it." Kelsey winked.

Glo laughed. Because she was right. It was time to stop living in fear. To give away her heart.

And to let her light shine.

She got up and grabbed her toothbrush, opened the door, and headed into the hallway.

The hall opened up into a balcony that overlooked the great room. The kitchen was dark, Gerri having gone to bed, but Glo spotted Ford and Tate sitting in the leather chairs.

Ford's voice drifted upstairs. "She's going to get herself killed, and I have to stand on the sidelines and watch. And it'll kill me, bro. I can't believe I let myself get in this far."

She turned, was walking to the bathroom when she heard Tate's voice. "Yeah, I get that, bro. I fell for the wrong girl once and it blew up in my face. I got sucked in to her world, and pretty soon I was in over my head, with no way out."

"I guess I should be glad it died before it really got started because we could have had a real mess." But Ford leaned forward in his chair, his face in his hands like he wasn't glad in the least.

"I hear you. It's like I can't get my footing. I want her— but I'm so afraid of making a mistake too. Of walking into an ambush or doing something stupid. She's amazing, but… yeah, she could be the death of me."

Tate ended with a laugh but Glo froze, the words a hot ball in her stomach.

Yeah, well, she'd see about that.

10

Tate could feel it, the niggle, the itch creeping up his spine that this night could go very, very badly.

He'd even alerted Sly, who stood opposite him up in front of the massive stage, tucked into the discreet shadows of the Bridgestone Arena in Nashville.

In front of him, twenty thousand country music stars, celebrities, and fans filled the arena, the glittering spotlights glaring down into the audience. He could only see the first thirty or so rows, but Glo and her entourage were sitting just ten feet away, and that's what counted. Besides, Sly had worked with the crew of the stadium and not a few other personal security teams.

Still, something stirred in his gut.

Please, he just wanted to get Glo home safely.

Maybe then she'd shake out of the strange arm's length freeze going on between them. It might be his imagination, because sure, they'd stepped out of never-never land and right back into the scrutiny of Senator Jackson and her henchmen, but Glo, too, seemed off.

She'd gone back to calling him by her nicknames. Champ. Rocky. The Rock. And a few strange ones like Bullwinkle, Tiger, and yesterday evening's Bono.

Of course, he'd been trying on the strange glasses Sly had procured for them, something to stop the glare of the spotlights. Orange wraparounds and yeah, maybe he looked a little like Bono.

She'd walked out to the estate's security booth and told the team she was going riding.

He'd volunteered to ride with her, but Rags got up and grabbed the keys to a four-wheeler.

Meanwhile, he and Sly had gone over tonight's plan. Again.

And while he hadn't expected to be her date—he could hardly keep an eye on her while sitting beside her—he wasn't exactly sure why she'd chosen Sloan to sit with her.

Maybe that accounted for the roil in his gut.

Cole Swindell finished playing, and the audience cheered as he ran down the thrust to the main stage. The spotlight flashed to Carrie Underwood, dressed in yet another outfit, and suddenly the worry in his gut ignited.

"And to present the award for New Group of the Year, please welcome Senator Reba Jackson."

"What?" The voice came through Tate's headpiece and he nearly winced at Sly's shout.

Agreed. What the—

Tate glanced over and sure enough, the senator walked down the stairs in the center of the stage and over to the mic. She wore a long white dress, like she might be a virginal offering, her shoulder-length amber red hair down, and raised her hands to calm the applause.

Like mother, like daughter, Glo was breathtaking tonight in a crazy teal dress that was both short and long, with a sort of skirt that overlaid the back of the sleeveless dress, and a pair of glittery gold heels that were so high he'd wanted to reach out for her elbow and steady her.

Of course, she hadn't needed it, Sloan filling in just fine.

And at the moment, the man was smiling, a weird look of satisfaction on his face.

Tate frowned.

Especially since Glo had gone nearly white.

"Hey, ya'll," said the senator, her voice pearly smooth in the mic. "I know this is a surprise. I wasn't actually supposed to be here tonight. I spent the day with the good folks from Atlanta talking about how we're going to make America a safer, better place, right?"

More cheers.

He looked at Kelsey, seated next to Glo. Her mouth was open, her eyes pinned to Reba. And next to her, his outrageously lucky big brother Knox, who'd flown their ranch plane down to Nashville, fit perfectly into the superstar boyfriend persona.

While Tate stood on the sidelines like the hired help.

Which he was.

"And that means I'm not going to stand down and be afraid, even when there are threats against me and my family!"

More cheers, galvanizing the American spirit. People loved a fighter.

"When I got the call from Carrie today asking if I'd present tonight's award for New Group of the Year, I was thrilled. Because we all love to encourage new ideas, new dreams, right?" More applause.

"But more, I understand how things can change in this world, and I want to be the person who can adapt, change with them, and show up when people need me."

Oh, for cryin' out loud. Tate tried not to roll his eyes, kept his face unmoved. But, really?

"Which is why, before we announce tonight's winners, I need to let you in on a little secret." She leaned into the mic, close, and whispered, "Promise not to tell anyone until tomorrow, when we make our announcement?" Laughter from the audience.

And his stomach clenched, a fist inside—

"Okay then. You're the first to know." She took a breath. "In the race for president, I've found the political party that I've long aligned with to be not hard enough on foreign policy, not willing to draw a line in the sand to put America first. So, as of tonight, I'm switching parties. And not only that, I'm doing it with the endorsement of Isaac White, my co-contender, the senator from Montana. I promise, I still believe in a fairer, safer America, but now with a party that also believes in a stronger America!"

More applause, but Tate had to wonder if it wasn't simply because of the emotion in the room more than her announcement. He didn't exactly follow politics, but it seemed that both parties were a mess. It didn't matter which camp you lived in, you did what was right, regardless of your affiliation.

Still, it felt like an odd place to make the announcement… unless he accounted for the audience watching. Country music fans. People who also believed in a stronger America.

Shoot, he believed in a stronger America.

But he also believed in Glo having her moment in the spotlight, and his mouth tightened as Glo offered a wide grin and clapped as if she wasn't completely blindsided.

She had her stage face on.

"Now, for tonight's award!"

The video queued up and announced the nominees. On the jumbotron in the back, Tate caught the Belles' stage photo. Glo wore a painted tattoo down her arm, an all-leather getup, her hair a white halo.

He loved all the versions of her, but for a second, the memory of her in faded boyfriend jeans, a T-shirt, and bare feet sitting on a stool in his mother's kitchen, stealing a cookie, might be his favorite.

"And tonight's award goes to—"

He held his breath.

And then Kelsey was on her feet, launching into Knox's arms, and Dixie and Elijah Blue high-fived. Sloan pulled Glo up to embrace her.

Or at least Tate thought so, until Sloan grabbed Glo's face and popped her a kiss, right there in front of the entire crowd. Phone lights flashed, and Tate fought to keep his face impassionate.

Get your hands off her, Slick.

He'd nearly delivered that exact threat tonight when Sloan showed up at the house, dressed to the nines in a tuxedo and bow tie. He wore a little scruff on his face, like he might be trying too hard.

And of course Glo needed a date tonight. But why she'd picked Slick—

Tate blew out a breath as she and the Belles took the stage, along with Elijah Blue and Carter. The senator gave her a hug, an air-kiss, and stood back, beaming.

Tate kept his eye on the audience, watching. But no one jumped up with a semi-automatic. No rumblings of the floor underneath them suggested a bombing. Just the thunder of his heartbeat as he watched Sloan smirk.

He'd set it up—Tate knew it in his gut. This little stunt to make sure Reba got the limelight. And maybe it wasn't a big deal.

But it burned inside Tate for the rest of the night. Watching Sloan settle his arm over Glo, his proprietary behavior extending to the way he settled his hand on the small of her back as they exited.

Tate stood by just in the wings, as the press took pictures of the Belles, with their entourage and without. Sloan added a few with Glo and her mother. Reba looked like she'd won her own award, for the grin on her face.

They finally extricated themselves, moved out of the building, back down the red carpet still thronged with fans, and into the limousines pulled up at the curb. Carter, Dixie, and Elijah Blue climbed into their limo. Sloan stood at the door and turned to Glo. "Where to first, darlin'? The Sony party? The Big Machine Label Group?"

For the first time, Glo shot a look Tate's direction, her expression stricken. "My feet are tired—"

"Take off your shoes. You'll be fine." Sloan all but pushed her into the limo.

Kelsey glanced at Tate also, as she climbed in. "Don't give up on her now," she said, and he frowned.

Knox clamped him on the shoulder as he followed her in.

Tate climbed into the front, next to Rags. "Did you know about this?"

"The after-parties? No. But whatever the boss wants."

Tate wasn't quite sure who the boss might be tonight.

They ended up at the Sony gig, held in an old church just a few blocks from the arena in downtown. The entourage got out, and Tate followed them into the packed venue. Paper chandeliers hung from the beamed rafters, and at the front of the expansive room, Kenny Chesney got up and took the mic, singing one of his newest hits.

Sloan had hold of Glo's hand and pulled her onto the dance floor. She wore one of her fake smiles but obliged as other celebrities danced around her. Tate spotted Benjamin King, a singer who had filled in a couple months ago when the Belles were recuperating from the traumatic bombing.

Benjamin was with his wife, a tall redhead, and their daughter, Audrey, talking to Brad Paisley. Ben must have seen Tate, because he nodded, catching his eye.

Wow, he so didn't belong here. But as long as Glo was here, so was he.

"We're a far distance from the ranch," said Knox, coming up to him. He handed him a can of Coke. Tate drank it and crumpled the can in his fist.

"She only went out with Sloan because she needed a date."

"I know."

But maybe Sloan didn't, the way he hung onto Glo. For her part, she seemed stiff, and almost annoyed, even as she played the role of belle of the ball.

Glo mingled, talked with Sony executives, took a selfie with Miranda Lambert, and Tate caught her laughing at something Brad Paisley said. Carter, their manager, was glad-handing and introducing them to producers.

The entire thing had Tate edgy and raw. He just wanted to get her home and…and congratulate her.

Break a couple rules, maybe.

But only after he knew she was safe. Because sure, there hadn't been a hint of a threat recently, but it didn't mean some other crazy wouldn't try something, especially after the senator's announcement tonight.

Okay, he was probably reaching. Giving himself a reason to stay in her life. Because he'd given the picture of the man he'd seen in the background of the last fundraising event to Sly. He'd checked it out but found nothing and dismissed him as a bystander. Probably he was right.

Probably.

They left the party after two hours. Dixie and Elijah Blue grabbed an Uber for their hotel, and the rest headed over to the Musicians Hall of Fame to Universal's gig. Tate spotted Luke Bryan, a guy whose music he actually listened to, onstage as Glo worked her way behind Carter through the crowd.

Sloan had folded his hand into hers like they belonged together.

He saw Glo ease hers away. But not before Sloan put his hands on her shoulders and leaned in for a photo.

Tate stuck his hands in his pockets.

"Kelsey and I are bugging out," Knox said after Carter had introduced them to a slew of executives. "We'll grab an Uber to our hotel."

Tate checked his watch—it was well after 2:00 a.m.

Glo must be exhausted.

Time to wind up this pony show.

He wove through the crowd, still going strong, and found Sloan standing with his arm around Glo's shoulders. "Sir," he said, keeping his voice even.

Sloan turned and frowned.

"I think we should be going."

"I think you need to step back, Security."

Glo was talking with one of the artists from Little Big Town. She glanced at Tate as if hearing the conversation, and something of gratitude streaked through her eyes.

And that was just *it*.

"I don't think so," he said and reached past Sloan. "C'mon, Glo. You're exhausted. Let's go." His hand closed around her arm.

Sloan pushed him back. "Get your hands off her!"

Whoa—*what?* Tate stepped back, held his hands up,

frowning.

Glo stared at Tate, a little horror on her face.

"Sorry," Sloan said to the group. "We've had trouble with this one. Gets a little handsy with Glo sometimes."

Handsy? Oh, he was going to dismantle the guy.

"Stop." Glo turned and pressed her hand to Sloan's chest. "Tate's right. I'm tired. Let's go."

Tate's jaw clenched, and Sloan's eyes narrowed, but Sloan turned to Glo and nodded. "Of course, honey," he said.

Honey?

Tate drew in a breath and followed them outside, through the crowd.

The downtown lights lit up the night, the air warm and woven with the smells of late spring. He opened the limo door for Glo and Sloan, but as soon as Glo got in, Sloan shut the door and turned to Tate.

"We're going back to my place, and you're not invited." He pressed three fingers into Tate's chest. "So, get lost."

"No, actually, you're not. Glo is my responsibility tonight, and she's going home."

Sloan shook his head. "I don't know who you think you are, hotshot. And yes, I know all about your little weekender in Montana, but Glo is back in her real life now, and here I'm in charge."

"I'm sorry, but unless you're flashing a badge, Glo is free to do what she wants." He clamped his hand on Sloan's shoulder.

Sloan gave him a push as he opened the door.

Glo was already on her way out. "What's going on?"

Sloan turned to her. "I told you this guy was trouble, Gloria. Do you have any idea who he used to work for?"

She frowned at Sloan, then Tate.

Tate's mouth opened, belly punched. "What are you talking about?"

But Sloan wasn't looking at him. "The Bratva. The Russian mafia. And you know what he did—?"

"Shut up," Tate said quietly. "Just—shut up."

"He was an enforcer."

Tate turned to Glo. "I worked security."

"He broke knees for a living."

Tate turned back to Sloan. "You don't know anything."

"I know *everything*, tough guy. I know about Slava and Yuri Malovich, and I know about the girl. What was her name? Oh, *Raquel.*"

Tate's mouth tightened, but the name hit him like a center punch. "Don't."

"He murdered a woman. The woman he was living with—"

"No, I didn't—" But no, he couldn't have this fight here, on the sidewalk. He turned to Glo. "Glo, I would never—"

She was nodding, so much trust in her eyes. "I know—I—"

And he couldn't take it one more second. Couldn't take Sloan's hands on her, his breath in her ear, the idea that he'd put his mouth on hers.

"I love you, Glo." And that's when the screaming started in the back of his head. The words *No* and *Stop* and *This is a bad idea.*

But he ignored them all, pressed on by the memory of Sloan kissing her as she stood to receive her award.

He curled his hand around her neck and kissed her. Something primal and possessive and no, it wasn't at all the right thing to do, but she was his, and, and—

He *loved* her. That thought took root and spread through him. She made him feel like he wasn't impulsive and dangerous, and he wasn't letting her go home with Slick, no matter what it cost him.

She'd frozen, and that was his first clue that maybe—

Aw...

Because this wasn't about Glo, but the fact that...that she belonged to him.

Your mother doesn't own you, Glo. His own words stung him just about the time Sloan grabbed him by his collar and yanked him back.

"Have you lost your mind?"

Maybe. *I'm so afraid of making a mistake, too…doing something stupid.*

Sloan's fist slammed into his face.

The pain exploded into his skull, and he stepped back, drew a breath, shaking off the gray that splotched his vision.

Oh, he was going to—

"That's enough." Rags's voice cut through the fog. He probably saved Tate from an assault charge because the man stepped between him and Sloan, turned to Tate, his hands on his shoulders. "Step back, man. *Back!*"

Out of the corner of his eye, Tate spotted the crowd gathering. And a few cell phones out.

Nice.

"He doesn't get in this car," Sloan snarled. "Leave him on the street."

"No," Glo said, and Tate looked at her. She pressed her hand to her lips, as if reeling from the kiss.

Yeah, him too, but for an entirely different reason.

"No. I'm going home, Sloan."

"Glo—" Sloan started.

She gave him a look, her mouth tight. "I'm tired. And this has been…" She swallowed, something raw and almost broken on her face. "A big night."

"Then I'll go with you," Sloan said.

Hardly. Rags's hand tightened on Tate's shoulder and he pushed Tate back.

"No. Thank you, but I think I need to be alone."

Sloan glanced at Tate, but Glo interjected, "Really. Alone."

As if from *him* too. Tate stared at her, but she shook her head, tears in her eyes.

Oh no, what had he done?

Clearly, he'd just made a bigger mess of things. Tate drew in a breath, nodded. Allowed Rags to push him away, into the front seat.

In a moment, Glo climbed into the back.

He wanted to weep when she raised the partition. *Glo—?*

Then she turned on the radio, and he listened to country

songs break his heart all the way home.

Glo dreamed of it all night long.

Tate, turning to her, so much earnestness in his eyes. Wrapping his big hand around her neck.

I love you, Glo.

His kiss, not gentle in the least, but as if he'd been holding it in all night, waiting, angry, desperate—

She could hardly blame him. She'd wanted to do the same thing. Watching him watch her had sent a tiny fire through her, and the agony in his eyes as he watched Sloan put his hands on her tore her asunder.

She'd cast him a look right after Sloan kissed her and felt a little sick at his drawn expression. She hadn't seen the kiss coming—if she had, she would have dodged it. But there she was, in front of millions, trapped.

She could hardly push Sloan away in front of the entire world.

And especially not with her mother looking on. Her mother, who'd suggested she take Sloan for appearances. At the time it seemed smart.

Especially with Tate's words ringing in her ears. *I'm so afraid of making a mistake too. Of walking into an ambush.*

Never mind his fears that she'd *be the death of him.*

So maybe yes, she'd harbored a little hurt when she asked Sloan to accompany her, but Tate did have to work. And she'd only wanted to keep him out of the limelight so he could do his job—not torture him again.

She never thought that would entail Tate following her from one after-party to the next, watching Sloan hold her hand. Put his arm around her and…well, when he closed the door on Tate after their last event, she knew he was up to something.

She never expected a showdown. For Tate to turn to her, his voice almost desperate and definitely impulsive. *I love you,*

Glo.

Admittedly, it shook her, right down to her core.

This man.

Loved her.

But as soon as Tate touched her, she felt like she had entered a little knock-down-drag-out and she'd been shoved between the two men.

A little like she'd been caught between her parents once upon a time.

She hadn't wanted to make a scene. And in the back of her mind, she saw a GIF of the kiss going viral across the Twittersphere.

So, she'd frozen.

But she felt Tate's shock when she didn't respond. By the time she caught up, he'd let her go.

No, Sloan had *yanked* him away.

And that's when his words registered. *I told you this guy was trouble, Gloria. Do you have any idea who he used to work for?*

Oh, she'd felt like a fool in that moment. Because all the lies she'd told herself about Tate simply shattered, as if she'd been punched.

He broke knees for a living.

And as Tate looked at Sloan—right before Rags dragged him away—she believed it.

It scared her a little. Because she had no doubt that if he wanted to, he could break every bone in Sloan's body. He'd been a Ranger, after all.

Maybe she didn't know Tate as well as she thought she did.

Or maybe she knew him just well enough to know that this wouldn't be the last time he'd be in danger.

Or put her in danger, maybe.

She'd spent far too long staring at the ceiling, thinking about his fight with Slava.

But, *I love you, Glo.*

Yeah, those words, his voice, seared through her, finding her bones.

She rolled over and hit her pillow, painfully aware that the sun had crested in through the blinds of the guestroom.

Daylight meant she'd have to…well, say something to Tate. The poor man had left his heart out on the street last night. It was all she could do to not launch into his arms. But that would certainly look unseemly after she'd kissed Sloan. She was enough of a politician to figure that out.

She didn't want to look to see if he'd spent the night on a lounge chair. Probably. Maybe.

The last she'd seen of him, he'd been carrying her up the stairs, Rags holding her shoes after she'd fallen asleep in the car. And she'd simply let herself sink into his warm chest.

Maybe she shouldn't have had so much champagne, either. But people had been glad-handing her all night, and Sloan kept plying her with champagne, and what could she do, say, No, I'm not going to toast with you?

And now her head hurt thinking about it. She pushed herself up and went in search of aspirin in the adjoining bathroom. She was working the child-slash-adult-proof top off when she heard the voice echo from the living room downstairs.

"Oh…my…*Gloria!*"

She stilled. Looked at herself in the mirror. Yeah, that was pretty. She hadn't taken off her makeup, and her hair resembled something out of the sixties, teased and definitely annoyed.

"Are you kidding me?"

She was wearing a T-shirt—she did remember pulling that on last night before falling into bed—and now pulled on a pair of pajama bottoms and grabbed a bathrobe.

"Gloria!" The voice turned shrill, and Glo yanked open her bedroom door.

"Calm down, Mother. I'm coming."

She strode down the hallway and down the stairs and only then did she see Sly walking in the back door, followed by Tate, whose hair was just long enough to resemble her own. He wore a black T-shirt, jeans, and was barefoot.

Clearly, yanked out of bed .

"He's here, ma'am."

Glo's attention went to her mother, who sat on the white sofa and set her iPad on the glass coffee table. "Please tell me that isn't a picture of you...two...*kissing*."

She looked at Glo, then at Tate. Back to Glo. Who hazarded a glance at the iPad.

Oh, that was a lip lock all right. Tate's hand around her neck, pulling her in tight. Hers inside his jacket.

"Yes," Tate said quietly.

Her mother drew in a breath and slowly rose from the sofa. Picked up the iPad. "And this one?"

She flashed to a shot of Rags holding Tate back, a darkness in his eyes that could still send a shiver through Glo.

"That would be me after Sloan hit me."

"I'd say you deserved it."

"Mother—"

Reba looked at Glo, raised an eyebrow, then back to Tate. "Have you no consideration at all for Gloria's reputation? What this looks like?"

"It looks like Glo kissing the right man, finally." Tate's eyes sparked.

Sly put a hand on Tate's shoulder.

"I know this may be hard for you to understand, Mr. Marshall, but Gloria is part of a bigger future than you are. She is on the way to the White House, in some capacity. If I should win this election, she'll be called on to lead organizations, lend her name to social projects."

She would? Glo stared at her mother. "Mother, I'm not a politician."

But her mother seemed not to notice her. "And perhaps Sloan was a little hasty in declaring his feelings for her, but you, Mr. Marshall, made me a promise. As did I."

Tate's mouth tightened. "Listen. I—"

"Can't seem to control yourself. You're impulsive and heedless, and you get people hurt." She tightened her jaw. "*Killed.* Don't you?"

He stared at her, stricken, and suddenly Glo didn't know who to panic for—Tate or herself.

He shook his head.

"Like your entire squad?"

He drew in a breath, as if she'd stabbed him.

"Mother!"

Her mother held up her hand.

"And there's the matter of a woman named Raquel Morris? Found dead in your apartment in Vegas?"

Tate's mouth tightened. "You don't know the whole story."

And she heard Sloan's voice from last night. *He murdered a woman. The woman he was living with—*

He turned to Glo. "I didn't...I mean...she was—"

"Collateral damage. From your violent lifestyle." Her mother looked beyond him and motioned Rags into the room. He was carrying Tate's duffel bag and a briefcase. He set them on the floor beside Tate, who glanced at them.

"I don't want my daughter to be more collateral damage." She walked over to Glo. "How's that eye healing, honey?"

"Mother, that was an accident."

She looked at Tate, the bags on the floor, and a hand tightened around her throat. "No—"

But Tate had shrugged away from Sly and taken a step toward them. "You know, I've been thinking a lot about how the Bratva found me that night, and it occurred to me that your boy Sloan sure knows a lot about my life. And according to my sister, RJ, he knows a few Russians. The kind with connections. I'm wondering just how Slava got Glo's room number."

Her mother looked at him, her face unmoving. "You're just an easy man to find, I guess, with all the destruction you leave behind." She put her arm around Glo. "All the broken hearts. Did you love Raquel too?"

Tate blinked. Swallowed. Nodded.

And Glo wasn't sure why that felt like a fist in her chest. She wasn't unaware that Tate had a life before her. But...

But he never talked about anyone else.

Or rather, he had, if she'd been paying attention. *I fell for the wrong girl once and it blew up in my face. I got sucked in to her world, and pretty soon I was in over my head, with no way out.*

Tate's voice got very quiet. "Oh, you are good, Senator. Very good. I can't believe how well you played this. Bringing me in, acting like you're giving me a chance when all the while you were trying to make me lose it. Making me follow Sloan and Glo around, knowing it would drive me crazy, hoping I—"

"Did exactly what I know men like you do? Get yourself into trouble? Gloria is a smart girl, but she has a hard time seeing the truth. She has a type—men who are beneath her. Who will eventually leave her and break her heart. She needs someone—"

"Like Sloan?"

Reba lifted her shoulder. "Someone steady. Someone who can see her potential."

"She won a freakin' industry award last night. I think the entire world can see her potential."

Glo didn't know whose words to lean in to. "I'm standing right here, for Pete's sake. I'm not a child—"

Except, no one seemed to be listening. Tate held up his hand, clearly schooling his voice. "Listen—"

"No, you listen!" Her mother rounded on him. "You forget yourself, and what you're here for. It's not to destroy Gloria's life—it's to protect it—"

"From what? The lies you told me about the Bryant League?"

She blinked at him. As did Glo. "What lies?"

Tate's eyes sparked. "I did my research, Senator. The Bryant League was never after you. They haven't even been active for over a year. Nothing. They weren't responsible for the bombing—frankly, I'm not sure it wasn't all just a convenient story to get Glo to come home and get sucked back in to your world."

"How. Dare. You!"

"I'm not usually this stupid, but apparently, I panicked. Well not anymore—I quit."

Wait. Glo's breath rushed out. What—? *Wait!* "Tate, no—"

"Save your breath, lover boy. You're fired."

"No. Wait—Mother." Glo turned to her mother, her throat closing. "Tate—"

"He's trouble, Gloria. Certainly, you can see that."

She looked at Tate, shook her head. "Don't go. Don't quit. Stay—"

But his eyes had darkened. "No, Glo. This won't work. I can't stand on the sidelines watching you with another guy—"

"I don't want another guy, Tate—I want you—"

"Please, Gloria. Don't embarrass yourself."

"Come with me." Tate took a step toward her. "We'll go back to the ranch—you can write, the Belles can get back together."

"I am in the toughest political race of my entire career, and if you hadn't noticed, last night I switched parties. I need my daughter here, by my side." Glo's mother slid her hand into Glo's.

Tate's gaze never moved from hers. "Your mother is manipulating you, Glo."

"Don't be absurd. If anyone is manipulating you, it's this man. This is not your life, Gloria. You have a future. Don't let him throw it away."

If you love me, you'll stay. The words rebounded in her head, and for a second, she was weeping into David's chest. Then, to her horror, the words emerged in a choked whisper. "If you love me, you'll stay."

His breath caught. "Really? C'mon, Glo." His eyes were hard in hers. "This can't be what you want. Where did the woman who used to paint on a tattoo and wear leather onstage go? I miss that girl. Now…you've vanished. You're all things to all people. But who are you? And what do you want? Me? Your mother?"

Her mouth opened.

"See? I told you—he only cares about himself. Which is why he's going to get you into trouble," her mother snapped. "Get out of my house."

A muscle flexed in his jaw. He narrowed his eyes and walked over to his duffel and picked it up, threw it over his shoulder.

Looked at Glo.

"Please, come with me, Glo."

Her lungs stopped working. Yes—yes—

"I meant what I said last night. I love you. I have for months, and I...I'd give my life for you." His eyes were broken, reddened. "Please." He held out his hand.

Her mother's hand remained locked in hers. "I need you Glo. More than ever." And, to her horror, her mother's voice broke. "Please stay. Help me change the world."

She looked at her mother.

"Tate is impulsive," her mother said. "Sure, he's brave, but the kind of bravery is going to get him killed. It almost did, in Vegas. He'll die, just like David. And then where will you be, Glo?"

She drew in a breath. Looked at Tate, her eyes blurry. "Tate, I..."

Tate's jaw tightened, and he dropped his hand. "Wow," he said quietly. "Did I read that wrong." Then he picked up his briefcase and headed barefoot out the front door.

Don't go! She wanted to scream it, but the words clogged inside her. *If you love me, you'll stay.*

Sly closed the door behind Tate.

Her mother pulled her into a hug. "It'll be okay, sweetheart." She leaned back and met Glo's eyes. "Let's have some breakfast. Then you need to pull yourself together. We have work to do."

11

Ford leaned against the kitchen counter, the morning sun streaming into his tiny base housing apartment. He might have more room in a Zodiac. "I'm telling you, RJ, the drive back to San Diego was the worst eighteen hours of my life."

And after BUD/S Hell Week and SERE—Survival, Evasion, Resistance and Escape—training, that was saying something. But at least during training, once he pushed past the physical agony, it became a head game of survival.

He didn't know what sort of head game tactics, what sort of strategy to use to repair the gigantic blowhole between him and Scarlett.

Ford had his phone propped up on his counter as he boiled a half dozen eggs. He'd eat them after his run, and in the meantime, he'd taken the FaceTime call from his sister. And filled her in on the details of the wedding.

He may have mentioned Scarlett. And omitted the kiss but added in the cold front that had blown in between them after he'd...well, he wasn't sure what he did. Been a gentleman?

Or maybe it was because of his not-so-subtle opinion of her crazy rescue swimmer idea.

"Eighteen hours of small talk about football teams and fast food and the occasional bad drivers." No, eighteen hours of thinking about her in his arms, the way she'd said *Kiss me, Navy.*

The taste of her still on his lips.

I want this. Just this, right now.

Yeah, well, he was a red-blooded male, and he'd wanted to say yes with everything inside him. But he'd made himself promises about the man he wanted to be a long time ago.

Besides, he definitely wanted more than right now with Scarlett, and all he saw ahead of them were tangles.

"I'm sure she's not blind, Ford. It's not like you are Mister Socially Progressive."

"What's that supposed to mean?"

His sister was sitting in what looked like an old-world tavern, her earbuds attached to the phone, probably to muffle the ambient noise. But he could definitely hear another language—it sounded Slavic in tone. Maybe she was at a trendy DC bar. She wore her dark hair up, little makeup, and spoke with the phone close to her face.

"It means that you're a typical male. You don't believe women should have dangerous jobs."

"What are you talking about? You were right there beside us, herding cattle on horseback, learning how to rope and wrestle steer to the ground for branding. I never cared if you got hurt."

"Thanks for that. But I also beg to differ." She raised an eyebrow.

Oh. She was talking about *that.* He drew in a breath. "That was different."

"That was you protecting me. Not wanting me to get hurt."

"We were in a cave, and I hadn't a clue how to get out," he said.

"I got us into the mess—"

He held up his hand. "Stop. Please, let's not go back to the worst day of my life. Can we please just acknowledge that she's going to be jumping into the middle of the ocean to rescue a drowning sailor who probably wants to use her as a buoy? RJ, people die in *training.*"

"I know. Believe me, we looked at the stats when you

went to BUD/S. Prayed you through it. I woke up with the nightmare of you drowning more times than I can count."

He made a face. "Sorry."

"Yeah, well, between you and Tate, I'm surprised that Ma is still talking to us."

"Let's not forget Reuben and his smokejumping. He started it all."

Someone brought her a drink. She thanked him, and he thought he heard Russian. Interesting. She took a sip of what looked like tea in a glass. "Listen, I need to go, but I can't get a hold of Tate. I called him, but my number is...unfamiliar, and he might have thought it was a telemarketer. I didn't want to leave a message, and I'm not sure when I'll be able to call again, so could you pass on some information to him?"

He didn't know where to start with his questions, so he nodded.

"He sent me a picture of a guy he saw in a crowd, someone he thinks is connected to the Bryant League, a domestic terrorist group who he thinks is targeting Senator Reba Jackson."

"He told me about the bombing," Ford said.

"I ran facial recognition software on the picture, and it pulled up a hit. He's ex-Marine, scout sniper. Graham Plunkett. We missed his association with the Bryant League—his brother is a member, but that took some digging because Graham has a different last name than his brother, Alan Kobie. Different fathers. Alan is the son of the mayor of San Antonio. But here's the interesting part. Kobie was an EOD Tech for his first deployment before he got an other-than-honorable discharge. I don't know why no one picked that up before, but I'd pay attention."

Explosive Ordinance Disposal. Yeah, hello. Red flag, anyone? "So, what are you saying?"

"Just that maybe, even if the Bryant League isn't behind this, these two guys might be still in play."

"I'll pass it along. Tate and Glo went to some big award show last night, so my guess is that he's sitting by the pool somewhere, nursing a late-night headache."

She laughed. "Probably."

"But I can promise you, he's not going to let anything happen to Glo. Not the way he behaved with her at the wedding."

"Really?"

"Let's just say, Tate finally found his girl."

"I like that Glo. She's a tough—and beautiful—cookie."

He might say the same about Scarlett.

"Okay, well maybe it's not a big deal then, just pass it along when you can." She looked away from the camera again, and this time a frown crossed her face.

"Where are you?"

She glanced back at the screen and seemed to consider his words. Then she set her phone down faceup, her fingers blocking the view, but for a second, he saw the surroundings. A pub with arched ceilings and a mural on the wall.

Then a face. Partially obscured by a newspaper that held a cone of fries, but dark hair, cut short, and dark eyes. He wore a short-sleeved shirt, and the shot revealed a tattoo that wound up his arm.

Ford only got a glimpse, but it looked like a bone frog.

Just like that, she cut the connection.

Huh.

He turned off the heat under his eggs, dumped them into a bowl of ice water.

Sat on the counter stool of his apartment and dialed Tate. No answer. It went to voicemail. He didn't leave a message.

You're a typical male. You don't believe women should have dangerous jobs.

Okay, maybe. Ford had awoken in a sweat the night after Scarlett had told him her plans, hearing old screams echo through his brain, and found himself downstairs in the darkness, searching for a glass of water and something for his pitching stomach.

He didn't know why, but he'd gone into the family office attached to the kitchen. His father's pictures still hung on the wall, especially the crazy family Christmas picture, taken so many years ago. He'd been eleven or twelve and of course sat next to Ruby Jane in front of the stone fireplace. Ma had made them all wear ugly Christmas sweaters—save Wyatt who got out of it by never taking off his favorite hockey jersey. Providential that he went on to play for the team he loved—the Minnesota Blue Ox.

Tate, of course, was grinning, holding a couple of rabbit ears over Knox's head.

Knox stared into the camera, way too serious. The do-gooder. He looked just like their dad, with the full head of hair. Except Dad sported a Tom Selleck mustache and black hair.

Knox had his wisdom and his voice too. Standing there in the office, with the wide wooden desk, the leather chair, the bookcases stacked with Louis L'Amour novels and old Bible commentaries, Ford could practically hear the old man.

Ford, climb out from under that desk! There's work to do!

He grinned against the memory. And the six-year-old who'd emerged, a couple of plastic six-guns attached to his legs.

Hiding from the bad guys?

No. From Tate and Wyatt. They're going to throw me in the river.

He could nearly hear his dad's laughter.

Courage isn't about hiding. It's about who you put your faith in. C'mon.

He couldn't remember the rest, but it probably ended with his father finding Tate and Wyatt and making all of them mow hay or clean the barn or even ride fence.

His answer to keeping his boys out of trouble: ranch work.

Probably why Ford left for the military immediately after high school, pushed himself into the SEALs. Hard work saved the day.

Saved him from himself.

Although he'd been ready to hide again when he'd gotten back to the house with Scarlett. Anything from knocking on the door to the den and taking her up on the offer he'd seen in her eyes.

He'd finished his water, put the glass in the dishwasher, and headed upstairs.

Slept a few scant hours, rose, and hit the road for a run. By the time he got back, Tate and Glo had left for Nashville.

And Scarlett had packed her duffel for the long, agonizing ride home. When he'd left her off at her house, he'd wanted to offer to help her with her tire, but she'd grabbed her duffel and waved him goodbye and yep, that was it.

He'd driven home, flopped into bed, and tried not to debrief for the next six hours what, exactly, had happened.

Now, five days later, he was still trying to work out the stiff muscles around his ego, not to mention his body.

He left the eggs to cool, changed into his running gear—a pair of compression shorts, running shorts, and a loose T-shirt—and stretched out his muscles in a run along the boardwalk of Coronado Beach. The sand rakes were out, gathering up the seaweed and other debris that collected with the tide, and a man ran with his dog down by the foamy surf. Tent and beach chair vendors dragged their offerings out of their shacks, and the ocean ran deep blue over the creamy sand. A few bicyclists passed him, and out in the water, early morning swimmers fought the gentle chop.

Eight miles, according to his Fitbit. His body was soaked, so he veered into the sand and ran straight for the surf. Toed off his shoes and pulled off shirt and dropped them on the beach before he splashed out into the waves.

Cool, refreshing, and maybe this was exactly what he needed to get Scarlett out of his system. What happens in Montana stays in Montana—wasn't that what Tate said?

Ford dove in and swam under the waves, straight out into the deep—long strokes before surfacing and gulping in the fresh air.

He bobbed there, free in the ocean, kicking slightly to keep himself from slipping under. Although, that was okay too. Just under the waves, floating, almost like flying.

He'd learned how to float in BUD/S. How having his head under the water and kicking up for a breath conserved energy.

He let himself go, the waves pulling him, nothing of a current in the depths.

"Hey!"

He heard the voice as he surfaced for air.

"Hey, are you okay?"

He turned, shaking the water from his eyes, and spied someone swimming toward him. She wore a swim cap, as if she might be out exercising, and it took him just a second for his brain to clear and settle on recognition.

Scarlett?

She was freestyling toward him, power in her strokes, and as she drew closer, she pulled up, clearly surprised to see him. "Ford."

"Hey, Red. What are you doing here?"

She was close enough for him to see she wore a one-piece athletic suit, and hello, of course she was out training. Didn't she have a PRT this week sometime?

The elite physical entrance exam to be a rescue swimmer.

"I'm just finishing up my mile swim."

Right. The waves had brought him in close enough to touch bottom, and now his feet settled on the sand. "I was on my run."

"You looked like you might be having a cramp or something."

He stared at her, then laughed. "Right. It's a treading water technique—you'll probably learn it." And with those words, it occurred to him... "How is your PRT training going?"

The sun had found her nose, left a little red there, and the water clung to her long lashes. Small yet powerful in the water, and he tried to wrap his brain around her staying above water in the high seas.

He should head back to shore before he did something crazy like grab her and beg her not to do this.

"Actually...I need practice in the buddy tow." She looked

away as she said it as if there might be other potential drowning victims.

The buddy tow. Yeah, that was a washout evolution in BUD/S during which people could be DORed, or rolled back to start training again, if they didn't execute it correctly.

Right.

"Okay, listen. Remember—when you're in the middle of the ocean and someone is panicking, you're their only life support. So they're going to attack you." He met her eyes for a moment, meaning in them. "You gotta be able to break free. It's called the Head Escape Method." He approached her and grabbed her hands, kicking her out deeper. "Now, push me underwater."

She frowned.

"If you don't do it, I will."

She grabbed his shoulders, pushing him under the surface. He slipped out from under her clinch, grabbed her hips, and turned her. Then he grabbed the back of her swimsuit, pulling her up to the surface to tow her.

When he let her go, she was breathing hard, but smiling. "I wanna try that."

"Okay, just once. When I grab you, I want you to tuck your head, put your hands under my elbows and push me up and away. Then grab my hips and turn me around. Don't be afraid to put some oomph into it. You're there to save me, not be polite."

He sank in the water and she dove for him. He grabbed her shoulders, but she ducked her head, shoved her hands into his elbows, dislodged his hold, and turned him around, pulling him against her as she kicked to the surface.

Oh, she was a fast learner.

And sure, he'd probably been easy on her, but a taste of triumph wouldn't hurt her.

"Good job," he said as she let him go.

"Let's go again."

"No. Right now, I just want you to practice the cross-chest carry. The trick here is to keep my head above water.

As the victim, I must be able to continue a normal breathing cycle. Remember, whatever you do, don't let me get a grip on you to pull you under."

He lay on his back, and she swam up next to him, her body against his, and tucked her arm over his shoulder, grabbing under his arm.

He was Andre the Giant in her arm as she began to swim, pulling him along. How he wanted to help her, to keep his hips up, to add a kick to her efforts. "Try and keep me planed in the water. It'll be a lot less work."

She swam parallel to the shore, the waves splashing over his face as she skip-breathed, taking every other breath.

"Try a scissor kick."

"Try and pretend you're dead."

"If I'm dead, it's not a rescue."

He hoped she was smiling. But she was getting it, his face not bobbing as much into the water, her arm fixed across his body. She towed him a hundred yards down the shoreline, maybe more before she let him go.

He sculled the water, watching her catch her breath. But she was grinning at him. "Thanks, Marsh."

Teammates. Right. Maybe he should remind his heart, not to mention the rest of his body, because everything inside him wanted to offer to buddy tow *her*, maybe right back into his arms. *I'm not that guy, Red.*

He still wasn't. "When's your test?"

"A week from this Saturday, in the morning."

He nodded. "You got this. They'll hone your technique when you get into training." He tried not to let the words tighten a noose around his chest. "I gotta get back to…uh…"

She splashed him. "Right. Thanks for your help."

He wanted to ask her what she might be doing for dinner, or even how her mother was, but that would bring up everything they'd left behind in Montana. Where it should stay.

Except, he just couldn't stop himself. "I'll help you—we can meet in the mornings, and I'll let you rescue me."

So much surprise and hope filled her eyes he felt like a

jerk for not believing in her.

"Thanks, Ford."

He didn't trust himself not to offer something else, like a ride home, dinner, his heart, so he splashed her back, winked, and swam to shore.

He picked up his shoes and shirt and walked over to a shower, cleaning off before he pulled his shoes on. Rinsed out his shirt and pulled that on too.

His gaze found her then, swimming freestyle in the ocean. And for the first time, he really wanted her to make it.

———————◆———————

Tate sat in the hotel sauna, silent, letting his thoughts stew.

A smart guy would know when to surrender. To slink out of town, the broken pieces of his stupid, impulsive heart in his hands, and not look back. Tate should hop on a plane and head down to San Antonio, where he'd left his truck after the impulsive decision to take on the gig as the Yankee Belles' security.

That guy might have a chance of gluing his life, not to mention his sanity, back together instead of spending the past week ignoring the niggle in his gut that this wasn't over.

Not him and Glo.

Not even the threats against Glo.

But apparently, Tate wasn't smart, because all the evidence suggested otherwise. Here he was, hanging around in a town where everywhere he looked, Senator Reba Jackson's face on billboards and yards signs reminded him of his mistakes.

It didn't help that Glo had turned into the darling of CNN, appearing in the news almost constantly this week as she hit the campaign trail with her "bold and innovative" mother.

Reba's changing of political parties was being heralded as the move to "unite all women." Apparently with her moderate stance, she still appealed to her base and had gathered in the women of her new party.

Glo and Slick were definitely a team because Tate wasn't unaware of his presence in the camera shots standing next to her, his hand always on her back. Or her shoulder.

Holding her hand in raised victory.

Like he belonged there.

As for security, Tate occasionally caught glimpses of Sly or Rags or even Swamp as they hustled Reba and her entourage into a nearby transport. However, since his outing of Reba's lies, apparently everyone was breathing a sigh of relief.

Clearly, they were bypassing the lies part. But she was a politician—no doubt she'd slithered her way out of any culpability.

The sauna door opened, letting cool air from the hotel locker room in to the steam room. The newcomer sat on the lower bench and picked up a scoop of water. "Do you mind?"

Tate didn't say anything, and the man poured the water over the hot rocks of the sauna stove. Steam rose, and the sweat on Tate's skin boiled. He hung his head. His knee was starting to loosen up, along with the stiffness of his muscles after his run today. And last night, he'd gone to a local gym and warmed up a heavy bag, putting everything of the past three frustrating months into his punches.

A little of it was directed at the nightmares that left him knotted in his sheets at night. Jammas and sometimes Raquel and even the bombing in San Antonio. Never mind the daymares that he saw every day on the news.

He was sort of a glutton for punishment, maybe, because he even had a news alert on his phone with Glo's name.

Yeah, he should get on the road. He wasn't sure what he might be waiting for. Glo to run after him, tell him that she was wrong? That she loved him?

The worst part was—he got it. He wouldn't choose him either. Not with her bright, shiny future ahead of her.

More than a few of his punches had Slick's face on them.

Tate breathed out again, aware that his heart rate was rising, probably faster than it should.

Or maybe that was just him, reliving the moment when he decided to make Glo choose. *You're all things to all people. But who are you? And what do you want? Me? Your mother?*

Yeah, that had been a brilliant moment of following his gut right into heartache.

He closed his eyes against the image of her shaking her head, her meaning rising to fill his chest with darkness.

No, I won't go with you.

I won't trust you.

If you love me, you'll stay.

He shook his head. He did love her. And if he hadn't let his pride get in the way, he might have been able to convince Reba to let him stay.

Maybe.

Probably not.

They were all right. He was impulsive, and probably it wouldn't be long before he…well, before he got her hurt. Somehow.

He ran his hands through his sopping hair, ready to leave, when the door opened again. He looked up and drew in a breath at the man who met his eyes and settled in beside him.

Rags waited until the other man left before he spoke. "Sly said you were here."

Rags wore a towel tucked at his waist, and for the first time, Tate noticed a scar on the man's upper body, near his shoulder. Rags might have seen his gaze slip over it because he pointed to it. "IED. Shrapnel. Kunar Province."

Tate pointed to the scars on his knee. "Paktia. Ambush."

"Can't be worse than what went down at the Jackson place."

Tate lifted a shoulder.

"For the record, I was rooting for you."

He glanced at Rags. "Who are you—Friar John?"

Rags frowned.

"He's the messenger sent to tell Romeo that Juliet is faking her death to be with him…never mind."

"Wow, you got it bad. If you're thinking of sucking down

244

poison."

"I'm fine."

"And so is Glo, by the way."

"Thanks. That's just what I want to hear."

"I just mean that she's still alive. No danger. I'm not sure she's...well, she seems to have thrown herself into her mother's campaign."

"I can see that. She's all over the place."

"We've been in three states in the past forty-eight hours."

"Good for you. What are you doing here?"

"Sly sent me."

"He couldn't call?"

"You tell me. He sent me on a field trip to the catering company for Liam Anderson's party where I passed around the photo you pulled off the photographer's phone." He lifted the water ladle.

Tate nodded.

Steam lifted off the rocks, settling into his bones. He should probably leave, his lungs parched now.

"Apparently, your guy with the tattoo was on the setup crew that night. At least three people remember his ink. And he vanished after setup, so Sly thinks you're onto something."

Tate's jaw tightened. "Did you pull a name from the caterers?"

"Yeah. We tracked it and it was an alias. But..." He ran a hand around his neck. "Sly said if you wanted to follow your hunch, he could use you in San Diego."

Tate's head swam a little. "San Diego?"

"The National Convention. It's this weekend, and the setup crew is headed out tomorrow. We could use your eyes—no one else has seen this guy."

"I don't remember seeing him in person in San Antonio. That was my brother. But I remember the pictures and Knox's sketches."

"And he can't be hard to miss with the tat."

"It's a big crowd."

"A rowdy crowd too. Something big is going down with

the Jackson campaign. It's all behind closed doors, but Isaac White—the other presidential contender—has been out to the house twice. They think that maybe he's going to be her VP."

Tate climbed down from the benches and braced his hand on the wall. He didn't have to ask if Glo would be there.

"When do you want me?"

"I'll call you with a sit-rep."

"Thanks, Rags." He pushed out into the shower area and turned on the water, cold, his body shaking.

He shouldn't have left Glo. Shouldn't have let his pride—even his anger—get him fired. He slammed his palm into the wall and let out a shout. Hung his head under the spray. It sloughed off the sweat and frustration of the last few days but left him cold and edgy. He tucked his towel around him as he walked out to the locker room area.

Opening his locker, he pulled out his clothing, and grabbed his cell phone. He needed flights to San Antonio, pronto. He wanted to track down this guy from the source.

That's when he noticed the missed call from Ford.

Rags exited the sauna and headed for the shower.

Ford picked up on the first ring. "Bro. 'Sup?"

Tate didn't know where to start. "You called."

"Right."

Tate heard clinking in the background. Probably his brother cooking up something gourmet.

"RJ FaceTimed with me a few days ago. Told me to call you with some information—"

"And you're just now calling me?"

"Hey! I'm not your personal secretary. I got called out on training. Sorry."

Tate ran his hand across his face. "Naw, I'm sorry. I'm not in a good place. Just tell me what she said."

"She said she tracked down the guy in your photo and that he was ex-Marine, sniper. Graham Plunkett. His brother is Alan Kobie, who is a member of the Bryant League. And—here's the important part. Kobie was EOD."

Which meant, he knew how to make bombs.

"How did we miss this?"

"Maybe it's because Kobie is the son of the mayor of San Antonio?"

"So politics as usual." Tate wanted to hit something. "You around for a while?"

"I have training, but I'll be in town. Why?"

Rags walked into the locker room area, a towel around his hips.

"Throw some sheets on the sofa. I'm on my way."

Tate closed the phone.

Rags's gaze was on the ink across his chest. "Surrender is not a Ranger word."

"No," Tate said as he got up and tossed his towel in the wire basket. "No, it's not."

Last time Glo stared out the window of a hotel room, she had just kissed Tate Marshall. Had started to believe that she might be the special one. That her life was going to change.

The thought brought her up, back to herself, to the current view of San Diego—the pool, the ocean, and the multitudes of high-masted sailboats moored in the harbor—and the chatter around her in the VIP suite of the Hilton Bayfront. To Sloan making arrangements with Nicole about tonight's event. The private dinner was a warm-up to the big stage event tomorrow night, but it still had her stomach in a knot.

I think Gloria should give a speech.

Yeah sure, Mother, great idea. But here she was, twenty-four hours later, her name on the program.

She'd even tried to appeal to her father, but he'd just sat across the table, giving her a shake of his head.

How did she get in this far? She never really wanted the limelight, not really. Just wanted to be with Kelsey and Dixie. And yes, she'd wanted to be with her mother.

But most of all, she wanted to be with Tate. His absence

this week as she attended her mother's events, clapped, even introduced her—yes, she could see the slow sinking into the mire—and especially in the evenings as she sat in her darkened room wishing he might be on his chair beside the pool, left a widening hole in her.

Please, come with me, Glo.

Oh, she'd hurt him, and she knew it. But she'd made her choice. She'd have to live with it. She glanced at Sloan sitting at the conference table, dressed in a blue oxford, the sleeves rolled up above his forearms work-style as he bent over her stupid speech for tonight. He must have seen her looking at him because he glanced up. Smiled at her.

She smiled back. Clearly, she'd been too hard on Sloan. Sure, he was overly protective of her, and her mother, but that was his job. And, he'd been her groupie before anyone else knew her name.

He seemed to respect her aching heart, too, because he hadn't tried to kiss her, not once this entire week. As if giving her space.

He went back to his work, and she slipped into one of the anterooms that overlooked the pool. A balcony jutted from their second-story VIP suite they were using as a greenroom. She toed off her heels, picked up her phone, her earbuds, and stepped outside.

The sea salted the air, and the humidity, along with the heat, blanketed the afternoon with a sort of sogginess. Down at the pool, kids splashed. She measured the drop down. Two stories. Not a terrible drop, but nope, probably too far. Still, her entire body longed for the cool water.

Something to wash away the heaviness in her soul.

Where did the woman who used to paint on a tattoo and wear leather onstage go? I miss that girl. Now…you've vanished… And what do you want?

Tate was haunting her. She put in her earbuds and queued up her Pandora. Sat on the lounge chair and watched a seagull stalk a plate of food.

The husky blues voice of country singer Benjamin King

came through her buds.

We said goodbye on a night like this
Stars shining down, I was waitin' for a kiss
But you walked away left me standing there alone
Baby I'm a'waiting, won't you come back home…

It brought to her mind the explosion of their tour bus during a gig in Mercy Falls, Montana. Ben had invited them to his house to regroup and talk to the local police.

She'd never expected Tate to show up, practically banging down the door of Ben's lodge home to get to her. He'd crossed the room in giant strides of panic, his eyes pinned to hers, and she'd half expected him to sweep her up in his arms, the anger and fear radiating off him nearly palpable.

She might have lost her heart to him the night when he'd cornered her in the kitchen of his family home. When she'd offered him a cookie.

He'd wanted something else, she knew it, but she'd ducked away, afraid of the emotions between them.

Afraid of losing her heart again to a man who could walk away with it.

Her eyes filled as King reached the bridge in the song.

I need you, I need you, I need you
Don't say goodbye
I need you, I need you, I need you
Can't live without you
I need you, I need you, I need you
Come back to me tonight.

She drew up her knees, staring out toward the ocean, hearing Tate's pleading. *I love you. I have for months, and I…I'd give my life for you.*

Her phone vibrated, and she looked down to see Kelsey's name on the screen. She accepted the call and the music died. "Hey."

"Hey."

Silence.

"So, you heard then."

"No. I guessed. I saw you stumping for your mother, and Tate was nowhere to be seen. Is that my imagination?"

"He left me."

A beat, then, "Tate *left* you? C'mon—"

"He kissed me, and the media found out, and Mother—"

"Oh. Glo."

"Yeah. And then he was quitting and walking out of my life and…" She shook her head. "It doesn't matter. He's trouble. Did you know that the last woman he protected was *killed?*"

"Knox told me the story. She wasn't a woman he was protecting. She was his girlfriend."

Glo nodded. "He was in love with her."

"Which probably gives a good reason why he's a little rabid about protecting you."

"Well, the threat is over—or it never was. The Bryant League wasn't behind the bombing, and all the rest of the crazy moments have been, well, just crazy moments. None of it is connected. I'm perfectly safe."

"Even from Sloan?"

"Sloan? Please. He's harmless. Protective, but that's all." Poor man—he deserved better from Glo.

"What are you doing tonight?"

"It's a dinner for my mother and Isaac White. Don't tell anyone, but my mother is going to be announced as his running mate."

"Your mother agreed to be VP? You're kidding. What about President Jackson?"

"He was leading in the polls, and the party put their heads together and decided he had a better chance. But yeah, she'd been planning it since before Vegas. In fact, the rumor about the Bryant League, even if it wasn't true, helped turn the tide her direction. Made her both sympathetic and tough and gave her a base with her new party. And her female voters have come over with her, so…it's a strong ticket."

"Oh my, who are you?" Laughter from Kelsey's end of the phone and with everything inside her, Glo wanted to be with her, curled up on the leather sofa of the Marshall home.

"I don't know," Glo said, the words just rushing out. "I… oh, Kels, I made a terrible mistake. Tate asked me to go with him and I said no."

A hiss at the end of the phone. "Oh boy."

"Poor man stood there practically letting his heart bleed on the floor, and I…I did nothing. My mother was standing there telling me how much she needed me and I…I even asked him to stay and…"

"Your mother fired him."

"I know. I *know*. But it was David all over again, though. Me begging him to stay, him walking away. And I just…I got angry. I couldn't believe after all his promises that he was just…just *leaving*." She sighed. "I should have gone with him. I don't know why I didn't."

"I do. All your life you've wanted your mother to choose you. And suddenly she does, and you're going to throw that away?"

"For Tate. The man who would protect me with his life, and I just stood there and shook my head."

"For Tate, the man who has a scary past that shows up in Vegas hotel rooms. I know that wasn't his fault, but Tate has a lot of skeletons. The kind that gets people he cares about hurt."

She closed her eyes. "Don't say that."

"His girlfriend was killed because of a choice he made."

She swallowed. "Whose side are you on?"

"Yours, honey. I'm just giving you a brutal dose of reality."

"Feel free to take it down a notch."

"How about this. I like Tate. A lot. He's a Marshall. And I do think he'd die for you, Glo."

"That's not making it better."

"I'm sorry."

"It's just…he asked me who I was. Accused me of being

all things to all people."

"You are. You show up in people's lives, you stick around, you are who they need you to be. Tate needed someone who believed in him, despite his scars. And that was you, Glo."

She still believed in him. "He believed in me too. He liked the Glo I was, with the leather and the tattoos and the sappy country songs."

Kelsey's voice turned soft. "She was my favorite too."

Tate's words at the door, softly spoken, tunneled in and drew blood. *Wow. Did I read that wrong.*

No, Tate you didn't.

But maybe Glo didn't know who she was if she didn't have the Belles and her sister and her mother…and Tate.

"I guess the question is—is loving Tate worth the trouble he brings?" Kelsey asked.

"You sound like a country song."

Laughter. "Listen. I'm not really talking about Tate's past, or even life, but rather…the trouble with love is that it's always going to involve risk. You putting yourself out there, not knowing if you'll be loved in return."

"That sounds like something you said in Vegas when you talked me into singing my song. Which started this entire fiasco."

"I think my words were something along the lines of stop being so afraid and sing your song. I can't be responsible for what happened after that. But I think it's more than just putting yourself out there to let Tate love you… What if you stopped blaming yourself for Joy's death and just…just let God love you?"

"And now you've been around Knox and his family too long."

"Not long enough. But you've spent your entire life showing up for everyone else. What if you let God show up for you? Show you that you don't have to do anything for Him to love you."

"I think I'd be setting myself up for another broken heart."

"Glo—"

"No, Kels. Why would God show up for me? Please… How are things with you and Knox?"

A pause, then, "Would you be upset if we eloped?"

Glo drew in a breath. "Really?"

"I don't know. I think he might ask. And if he does, I'm saying yes."

"But it's only been a few months—"

"I've waited for this man my entire life, Glo. He's the one. He makes me feel safe and, most importantly, I like the person I am with him. He made the songs stir out of my soul."

"You should write that down."

"I have. I am. I have a slew of songs for you to put music to when we get back together. Please tell me it's soon."

A knock came at the sliding door behind her and she turned. Sloan was standing there, pointing to his watch.

"I don't know. Maybe a few more months. After my mother gets elected."

"Glo—give God a chance."

"I gotta go, Kels. The VP is waiting." She hung up before Kelsey's words found too tender soil.

As it was, her question dug deep and hung on as she opened the door to Sloan.

What if you let God show up for you? Show you that you don't have to do anything for Him to love you.

God didn't work that way. Really. She knew from personal experience.

"Ready for an amazing evening?" Sloan said. He'd rolled his cuffs down and donned a coat. "I promise, it's going to change your life."

Yeah, that's what she was afraid of.

12

P lease don't let her be the weak link here.

"You look amazing, by the way," Ford said as he held out his hand, completing their operational disguise. Scarlett took it, and he wove his fingers between hers, like they might be an actual couple.

Scarlett still wasn't sure how she'd gone from her runners and a T-shirt to being mic'd up and wearing a glamorous dress that could have been worn by a movie star during some red-carpet event. When Ford had brought it over, along with his brother and their crazy idea, she'd been stretching out after her mile swim along the coast.

Feeling pretty invincible.

She was going to nail the PRT. Not just the swimming, pull-ups, and push-ups, but the buddy tow too.

All because of Ford. Because he'd flipped a switch and decided to play on her team. Not only had he helped her get her car running, but he'd shown up every morning for the past week for buddy tow training, instructing her on technique, giving her tips, and cheering her on until today she swam all two hundred yards towing him, his face above water the entire time.

She could even take him in the freestyle swim—his combat crawl was too bulky for him to keep up with her.

Which meant when he'd asked her for help catching, uh, a *terrorist,* of course she said yes.

Because she was on his team too.

Hooyah!

"Can you guys hear me?"

Tate's voice came through the mic from somewhere inside the Hilton San Diego Bayfront.

They'd scoped out the place yesterday as tourists, walking down the boardwalk, then into the grand arching gold-and-teak lobby, taking the escalators to the second floor where tonight's private event would be held in the Indigo Ballroom. They peeked into the meeting rooms across from the ballroom, then wandered out to the terrace, two stories high and overlooking the pool.

Scarlett had stood staring out at the ocean, smelling the breezes, acutely attuned to Ford and Tate chatting behind her, and had to remind herself that she was here to catch a bomber.

Not dance the night away.

Not eat shrimp cocktail and monk fish.

And definitely not to fall for tall and handsome Ford Marshall, who would be dressed to the nines in a tailored tuxedo.

Tate had shown up three days ago with a crazy story about a bomber and Glo, whom he was no longer protecting—well, officially, because the guy had Personal Security written all over his face. Scarlett believed every word of his crazy story when he outlined the plans, complete with blueprints and contingencies, on her kitchen table.

They'd go in undercover, as guests via tickets Tate had procured for them, and keep their eyes out for Graham Plunkett, aka, the man with the fire tattoo.

She could see it in Ford's eyes—he wasn't entirely sure that Tate wasn't a little off his rocker. But brothers stuck together, and Ford had the night off, and she had a sneaking suspicion that he had something else on his mind too.

Because she couldn't deny the tiny spark that still simmered between them. And why not—she'd spent the week with her arm around his amazing chest, towing him to safety, his body tight against hers.

His big, muscled body that possessed nearly no buoyancy. He hadn't even helped her once by kicking—had made it worse by letting out all his breath, becoming dead weight in the water.

As if he really wanted her to blow her instructors away.

More than once when they reached shore, she'd wanted to keep hanging on. Wanted to take him up on the offers to have breakfast together or maybe go for a run.

She was already having a hard time keeping herself afloat around him.

And then he had to show up on her doorstep in her imagined tux. Only in real life, he wore a gray suitcoat, a pair of dress pants, and a gray tie. The man should wear that kind of uniform every day—the guy could sell calendars.

And that's when the entire thing turned into a fairy tale.

She blamed the dress too.

The amazing, black tulle dress with an embroidered corset and sheer top and okay, Scarlett had never felt invincible before in a dress, but this conjured up emotions that her Navy uniform didn't have a hope of eliciting. To think she hated wearing dresses. She'd only donned the last one because it had been Reuben Marshall's wedding, and even that had been a ten-year-old black thrift store affair.

But this dress…

Ford let her hand go, opened the door for her, then she slid her hand over his arm, like it might be a real date, and headed into the hotel lobby. The chamber music of a string ensemble drifted into the space as they took the escalator to the second floor.

"I hear you, Tate," Ford said, turning to her as though he might be saying something. They were using a tiny earpiece, and Tate had wired the transmitter and her microphone into her beaded necklace and connected it all via Bluetooth to the phone in her purse.

No screaming tonight.

"Where are you?" Scarlett said, glancing at Ford. He had

found her eyes, was smiling.

Clearly, he was enjoying himself too.

"I'm inside the ballroom. I checked in with Sly and the guys, and they're with Reba and the others in the greenroom across from the Indigo. Mingle, and keep your eyes peeled."

Ford took her hand again as they reached the top of the escalator, assuming the role he'd taken at her mother's place.

Boyfriend.

She tried not to remember the way his hands tangled in her hair when he'd kissed her.

White-gloved bouncers stood at the door, and Ford handed them a couple invitations.

The place rivaled any of the Vegas glamour she remembered from her childhood—gold carpet, brocade wallpaper. White table linens at fifty or more round tables were set with gold plates and long-stemmed glasses, each centered with a spray of red, white, and blue roses. And at the end of the room, a row of American flags crossed a long platform. Covered wings blocked the back doors and served as entrances to the platform.

Already, conversation filled the room, bedecked guests at high-top cocktail tables. She shot a look around the room and spied Tate. He wore an unobtrusive black suit jacket, a matching vest and pants, and a blue shirt, accented with a dark blue tie.

Yes, the Marshall men knew how to clean up, in and out of flannel.

He nodded to them, then grabbed a flute of champagne from one of the waiters and started searching the room.

It made sense, maybe, this idea of having a man undercover. Plunkett might veer around regular security, but he wouldn't know Tate and especially Ford and Scarlett were watching. They all looked like upscale millennials paying attention to politics.

Ford handed her a flute of champagne, and Scarlett held it but didn't drink.

Rules. She had them for a reason.

And especially on nights like this that could cajole her into believing she might be someone else. *What do you want, Red?*

Ford's question came back to her as they wandered the room. As more than a few sultry blondes cast an appreciative eye on her "date."

She couldn't deny a weirdly possessive pride.

They conversed with a couple from San Francisco. A man from Arizona, and a cowboy from Wyoming with whom Ford talked big cattle.

In this world, she forgot that he had cowboy in his blood.

By the time dinner was served—prime rib and asparagus—she had tried to put her eyes on every attendee, even excusing herself after dinner to go to the restroom and scan the crowd.

"Sorry, Tate," she said, standing at the edge of the room. "I don't have anything."

"Me either." Tate bore the tiniest edge of frustration in his tone.

She was winding around the tables, dodging servers clearing plates, when a man came up to the mic and tapped it on. Tall, handsome, with dark brown hair and a warm smile.

"Hey, everyone. Welcome to tonight's private event. I hope you enjoyed dinner. We have a lot going on tonight, but I wanted to kick off this evening's fun by inviting our host and hostess, Senators Isaac White and Reba Jackson, to the stage."

He backed away, clapping, and the crowd rose to the entrance of the two candidates. Which seemed a little weird since, weren't they running against each other?

Isaac welcomed everyone first. A handsome man—dark hair, graying at the sides, and a body of a thirty-year-old. She'd seen him on television a few times. Military hero, a former SEAL, rancher, and political conservative. According to rumors, he ran tough mudders and still broke his own horses.

No wonder Ford liked him.

Senator White offered a few words of welcome, then

tossed it off to Senator Jackson. A beautiful woman with her blondish red hair, she wore it up, tidy but casual, and a high-necked black, sequined dress that fell all the way to the floor and outlined her model-curved body.

She gripped the podium in both hands. "Hello, California! Are you ready for victory?"

A searing high-pitched whine split the room. She clamped her hand over the mic, cutting off the noise. The sound died.

A bus boy came in and retrieved their plates as a technician slipped onstage, carrying another mic, and replaced it.

"Sorry about that," Senator Jackson said as she spoke into the new mic. She indicated the lavalier mic pinned to the collar of her dress. "I guess I *really* want to be heard."

The crowd laughed. "We have a fantastic evening planned for you…with some excellent speakers, including my daughter…"

The crowd offered more applause.

"Would you like to meet her?"

Scarlett reached her seat and sat down as Senator Jackson turned and gestured offstage.

Glo Jackson owned the room. To be able to sashay onto a stage with that much poise, that much confidence…

"You okay there, bro?" Ford said, and she looked around to spot Tate.

Poor man was standing to the side, near the doors, his eyes glued to the stage, nearly white. Of course he knew she'd be here—that wasn't a surprise.

Maybe he was simply undone by the impact of Glo shining under the bright lights. She wore a white dress that hugged her body, black heels, and diamonds at her neck and ears. With her hair curled and tufted like it might be a halo around her head, she looked like a princess.

Scarlett felt like Cinderella next to her.

Even in her amazing dress.

Ford put his hand over hers on the table and squeezed.

Glo air-kissed her mother and waved to the audience.

"Isn't she beautiful?"

Glo rolled her eyes to her mother's praise.

"And I'm not the only one who thinks so."

She stepped back and the tall, dark-haired man who'd introduced them leaned in to the mic. "I do too. And I plan on marrying that woman."

Glo glanced at him. Her smile remained intact, but Scarlett could recognize a woman surprised.

"You know how it is. When you meet the right one, the one you've been waiting for your entire life? Suddenly it doesn't matter if it's been weeks, or days, or even hours—you need that person in your life. Need their smile, their laughter, their wisdom. Need the way they make you feel invincible."

Like she might be seduced by his words, Scarlett looked at Ford. His strong jaw, the way his fingers curled in hers, so natural, as if they belonged entwined.

She needed him. And not just as a teammate, but...

He picked right then to look at her. To meet her eyes with his devastating gaze and yes, he could probably see right through to her soul, but she could see his too.

What do you want, Red?

"In fact, what do you say I ask her right now?"

No...no...even Scarlett, who didn't have a romantic bone in her body—okay, maybe a few, but really, she'd never dreamed of roses and sunlit beach walks—knew this wasn't the way to a woman's heart.

Except, maybe, if she craved the limelight.

The room exploded in cheers as he stepped up to Glo and took her hand.

Went to his knee.

The applause died, the audience straining to hear his words. "Gloria Jackson. We've known each other since childhood. I love you, and I know you love me. I think the only way to kick off this victorious campaign is one way..."

He produced a box and opened it. "Marry me."

Glo let out a breath.

Scarlett couldn't help but find Tate again. Oddly, his space by the door was vacated.

She turned back just in time to watch Glo look at the audience, grin, and say, "Aw. Now if that isn't a country love song, I'm not sure what is." She winked, then pulled the man up by his collar and gave him a quick kiss. Turned again to the crowd. "I think that answer is going to have to be in private."

The man waggled his eyebrows but pocketed the ring.

Senator Jackson stepped back up to the mic, clapping, but Glo put her hand around her mother and leaned in, taking her spot. "How about if we get this party started with some real music while bussers clear our tables."

The senator appeared a little startled but stepped back in a moment, clapping.

"Where's Tate?" Ford asked, turning to face Scarlett.

She didn't have to answer. Tate's heavy breathing sparked through the earpiece.

"It's the sound guy! I'm in the stairwell. He's getting away!"

He'd had a choice—storm the stage or track down Plunkett.

Tate's brain had stopped for a full second when the man came onstage because he'd glimpsed, from his vantage point, Glo standing in the wings, and...

She was so beautiful it hurt. Just clawed at his chest, like his heart might be ripping from its moorings. He couldn't breathe, couldn't think, and nearly ignored the sound guy.

Nearly. Might have missed him altogether had the man not turned and walked back offstage just as Glo stepped forward.

He wore a gray collared shirt with the logo of the sound company on the front, neatly buttoned all the way up. He must have tried to hide the tat with makeup, but the uniform had smudged enough off for Tate to spot bright orange lipping above the neckline.

Please let him be right.

He started to make his way to the door as Sloan stepped up to the mic. *You know how it is. When you meet the right one, the one you've been waiting for your entire life?*

Yeah, he knew.

Because he'd never loved anyone like he loved Glo. Needed anyone like he needed Glo. Yeah, her smile, her laughter, but also the way she believed in the good, the hero in him.

And right then, he'd wanted to rush the stage. Scoop up Glo and make off with her like he might be a crazed fan.

True fact.

But that would be impulsive and fanatical, and he'd not only get tackled by Rags, doing his job, but Plunkett would get clean away.

His words to Glo in Montana found him. *I promise you right now—I'm not going to let anything happen to you...or me.*

He was keeping at least one of those promises.

He was pushing out the door when Sloan said, *In fact, what do you say I ask her right now?*

No—what? The blood drained right out of him as he'd glanced at Glo.

She was smiling.

And for a long, painful second, Tate watched his hopes crash and burn onstage. *I love you, and I know you love me. I think the only way to kick off this victorious campaign is one way...*

He couldn't watch this, the betrayal like a knife through his chest. Wow. Just, really, *wow*. How had he gotten sucked so far in that he hadn't seen that coming?

Maybe he had. Maybe he just hadn't wanted to.

Just like Jammas, he'd wanted to believe the best.

Tate pushed out the door and into the hallway.

He ran around to the main hallway and spied a bouncer near one of the exits. "Did you see a sound guy come out of here?"

The man frowned and shook his head, and it occurred to Tate how often people never noticed the people behind the scenes.

He spied the door closing to the stairwell down the hall.

He turned and sprinted to follow, slamming open the door.

Plunkett was two flights down, taking the stairs down two at a time.

"Where's Tate?" Ford said in his ear as Tate scrambled after Plunkett.

"It's the sound guy! I'm in the stairwell. He's getting away!" He didn't want to ask what Glo's answer was. "Scarlett, grab security and tell them to lock down all the exits."

"Do we have a bomb threat?" Scarlett's voice was hushed, but he heard music and applause behind her words.

Perfect. It was probably a yes.

"I don't know yet." He hit the second landing, took the rest of the stairs down in four big steps.

The sun glared off the cement deck of the patio, and he blinked against it, adjusting his eyes as he sprinted after Plunkett, running hard for the end of the building.

"Hey!" Tate wanted to startle him, jerk him out of his escape path, maybe alert local security.

It worked. The man glanced back and leaped toward another door, fleeing back inside the building.

Tate reached it—another stairwell.

"He's coming back up the stairs. Ford, you'd better be there."

"On my way."

The man's steps pounded above him as Tate gripped the rail and launched himself, two steps at a time, up the cement steps.

A shout echoed against the walls as a door slammed open. Grunts, a curse, shouts.

Tate came up the stairs and nearly bought it when an axe sailed his direction. It bounced off the wall and skidded down the stairs. Plunkett must have pulled it off the wall.

Tate stopped, breathing hard, heard more pounding as Plunkett thundered up another flight.

He wanted to curse when he found the stairwell handle destroyed. Ford was on the other side, banging his fist on the door.

"Get to the roof!"

He scrambled up behind Plunkett, ready to duck, but the man had a two-flight gain on him.

The other man's steps had died by the time Tate reached the third floor, and he took a guess and launched out into the fourth.

The floor was empty, a yawning conference space that led out to a balcony overlooking the pool area.

He spied a man standing at the edge of the terrace, against the white cement railing, wearing a gray shirt, his body paint swiped off. Empty tables and chairs, conversation groupings of wicker, stood between them.

"Plunkett!"

The man turned, sweaty and desperate.

Yeah, Tate remembered him now. And not just by his picture, but three months ago, in the bar in San Antonio where he'd bellied up next to Kelsey, Glo's bandmate. Stalking the Belles even then.

Remembered the tattoo, sure, but also the way he'd looked at Kelsey, eying her up, cocky, as if he knew something.

He wore the same look now, and it raised the fine hairs on the back of Tate's neck. "What are you doing here?"

Plunkett lifted a shoulder, glanced over his own, then back to Tate. "Can't you read?" He pointed to the emblem on his pocket. Event Sound and Lighting, with a little lightning bolt on the logo.

Tate shook his head. "Then why the sprint?"

Plunkett shrugged. "I know you secret service types. Tough guys, trying to show off. But I'm not running now."

He was leaning against the half wall of the terrace, with a four-story drop behind him. Although with the high ceilings of the hotel, it felt more like eight.

And that felt...odd. Why run up here? Maybe they weren't in any bomb danger.

Although, he had been leaving. Tate walked out onto the terrace. "Listen. This doesn't have to end with anyone getting hurt. Just tell me what's going on, and we all walk away. You got to terrorize the senator a little, but in the end, no one dies, right?"

"Everyone will die if Jackson is elected." He looked away. "She's behind it all."

Tate kept his voice cool. "Behind what?"

Plunkett met his eyes then. "You know they fight until they die, right? They don't surrender. Ever."

He frowned. "Who?"

"The Russians."

"We're not in a war with Russia!"

"We will be if Jackson wins."

And then he got it. "It's because Jackson is on the National Security Council?"

"No. It's because she only wants power. And she'll do anything to get it—including start a war with Russia. Nothing puts a president in power more than a war."

Right. The man had survived a war—and come home angry. Even delusional. Tate held up his hands. "Listen, pal, I'm sure she'll be glad to listen to your side of things. Just... how about you tell me what you're doing here."

Plunkett shook his head. "It's too late, man. The lies have already started."

Tate frowned just as Plunkett turned, grabbing the edge and hoisting himself up—

"No!" Tate rushed him, grabbed him, and that's when he realized it might have been a trick. Plunkett rounded on him.

Tate just barely deflected his punch.

Plunkett got a knee into his gut, but Tate grabbed him around the neck and spun him around.

Tate took him down, landing hard against a table. A couple chairs skidded away.

Plunkett's breath whooshed out of him, and Tate managed to get a shot in.

The man got a leg under him and tossed him, but Tate landed on his feet.

His ribs burned, old wounds surfacing, but he ducked as Plunkett's fist arrowed toward him.

And that was just *it*. Tate wrapped his arms around the man's girth and pedaled him back against the wall. He sent a couple jabs into his gut, then punched his hand into his jaw. "Stop. It's over."

Below, a few people spotted them, and screams lifted.

"It's just started," Plunkett snarled, burying his fist into Tate's side, but Tate grabbed his hand, trapping it to the wall.

"You think I'm the only one?" Plunkett spit out.

"We know about your brother. He's next, big man."

Plunkett brought his knee up. Tate dodged it, but the movement unbalanced him.

Plunkett roared to the advantage, rolled, and in a second had Tate pressed against the wall, pushing him over.

Tate's feet lifted off the ground.

No way, pal. Because he'd made promises to Glo.

He sent his palm into Plunkett's jaw, and the man's head jerked back. Then Tate jerked his knee into Plunkett's abdomen and dropped.

Plunkett rebounded. Lunged, and his own momentum sent him over the edge.

But not before he hooked Tate around the shoulder.

Tate followed Plunkett over the edge.

Ford made it to the roof just in time to see Tate go over. "Tate!"

He plowed over a chair, ran across an outdoor sofa, and reached the edge of the terrace.

Tate dangled by one arm.

Ford wanted to weep.

He leaned over the edge and grabbed Tate's belt. Hauled him up and over the edge. Instead, "You okay?"

Tate dropped in a heap, breathing hard, and Ford slid down beside him. "Now I am."

"What happened?"

"I don't know. I'm not sure if he wanted to jump or not,

but—" Tate lifted a hand as if to say, *Survey the handiwork.* He leaned his head back against the edge. "I can't look. Is he—?"

"He missed the pool and landed on the concrete. There's some screaming going on."

Tate ran his hand—shaking, Ford noticed—across his head and pushed to his feet.

"Sorry, bro. I should have been here sooner. They locked all the stairwell doors when Scarlett alerted security to the threat. I had to get them to open one. Did he say anything? *Is* there a threat?"

Tate headed toward the door. "I don't know. Said something crazy about Jackson's involvement in Russia, but I'm guessing it's part of their conspiracy agenda—"

"And the bomb?" Ford ran after him.

"He said it was too late. The lies already starting—"

"The microphone. He changed out the mic!"

Tate wore horror in his eyes.

Ford directed him toward the other stairwell.

Music spooled out from the ballroom, something country. Scarlett spotted them from where she stood outside the doors, her heels off, and ran over. "Did you get him?"

"Tate did. Sorta." Ford liked how she was grabbing his jacket, like she might be worried for him. "He's dead."

Tate was charging toward the door. Ford grabbed his arm. "Stop. Listen. We need to evacuate everyone without a panic. And we don't even know that there is anything wrong with the mic—"

"What's with the mic?" Scarlett said.

Tate rounded on her. "What did she say?" He looked at Ford. "Did Sloan propose?"

Scarlett nodded.

"Did she say yes?"

Ford blinked at him, then understanding dawned. "She said...she didn't say anything."

"No yes?"

"And no, well, no."

"No yes is a no," Tate said and turned back to the door.

Took a breath.

"She got Sloan offstage, then returned to the mic and said something about how this country needs to have a little faith. To take a risk on a team of people who were ready to put their pasts behind them. Then she announced that her mother was going to be Isaac White's VP."

But Tate didn't seem to be listening. He pressed his hand on the door.

Ford frowned at Scarlett, who shrugged. "The senator said a few words, and then Glo got back up and she said she was going to sing a song."

"It's our song," Tate said quietly, his voice a little broken. "She hasn't sung it since Vegas."

She was singing a cappella.

She...don't wanna cry,
But she ain't gonna fall for another guy.
It's too hard to be apart
Not after she's waited for...one true heart...one true heart...

He turned to Ford and pressed his hand on his shoulder, his eyes shining. "One true heart."

Ford had nothing, watching his brother unravel. Then Tate opened the door, stepped inside, and the rest of the song wound out into the hallway.

He said I'm leaving, baby don't cry.
No, Stay with me, please don't die.

The door closed behind his brother.

Always, forever, together, with me
She lay in his grass, clutching eternity.

"It's sort of romantic," Scarlett said. She offered a tiny smile.

Ford wanted to reach up and trace his finger down the

groove in her face, run it over her lips.

Wanted to curl his hand around her neck and pull her to himself.

Always, forever, together, with me.

He didn't know what the words meant, but he liked them.

After this was over, they were going to have a serious talk about complications and happy endings. "We need to evacuate the ballroom. And if there's a bomb, we need EOD here."

"I'll call Commander Hawkins."

He couldn't stop himself from squeezing her hand before he stepped into the room behind Tate.

Who was standing next to Sly, Tate's old boss. Ford had met the big man yesterday, found him to be the kind of guy Ford could take orders from.

Sly fielded Tate's words and nodded.

And now all eyes turned to Tate as suddenly Glo—on-stage—smiled, her gaze on her former bodyguard.

She...don't wanna try,
It's too hard to fall for another guy.
But you don't know if you don't start
So wait...for one true heart...one true heart...

Tate had managed to work his way toward the front and stood at the side of the stage as Glo's last tones died.

Wow, the woman had a voice. But more, she had heart. The kind that Tate deserved—brave, strong, and even a little feisty. Ford remembered how she'd deflected the other man's proposal with both grace and wit.

Ford caught up to Tate as he stepped onto the stage.

The look on Glo's face suggested she might kiss his brother in front of the entire audience.

Instead, Tate covered the microphone with his hand, leaned down, and spoke into her ear.

She drew in a breath and looked past him to Ford.

"Right now?"

Tate nodded, and she turned to the crowd, took a breath. Smiled.

Tate removed his hand.

"Ladies and gentlemen. We'll now adjourn to the court-yard outside where dessert is being served," Glo said, clearly wanting to keep panic from ensuing.

Ford raised an eyebrow and glanced offstage, behind him to where Sly had cornered Senator Jackson. Senator White had vanished, but he wasn't Ford's responsibility.

Getting everyone else out alive—yeah, that was on him. And Scarlett.

The guests began to leave.

"You there, Red?" Ford said into his mic.

"I called Nez and the team. They're calling in the EOD guys. Nez is on his way."

"Stay out in the lobby until we know what we're dealing with."

Silence, and he knew she wasn't happy with his words. But he needed her safe. And yes, in his ear, helping him sort this out.

Tate had reached for the mic, but Glo was already inspecting it. She turned it over and flicked the Off switch.

The sound died, but the light remained on.

"That's weird." She started unscrewing it.

"Glo—" Tate said.

She edged him away with her shoulder. "I know how mics work. This one is too lightweight to have a bomb in it—"

"What do you know about bombs?" Tate reached over her shoulder and pulled it away from her.

"Hey!"

He handed the mic to Ford, who examined it while Tate rounded on Glo. "You need to leave too."

"I'm not leaving."

Sloan came onto the stage then, and Ford stepped back, watching out of his periphery in case this turned ugly.

"Glo, you're leaving with the rest of us." Sloan reached out and took her arm.

Ford had the bottom open and examined the contents. "She's right. There's no explosive in here."

"What kind of game is this, Marshall?" Senator Jackson strode onto the stage. "You ruin my event—"

"Get out." Tate rounded on her. "Get out of here right now."

Oh. Ford knew that voice. Tate had used it a few times on him in his youth when he'd found Ford in his room.

Ford raised an eyebrow as the senator recoiled. "Fine. C'mon, Gloria."

"I'm not going, Mother." She slipped her hand into Tate's. Ford noticed Tate didn't close his hand around hers.

"Glo—" Tate started.

"No. Listen, bossy pants, I should have never let you walk away, and I'm not leaving you now. Or ever."

Tate blinked at her, and Ford sort of wanted to high-five her.

Except, well, Tate was right.

Ford walked up to Glo. "Sweetheart. I know you're crazy about my brother. And it's about time, but the fact is, you need to leave. For *his* sake. Because he won't be able to think with you here. Trust me on this."

She stared at him, then Tate, who nodded.

"Fine." But then she reached up and pulled Tate's head down.

And gave Sloan his definitive answer to his proposal, right there on the stage. Hel-*lo*. Ford averted his eyes and headed over to a table with the microphone. But kept an eye on Sloan just in case the man didn't take *No way, I love another man* for an answer.

As it were, Sloan's mouth tightened, and he shook his head.

Glo let Tate go. "Promise me you'll stay safe."

He took her face in his hands. "I promise to do everything I can to come back to you."

"You'd better, Captain America. Because I don't want to spend the rest of my life pining for you." She kissed him again, hard. Then turned and left the room.

Ford's chest tightened as he watched her go. He pulled out the battery and noticed another set of electrodes attached to the battery.

He eased the assembly out onto the table.

Two wires attached to a tiny timer, the count at two minutes, forty-eight seconds.

His entire body went still, only his heartbeat thundering in his ears.

"No time for EOD," Tate said.

"Tell me what's going on," Scarlett said, her voice soft, solid in his earpiece. He looked up and spied her standing at the door, watching him through the glass. She had a cell phone pressed to her ear, probably talking to Nez.

"There's a timer," Ford said. "It's attached to a battery, counting down. My guess is that it's on a frequency, and when the count gets to zero—"

"Boom," whispered Tate.

"You should leave, too, bro," Ford said.

He got a look that might as well have been sign language.

Scarlett was relaying the information. "Nez is on the line. Says to describe the timer."

Ford knelt and used a fork to turn the mechanism. "It's a simple digital timer with a chip on the back. It has a number on it."

"Read it."

Scarlett repeated it to Nez.

Ford looked up. "Tate, really—"

"This is my gig. If anyone is leaving, it's you. I should've never gotten you into this in the first place."

"Are you kidding? I've wanted to do superhero stuff with you ever since Dad told me about that time you fell off your horse and walked around the house for two days like you might be invincible. He said you had a hero streak a mile wide."

Tate frowned. "He did?"

"Yeah. Dad told me that out of all his boys, you were too

much like him. Stubborn and tough and didn't know when to quit. Which was probably why he was so hard on you, I'd guess. But I got it in my head that I wanted to be like you—well, without some of the trouble."

Tate smiled, still the frown in his eyes.

"Ford, I have an answer for you," Scarlett said.

"Go ahead, Red."

"That's a common control system switch. It's used for things like temperature control circuits to turn off or on an engine. When the clock reaches zero, the chip will send a signal to the remote detonator."

Boom.

"So, we just have to cut power to the clock to deactivate the chip."

Tate was crouching next to him.

"No, you have to cut the power to the chip. Because if you cut the power to the watch, the chip will think the timer is at zero—"

"And *boom*," Tate said, listening in with his earpiece.

"I've got two cords. One is blue, one is white. Can't I cut them both?"

"Not precisely. They would have to be cut at the same time down to the ten-thousandth of a second. Even if you put them in the cutter at the same time, one will be cut just prior to the other. There's no physical way to make it happen at the exact same time."

"Okay, so, which one is the power to the chip? Blue cord or white cord? Yes, we're playing *that* game."

Silence.

"Red, you got anything for me?"

"Don't know, Ford. And neither does Nez."

Perfect.

He picked up a steak knife from an uncleared table. Looked at Tate.

Then to Scarlett. She had her hand on the window, her eyes wide in his. And he heard her words. *I want this. Just this, right now.*

Him too. Maybe he didn't have to be the guy who always had to figure out everything. And no, he wasn't going to suddenly abandon everything he believed in, all his promises to himself, but maybe he could follow his gut a little.

Let go and live.

That worked out sometimes too.

"Which one, Red?" he whispered. "Tell me which one."

She drew in a breath. "The white one. For hope."

He nodded and slid the knife under the wire.

Beside him, Tate tensed.

Then he cut and waited for the world to explode.

Glo had been set up—maybe not by Tate but definitely by Sloan.

As soon as she walked outside the ballroom, Sloan directed Rags to grab her and drag her away from the trauma inside, leaving Scarlett to crouch beside the door, watching and relaying the events to whomever she talked to on the phone.

"Let me go!" Glo had kicked Rags in the shin, but he'd simply pulled her up into his arms and held her in his Hulkish embrace as she battered him. "This is kidnapping!"

"I'm sorry, ma'am," Rags said as she pushed against him.

She wouldn't slap him—that wasn't fair—but when they reached the escalator, she said, "Fine—fine. Put me down. If people see you dragging me away, they'll panic."

Still, it took a look from Sloan, the betrayer, before Rags would set her down. He steadied her with his hand on her arm as they rode to the main floor.

The security had led everyone outside, to the grassy park area beyond the hotel. A few of the women had taken off their shoes. Servers walked around with desserts on trays. The sun had just started to sink into the ocean, a bloody red upon the water. The chamber orchestra had reset up, Nicole at the helm of the disaster, as usual.

The whole thing felt a little like the sinking of the *Titanic*. Ford and Tate were inside disassembling a bomb, and—

"Are those sirens?" her mother snapped and turned to Sloan. "Make them go away."

"Mother. There is a bomb in the building. Of course we need police and sirens!"

Reba turned to her, swallowed hard. Then blew out a breath. "Yes, of course." She reached up to her neckline and unclipped her mic. "Come with me. I need your help to get this off me. I don't know why the sound guy mic'd me up if he was going to use the stand mic."

Glo followed her mother back into the lobby and down to the bathroom, Rags and Sly on their tail. She turned to them at the door of the bathroom and held up her hand. "Really. I got this."

Her mother was washing her hands, muttering. Blowing out controlled breaths.

"Mother." Glo stepped up and unzipped her to where the mic pack hung on her camisole. "It was a great night. Every single one of these people are here to see you. Because you... you're amazing. You fight for the underdog, and you give the voiceless a voice. That matters." She unclipped the mic pack and wound up the wire around it, setting it on the counter. "That's why people vote for you. Because of your character. Not because you throw them a great party."

Her mother looked up, drew in a breath. "How did I get so lucky as to have two such brilliant daughters?"

Glo looked down and zipped her mother back up.

Reached for the mic pack.

But her mother grabbed her hand, stopping her, and turned, her back to the mirror. "I mean it, Gloria. After Joy died, a part of me died too. And I threw myself into public service, thinking it would fill that empty place inside. And it did, it does. But not enough. Not like having you around does."

Glo's eyes burned.

"But you carry that same light Joy had inside you. It

shows when you sing. And it shows…well, when you love other people. Like your band. And your father. And…Tate."

She looked up at her mother.

"I was wrong about Tate. He might be trouble, but he is also a hero." She touched Glo's cheek. "And he came all the way to San Diego. For you."

Even after she'd rejected him.

Glo's breath caught. *What if you let God show up for you? Show you that you don't have to do anything for Him to love you.*

"In fact, he never left Nashville. I know, because Sly was watching him."

Glo frowned. "Did you assign Sly to him?"

"Of course I did—"

"I mean, in Vegas too?"

"Yes. Because, well, I had heard about his reputation. I wasn't sure…"

"Where was Sly the night he was attacked?"

"I don't know. I was on a flight from Pennsylvania that night. Sloan came in and told me about the attack. So I re-routed us."

"Sloan was on the plane?"

Her mother sighed. "Yes. I didn't want to…well, I wanted everything to progress between you two naturally…"

"When did Sloan find out about the attack?"

"Oh, let's see. It was after eleven, I think."

"11:00 East Coast time is only 8:00 p.m. in Vegas."

Her mother just stared at her.

"Mother—we didn't get attacked until nearly midnight. And you were there by morning."

"Maybe I'm wrong about the time—"

But something Tate had said…about Sloan and the Bratva… "Oh no!"

Glo scooped up the mic and headed out of the bathroom. Rags and Sly stood at the door.

She looked at Rags, then Sly, and took a chance. "Sly, where were you the night Tate and I were attacked in Vegas?"

Sly glanced at her mother, now following her from the

bathroom, then back to her. "I'm sorry ma'am...I was—"
He shook his head. "I was gambling. The show was over,
and I thought you were tucked in for the night." He appeared
distraught. "I'm so sorry, ma'am. I should have been there.
I checked in with Sloan, and he asked me where you were
staying. I told him I thought you were safe—the Bellagio has
top-notch security. He agreed and gave me the night off. If
I'd known..." He wore a tight ball of agony on his face.

Glo looked at her mother.

"Gloria—"

"I have to apologize, Mother. I thought it was you."

Her mother frowned.

"I couldn't figure out how the Bratva might have found
Tate—and I...I suspected you. But I didn't want to."

Her mother's mouth tightened. "It was Sloan. He had the
connections and your location." She had gone white. "He
knew I didn't like Tate, but I never thought...oh my..."

"I'll find him, ma'am," Rags said, and his expression
looked very much like Tate's when he'd told her he'd come
back to her.

Promises. Unspoken, but just as binding.

Tate. The bomb. She probably wore questions in her eyes
because her mother said, "What's happening, Sly?"

"Apparently, they've diffused the timer, ma'am, and security is searching the building."

Glo had already turned and headed up the escalator.

"Gloria!"

Tate was standing outside the ballroom with Scarlett and
Ford, and she took off running.

Tate looked up just in time to catch her up. "Babe."

"Not one more second," she said, pulling him tight
against her. "Not one more second without you."

"I agree," he said. "I agree." He set her down, catching
her face in his hands, those devastating blue eyes holding
her. "I completely panicked when Sloan... Scarlett said he
proposed?"

"Yeah. And for a second, I thought...this is all I could

hope for. A pseudo-happy ending doing what I should, but not what I wanted. And I stood there, and I thought…no. I wanted to wait for the song. For—"

"One True Heart."

She nodded. "And then I saw you standing there and…I knew I didn't want anything but the real thing."

"It is the real thing, Glo. I love you so much…I'd—"

"Die for me. I know."

"Or live. Whatever it takes to keep my promises."

His promises. "I don't know why you love me, Tate. But it's enough that you do."

"I do love you. And I know you're destined for amazing things. In and out of the limelight—whatever. I just want to be there, on the sidelines. Being the one who keeps you alive."

In spirit and body. Lighting her fire.

Yes.

"Forgive me for walking away from you, Glo. It was impulsive and prideful, and I should have told your mother that I was staying—"

"No. I should have gone with you. You're not trouble, Tate. You're…brave. And you've got such an amazing heart and frankly, I need a guy who isn't afraid of a little trouble."

He drew his thumb down her cheek and was bending to kiss her—*yes, please*—when Ford came up.

"You guys ready to go?"

"In a minute. I need to put my mother's mic away and grab my bag." She met Tate's eyes. "Want to come with me?"

He glanced at Ford. "Yes. Alone."

Ford rolled his eyes.

"Nez just arrived," Scarlett said. "And the San Diego bomb squad is coming in to sweep the building."

"The police are evacuating the building so don't take your time," Ford said to Tate, but he winked at Glo.

Yeah, she could get used to being part of the Marshall family.

She led the way to the greenroom/VIP suite where the

campaign team had gathered before the event, not sure how much she should tell Tate about Sloan.

She'd seen enough violence for today.

"Who did you say put that mic on your mother?"

Glo pulled out her access card as they reached the door.

"The sound guy. The one who fixed the mic on stage."

She opened the door and stepped inside.

Tate grabbed her hand and took off in a run.

She screamed, mostly in surprise, but with a little horror as he hit the glass door to the balcony without slowing. It shattered as it opened, and then he had his arms around her.

"Take a breath!" He clutched her to himself as he launched them off the balcony.

Behind them, the room exploded in a flash of fire and glass and timber.

They hit the pool, Tate's arms tight around her.

She'd forgotten to breathe, the water sucking her under, closing around her.

But Tate was right there, letting her go, pulling her to the surface.

She gulped air, a fish gasping. "What—?"

Tate was already dragging her away from the falling debris, toward the edge of the pool. He hooked his arm around her waist and practically carried her out and away from the destruction.

"Are you okay?" He put her down then, and turned her, his hands running over her arms, her body, then meeting her eyes. "Tell me you're not hurt."

She managed to get a shake of her head in before he pulled her into his arms, so tight she couldn't get her head around it all.

"What happened?"

Not her voice, but her thoughts, definitely. Ford was sprinting up the boardwalk from the park.

"The senator's mic—that was a transmitter." Tate wasn't letting her go, so she pushed against him. His entire body started to tremble, clearly an adrenaline rush. "It didn't make sense—our fifty-fifty odds were just too…easy. And the second mic—"

Scarlett had run up behind them, barefoot, and behind her, a tall Native American man, along with a couple more men.

"That's what the switch was for—it activated the transmitter in the senator's mic."

"I don't understand," Glo said. "Mother was mic'd in the greenroom, before the event."

"Which was why they needed a second transmitter to activate the first. When Plunkett brought out the second mic and turned it on, it activated your mother's unit. She was supposed to wear it until after her speech."

"And since it was under her dress, she'd return to the suite to remove it," Glo said.

"Which would then activate the bomb, in her room, as soon as she entered. They didn't want to take out the crowd. Just your mother," said Scarlett.

"And Glo, maybe," Ford said.

"Collateral damage." Tate looked a little pale. "I don't know why I knew to run—it was just…something inside me said get out of there." He turned to Glo again and pulled her against himself.

And she wasn't going anywhere, thank you very much.

Not without her bodyguard.

13

W hich one, Red? Tell me which one.
Ford's words from last night burned through her, a torch that ignited Scarlett to her core as she stroked through the water. Her shoulders burned, her legs fighting a cramp against the cool water.

Jerk.

He shouldn't have put her in that position. Shouldn't have looked up, their lives in his hands, and asked her to save the day.

Like he trusted her. Like he respected her.

Like she was on his team.

Four strokes and a breath. Four more, a breath. She wore goggles, and out of her periphery, in the quick moment it took her to gulp air, she spied the shore she paralleled. The buoy would be ahead another one hundred yards.

She'd already completed the on-land test—the push-ups, sit-ups, and pull-ups. Flying colors, but she'd always excelled in the core activities.

Endurance. That's what she failed at. Looking past the current pain to the goal. And knowing that she was making the right decision, not sure if her next step might crumble under her.

Life was a series of white cords versus blue cords, hoping she clipped the right one to keep the world from blowing up around her.

The white one. For hope.

She wasn't sure why she'd said that—a gut feeling, maybe, although after inspection, the bomb squad had deduced that the chip hadn't been intended to trigger a bomb, but rather to activate the transmitter inside the senator's lapel mic.

A transmitter that would trigger the bomb set inside an innocuous vase of decorative flowers in the senator's VIP suite. A bomb meant for the senator alone, regardless of the collateral damage.

Tate had uncanny instincts to have figured it out in the split second between entering the room and launching himself and Glo off the balcony.

But she could have picked the blue cord, and nothing would have gone *boom*.

It made her wonder if she worried too much about the impending *boom* in her life. If it kept her standing outside the room, staring at what she wanted through the window. And sure, Ford was trying to keep her safe, but maybe she was tired of being safe.

Fifty more yards. Her chest had tightened, her breaths coming in a burst of flame.

Tired of trying so hard, of taking care of everyone, of denying what she really wanted.

Ford. And yeah, the happy ending that came with him. Sure, it would be complicated, but…well, Ford knew how to navigate complicated. *And I'm all in…as long as you are.*

White cord or blue cord. It didn't matter as long as she was with Ford.

Teammates, and more.

She hit the buoy, grabbed the rope, breathing hard. Her instructor floated in a kayak nearby, clocking her. He gave her a thumbs-up.

"You have a three-minute rest, then you'll be towing your instructor Chief Petty Officer Peters to shore."

She cast a look at the man she'd be towing. He was about Ford's size, wide shoulders, blond hair. He wasn't smiling.

She gathered her breaths, put her head back in the game.

One more evolution.

You got this.

Two hundred yards to her future.

She blew out a few more quick breaths, filled her lungs a final time, then nodded her ready.

The instructor sank in the water.

She dove down for him, expecting him to lie limply, in need of rescue, but he grabbed her.

Remember, whatever you do, don't let me get a grip on you to pull you under.

She ducked her head and sent her hands into his elbows, dislodging his hold.

He let her go, and she turned him around, her arm around his chest as she kicked for air.

The ocean had turned choppy as the morning drew out, but it worked to her advantage as she towed her victim to shore. *Keep me planed in the water. Scissor kick.*

Ford's voice filled her head as she swam, her strokes even, her hip under her victim to keep him afloat. *I like you in my ear, what can I say?*

She heard the other trainees—two women, seven men—shouting at her from shore.

You look amazing, by the way.

Oh, brother. But still, the memory of him taking her hand, weaving his fingers through hers…

She *felt* amazing.

Her feet hit the beach. She dragged her instructor through the waves, pulling him all the way to the beach, then collapsed beside him, dragging in hot breaths.

A shadow cast over her. Another of her instructors. He wore a Navy hat, shorts, and a sleeveless shirt and gave her a hard look.

Please—

"You passed, Petty Officer Hathaway."

She rolled over in the sand, onto her elbows, wanting to weep. Her victim bounced back to life.

"Who taught you how to get out of the swimmer's grab?"

Peters said.

She climbed to her knees. "My teammate." Probably it wouldn't be prudent to add *my boyfriend.*

No, that sounded weird.

But what if…maybe it was time to do something crazy. To cut the white cord.

To release her hope in a happily ever after.

She walked over to a nearby picnic table where she'd left her gear. The other trainees were getting their times, talking with the instructors. She picked up her towel and wiped her face with it, then wrapped it around her shoulders.

Chief Petty Officer Peters came up to her, holding a water bottle. He rinsed out his mouth and spit onto the ground. "There's an opening in the upcoming rotation to Rescue Swimmer School in Pensacola. It starts next week. I can get you in, if you're interested."

Next week. She nodded.

"Good job today." He gave her a smile and headed over to the group of instructors.

Next week. And then she'd get her RS certificate, move on to aviation training and…

No more sitting on the sidelines.

Overhead the sky was clearing with the morning, blue with a scattering of clouds that looked hand-stirred from the heavens. A few beachcombers wandered the shore picking up shells, seagulls cried overhead. A dog barked, running to catch a Frisbee.

"Hey, Hathaway, want to catch breakfast?" One of the trainees called to her from the gathering nearby.

"Nope. I have other plans."

Like calling Ford with the good news. Maybe cajoling him over for some very unhealthy Cap'n Crunch.

Taking him up on that desire she'd seen stirring in his eyes when he dropped her off at home last night, after their debriefing with the FBI, who'd shown up way after the firemen put out the fire and bagged the body of the bomber. Thankfully, Ford had seen the altercation between them and defended Tate's actions to the police.

Ford had walked her to the door, the gentleman he was, as if they'd been on a crazy, high-action date, and stood on her doorstep like he had nearly a month ago when he'd offered to road trip her to Idaho. When he decided to walk into her heart and stick around like he meant it.

She'd perched on the step above him, almost eye level with him. He'd pulled off his tie and coat, rolled up the sleeves of his dress shirt, revealing his powerful, tanned forearms, and propped one foot on her step. "Thanks for…well, you saved my life, again."

She laughed. "Pick one? Really?"

"You picked the right one." He winked.

Yes, yes, she did. And he'd been standing right in front of her. The wind had stirred the scent of his aftershave, and he wore a hint of a five-o'clock shadow, his chest pulling at the buttons on his shirt, and she'd just wanted to step close, run her hands over those amazing shoulders, feel his arms close around her.

Lower her lips to his and taste that amazing smile.

Oh, she wanted more than right now.

What was she thinking—she wanted forever.

And she almost took it, right then. Except for Ford, who'd taken a breath, backed away as if reminding himself of the last time they'd had this moment.

"Good luck tomorrow, Red. I'm rooting for you." He took a step off the porch.

And what was she supposed to do, leap into his arms?

Maybe. Instead, she'd nodded. "Thanks." And watched him walk away.

Not today. Today she was invincible again.

She hiked up the beach to her car, the sand warming her bare feet, and unlocked her door, dropped her gear in her trunk. Then she got into the hot front seat, leaving the door open as she retrieved her phone from the glove box.

She pulled up her messages to text Ford, sending him a quick *I passed,* and was about to follow up with her invitation when she spotted the voicemail. Unknown number, a 801 area code, the same as her mother's from her days in Salt Lake City.

She opened the app and listened.

"This is State Trooper Troy Smith. I'm leaving a message for Scarlett Hathaway. Please call me as soon as possible..." He left his number, and she took a breath and dialed it.

He answered on the second ring and she identified herself.

He paused. "Ma'am, I'm sorry to have to tell you this, but there's been an accident..."

Scarlett leaned her head on her hand and listened to her future explode.

If someone wanted to take a shot at Glo, it would be tonight, right here in the middle of the San Diego Convention Center, as she took center stage after her mother accepted the vice presidential nomination.

Which was the only reason Tate agreed to go out onstage with her. Sure, the place was jammed with security, including their own force of Navy SEALs who'd agreed to step in for the evening—thank you, Ford. They mingled, plainclothed in the audience, their eyes peeled for trouble.

But Tate wasn't taking any chances. He had no plans to leave Glo's side.

Ever.

"You look nice," Glo said as she turned to him, smoothing down his lapels.

"I still can't understand why you wanted me in cowboy boots and my hat. I look like..."

"Calm down, Rango. You look like a hero."

He cocked his head, gave her a look, and she pulled off his Stetson and set it on her head, grinning up at him.

"Now that looks better. And, I like this." He touched the daisy she'd temporarily inked on her shoulder. She wore a white, off-the-shoulder lace dress that showed off her tan, and a pair of boots. "And this." He pointed to the Dobro, the instrument twined behind her. "Got a little something planned for the campaign?"

"Just tonight. Tomorrow, we're back on the NBR-X tour."

He could admit to some surprise today when Knox and Kelsey had shown up at the Hyatt, where Glo and the campaign team had relocated after yesterday's horror. Tate was still bunking on Ford's sofa but had risen early to take Glo to breakfast.

To lay down the ground rules.

He would be her security detail on the campaign trail. No questions, no argument, and especially no firing.

Because he also planned on getting close and personal with her. The kind of close and personal that included a ring and vows and a permanent say-so in her life.

If that sounded okay with her.

And no, he hadn't produced a ring—not yet. But he was a man who kept his promises.

Dixie and Elijah Blue had arrived early in the afternoon with most of the equipment, and Tate had sat in the sound check.

Apparently, it was time for the Yankee Belles to get back together. He'd never been prouder of Glo than when she stood up to her mother and told her that she wouldn't give a speech tonight.

That instead, she'd sing.

Which, after all, was what she was good at.

And yes, she liked the limelight, but only if she could share it, thank you. Besides, she had the perfect song for tonight, if her mother would just trust her a little.

Meanwhile, future VP Reba Jackson was onstage before thousands—no, millions, if they counted the television audience—giving her acceptance speech.

He'd missed most of it—the background of her life, the callouts to various supporters, the stumping against the other candidates—but Glo took his hand and walked him to the edge of the wings.

Reba wore a red dress, striking and powerful on her slim frame. She held the podium with both hands, as if she might be driving, and she probably had her speech memorized, despite the teleprompters.

He wasn't sure what she'd just said, but the audience—some in crazy hats, others with foam fingers—was alive, raising blue-and-white political signs. It felt like a football game, and for a second, the old buzz of standing at the edge of his high school stadium and hearing the roar of the crowd sluiced under his skin.

As if he might be at the edge of the biggest game of his life.

Maybe he was. Loving Glo. Being the man she believed in.

"You know what is going to change this country?" Reba said now. "People who won't give up. People who are willing to sacrifice and commit and keep showing up, even when it gets hard. People like my daughter's boyfriend, Tate Marshall, a former US Ranger who didn't give up when his unit was attacked, who fought his way out of an enemy village, towing a fellow soldier on his back, even though he was injured himself, and got both of them to safety. A true American hero who just yesterday saved my life and the life of my daughter."

Tate couldn't move.

"Tate, just step out here for a moment, and let America thank you."

What—uh—

Reba turned in his direction from the stage, and his chest hollowed. "No—"

"Yes," Glo said, looking up and grinning at him, her voice low. "Just…receive it, Tate. C'mon." She tugged his hand. And then, when he didn't move—still stunned—she pulled him out onto the stage.

"Try not to look like you're going to throw up," she said, and he swallowed, forcing a smile.

"Wave, Tate!"

A voice shouted from behind him, and he turned to look.

Knox stood on the side, next to Ford, Reuben, and Gilly, and even—his mother? *What?* Gerri was grinning, tears cutting down her face. Smiling.

Glo looked up at him. "Surprise."

"What did you do—?"

"I didn't do anything. You did. You showed up."

"I showed up because I love you. Not because I'm some great hero."

"Aw, Tate, that's what you don't see. You don't consider yourself a hero, because it's what you do. It's just who you are. But you *are* a hero and we all know it. It's time the world did too. So just *wave* for Pete's sake!"

He took a breath.

And lifted his hand to the world.

The applause thundered down over him, a wave of respect and acceptance, and he couldn't breathe. Reuben's words in the kitchen the night before he got married pressed into his mind. *When you show up with nothing and discover that you're loved because of who you are—that's when you realize what it means to be a son of God... It's pretty breathtaking...*

The words washed through him, hot and bold.

A son of God.

That's when you discover that you've inherited more than you could possibly imagine.

Yes. And as he stood there, put down his hand, he simply let the applause wash over him. Let it sink into his pores, his bones, his cells.

I'm proud of you, son.

Maybe his father's voice, maybe something more, but his throat tightened.

Thank you, Father.

Glo tugged his hand and turned him back to the wings.

His brothers stood there. So much alike—tall, wide-shouldered, dark haired. Strong, brave, wise—true cowboys.

And he'd spent his entire life wanting to be like them. Proving that he fit into the family.

Out of all his boys, you were too much like him. Stubborn and tough and didn't know when to quit.

So maybe he was more like his dad than he'd ever realized. Huh.

Tate entered the wings to the high fives and one-armed hugs of his brothers. His mother parted them and pulled him into a hug. "It's about time. Your father would be so proud. He always told me that you'd blow my socks off, if we could just keep you alive."

Tate swallowed the heat burning his throat. He leaned away from her, met her blue eyes. His blue eyes. But he had his father's grit.

And his Father's name. And that made all the difference.

"Thanks for putting up with me, Ma."

"Oh, Tate. You were the most fun." She winked and kissed his cheek.

Reba had returned to the mic, winding up her speech as Glo dragged him away into the shadows.

"Surprised?"

"Glo, I—"

"Love me. I know. Me too. I just wish I had a medal to give you."

Then she stood up on her toes and kissed him, her arms around his neck.

And he was the guy who got all the luck, got the girl of his dreams, got the happy ending.

In fact, maybe he was even the hero of the story.

Glo leaned back, her eyes shiny. "Now hang on to your hat, cowboy. Because it's time to get this party started."

Then, as her mother waved her arms to the crowd's applause, Glo grabbed her band and headed to the stage.

And Tate stood on the sidelines, keeping his eye out for trouble.

Night hung over the skyline of San Diego, the breeze fragrant with ocean and the sultry smells of early summer.

He should be out riding his motorcycle, Scarlett's arms wrapped around his waist.

Instead, Ford was stuck at the after-party of tonight's big political performances, in the conference suite of the Jackson campaign, country music and conversation winding out onto the balcony.

He didn't know why his gut tightened as Scarlett's prerecorded voicemail message came over the line. Again. "Leave a message, I'll get back to you."

His message couldn't be left over the phone.

I need you, Red.

That truth had never felt more solid, more compelling than when he'd held their lives in his hands and turned to her. Her voice in his ear, soft, sure—yeah, he needed her.

He should have told her last night as he'd stood on her front steps. She still took his breath away in that black dress, and when she'd looked at him with such light in her eyes, laughing when he told her that she'd saved his life, again, he'd just wanted to wrap his arm around her waist and pull her to himself.

Taste that laughter.

You picked the right one, he'd said. But really he meant... *Pick me. Right here, right now.* And sure, tomorrow might be complicated, but she was worth it.

They could figure it out.

But maybe not until she passed her PRT. He knew what it felt like to need to focus on a mission, to not let anything distract him from the goal.

The breeze had swept her perfume his direction. He'd taken a breath, needing to put some space between them.

Good luck tomorrow, Red. I'm rooting for you. And yes, he was, but not without a sense of panic.

She could leave him.

Her gaze had followed him as he'd stepped off the porch and he nearly stopped, nearly tossed all his mission sense, closed the gap, and ran back up the steps.

Nearly lowered his mouth to hers, caution thrown to the

night settling around them, nearly let go of his heart and kissed her.

The feeling could consume him, so he'd turned and fled to his truck.

But tonight...tonight was different.

I passed. He'd received her text this morning.

The words found his gut, settled there.

Maybe if she knew how much he needed her... Not that he wanted to hold her back, but she *was* a part of the team. His team. And sure, he could work with anyone, but knowing that she was watching his back, that she'd break protocol to save his hide...

Even stick around when he held a bomb in his hands...

Maybe she was just exhausted after all her training. Ford should probably ditch the soiree and head over to her house.

Ford came in off the balcony, hanging up before leaving a message. He pocketed his phone into his suit pocket and headed over to the bar counter. His mother and Jackson's team had retired, but Glo and her band had hung around, inviting Ford and his SEAL team as well as the rest of the Marshall brothers in for some much-needed downtime.

Nez and Sonny were sitting at the stools, drinking Cokes. Over the bar, CNN news played, muted.

Levi, Trini, Cruz, and Kenny were in a knot talking to Tate, exchanging stories—apparently Trini and Tate had been in Afghanistan at the same time, knew the same people.

Ford walked over to Knox, who was in conversation with Reuben and Gilly, talking about their honeymoon in Hawaii.

"Gilly talked me into taking a discovery scuba class," Reuben said, his arm around his petite wife. "I saw a sea turtle, a shark, even a stingray."

"Going to exchange your wings for iron lungs?" Ford said, trying not to be bugged by Scarlett's silence.

His day had been consumed with security meetings and prepping for tonight's speech, and by the time he'd been able to sneak away to call her, his call flipped over to voicemail.

"I dunno, bro. Why should you have all the fun?" Reuben

said.

"I don't dive for fun," Ford said and immediately regretted his tone. "Sorry."

"You okay?" Knox asked.

Ford sighed. "Yeah. I just...I sort of thought Scarlett might like to be here." Or maybe not here, but with him. Celebrating. "I called her, but she's not answering."

"That's because she left town."

Ford turned. Nez had come up behind him. The master chief stood as tall as his brother Reuben, and it struck Ford for a moment how much alike they were. Pensive, in control, capable. Born leaders, despite their quiet demeanors.

"What?" Ford asked, trying not to let panic bleed through his voice. "How do you know that?"

"I got a call from Peters today—he was at the PRTs. I asked him for a status report on Scarlett because she works so closely with our team, and it looks like we're going to have to get used to someone else talking us through our ops. Peters hooked her up with an immediate placement in Pensacola."

Ford tried to act casual, to nod, like no big deal, but he felt Nez's gaze on him, as if the chief could see right through him. "She requested emergency leave sometime this morning, not long after. Maybe to give herself more transfer leave time."

Emergency leave?

Ford picked up his phone again, now worried. "If you guys will excuse—"

"Oh my—look." Knox's voice brought Ford's gaze up, and he followed Knox, who'd started walking toward the bar, his eyes on the screen. "Unmute the television."

Someone responded with the remote, and in a moment, commentary added to the visuals on the screen.

The shot was half screened—one side a grainy cell phone photo, the other an on-scene reporter, who stood in front of Saint Basil's Cathedral in Red Square in Moscow. "We don't have all the details, but the apparent assassination occurred last night as General Stanislov was exiting a popular restaurant in the Arbat district of Moscow. Stanislov is a member of the Troika, one of the top three leaders in the Russian government with the authority to release nuclear missiles. He is unhurt, but one security officer was killed, and another is in critical condition."

"Oh my," said Glo, who'd edged into their group. "My mother knows him. He's even been to our house. A moderate, politically, she says he's the reason that Russia hasn't pulled the trigger on us, or any other country. If he dies, there's a hard-liner waiting in the wings to take his place. It could mean the restarting of the Cold War, or worse."

The woman on the screen continued her report. "A cell phone caught this woman with a handgun, and she's being hunted in connection with the shootings."

"Is there any idea who this woman is, Cecily?" the host asked.

"No. But the police have put out a sketch, based on witnesses, and decided to release it, hoping someone might call in. We have a copy of it."

The sketch flashed on the screen, and the air left Ford's lungs.

Knox let out a "No way," and behind him, Reuben added a "What the..."

"That can't be right." Tate had left his group and come up behind Ford. "Please tell me that's not—"

"It looks like it," Ford said, and pocketed his phone. "I had a bad feeling last time I talked to her. Something didn't feel right."

The news flipped to the next story, and Sonny, the holder of the remote, muted it again.

"Do you guys know that woman?" Nez said, and Ford glanced at his brothers. Knox and Reuben were still shaking their heads, but Tate met his gaze with a dark, solemn look.

"I'm going to need my own emergency leave, Chief," Ford said quietly.

Tate nodded, and his expression hearkened back to his Ranger days. Lethal. Determined.

Ford looked at his team, who'd gathered around. He needed them all, maybe. But especially Scarlett. His gaze landed back on his chief.

"The woman in that picture, the one they're calling an assassin...she's our sister, Ruby Jane."

What Happens Next...

If Ford didn't get his head in the game, they were doomed. People were going to die. Probably him.

And, maybe his teammates, fellow SEAL operators with Team 3, right here on the rugged shoreline of the Caspian Sea, in the democratic Muslim state of Azerbaijan.

The team had dropped in sometime before zero-dark-thirty, making their way toward a cluster of buildings that made up Vigeo, an international boarding school perched on the seaside cliff. By the time the sun rose, Ford was crouched in the shadows beside the gymnasium doors.

It might have been a beautiful morning. Striations of crimson and burnt orange casting over the dark rolls of the Caspian Sea, if it weren't for the smoke that billowed from the still-burning chapel, the terrorists' first stop in their take over the school. It soured the air and the longer Ford waited, the more his gut roiled with the fact that children had died inside that chapel.

Twelve more children remained hostage in the gymnasium of the ancient stone and marble building.

The Team's job? Get in, eliminate the hostage takers, secure the packages and evacuate.

A mission that demanded his full attention.

Except, he shouldn't be here, not right now.

Right now he should be finding, and extricating, his twin sister from the clutches of the FSB—former KGB—somewhere in Russia.

So maybe his imagination had run a little wild with the word, *Russia*, but two days ago, CNN had reported the attempted assassination of a Russian General Boris Stanislov. Providentially, the accused—still at large—shooter was caught on a fuzzy street camera, and the image looked insanely like his twin sister Ruby Jane.

Right.

Not. For. A. Moment.

And sure, he hadn't talked to her—really talked—for years, but she was a *travel agent*. So, she'd probably taken some hapless tourists on an excursion and ended up in the wrong place, at the wrong time.

Crazy.

Still, the thought of his naive twin sister now missing and on the run from the FSB was enough to tangle his brain.

Where was his sister, and was she—please, God   still alive?

Author's Note

Be thou my wisdom, and thou my true word;
I ever with thee and thou with me, Lord;
thou my great Father, I thy true son;
thou in me dwelling, and I with thee one.

Ever feel like no matter what you do, it backfires? That some-how, despite your best efforts, you are standing outside of God's blessings, outside of his love. You're watching the family of God hang out in communion around the campfire, but you're still stuck in the darkness, not really a child of God but a refugee in the kingdom? Hopefully not, but let's face it—sometimes we look at others and feel *less than*. We don't belong. We're the misfits. The ones who aren't enough.

Just being honest.

I wanted to write a story about the fact that all of us—*all of us*—feel less than at some point in our lives. We all look at our lives and the mistakes we've made, the times when we weren't enough. Not enough for ourselves, not enough for others…

Not enough for God?

Hello. Never. Because yes, if *we look at ourselves, we will never be enough*. But if we look at what God did for us. Does for us. Saves us, protects us, blesses us, forgives us…

We are enough because He decided we are. I love what Reuben said to Tate, "When you show up with nothing and discover that you're loved because of who you are—that's when you realize what it means to be a son of God."

We only stand at the edge of the kingdom because we have decided that's where we belong. We look at others and compare. We look at our faults and give up.

But consider this—we are enough because what we lack, God fills up. You lack patience? That's okay. God has enough. Lack faith? God will give you what you need. Lack strength? Read Philippians. You are enough **because He is enough**.

To quote Gerri, "Heaven sees you! You don't need to do anything to get God's attention. You had it before you were born." And we love not to earn God's love…but because he loved us first!"

You are enough, friend. Because He has decided you are. Enough for him to save. To love.

To belong.

Stop lurking at the edge and step into the glow of the campfire.

I am so excited about this series, and my deepest gratitude for their help in creating it goes to my amazing SDG publishing team: Rachel Hauck, for her amazing encouragement and help on the journey. Alyssa Geertsen, my key beta reader, Barbara Curtis, for her almost magical editing, Rel Mollet, for her awesomeness in countless ways. I'm deeply grateful for my cover designer, Jenny @ Seedlings Design Studio, and my talented layout artist, Tari Faris. Thank you also to my fabulous beta readers (any mistakes are all mine!) Lisa Jordan, Lisa Gupton and Bobbi Whitlock. You all are fabulous! Appreciation also goes to my amazing Masterminds. You know who you are. Thank you for pushing me and believing in me.

Finally, to the Lord, who is always and forever telling me He loves me. I am His beloved daughter. Blow. My. Mind.

Thank you, dear readers, for reading book 2: Tate. I can't wait for you to find out what happens in book 3: Ford!

Susie May

Susan May Warren is the USA Today bestselling, Christy and RITA award–winning author of more than sixty novels whose compelling plots and unforgettable characters have won acclaim with readers and reviewers alike. The mother of four grown children, and married to her real-life hero for nearly 30 years, she loves travelling and telling stories about life, adventure and faith.

In addition to her writing, Susan is a nationally acclaimed writing teacher and runs an academy for writers, Novel. Academy. For exciting updates on her new releases, previous books, and more, visit her website at www.susanmaywarren. com.

Continue the Montana Marshall family adventures with FORD

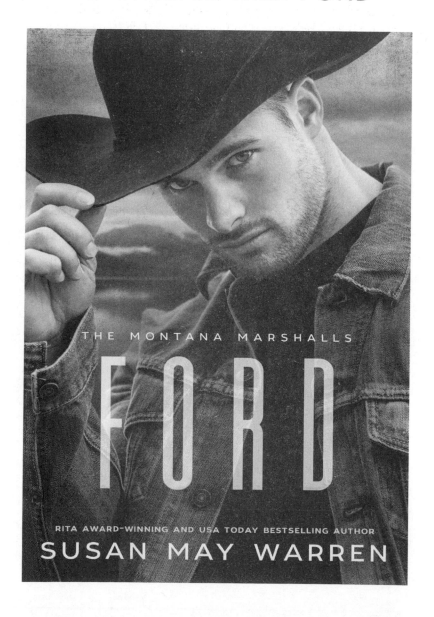

THE MONTANA MARSHALLS

FORD

RITA AWARD-WINNING AND USA TODAY BESTSELLING AUTHOR

SUSAN MAY WARREN

Navy Seal Ford Marshall isn't the kind to stand by and let a woman get hurt—especially when it involves his twin sister, RJ. So, when she makes the international news, accused of an attempted assassination of a Russian General, he doesn't care what it takes—he's going to find her and bring her home.

But he might need a little help, so he calls on the woman who has had his back during the last three years—Petty Officer Scarlett Hathaway, former communications expert-turned Rescue Swimmer candidate. She'll help him get into the country, watch his back, and…well, they might be able to have one last mission together before she leaves for a new life, a life he very much wants to be a part of now that she is off his team. Maybe he can convince her to give them a chance to kindle the spark that's simmered between them for years.

Scarlett Hathaway isn't sure what future she wants—not when she suddenly has to care for her little brother. Maybe she should quit the Navy and start a life with the man she can't seem to get out of her heart. So yes, she'll help Ford find his sister. And maybe, along the way, figure out if they have a future.

But finding RJ somewhere in the vastness of Russia with the FSB chasing them will push Scarlett beyond even her courage and make her question everything she thought she wanted…including Ford. What will it cost her to love a man who saves the world?

And when Ford is asked to choose between saving his sister, saving the world from a war, and rescuing the woman he loves…can he live with his decision?

The third book in the Montana Marshalls series will leave you breathless!

Available where books are sold
September 2019
Also available in ebook format